CRIME SCENE

I walked into the room, my eyes immediately going to the bed, to the dead woman. The sheet was still thrown back and I balled my hands into fists, digging my fingernails into my palms as I willed myself to walk forward, to take in the scene. The woman's peaceful head still rested calmly on the silky pillow, but now I could see that her neck was barely attached. There were horrible-looking bite marks on her collarbone and across her chest; the skin was puckered, torn, and purpled. There were double puncture wounds on each upturned wrist, and more blood than I had ever seen in any of Nina's blood-bank lunch deliveries.

"Who could have done this?" I whispered, unable to tear my eyes away.

Hayes looked sideways at me, his jaw set, that muscle twitching again. "I was hoping you could tell me."

I found myself stepping closer, examining the corpse. I pushed aside a crumple of torn, blood-soaked nightie and gasped.

There was a yawning, bloody hole just under the woman's left breastbone—and her heart had been completely removed . . .

UNDER WRAPS

The Underworld Detection Agency Chronicles

HANNAH JAYNE

KENSINGTON BOOKS
http://www.kensingtonbooks.com

KENSINGTON BOOKS are published by

Kensington Publishing Corp.
119 West 40th Street
New York, NY 10018

All Kensington titles, imprints and distributed lines are avail-
able at special quantity discounts for bulk purchases for sales
promotion, premiums, fund-raising, educational or institu-
tional use.

Special book excerpts or customized printings can also be
created to fit specific needs. For details, write or phone the
office of the Kensington Special Sales Manager: Attn.: Special
Sales Department. Kensington Publishing Corp., 119 West
40th Street, New York, NY 10018. Phone: 1-800-221-2647.

Kensington and the K logo Reg. U.S. Pat. & TM Off.

ISBN-13: 978-0-7582-5892-2
ISBN-10: 0-7582-5892-5

First Printing: March 2011

10 9 8 7 6 5 4 3 2 1

Printed in the United States of America

To my second-grade teacher
Vi Sullivan:
I don't know where you are,
but I'm here because of you.
Thanks for letting me keep writing.

ACKNOWLEDGMENTS

Wasn't it Hillary Clinton who said, "It takes a village to raise a writer"? Special thanks to my agent extraordinaire Amberly Finarelli and my über-patient editor John Scognamiglio; to the San Francisco Police Department and officers Gardner and Green from the Santa Clara Police Department—thanks for listening to my endless questions and keeping an (almost) straight face as I learned how to shoot. Thanks to the phenomenal staff at M Is for Mystery in San Mateo and Crema café in San Jose for allowing a poor writer to nurse a single cup of tea for hours on end. A special thanks to Heather Woods for always encouraging me to write on (even when I inundate her with six versions of the same scene) and to Prolific Oven Palo Alto for gently shooing us out at night. Thanks to CTS for not evicting me. To John and Oscar for your endless support—I'll be forever indebted, and to Joan who made all this happen (and brought the toilet paper to boot)—I couldn't have done it without you.

Finally, a very special thanks to my parents who may not have always understood but always encouraged, and to Jack and Lily who constantly remind me that it's impossible to feel self-important while cleaning out the cat box.

Chapter One

This was why I didn't do magic. Well, this and the fact that incidents like this wreaked havoc on my organic cotton-blend wardrobe.

I stood by while Nina perched on her desktop, hands on hips, teeth bared, dodging the singed-hair-smelling puffs of smoke that shot from Mrs. Henderson's scaled, flared nostrils.

Lorraine, the Gestalt witch and resident UDA Accounts Payable shark, was hopping from foot to foot, muttering a calming spell that made flowers bloom on the desk and then wilt under Mrs. Henderson's dragon-fire heat.

"Mrs. Henderson," I said, reaching out to soothe the eight-foot dragon. "I'm sure Nina didn't mean anything by her comment. If you would just let me help—"

Mrs. Henderson angled a surprisingly well-manicured claw at Nina and jabbed at the air in front of her. "That woman should not be allowed to deal with the public!" she spat, blowing a fireball from between pursed, candy-pink lips.

"Oy!" Lorraine yelped and scampered out the door, patting her smoking scalp while I watched Nina's small hands ball into fists, her dark eyes agape, glaring at the bowling-ball-sized hole burned into her hand-smocked blouse.

"This was an original!" Nina shrieked.

"Mrs. Henderson," I tried again.

Mrs. Henderson clapped a claw over her mouth, but I could still see the snaking smile on her thin dragon lips. "Sorry," she said. "That one really got away from me."

"If you think that I am going to change my mind, or wear"—Nina wrinkled her nose in disgust—"fire-retardant fabrics to deal with this, this—"

"Client," I offered.

"*Lizard*," Nina spat, "who can't hold her fire breath . . ."

I cringed as Mrs. Henderson's eyes bulged. "Who are you calling a lizard, Nosferatu?"

I ducked just in time to miss a spout of fire that engulfed Nina and fizzled on her cold, marble skin. She sniffed, the charred remains of her singed dress falling off and crackling to the desk, leaving her stark naked, stiletto heeled, and completely bald.

"Why you—"

I watched Nina rise up on her toes, her sharp fangs pressed against her Resolutely Red MAC lip stain.

"Nina!" I stepped in front of her just in time to catch a blast of Mrs. Henderson's fire. It balled around me, the orange-yellow flames held an inch from my skin. They crackled, white hot, then fizzled out.

Mrs. Henderson frowned, her tail flopping on the floor and upturning my potted spider plant. "I'm sorry about that, Ms. Lawson." She shrugged, her slick gray-green shoulders hugging her ears. "I guess it's a good thing you're immune."

So, not only do I not do magic, magic can't really be done *to* me. So, exit zombie love-slave spells, demonic possession, and Disney princess movies; enter standing in between a stark-naked vampire and an eight-foot dragon on a Tuesday afternoon.

"Mrs. Henderson," I said, using my most calming tone. "How about if I personally handle all your paperwork from now on?"

Mrs. Henderson eyed Nina and then pinned me with a yellow-eyed glare. "*All* of it?"

I nodded, holding out my hand. "Every last form. I'm sure we can get this all worked out for you"— I smiled beguilingly at Nina—"with no further problems."

Mrs. Henderson slapped her paperwork into my open palm. "Okay," she said, the heat still in her breath. "But expect me to file a formal complaint with Mr. Sampson about her!"

She turned around, sashaying her large, scaled behind out the door, her tail slithering on the floor behind her.

Nina jumped off her desk and shimmied into a lemon yellow sheath dress she yanked out of her handbag. "I swear, that woman!" she muttered.

"Nina—"

Nina raised what remained of her left eyebrow and then rubbed it vigorously until the hair started to grow back. "This is not my fault," she said. "That woman was smoking. Smoking in my office!"

I sighed. "Mrs. Henderson is a dragon. She can't really help it."

"Oh. So I'm just supposed to sit here, breathing all

that smoke for minimum wage? Oh, no." Nina crossed her arms in front of her chest. "Not in this lifetime."

She wagged her head, enviable locks of glossy black hair sprouting from her scalp, growing until she had a full head of waist-length hair.

I nonchalantly patted my Brillo Pad curls and lowered my voice, trying my best to offer a calming vibe. "Nina, you haven't breathed in one hundred and sixteen years. You're a vampire. And we don't make minimum wage."

Nina was unmoved. "You breathers are all so literal. Is it lunchtime yet?" She rose up on her toes and peeked over the counter that separated us—non-minimum-wage-making UDA staff—from them—the general demonic public.

"There's hardly anyone here," Nina said. "Let's take a long lunch. Abercrombie is having a sale. And all their male models are topless." She grinned. "And yummy."

I looked over the counter and did a sweep of the UDA waiting room. It was crowded, shin to shoulder, with the usual eleven o'clock crowd of minotaurs, gargoyles, Kholog demons, and trolls. I rolled my eyes at Nina, stepped up to the counter, and yelled "Next!"

"Ugh," Nina said, hopping up onto her stool. "You are no fun."

By 4 P.M. I had authorized the existence of two immortals, rubbed enough slobber off a hobgoblin's file to okay his power addition, and de-magicked a Salite witch who was caught trying to torpedo a Carnival cruise after she got salmonella at the captain's dinner. I glanced at the dwindling line of clients in the waiting room and then out the window, watching the gray of dusk replacing the gray of fall in San Francisco.

"Nina," I said, leaning over my station. "You're going to have to grab the rest." I nodded toward the window. "It's time to go up."

Nina blew out a sigh. "Kiss Sampson for me."

I slid a THIS LANE CLOSED sign across my desk, rummaged through my shoulder bag, and unwrapped a Fruit Roll-Up before heading down the hall toward my boss's office.

"Just another day in the life," I muttered under my breath as I skirted the microwave-sized hole in the linoleum where a wizard exploded six weeks ago. Really, could operations be *that* busy?

Like I said, I don't do magic. Hell, I don't even know how to program the DVR. I can't toss lightning bolts (so very witchy) and my flesh-eating abilities are limited to Popeyes Chicken and the occasional veggie burger. I don't have superhuman strength or immortality or X-ray vision or even a body that looks all that good in a leather bustier (a requirement for the vampire chicks). I have a goldfish named Tipsy (well, had—there was a run-in with a Llhor demon, but that's a different story) and an old Honda with a dent in the front. I can type eighty words a minute, make a mean pot of coffee, and chain up a full-grown man in thirty-four seconds flat.

That last one is important, since my boss is a werewolf.

I know what you're going to say: that werewolves don't exist. Only, they do. Werewolves, vampires, witches, trolls—pretty much everything you ever feared was under your bed? Yeah, they're real. But they're not under your bed. Generally, they're here: at the Underworld Detection Agency. We're kind of like the DMV for the demon world—long lines, lots of windows, forms up the wazoo. It's our job to get all the demons registered, documented, and legal and take care of any Underworld disputes. UDA is pretty forward thinking when it comes to demon life. We've got job counseling for the demon who has decided to leave the Underworld careers of terrorizing children and hiding under beds and move to something more permanent and substantial—like working the register at the Pottery Barn on Chestnut Street. We even offer a cutting-edge demon–human immersion program. It usually culminates with an exorcism on the part of the human, but still, it's a start.

What? You thought that demons were an unorganized bunch? Common mistake. Vampires are obsessive-compulsive. Witches are scatterbrained. Trolls are short tempered (and reek of mold); zombies can't be trusted for anything and are always losing their forms. Werewolves are organized—which probably explains why my boss, Pete Sampson, is not only the most respected man in the Underworld, but also one of the most respected men up there (that would be the so-called normal world). It also doesn't hurt that when he's human he's got warm, chocolate-brown eyes that crinkle when he smiles, a head full of lush, sandy blond, run-your-fingers-through hair, and a body that holds his Armani suits exceptionally well.

But, I digress.

The Underworld Detection Agency is located thirty-seven floors below the San Francisco Police Department—although most of the SFPD has no idea we're here. Though the regular world is pretty widely populated by members of the Underworld community, it's not something either world advertises all that much, lest Hollywood lose its stronghold on the demon-as-horrible-murderous-monster thing. And, there are a whole lot of Underworld inhabitants that solidly frown on dead–undead/human–non-human fraternizing. Something about warm blood and mortality weakening the demon gene pool. Those are the demons that spend most of their time in UDA lines, trying to force legislation that limits crossbreed marriage and touting the benefits of total world demon domination. They're *really* pushy.

Demon or not, every morning I pop into the elevator, and when the heavy metal doors open, it's just another day at the office of the undead.

Down here, amongst the demons, vampires, zombies, and stuff, I'm the anomaly. I'm five-foot-five while standing on a phone book, and I have a shock of red hair that makes me look a little like Kathy Ireland in her pre-K-Mart days or a lot like Carrot Top's kid sister. My eyes are lime Jell-O green and a little too small—when I was a kid I prayed for the bug-eyed look of a thyroid sufferer with no such luck. The only person in either world with skin paler than mine is my roommate's and that's because she's dead. Well, undead. That's why I'm the anomaly: short, red-headed, small-eyed, and non-demon. Flesh and blood. Alive. Nina calls us "breathers" or "norms," and every once in a while a clutch of vampire kids will break away from their sire and bet each other to touch me, shuddering when their cold, dead fingertips brush against my warm arm.

So I know you're wondering: What's a nice,

redheaded breather like me doing in a place like this? It's a question I ask myself every day when I'm tucked behind my desk at the UDA, pushing yet another form over to a slobbering hobgoblin who's eaten the first one.

Well, for starters, my grandmother was a seer. Of the crazy-scarves, crystal-ball, palm-reading type. Which, by the way, made me immensely popular in grade school—as everyone's favorite kid to pick on. When other kids' parents were talking new school clothes and soccer uniforms, my grandmother was talking auras and past-life regression. And although I tried my best to distance myself from Gram and wear the stretch pants and BUM sweatshirts of my (fashionably misguided) generation, the giant neon hand with the palm facing out in our front window didn't exactly scream "regular girl." So, after growing up in a household where séances were the norm and intuition was gospel, spending forty hours per week with the legion of undead wasn't exactly a far stretch. Besides, UDA was an equal opportunity (live/dead/undead) employer, and, with vampires making up forty percent of the office staff, dental benefits were amazing.

I was halfway out of my desk when I heard the *ding* of the elevator and Nina growl, "Well, hello, sailor . . ."

I turned and stopped dead in my tracks as the elevator doors peeled open and *he* stepped out. I blinked, taking in every inch of him in slow motion.

He was stunning in a dark blue suit, his shoulders broad, his tie smart and hanging against a trim stomach. His cobalt eyes were scanning the lines of demons, the centaur children milling about the waiting room, the staffers with curious heads poking through their own little glass cutouts. I sighed—then tried to hide it—watching as his dark hair curled sensuously over a strong forehead and licked at the top of small ears, perfect for nibbling. He sucked in a breath, his pink lips puckering gently, and my heart did a wild little tap dance and then sunk deep into the pit of my stomach.

"Hey," Nina said, strolling toward me. "Check out the norm!" Her ruby lips widened into a salacious smile. "He looks good enough to eat!"

I threw Nina an alarmed look because she's a vampire and if anyone looks good enough to eat, well, he could be dinner.

"I meant for you," she breathed, then patted her taut tummy. "I've already eaten."

The guy was tall—at least six feet—and I pegged him as a cop immediately as he assumed the tight stride of an officer on alert. Also, I could see his badge winking on his belt and a gun belt nestled against his waist. (Hey, if my instincts aren't as honed as they should be, at least my powers of observation are.)

His head was cocked and a U-shaped curl of glossy black hair fell over his forehead. I balled my hands into tight fists as suddenly all I could think about was running my fingers through that luscious head of wavy hair.

The cop's eyes locked on mine, and I sucked in an excited breath, and felt myself smooth my wild hair—and curse myself for another day of slept-late ponytail style. I straightened the hem on my black pencil skirt and dabbed on some lip gloss before I realized that I was primping.

"You love him," Nina hissed, her long black hair falling over one angular shoulder. She grinned at me, her eyes coal black and deep set, her mouth open, tongue playing with one razor sharp fang. "You *so* love him," she sang, twisting a red pen in her pale, slender fingers.

I rolled my eyes and fought to keep my grin welcoming and professional as the zombie at the front of the line frowned, checking her pockets for her paperwork.

"It was here a moment ago," she groaned. "I know it was. Ooh!"

"Pardon me," the cop said, his voice smooth and deep. "May I? I'll just be a minute." His dark eyebrows rose up kindly, and it seemed even the zombie went weak-kneed and stepped aside, offering her place in line.

"Yes," she said, nodding. "I can't seem to find my papers anyway. Sometimes I lose my head when it's not screwed on tight," she drooled, her milky white eyes locked on him.

"Thank you." The cop nodded to the zombie and then turned to me. "Hello," he said, inclining his head of dark curls toward me. "Do you know where I can find Mr. Sampson?"

I had an image of myself climbing up onto my desk, covering the cop's chiseled jaw and high, rose-colored cheeks with kisses, my fingers tangled in his mass of silky dark curls as my body pressed against his, fitting into the curves of his chest, of his trim, taut stomach, our hearts beating passionately as one. . . .

Instead, I opened my mouth and nothing came out. I smacked it shut, blinking dumbly into the cop's kind—but confused—face.

Nina shoved me, her bloodless hands cold on my arm. "Sophie works for Mr. Sampson," she said. "She can take you right to him. She was just going there right now as a matter of fact. Weren't you, Sophie?"

I tried to glare at Nina, but she was already engrossed with a hobgoblin who was slobbering all over her desk.

"Yes," I finally forced, "I can take you to see Mr. Sampson."

I looked up into the cop's beautiful blue eyes, and although I had no idea what swooning was, I was pretty sure I was doing it. I started to think of the two of us, hands joined, spinning in a meadow somewhere while the theme to *Love Story* played in the background.

"Miss?" The cop blinked at me, and I felt my face flush.

I did a mental head slap and decided that I really needed a hobby. And a boyfriend.

The cop frowned and leaned closer. "Are you okay?"

That's the thing about redheads. That's the thing about having milky-white skin. Every time I blushed or flushed even faintly, I'd go tomato red from my toes to my eyebrows. Think third-degree sunburn. Not exactly the cute, pink-faced tinge of an embarrassed brunette.

"I'm fine," I whispered.

I took a few deep breaths to steady myself before going to join the cop on the other side of the partition.

"Hi," he said, offering a hand. The top of my head barely cleared his shoulder and he stooped a little bit.

I took his hand—it was large and cool, his palm rough—and shook. "Um, hello. Hi. I'm Sophie. Sophie Lawson," I said, pulling out all the stops in my impressive vocabulary.

"Are you Mr. Sampson's secretary?"

I raised one annoyed eyebrow. "I'm Mr. Sampson's administrative assistant."

"Oh"—he raised both palms placatingly—"right, of course." His sinful eyes traveled to my vacated front-counter spot.

"I was just filling in," I said quickly.

"Right," the cop said. "Not really work for an administrative assistant." His grin—framed by full lips that made my mouth water—was wide and a little playful and just the tiniest bit smug.

"And you are?" I said, extracting my hand and crossing my arms.

"Hayes. Detective Parker Hayes. Police Chief Oliver"—Hayes's blue eyes slid skyward—"sent me down here." He grinned again. "I didn't even know *here* existed."

"Yeah," I said, turning on my heel, "follow me."

I tried not to pay attention to the hard set of the detective's jaw, to the way his dark hair snaked over his collar, to the slight scent of juniper and Ivory soap that surrounded him. *I'm so not doing this,* I murmured in my head. *Not interested at all.* And then, when we turned a sharp corner and Detective Hayes's hand brushed against mine, I thought, *Well, maybe just for a second. We can just be friends, right? We should be friends.*

I was about to name our firstborn when Detective

Hayes fell into stride with me. "So, you work down here all the time?" he started.

I nodded. "Four years now. Forty hours a week." I grinned. "Give or take."

"Give" meaning there were always an extra couple of hours tacked on around the full moon when I needed to double-check Mr. Sampson's chains and drop off a takeout box full of rare—as in raw—filet mignon. "Take" meaning there were always an extra couple of hours taken for lunch when Nina sniffed out yet another designer's sample sale in China Basin and dragged me down to try on armloads of skinny jeans and boho shirts at ridiculous discounts.

Hayes looked around. "Don't you find working here kind of . . . odd?"

"No more strange than any other office job," I said, nodding to Pierre, a centaur who also did the filing.

Hayes paused. "Okay, like that," he said, gesturing back to Pierre, his voice lowered. "How does a—a—"

"Centaur," I supplied.

"How does *that* get to work in the morning? It's not like he can hop on BART."

I snorted. "Of course not. Pierre drives a Chevy."

Hayes rolled his eyes, and I grabbed his elbow, leading him in a wide berth around a group of fairies and one pixie gathered around the water cooler.

"Just keep walking and don't make eye contact," I told him under my breath.

"Okay, wait. I might not know a lot about this stuff, but you're telling me to avoid *them*?" He looked back, eyeing the pink-and-pale-green-clad diminutive group, their voices high-pitched and impossibly sweet as they chatted. "You can't tell me you're seriously afraid of Tinker Bell over there. What'd they do? Get fairy dust in your eye or something?"

I kept walking but faced Hayes. "Fairies are *mean*. Everyone knows that."

Hayes remained unconvinced. "Mean? They're talking about cookies!"

I stopped dead in my tracks as the fairy chatter died. "Uh-oh," I muttered.

"What?"

"Fairies are very private. When disturbed by gawkers—"

"I wasn't gawking!"

"—or intruders, they can react very violently."

"Them?" Hayes swung around to the tiny, sweet-faced group, their wings twittering, littering the gray, industrial carpet with sparkly crumbles of pixie dust.

I grabbed Hayes by the arm again and yanked, hard. "Run!" I shouted in midstride, as the fairies— eyes narrowed, apple cheeks angry and flushed— flung themselves through the air toward us. Hayes and I ducked into an empty conference room, and he leaned against the door, doubled over, hands on knees. "Fairies are mean," he said, grinning. "Who knew?"

"They're a complete HR nightmare. Anyway, you should lock your doors when you leave here. And check your shoes. They can be surprisingly sinister."

"I can't believe you don't find this the least bit weird," Hayes was muttering as I made sure the coast was clear.

We stepped into the little foyer that housed my desk, a half-dead spider plant, and a red velvet fainting couch that Nina used for the (more than) occasional vamp nap. I gestured toward the closed door to Mr. Sampson's office.

"Here we are," I told the detective.

I knocked twice and then clicked open the door, poking my head into Mr. Sampson's office. "There's a Detective Hayes to see you, sir."

Mr. Sampson looked up, his brown eyes velvety and inviting. He raked a large hand through his blond hair and then patted it back in place, cocked his head, and smiled at me, holding one finger up.

"Not a problem," Mr. Sampson said to no one, his voice throaty, rich. "We'll get that taken care of right away. Thank you. I've got an appointment right now. I'm sorry, but I'm going to have to let you go. Yes—" His dark eyebrows rose, his eyes finding mine. "Certainly. I'll have Sophie look into that."

A rush of heat washed over me as I watched my name roll off Mr. Sampson's lips. I clamped my knees together and vowed to give up reading romance novels for good. Really—my hormones had gone into overdrive.

I suddenly had an image of my grandmother shaking a bejeweled finger at me (and they were all *real* jewels, by the way), saying, "Sophie Lawson, you are completely man hungry." Which is not entirely true. I'm just a firm believer in appreciating your surroundings. And it doesn't hurt if your surroundings have chiseled chests and happen to look excellent in an Armani suit . . . right?

Mr. Sampson looked at Detective Hayes and then tapped the flashing blue earpiece clipped to his ear. "Okay, good-bye," he said, before pulling the earpiece off and dropping it into a desk drawer. "Detective," he said, "so sorry about that. Come on in."

I nodded curtly at the detective and turned on my heel, but Mr. Sampson stopped me before I reached the door. "Sophie, why don't you stay, too?"

I led Detective Hayes into Mr. Sampson's office—a huge, groaning room with cinnamon brown walls and soft cigar chairs set around Mr. Sampson's elegant, enormous desk. The office could house any other upscale male executive—the impeccable, masculine décor, the walls laden with gold-embossed awards and framed degrees, the bookshelves lined with impressive leather-bound books, and the requisite crystal clock with ticking gold innards. Against the back wall there was a set of heavy metal chains, the innocent, brown paint covering a reinforced cement wall with steel rebar the size of bridge supports. Okay, that part might be slightly different from other offices.

Detective Hayes's eyes went wide as he stared at the chains, and Mr. Sampson followed his gaze, grinned, and shrugged lightly. "Occupational hazard. Why don't you have a seat, Detective?"

Hayes and I settled into identical plush leather cigar chairs opposite Mr. Sampson. I stifled a delighted Carrie Bradshaw grin and made a mental note to tell Nina about the hot-male sandwich I found myself in: Pete Sampson with his miles-deep, chocolate brown eyes, close-cropped ash blond hair, and *GQ* model build; and Detective Parker Hayes, rich blue eyes, chiseled jawline sprinkled with stubble, Roman god nose—I'd leave out the part about him being smug.

It's not that I was particularly man crazy (except for the hormone thing); it was more that when you worked in an office where the general male populace either smells of graveyard dirt or has a horn where no horn should be, it's rather exciting to be the bologna in a mostly normal hottie sandwich.

I crossed my legs at the ankle and tried to nonchalantly study Detective Hayes's severe profile as his eyes slowly scanned the office. He didn't say anything, and a muscle twitched against his well-defined jawline.

"Sorry," he finally said, tearing his eyes from the chains. "I don't mean to stare."

"It's still daytime," I told the detective. "You're fine."

I watched Detective Hayes force a smile and then paste on what must have been his professional face. "Sorry," he said again to Mr. Sampson. "All this"—his blue eyes trailed the office, the chains—"just caught me by surprise."

Mr. Sampson leaned back in his chair, his mouth curling up into one of his seductive, easy grins. "Understandable. Not a lot of people know about us down here. So, what is it that I can help you with? Chief Oliver said there is a case the force could use our assistance with?"

Detective Hayes cleared his throat and set his hat on his knee. "Right. Chief Oliver would have come himself but"—again, his eyes went to the chains—"he's leading the task force up top. He said you two were close." It was almost a question, and I knew what Detective Hayes was getting at: How is it that the San Francisco chief of police could buddy up with the sometimes-werewolf head of the Underworld Detection Agency?

"They went to college together," I blurted.

Detective Hayes blinked at me. "Excuse me?"

Mr. Sampson smiled kindly at me. "Sophie means that Chief Oliver and I went to college together. We were roommates, actually. While our careers generally no longer intersect, it happens occasionally. So, Detective Hayes, exactly how do you and Chief Oliver think UDA can be of service to the police department?"

"Well"—the detective licked his lips, looking from me to Mr. Sampson—"there's been a murder."

I yawned and settled into my chair.

"Forgive me," Mr. Sampson said, his voice smooth and melodic, "but this is San Francisco. Saying there has been a murder is akin to saying there is fog, isn't it?"

"Yes." Hayes nodded as a blush of pink crawled over his cheeks. I sucked in a hollow breath as my heart thumped.

"But this one is different. A businessman—an attorney, actually. Murdered in his office. And all his blood had been drained."

Chapter Two

"Vampire," I whispered, raising one alarmed eyebrow.

"That was our first thought, too," Hayes said, his blue eyes intent on mine. "Well, not our *first*, but . . ."

Mr. Sampson and I nodded.

"But there are no puncture wounds on"—Hayes absently gestured toward his neck—"the body."

Mr. Sampson looked unconcerned and began to shuffle papers on his desk. "The old puncture wounds on the neck have become rather archaic and cliché. Very Bela Lugosi. Everything evolves."

"It happened in broad daylight," Hayes went on, and Mr. Sampson paused.

"That's a bit odd, but not impossible. Sophie, why don't you get the file of active vampires within the city limits for the detective?"

I stood up and then sat down hard when the detective said, "Wait. There's more."

Hayes reached into his pocket and pulled out a small, leather-bound notebook and began reading from it. "Eight days ago there was another murder. A drifter, we think—we haven't been able to ID him yet.

White male, midthirties, pretty physically fit. His throat was torn out."

I gulped. Somehow, I find the walking dead far less frightening then the *dead* dead.

"His limbs were basically shredded."

Mr. Sampson straightened.

"Claw marks and"—the detective's voice dropped—"bloody paw prints surrounded the body."

"Paw prints?"

Hayes swallowed and nodded. "Large. Canine or"—his eyes flashed—"wolf, maybe."

"That's not possible," I said, surprised at the shrill sound of panic in my voice. "I chain up Mr. Sampson every night, and there are no other active werewolves in the vicinity."

Mr. Sampson's mouth was set in a hard, thin line. "Go on," he told Detective Hayes.

"A woman—a known drug user, so not entirely reliable—said she saw the murder. Well, sort of. She was in the upstairs window when she heard the vic scream. She said it was bloodcurdling, not like the usual screeches and howls on the street. She went to the window within a second or two and the vic had already been torn apart. Then she saw what she described as a large dog running off the premises."

"A dog?" I said, leaning forward.

Detective Hayes nodded at his notebook. "Like I mentioned, the body was pretty badly torn apart. But . . . and I'm sorry, but this is pretty gruesome—the victim's eyeballs had been removed." Hayes wagged his head. "We haven't recovered them. Whoever did this removed them and kept them."

My stomach lurched and I gasped. "He took the eyeballs? That's disgusting!"

Mr. Sampson looked at me sharply, and I felt myself

redden, embarrassed. "I mean . . ." I sucked in a breath and then pushed it out, shaking my head. "No, really. That's just completely disgusting."

Detective Hayes looked at me, his blue eyes sympathetic. "We see a lot of odd things in the city, a lot of murderers who take things—souvenirs—from their victims. Usually jewelry, an item of clothing, a driver's license. But this—" He slowly shook his head, lips pursed. "This is extreme. Unsettling."

I chanced a glance at Mr. Sampson, who had his fingers laced together, his brown eyes set hard. "And what about the second murder, the attorney? Were there any witnesses?" he asked.

Hayes shut his notebook and tucked it back into his chest pocket. "That's just it. No witnesses on the second murder even though it happened in a busy office during the day. No one saw anyone go in, no one saw anyone leave. There were security cameras everywhere."

"And?" Mr. Sampson raised an interested eyebrow.

"And there is nothing on them."

Mr. Sampson pushed out a long sigh.

"So we're dealing with a rogue vampire *and* an undocumented werewolf?" I swallowed heavily, my stomach starting to churn. "Good grief."

"Actually"—Detective Hayes sat on the edge of his chair—"that's why I'm here. We're not sure what we're dealing with, although we're growing increasingly certain that it isn't human."

"Why is that?" I knew it wasn't my place, but I was interested—arms-crossed, edge-of-my-chair interested. "Why can't it be human?"

"I suppose it could," Mr. Sampson supplied, "but that would be unlikely. Especially with the bodily harm in the scenes you described. Was there any blood lost on the carpet, Detective? Any blood lost anywhere around the second victim?"

Hayes shook his head. "Not a drop."

"And the other victim?"

"He was a good-sized man. If the druggie—uh, witness—was right about the time of the scream and the time she saw the body, only seconds passed. One scream and the man was shredded from head to toe. That's not easy to do in such a short amount of time. And given the amount of destruction? I'd call it very nearly impossible."

"And the eyeballs," I said, my stomach gurgling. "Don't forget the eyeballs. That had to take some work." I looked from Mr. Sampson to the detective and swallowed thickly. "Right?"

Mr. Sampson sat back in his chair. "I see. So, Police Chief Oliver is looking to check into our files?"

"Actually, Chief Oliver has put me in charge of the case and would like us to work together."

"What does he want us to do?" I asked, my mind already plugging my smiling mug into the opening credits of *CSI: San Francisco*, with Detective Parker Hayes as my love interest—er, partner.

"If we have access to your files, and maybe your . . . expertise with the, the kind of"—Hayes swallowed—"*people* we might be dealing with in this case. Well, we think things will run much more smoothly if you and I could work together, Mr. Sampson. It's obvious you have a wealth of knowledge in this field superior to anything we can glean."

I glanced at the beautiful old calendar over Mr. Sampson's shoulder; the one that showed an opal moon moving across a slick, blue-marble night sky and documented the changes of the moon.

"I'm afraid I can't do that," Mr. Sampson said,

splaying his fingers on his desk. "It just wouldn't be"—he paused—"prudent for me to be out, above ground, at this time."

"I can help," I heard myself blurt.

Both Mr. Sampson and Detective Hayes swung their heads to look at me, and I started to stutter.

"I—I—I mean, I know—I'm on top of all the Underworld documentees and conflicts and I can move up there"—I gestured toward the police station, thirty-seven floors above us—"without raising suspicion. Or without . . ." All of our eyes traveled toward Mr. Sampson's set of chains. ". . . having any issues. Really, I can help."

That's right, I thought to myself, *Sophie Lawson: CSI.*

Mr. Sampson nodded his head slowly. "She's right. Miss Lawson very likely will be your best bet. She can move freely in both worlds at any time."

I stood up slowly. "I can still come in, sir," I said to Mr. Sampson, "and chain you up. And handle all my paperwork and everything." I was already thinking about borrowing a pair of Nina's stiletto knee-high boots and her black leather duster. That's totally *CSI,* right?

I noticed the muscle jerk along Detective Hayes's chin again when Mr. Sampson grinned and wagged his head. "Nina can do the honors for a while with me and you'll still check in."

Hayes gripped his notebook. "Sir." His eyes traveled to me and looked me up and down in a less than flattering way. "Miss, with all due respect, the department can't risk putting a civilian in danger."

"The department can't risk the general public finding out that there is a supernatural animal out there, draining people of their blood and ripping out their throats."

"And eyeballs," I quipped, certain my usual sallow color has dipped to . . . more sallow.

"Sophie is going to be your best bet, Detective Hayes. She is one of the only of your kind who can sense a supernatural presence and not be affected by it."

Detective Hayes frowned. "My kind?"

"Breathers," I supplied. "Regular folks."

"The population in general can't see magic, can't see demons unless we allow them to. It's what we call veiling or shielding."

"Would this veiling work on technology? Like the security cameras not seeing our first victim's murderer?" Hayes asked.

Mr. Sampson nodded. "Yes. But veiling doesn't work on Sophie."

I grinned, feeling a weird mix of pride and shame.

"Occasionally, there are people who can straddle both worlds. It's rare, but Sophie is one of those people. You need her, Detective Hayes."

My stomach lurched when Mr. Sampson eyed the detective.

He *needed* me.

Suddenly all the romance of becoming a super sleuth was replaced by an image of those poor men—actual, dead people—outlined in chalk and crime-scene tape. I gripped the sides of the chair and sat down again. "Maybe this isn't such a good idea." Besides, I was really more flannel pajamas and bunny slippers than leather duster and stiletto boots.

"You'll be fine," Mr. Sampson said, obviously unconcerned. "I have no doubt that Chief Oliver will keep you safe and Detective Hayes here will teach you everything he knows."

"Great," Hayes and I both muttered.

Mr. Sampson smiled, but my stomach was too busy playing the accordion to revel in the warm creases at the sides of his eyes.

"All right then, everything is settled. Sophie will help you with whatever you need. You'll have access to all of the Underworld files."

I forced a smile. "I'll start gathering them up."

The room fell into silence as we all sat, smiling politely and staring at each other.

"Oh." I stood up quickly. "Will that be all?"

Detective Hayes stood, reluctantly tucked his notebook in his back pocket. He reached out and shook Mr. Sampson's hand.

I led Detective Hayes from Mr. Sampson's office. "So," I said casually, "I guess we're going to be working together. How are we going to work this? Should I come up—"

"Like I said, Miss Lawson," he started, cutting me off smoothly.

"Sophie," I interjected.

"Sophie." Detective Hayes seemed to bite out my name, his lips held tight. "I don't know about this veiling and shielding stuff, but honestly, I don't know how much help you're going to be. Don't get me wrong, I appreciate you wanting to help, but I really think you'd be better off staying down here. Nobody wants you to get hurt, and this is police work."

All that was missing was a lollypop and a placating pat on the head.

I crossed my arms and stopped walking. "Police work? Don't you mean man's work?"

"You said it, not me." Hayes's eyes scanned me and

his big hand cupped my shoulder. "This is dangerous. Whoever is doing this is not playing games, and the last thing I want—or need—is anyone else getting hurt. No one is going to be helped if I have to worry about my 'partner.' I appreciate your offer, though." Hayes turned around, striding down the hall.

My skin bristled. "Do you know how vampires feed, Detective? Or that werewolves have the ability to change every night—not just at the full moon?"

Hayes's pace slowed, and then he stopped, turning slowly. "Excuse me?"

I jutted out one hip, resting a hand on it. "You don't know a thing about the Underworld or the people living in it. All the detective training in the world isn't going to help you against one of them."

The detective's cheek pushed up in an amused, gorgeously annoying half smile. "Is that so?"

"Have you ever seen a zombie, a hobgoblin, a troll?"

I could practically see the wheels turning in the detective's head, working it out.

"No," he said slowly. "But—" Hayes started and then stopped when I raised both my eyebrows, expectantly.

Hayes's grin went full. "All right, Lawson, looks like you've got yourself a partner. Meet me up top at noon."

That's right, I thought, grinning smugly to myself. *Sophie Lawson, CSI.*

Hayes spun on his heel and called over his shoulder. "Just do me a favor and try not to get yourself killed, okay?"

I took a step forward and realized my knees had gone rubbery.

Chapter Three

I returned to my desk, the rapid beat of my heart having slowed to a near normal pace, my revelry in wild, gun-toting crime raids with Parker Hayes almost over. I plopped down on my chair and cracked open a Diet Coke, then dropped my head into my hands.

"Well?" The voice was cool and right next to my ear, and I almost jumped out of my skin.

"Holy crap, Nina, you should wear a bell or something!" I gripped my thundering heart with my hand, and Nina sat down on the edge of my desk, her long, milky-white legs dangling.

Nina is a vampire—a 167-year-old vampire—and my very best friend. She was turned in 1842 and before that was a twenty-nine-year-old foul-tempered Parisian heiress who climbed out her bedroom window one night to meet a dark-eyed stranger. Two months after that, Nina, the newly made vampire, caused the Massacre of Elphinstone's Army. You could never tell it by looking at her, though. She's just barely my height but supermodel-skinny with waist-length black hair, a little ski-jump nose, a heart-shaped red mouth . . . and fangs.

"Tell me everything and don't leave out a single, juicy detail. He smelled good, didn't he? Different"—Nina's dark eyes scanned the ceiling—"not like your standard breather. It was like . . ."

"Smoke and toasted almonds and cocoa. Not that I really noticed," I said quickly.

"So spill! You were gone for an age with Mr. Yummy Cop," Nina said, lacing her fingers together and leaning into me.

"Actually"—I wiggled a file on demons in unincorporated San Mateo County out from under Nina's butt—"he's not a cop, he's a detective."

Nina licked her lips. "Even better."

I reached into my desk drawer and shoved a Fiber One bar in her hand. "Eat this. You're obviously starving."

Nina glared at the Fiber One bar, fangs bared, and dropped it as though it were holy water. "Gross," she said, wiping her hands on her dress.

I shrugged. "Sorry. It's the best I could do. I don't have any Plasma Pops here."

Nina's eyebrow twitched and she pursed her lips. "Stop stalling, start spilling."

As much as I wanted to brag about my Sampson-Sophie-Hayes manwich, the details of the murder—and the bloodless, eyeless bodies—trumped my lust-o-meter, and I shivered.

"There's a murderer in town," I said.

Nina rolled her coal black eyes. "Big deal. There's a million murderers in this town. Get to the cop." She grinned. "Did he take off his shirt?"

"Nina! We were with Sampson."

Her jaw dropped, her pointed incisors glistening. "Did *Sampson* take off his shirt?"

"No one took off their shirt!" I lowered my voice. "Like I said, there's a murderer in the city and the PD is concerned it's supernatural."

Nina looked only slightly interested—although whether it was in my story or her cuticles I couldn't tell. "You should check with the zombies. They can get so rowdy."

I began stacking files and shoving them into my shoulder bag. "Nah, zombies are totally adherent."

"When they're on their first brain." Nina jabbed at my files with one perfectly manicured cotton-candy pink fingernail. "What are you doing with those? Aren't they confidential?"

"The PD wants Sampson to work with them, but he can't. Too risky to be out after dark, especially if he's examining crime scenes with that much blood."

Nina licked her lips, and I pretended not to notice.

"So, I'm working with Detective Hayes on the case. Bringing in some of the files that we have. Thinking maybe we can locate the perp—I mean perpetrator— from some of our adherents. I figured we'd go through the relevant UDA files and see if there are any clues."

I loved how detectivey I sounded.

Nina pressed her pale hands to her open mouth, her thin black eyebrows shooting up. "You're kidding me!"

A little twitter of pride slipped through me, and I hid my smile behind a stack of file folders. "Really, Nina, it's no big deal. The PD needed some help, and frankly, I'm the only one who can do it."

How totally CSI am I?

"No big deal?" Nina hopped off my desk—her landing didn't make a sound—and turned to me, her palms pressed against my file folders, pinning them to my desk. "You are going to be nose to nose with that hot cop for, for days, weeks, maybe *months* on end and it's no big deal?"

I hadn't thought of that.

Me and Parker Hayes, alone together for days, weeks, *months* on end? I imagined us head to head in his office working on the case, the Styrofoamed remains of our on-the-go dinner spread before us . . . huddled together in his squad car, rushing off to crime scenes . . . showering together, first thing in the morning. . . . My mouth went dry, and I found that I was twirling a long strand of red hair around my index finger—my number-one nervous tic. I shoved my hands into my jacket pockets.

"The detective isn't that hot close up. And he's certainly not all that hot about having me tag along, so I doubt we'll be spending all that much time together anyway."

So much for our morning shower.

"Still"—Nina's cold eyes skimmed over me skeptically—"if you're going to run into him again, you really should change your outfit."

"I'm not going to change for him!" I said, indignant. "Besides, he's already seen me once today. And," I said, standing, "I look fine."

Nine crossed her arms in front of her own midnight blue vintage Valentino wrap dress—vampires are total fashion whores—and shrugged.

"You do look fine," she mused, "just so *secretarial*."

I stood up and hauled my shoulder bag over one arm. "I'm an administrative assistant," I spat.

"Fine," Nina said, stretching out one long, lean leg and examining her newest pair of Jimmy Choos. "At least—" She dropped her foot and leaned into me, her dark lips ice cold as they skimmed my neck. She unbuttoned the top two buttons on my white blouse. "Show some skin."

Nina cocked her head and smiled at me, then batted her eyelashes sweetly. I narrowed my eyes. "Now what?"

"Since I helped you, you want to help me?"

"Helped me?" I raised my eyebrows, then blew out a resigned sigh. "What do you need?"

Nina held up her thumb and forefinger. "Eensy weensy favor."

I set my shoulder bag back on my desk, certain that Nina's "eensy" was never anywhere near "weensy."

"Oh, no. Every time you need a favor I end up trapped in a demonic vortex or on a blind date with a Minotaur."

"The Nordstrom half-yearly sale is *not* a demonic vortex, and besides, you said you liked Keith!"

"He ate my purse!"

Nina held up her hands. "Okay, okay, it's not a shopping excursion or a date, I swear."

I narrowed my eyes. "On your undead soul?"

Nina raised a single brow.

"Damn it. Okay." I sighed. "What do I have to do?"

"My nephew is going to be coming into town—"

"Nina! You have a nephew?" In all the years that Nina and I had been roommates and best friends, she had never spoken of her family. "You never mentioned a nephew!" I furrowed my brow and frowned. "Wait. How do you have a nephew?"

She crossed her arms in front of her chest. "The same way anyone else has a nephew."

I blinked at her.

"I have—had—a younger sister, Agnes. Her son is Louis, my nephew."

"But wouldn't he be like . . ."

"One hundred and twelve. But perennially sixteen."

"He's a vampire then?"

Nina nodded, a flicker of sadness marring her perfect marble features. "Thanks to me."

I waited for her to continue. She looked away, avoiding my gaze, and slumped against her desk.

"Agnes knew what had happened to me—what I had become. Right after I was changed, I left home, left my family. I had to. But almost twenty years later Agnes tracked me down. It was weird seeing her. She was my baby sister, but her hair was gray and her skin loose and here I was." Nina shrugged her small shoulders, gestured to her eternally young facade. "She begged me to come home with her—her son, Louis, was sick. At that time, there was no cure for polio, no vaccines. It was a death sentence, or in the very best of situations, crippling. She begged me to change him."

"She wanted you to kill her son?"

Nina's eyes were fierce. "At that time, it was the only way to save him. I didn't want to, but she was my sister. I had already caused her so much pain. I couldn't watch her watch him die. It was excruciating to watch a mother—my sister—helplessly standing by while her son withered and just waited to die."

"So you changed him?"

Nina nodded and smiled wistfully. "The polio was

gone. Louis was strong again. He was going to live forever."

I tried to smile. "Well, that's nice that you were able to do that . . . for them."

"Always nice to damn your family."

"Nina—" I tried to be sympathetic, but she held up a silencing hand.

"So, the favor. He's going to be here in San Francisco. Can he stay with us for a little while? He's been having some trouble with the vamp family he's been living with back East. They move around too much, are always dropping in with a new coven. I just think he needs some stability right now."

"Yeah, of course he can stay with us." *What's more stable than a vampire, her breather roommate, and a city with a psycho killer on the loose?*

Nina grinned.

"Okay, it's settled. Louis stays with us. Now I've got to meet Parker—" I tried to turn, but Nina put one cold hand on my forearm and batted those lashes again. I sighed. "Okay, Nina. What now?"

"Another eensy weensy—"

"Spit it out."

"Can you pick him up from the Caltrain station? I would do it, but I've got so much work. . . ."

I jutted out one hip. "You mean you have a date?"

Nina smiled sheepishly. "It just came up. I met him at Cala Foods. . . ."

"Why do vampires need groceries? Oh, never mind. What time does his train come in?"

"Six thirty. Oh, Sophie, you're the best!"

"I know. Wait, how am I going to recognize him?"

"He's a vampire."

I put my hands on my hips.

"And a teenager. He'll be easy to spot, I promise. Besides, I told him what you looked like, so he'll be keeping an eye out for you, too." Nina hugged me to her. "Ooh, thanks again!" She turned on her heel and started for the door.

"Wait!" I said. "If this date just came up, why did you already tell Louis what I looked like?"

Nina's smiling face remained unchanged. "How about I buy you a kitten?" she asked, dodging the issue.

"No," I said, drawing out the word. "No kittens. Just be glad I like you. I'll pick up Louis and he can stay with us as long as he likes." I shrugged. "Besides, it might be fun having a kid around for a bit. Should we get some movies or something? Something for him to do? What do teenage boys like?"

Nina smiled. "Teenage girls. Anyway, Louis can entertain himself. He's one hundred and twelve years old . . . and a little troubled."

I felt my eyes bulge. *How much more troubled can a vampire get?*

"But he's super, duper nice," Nina said. "For a vampire. Thanks again!"

"Nina!"

She hurried for the door, holding up a yellow legal pad and pen. "Can't talk, going to be late for my meeting. You're such a doll, Soph, thanks! I totally owe you my afterlife!"

When I stepped out into the hall I was stopped when a fist full of drooping chocolate cosmos was rammed against my thigh. I paused, and Steve stepped out from behind the offending bouquet, a slick grin spread across his graying troll face, his yellowed, snaggle teeth exposed.

"These are for you." Steve wagged the flowers in front of me, and I stooped down, plastered a smile on my face, and buried my nose in the chocolaty scent of the flowers. Anything to avoid the swamp-mud/aging-gym-sock smell of troll.

"Thanks, Steve," I said. "But you know UDA clients are not supposed to be back here." I pointed to the front office. "You're supposed to stay behind the partition, remember?"

Steve shrugged. "Steve will always be where Sophie needs him to be."

"That's the thing, Steve. What I need is for you to be behind the partition." I tucked the flowers in a clean mug I snatched from Nina's desk while I held my breath. "I mean, I really appreciate the thought and that you like me and all. . . ."

Steve wagged his head, his milky eyes big. "No, Steve doesn't like Sophie." His pointed tongue darted across thin, charcoal-colored lips. "Steve loves Sophie. Steve thinks that Sophie just may be Steve's soul mate."

I sighed. "Thank you. But you know you really can't be popping up everywhere I am, Steve." I looked both ways, sidestepping Lorraine, the witch/accounts receivable head, as she came barreling down the hall. "UDA has strict policies."

Steve grinned again, tapping his chest. "That's why Steve has an exclusive contract with UDA." He made his hands into fists and rammed them onto his hips proudly.

I swallowed. "A contract? With UDA?"

"We're furniture movers."

I looked skeptically at Steve, his half-bald head

barely clearing the top of my thigh. "Furniture movers, huh?"

Steve nodded, then inclined his head toward me. "So Steve can be close to Sophie all day long."

I stepped back, working to avoid the moldy scent that wafted each time Steve moved. "Wow. Well, Steve. Good luck with that." I patted my shoulder bag. "I've got some important business to take care of, somewhere that's . . . not here. But I'm sure I'll be seeing you around."

He raised one caterpillar eyebrow hopefully. "Perhaps for lunch?"

"No."

His other eyebrow went up. "Perhaps for a little wink wink, nudge nudge in the supply closet?"

"Good-bye, Steve."

"Steve will be waiting for you, Sophie! Steve will always be here waiting for Sophie."

I spun on my heel, trying my best to forget about Steve, standing three feet tall in the UDA hallway behind me, grinning salaciously, gray troll eyes staring me down.

I kept my head down, shrugged my bag over my shoulder, and hopped into the elevator with a hobgoblin and two pixies. We rode up in silence, three sets of eyes all fixed on the digital readout going backward. When the doors opened at the police station we shuffled out, exchanging positions with two female cops on their way to the garage. The dark-haired woman jostled against one of the pixies. I sucked in my breath as the pink-haired pixie flushed angrily and narrowed her eyes, but she stepped out without making a scene. As the doors slid closed, I heard the cop murmur, "I never know what to call them. Midgets? Little people?"

"I don't know," said the other. "Anyone under three feet tall gives me the creeps. My kids included. Do you want to get a latte?"

Chapter Four

The San Francisco Police Department was housed in a cavernous room with desks every ten feet and uniformed officers threading their way past the occasional plainclothed employee carrying stacks of manila file folders. There was always a phone ringing or a radio squawking, and whether or not there was an actual crime spree going on, the officers were always ready to move. I sucked my breath in as a uniformed officer shimmied by me, his head cocked as he listened to the radio cradled on his shoulder, the butt of his gun brushing up against my hip.

"Excuse me," I muttered, jumping out of the way. "Sorry."

My heart thumped as two officers pushed through the heavy glass doors and led a sullen-looking woman in, her hands in cuffs behind her back, her hair matted, eyes looking caged-animal wild and rimmed with smudged black liner.

"I swear," she was saying as the officers led her past me, "I'm telling you exactly what I saw. It was flying. It was a person and he just *flew* away."

"Just like last week," one of the officers answered back, his boredom obvious. "What was it then? A dog the size of a couch, jumping over a car? You and Superman, lady."

The woman fought against the officer clutching her arm, and I heard her handcuffs rattle. She stopped in front of me, her eyes wide, intense, and terrified.

"You believe me," she said, sniffing, moving her flushed face just inches from my own. "I know you do."

I stepped back, my stomach souring as much from the overpowering smell of alcohol and urine wafting from the woman as the intensity of her eyes, the biting truth in her words: *You believe me. . . . I know you do.*

The officers ushered the woman out of the way, and I beelined toward what seemed to be the front desk. I cleared my throat at the top of the officer's bent head.

"Good afternoon. I'm here to see Detective Hayes," I said.

The officer didn't look up.

"Excuse me," I said again, a little louder. "I need to see Detective Hayes."

The cop looked up at me, and I blinked twice.

He was twelve.

Maybe not twelve, but certainly not old enough to be strapped into an officer's uniform and running the front desk—even if he was just doing a Sudoku in yesterday's *Chronicle*. His small hazel eyes were red-rimmed and set too far apart. His nose was thin and freckled and a few stray whiskers—a petty attempt at a beard?—grew in odd angles above his upper lip. With his close-cut cropped strawberry-blond hair and big ears, he looked like an odd cross between Opie and Butthead. Or maybe it was Beavis; I could never remember which one was which.

"I'm sorry, miss, what was that?" Opie asked me.

"Um, Detective Hayes," I said for the third time, then patted my shoulder bag affectionately. "We're working on something." I straightened my shoulders and stood up taller. "A case. We're working on a case together."

Opie raised one red-blond eyebrow, and I forced the polite smile I used for gargoyles—hard-headed, stubborn, immovable gargoyles—and nodded. "Do you know where I can find him?"

Opie jerked a thumb over one shoulder, his hazel eyes never leaving the top of the blouse I forgot to button. I pinched the fabric together over my breast and narrowed my eyes on the officer. "Officer?"

"Down the hall, on the left. You'll see the sign."

I turned to leave, but Opie stopped me. "Ma'am?"

I bristled, and then reminded myself that to the police force under fifteen, I *would* be a ma'am.

"You'll need to fill this out first, please." Opie slid a clipboard toward me, and I sighed, filling in the obligatory information, then clipped the little plastic badge he gave me to my jacket.

After two wrong turns and several glares from angry-looking hooker types being led around by their cuffed arms, I found the correct hallway and Hayes's office. There was a folded piece of paper Scotch-taped to the frosted-glass door, the name DETECTIVE HAYES scrawled on it in black Sharpie.

"How very Barney Miller," I muttered before knocking quickly.

"'S'open!" I heard Hayes bellow from inside.

Okay, here's the thing. Like I said before, I'm not man crazy. But the sound of Detective Hayes's rich voice floating out did something to me, and every hair on the back of my neck stood up, every nerve ending pricked—especially the ones in the nether regions I cared not to mention. I wondered what that voice would sound like first thing in the morning, gruff with sleep, whispered in my ear.

"Come in," I heard again.

I shook myself from my fantasy and pushed through the frosted-glass door.

Hayes was leaning back in his ancient leather office chair, his feet resting on the corner of his desk, ankles crossed. His dark eyebrows were knitted and intense as he scanned the papers stacked in his lap, his perfect teeth chewing on his full bottom lip as he read.

I steadied myself against the little flutter I felt when his crystal blue eyes glanced up from his work and settled on me; I gripped the strap of my shoulder bag even more tightly when his face broke out in a warm, genuine grin that made my knees go medically oozy.

"You made it!"

I slung my bag onto one visitor's chair and slunk into the other.

"How do you manage around here? The environment is so hostile!" I shuddered and pulled my jacket tighter across my chest, and edged my chair a little farther back when I noticed the outline of an ankle holster against Detective Hayes's left pant leg.

A half smile cracked across the detective's face.

"This from the woman whose coworkers are blood suckers."

I rolled my eyes.

"And clients are monsters."

"Demons," I corrected, "and you shouldn't judge until you know one."

Hayes crossed his arms. "I could tell you the same thing."

"I'm sure you have a very friendly bunch up here," I said, doing a quick mental scan of the office: Cardboard file boxes. Super Big Gulp cup. Deeply stained coffee mug. Obligatory framed motivational poster propped on the floor behind the desk. No grinning, happily-ever-after wedding picture. No glossy black-and-white of a supermodel girlfriend. No "Proud Parent Of" bumper stickers, no five-by-sevens of a fat Michelin baby with cute brown curls and Detective Hayes's bright blue eyes. *Not* that I was interested. I let out the tiny breath I didn't know I was holding, and Detective Hayes raised one concerned eyebrow.

"Everything okay?"

I licked my dry lips and avoided his ice-blue stare. "Of course. Just checking out your office."

Hayes grinned again, leaning back in his chair and opening his arms. "Well, it's not exactly as posh as the UDA offices. I don't know if you know this, but us humans aren't always great decorators. I hear vampires really have a knack for that. Am I right?"

I rolled my eyes and Hayes chuckled, settling a coffee mug on a stack of boxes. "Besides, I just moved into this office not too long ago. They had me in a utility closet before this."

I was at a loss for witty banter, so I began rifling through my bag and stacking the file folders I had brought onto his desk. I decided it was best to go all business, especially since every flash of Parker Hayes's blue eyes or sexy smile seemed to make my heart thump painfully while putting my female parts on high alert.

"Okay, so I went through our files and I figured we'd start with the most likely candidates—or—suspects. So, I brought you—"

"No, not yet." Hayes was holding his hand up, palm forward. His sat up straighter, pulling his legs from the desk and planting them firmly on the ground. "Lunch first, work later."

I didn't move, and he chucked me softly on the shoulder. "Come on, I'll even buy."

"Such a gentleman," I said, sliding the files back into my shoulder bag and standing up. "Shouldn't we get to work right away? Isn't this kind of pressing though? The case, I mean?"

Hayes headed out the door, and I nearly had to run to keep up with his long, purposeful strides.

"The case is definitely pressing. And lunch is more pressing. Besides"—he patted his trim stomach—"I work best on a full stomach."

We walked outside into the moist San Francisco air and stood on the curb, waiting for traffic to pass. Hayes had his hands in his pockets, his lips and forehead puckered as he thought.

"So explain to me again how the UDA operates. And what is it, exactly, that the Underworld Detection Agency detects?"

I shrugged. "We detect paranormal activity to some extent. And more or less, we detect who and what is traveling through the Underworld or becoming active in the other world."

Hayes smiled. "The Overworld?"

I looked both ways and then stepped into the street. "Frankly, this world is rather wrapped up in itself. It doesn't really recognize the Underworld as actually existing, so it's pretty much just 'the world' up here. As for how we operate . . ."

Hayes reached out and grabbed my shoulder, his fingers digging into my flesh as he yanked me back and a rusted-out van zoomed past us.

"Whoa," I said, my heart pounding. "That was close." I looked at Hayes's fingers on my shoulders as his grip softened, but he didn't move his hand. "Thanks," I said.

Hayes didn't look at me, but he was smiling. He dropped his hand to his side, leaving a sudden cold spot on my shoulder where his palm had been. "So you were saying . . ."

"Right. How we operate . . . well, it's a little like the Social Security office, I guess. Demons register themselves with us. Once you're on the UDA radar, you're entitled to all the perks of the Underworld—unemployment, workers' comp, protection from labor and personal disputes . . ."

Hayes steered me toward the double doors of the Fog City Diner and paused. "Demons get workers' comp? In case what? A vampire breaks a fang on a particularly stubborn artery?"

I rolled my eyes. "Very funny. The UDA just works to keep a sense of order and harmony in the Underworld. We allow demonkind a little protection from a regular world that really disregards them."

"Until they scoop your eyeballs out."

I rolled my eyes. "Can we just get something to eat now?"

We walked into the warm diner, and I inhaled the comforting scent of club sandwiches and too-crisp French fries, smiling. "Smells good," I murmured.

Hayes nodded and held up two fingers to the woman behind the counter. She grabbed two menus and a couple of place settings, then beckoned for us to follow, leading us to an empty table by the window.

We slid into the booth and Hayes handed me a menu. He scanned his while I played with the laminated corner of mine, my stomach churning, my mind going a million miles a minute. Hayes looked up, eyebrows raised.

"What's wrong? Oh, don't tell me. You're vegan or something, right? Fruitarian? Only eat orange things?"

I wagged my head. "No. Nothing like that. What's a fruitarian?"

"Girl I dated in college . . ."

I looked up expectantly, but he just shook his head and went back to reading his menu.

"I guess I'm just a little nervous," I said.

Hayes grinned at me—a wide, lady-killer grin. "Really? I couldn't tell." His cobalt eyes traveled to my hand, to the loop of red hair wound absently over one finger. I quickly dropped the lock of hair and sat on my hand.

"Nervous tic," I said. "I hate it."

"Actually, I think it's kind of cute."

My heartbeat sped up, and I sat on my other hand.

Hayes shrugged, scanning his menu again. "So what's there to be nervous about? I'd tell you if you had spinach stuck in your teeth or something."

I blew out a long sigh. "There's a killer out there. Doesn't that bother you even a tiny little bit?"

Hayes turned over his coffee cup, and the waitress came by, giving him a nod and sloppily sloshing coffee into his mug.

"Honey, there's murderers everywhere." He lined up three sugar packets and dumped them into his cup, clinking his spoon against the mug as he stirred. "It's just another day at the office."

"But these are different—and don't call me honey," I said, my voice a hissing whisper. "Eyeballs are missing. Blood is missing. People are being torn apart. You can eat when people are being torn apart?"

I looked up to see that the waitress had returned and was working on a piece of Hubba Bubba, blowing large bubbles and then sucking them in.

"Are you guys ready to order?" she wanted to know.

I gulped. Either she didn't hear my comment, or I was the only one in the entire city worried about a supernatural predator hunting the San Francisco streets.

We placed our orders, and Hayes sipped his coffee, staring over the rim of his mug at me. "So what's your story, Lawson?" he said finally. "How'd you end up a secretary at a place like the UDA?"

I rested my arms on the table, lacing my fingers together. "Sophie. Lawson sounds way too *Law & Order*. And, I'm not a secretary. I'm an administrative assistant. An executive assistant if you really want to get technical." I sipped my water, pleased.

Hayes's lip curled into another one of those delicious half smiles, and I reminded myself that this was business, and that when Parker Hayes wasn't looking sexy and brash in his navy blues, he was kind of an anti-demon asshole.

"Sorry, of course—executive assistant. So, how'd you decide on pushing papers in the demon underground?" he asked.

"It's amazing what you can find in the want ads," I said, averting my eyes and tearing my napkin to shreds.

Hayes continued to eye me, and I breathed a little harder, pinned under his steady gaze.

"Well, first of all, I could get down there."

Hayes sipped his coffee and shrugged. "So what does that mean? Lots of people can use elevators."

"Nice. Theoretically, you can only get into the Underworld if you've got"—I bit my lip and glanced out the window, trying to choose my words carefully— "some supernatural in you."

"What?" Hayes snorted. "You're some kind of demon, too? I never would have thought. . . ."

"Keep your voice down!" I hissed,

"Sorry. It's just that you look so regular."

"Awesome," I said dryly, "regular. That's what every woman wants to hear about herself. And no, I'm not a demon. Well, yes, I guess I am—sort of. I think."

Our waitress came back, a large white plate balanced in each hand. She eyed me as she slid my salad in front of me, and I got a big whiff of grape-scented Hubba Bubba as she snapped a bubble.

"Can I get y'all something else?" she asked.

"No, thanks," I said, smiling politely.

Hayes popped a French fry in his mouth with one hand and shook a bottle of ketchup with the other. "So what are you? A leprechaun?"

Anger roiled in my stomach, and I could feel my

usually creamy white skin turning red. I dropped my fork. "I am *not* a leprechaun."

"So? What are you then?" He cocked his head, looking me up and down.

"My grandmother was a mystic—a seer. But then she lost it."

"Her power?"

"Her mind."

Hayes chuckled, settling back into the booth. "How very Psychic Friends Network. You know, I've always thought that if those people really were psychic, they'd call me when I had a problem." He grinned, enjoying his joke.

"She would have called you."

Hayes pursed his lips.

"The palm reading, fortune telling—that was kind of her day job. But she had real powers. She was pretty well known in the Underworld for it. She could really see things."

Hayes nodded but looked entirely unconvinced. "So, can you do it too, then? See the future and stuff?" He raised one eyebrow. "Can you read minds?"

I glared back at him. "I think I might be able to read yours."

He laughed, shoveled another handful of fries into his mouth. "There's that leprechaun spunk I like so much."

I felt my lips go thin and tight. "I. Am. Not. A. Leprechaun. And no"—I wrapped my hands around my water glass and stared at the ice cubes bobbing inside—"I don't have any powers. Yet. Or, maybe I never will. It's kind of hard to tell. I'm working on it, though. I mean, there might be something; it just hasn't happened yet. Anyway, after I graduated—USF"—I smiled, proud—"the only jobs open for an English major were paper boy or barista."

Hayes leaned back in the booth and smiled kindly. "I think you'd make a great paper boy."

I rolled my eyes, continuing. "My grandmother kind of talked me into the job initially—introduced me to Mr. Sampson and all. I thought it would be a quick thing, like a summer internship. You know, until I could write the great American novel or start teaching English in Spain. But as it turns out"—I shrugged—"I fit in really well down there, and I really like it."

"Well, score one for the leprechaun."

I resisted the urge to slug the smug grin off Hayes's face.

"So where's your grandma now? Pleased as punch you leash a dog like Sampson for a living, I'll bet."

I felt my muscles tighten, my arms going leaden under the anger. "You've got a lot of nerve, you know? Sampson is a werewolf, not a dog," I said, working hard to keep my voice low and even. "And my grandmother passed away, thank you very much." I blinked furiously, feeling the hot tears well, the growing lump choking my throat.

Sophie Lawson: tough chick or emotional invalid?

"Oh, hey." Hayes handed me a napkin. "Sorry, I didn't mean to make you . . ." He shifted uncomfortably. "What about your parents?"

I shrugged again. "My mom was a seer, too, but she hated what she could do. Sometimes—I've been told—it can get really hard to live with. Seeing all the things that people work so hard to keep hidden. It can take a lot out of you. All Mom wanted was a little normalcy. So, one day she met my father, a very normal professor of mythological anthropology at Berkeley. Nine months later I was here and dear old Dad was realizing that he wasn't exactly cut out for fatherhood."

"That's rough," Hayes said.

"Oh, he gave it the old college try, though." I wiggled four fingers. "He stayed for four whole days after I was born."

"Wow. Four?"

"My grandmother said he left because after four days, I didn't show any signs of magical ability. I guess that's what he was looking for in a spawn."

Hayes stopped chewing. "Do you really believe that?"

"I believe that after four days I didn't show any signs of the ability to change my own diaper. I think that was more bothersome. So, he took off. A little less than a year later my mother died." I smiled wistfully. "Grandmother, again, went to the magical extreme: my mother died of a black heart—a love spell gone wrong. I tend to lean toward the slightly less magical explanation of a steady diet of Chicken McNuggets and a pretty solid family history of heart disease. But there isn't any way of convincing Gram of that. Or there wasn't."

"I'm really sorry," Hayes said softly. "But your grandmother raised you? That must have been good, right? She sounds like she really cared about you."

"She did, and living with Gram was okay." I gritted my teeth, my mind working: *Every child should be raised in a house with a giant neon hand, palm highlighted with stars and hearts, in the living room window and a crystal ball in the dining room. Kids flock to children who are different and odd . . . and then beat them up.*

"Sophie?" Hayes's head was cocked.

"Oh." I blinked. "Sorry." I stabbed at a piece of chicken and popped it in my mouth. "This place is great," I said, chewing absently, not tasting my food. "So, I spilled. Your turn. What's your story?"

Hayes's blue eyes touched mine, then flitted across my forehead, avoiding my gaze. "Nothing as interesting as your life," he said. "I'm just a local guy, been around this city for . . . forever, pretty much. I'm just your basic, run-of-the-mill cop. Boring."

I nodded, but he didn't continue. "Oh."

Hayes had a handful of French fries in his mouth before he stopped chewing and stared at me, panic in his wide, cobalt eyes. He swallowed slowly, little bits of salt glistening on his lips.

"You know when you said you could get down to the Underworld?"

I nodded, sipping my water.

"Well," Hayes continued, "if you have to be . . . *you know*, to get down to the Underworld . . . how come I was able to?"

"I don't know. I guess I just assumed you were dead."

Hayes gasped. "You think I'm dead?"

The waitress's head snapped up as she passed again, and I smiled politely, watching until she was out of earshot.

"You think I'm dead?" he repeated in a desperate whisper.

"Okay, undead, whatever."

"I'm not!" Hayes was indignant. "Feel this." He wrapped his palm around my wrist. "See? Flesh and blood."

"Okay." I pushed a crouton off my plate and stabbed a piece of lettuce. "Sure."

"No, seriously." Hayes was standing up and pushing me aside, sliding next to me in the booth. "Feel." He grabbed my hand and slid it between the buttons of his navy blue shirt, so my fingers rested against the soft cotton of his undershirt. He pushed my palm flat, his hand over mine.

I resisted the urge to ogle. His chest was firm and taut and wonderful, and his heart thumped underneath my palm—warm—and very much alive.

"So you're not dead," I said, trying to squelch down my giddy goose bumps and control the tone of my voice.

Hayes's voice was thin, his eyes big, terrified. "Then what am I?"

"A big girl."

Hayes's eyes flashed and I sighed. "You can get down as a normal person—Nina calls 'em breathers— if someone who can go down sends you down. They're able to temporarily loosen the veil on the breathers." I went back to stabbing at my salad, and glanced through my lowered lashes to see a look of utter relief flood across Hayes's face—and then he panicked again.

"The chief is a demon?" he asked. "Is that how he knows Sampson?"

"I don't know if the chief is a demon," I said, mouth full of salad. "He and Sampson met in college, just before Sampson was bitten. They were college roommates."

Hayes's eyebrows rose expectantly.

"Sampson was bitten and changed into a werewolf in college. Now, can we just have lunch and then get to work? The sooner we crack this case, the sooner you can be done with the Underworld and go back to believing that the things that go bump in the night are just harmless human rapists, sadists, and murderers."

"That's all I ask," Hayes said, sipping his coffee again.

Chapter Five

After lunch at the diner, we headed back to the police station. Hayes handed me a Styrofoam cup filled with horrible coffee, drank his down in one gulp, and told me to hold steady.

"I'm going to go grab our files from downstairs. Can I get you another cup?" He gestured toward my still-full cup, and I wagged my head, forced a small gulp just to be polite. When he left I dropped the greasy mess into the trash can and shuddered.

I was making myself comfortable in a cracked pleather chair in the police department conference room when Hayes came in, carrying a groaning cardboard box packed with file folders.

"This is all we've got on the case so far," he said, dropping the box with a thud.

"Looks like a lot."

"Looks like a haystack." Hayes nudged the box. "It's our job to go through here and figure out what's pertinent and what's not, what's part of the case, what's helpful, etcetera, etcetera. But"—he reached into the box and extracted a grease-soaked white pastry bag—"I did bring dessert." He shook the bag with a grin.

I smiled. *A man with a heartbeat, a chiseled chest, and a penchant for sweets? Sophie Lawson hits the jackpot.*

"Well, aren't you the gentleman?" I said in my best attempt at sultry.

"I am. But the jelly-filled one is mine."

Hayes reached into the bag, extracted a sticky, glazed concoction, and stuffed the entire donut into his mouth, chomping down. I quickly shoved the file box aside, just in time to avoid a splat of blueberry jam as it dribbled from his chin and dropped onto the table.

"Be still my heart," I said, feeling instantly sticky.

Hayes sat down next to me. "Try your best not to fall in love with me." He pushed the bag toward me as he chewed. "Donut?"

I picked out a pink-sprinkled one and tried my best to nibble daintily.

"Pink sprinkles. I totally had you pegged," Hayes said, smiling down at the table.

I rolled my eyes, shoved the rest of the donut into my mouth, and dug into the file box.

"Interesting," was the only thing I could think of to say as I sifted through the first overstuffed folder. I pulled out a few yellowed newspaper clippings, some crime-scene photos, a Starbucks receipt, and a GO WITH GAVIN bumper sticker. "Don't you guys have any organizational system?"

"Yeah," Hayes said, gesturing toward the ragged box. "Put. In. Box." He dipped his pincher fingers into the pastry bag. "Do you mind if I have another?"

I shook my head. "It's no wonder you can't find this

guy," I said, wrinkling my nose as I pulled out a folder covered in grease and coffee stains.

I'd struck a nerve. "Look, lady, we do the best we can. It's not like we've got people lounging around the office, just waiting to file the latest. We've got a community to protect. A very large metropolitan community. What have you got? A couple of witches? The bogeyman? A vampire here and there?"

I pushed a neatly organized stack of UDA files toward Hayes and fished a few more out of my shoulder bag.

"I have just over twelve thousand actives. Twelve thousand and seventy-one, to be exact. Demons, vampires, witches, goblins . . ." I couldn't help but feel a little smug as Hayes's eyes went wide at the orderly stack I presented.

"Don't worry; I didn't bring in all our files. I'm pretty sure whatever is out there"—I suppressed the smallest shudder—"isn't the work of any centaur, gargoyle, or troll. Those are generally our less volatile groups."

"Wow," he said, wiping donut grease on a nearby file. "You guys really are organized. That's impressive."

"Forms up the wazoo," I said, shrugging. I eyed the stack, then picked out all the ones marked with a bright red flag. "These ones are the active vamps. Everything we need should be there—original birth dates, sires, crossovers—"

"Crossovers?" Hayes's dark brows rose a millimeter.

"When a breather goes vamp," I explained.

"Vampires remember that kind of stuff?"

"Initially, yeah. Five hundred years into their afterlife, the 'rebirth' details can get a little foggy. But at first it's pretty easily traceable. You wake up one morning with no breath and bellbottoms on? You were crossed over in the seventies. Ditto if you've got go-go boots or love beads."

"I see."

"There is information on current residences, jobs, skill sets, languages spoken, etcetera. Everything should be listed in the file."

Hayes swallowed thickly. "They work up here?"

I shrugged. "They work everywhere. The short order cook over at Fog City is a werevamp."

Hayes's eyes bulged. "Tiny? I thought he was a drag queen."

"He's that, too."

Hayes paled a little bit, and I blew out a long sigh and cocked my head, eyeing him. "Listen," I said, "there are a lot more magically inclined people out there than you think."

"Oh no," Hayes started. "I've seen a lot of weird things in this city—Elvis, the Easter Bunny on the Fulton 5, Mrs. Claus walking down the Haight with Santa in a dog collar in the middle of July. Even with that veil thing, I don't think I would miss seeing a vampire on Market. Or a troll."

"And what would you think if you did?"

"I'd think that I've definitely been working too hard."

I smiled. "Well, there you go. You're not expecting to see them, so you don't see them. That's how the veils work for the most part. It's not really that big of a deal."

I didn't think it was possible, but Hayes's complexion went a few shades lighter. I rested my hand on his. "They're just like you and me."

He opened his mouth to protest, and I held up one silencing finger. "Okay, maybe not *just* like. But the people of the Underworld want to live their afterlives just like anybody else—steady job, comfortable den with a white picket fence, minivan . . ."

"And two-point-five demonic kids?"

I ignored him. "The majority really doesn't want any trouble."

"Except for the small minority that wants to rip out people's throats, gobble up their eyeballs, and suck out all their blood."

I crossed my arms in front of my chest. "Kind of like the small minority of the human population, right?"

"Touché. Okay," Hayes said, a little bit of the color returning to his chiseled cheeks. "Where do we start, then?"

"Here," I said, handing him a thick stack of files. "Red flags are vampires. Yellow, zombies; blue, hobgoblins; green, witches; pink, other. We're not too sure what we're looking for, so I brought the most likely candidates. Vampires, obviously. But the zombies and hobgoblins can cause similar destruction and the witches—well, you generally want to stay on their good sides."

Hayes licked his lips and grinned. "What about mermaids? Do mermaids exist?"

I raised one annoyed eyebrow. "Why don't you jump into the ocean and find out?"

Hayes stifled a grin, taking the files. "Note to self," he said under his breath, "Lawson is anti-mermaid."

I shifted my eyes to Hayes, who ignored me. He was shuffling through the first set of documents. "I can't believe that demons adhere to this kind of structure."

"Well, vampires are very rule oriented," I said, rolling my hair into a loose bun.

Hayes looked skeptical. "I find that hard to believe. Soulless bloodsuckers, rule oriented?"

"Soulless bloodsuckers who won't come into your home unless invited. They are also compulsive counters, obsessively neat, and very polite." I rearranged my files, feeling a heat creep up the back of my neck as Hayes's knee brushed mine. "That kind of adherence to etiquette is quite endearing."

Hayes didn't look at me. "I suppose," he muttered.

I frowned at the UDA files. "If we don't find what we're looking for in here, I can send out a satellite request for files from the other offices."

Hayes blinked. "There are other UDA offices?"

"Of course. UDA is worldwide. You should see our Transylvania office."

"And are all the other offices"—Hayes's eyes shifted—"underground?"

"No. The one in Spokane is in the back of a Wal-Mart." I grinned when Hayes raised his dark brows. "Most of the offices are underground. It just makes our clientele feel more . . . comfortable. More able to be themselves, I guess. They don't have to worry about keeping up veils or shielding when they're underground. Not a lot of breather counterparts stumbling into the underground offices, asking to use the restroom." I offered a reassuring look.

Hayes shook his head. "I don't think I'll ever understand the Underworld."

I picked at another donut, popping a bit of pink frosting into my mouth. "You know all you need to. Demons exist in every aspect of your daily life—"

"And I should stay away from fairies." He grinned.

"Everyone," I said, breaking off another piece of donut, "should stay away from fairies." I smiled back at Hayes, my resolve softening as I studied the warm, pale blue flecks of color in his eyes.

Our moment was broken when there was the sound of shuffling papers, then a chirp from Hayes's cell phone, and then Chief Oliver was standing in the doorway, his lips set in a hard, thin line. He knocked on the door frame and looked in at us.

"There's been another murder," the chief said solemnly.

My mouth went dry and my palms started to sweat. Hayes stood up and grabbed his coat. He glanced over his shoulder at me while I began collecting my files.

"We don't have time for that," he said. "Come on."

"Don't worry. I don't have to be down at work for the rest of the day so I can stay around and clean up—"

Hayes cut me off. "You *are* at work. This is our case." He took my elbow, and I stood, numbly beginning to follow him.

"We're going to the crime scene," he told me.

"Crime scene?" I mumbled. "You mean, the scene of the crime?" My stomach dropped into my knees.

Hayes roughly put his arm across my shoulders and pulled me toward him, a hint of a smile on his moist lips. "Lawson, you're a natural."

My hands were gripping the seat as Hayes squealed the squad car out of his parking space and roared out of the lot.

"Shouldn't you put your sirens on?" I asked, trying to keep my voice an octave below hysterical.

"The guy's dead. He's not going anywhere."

I must have paled considerably—or gone completely green—because Hayes blew out a resigned sigh and clicked on the lights and sirens. Then he sunk the accelerator to the floor and we jerked through an intersection, cars screeching around us, action-movie style.

"He's dead, remember? Not going anywhere? This is not a chase scene from *Cops*!"

"If only," Hayes muttered as we reached the commute gridlock on Market Street. I saw heads swinging in our direction, tourists hugging their GAP purchases to their chests, civilian cars peeling to the sides to let us through as our police sirens howled.

I started to feel Hayes's adrenaline, and as we sliced through town, I tried to hold back a grin.

"Can I get a set of these lights and sirens for my Honda?" I asked, poking at the ceiling. "It would seriously cut my commute time in half."

Hayes chuckled and took a corner at record speed and I rolled into him, my seat belt cutting off my circulation, my head thumping against his chest. His firm, soap-smelling chest. I breathed deeply, hoping my olfactory ogling wasn't completely obvious.

"You women are always turned on by danger," he said, staring down at me with a seductive grin.

I struggled to sit up, to keep myself from getting too comfortable, nestled against his chest. "As if," I managed to mutter, letting my heartbeat slow to a normal rate.

After a few minutes, Hayes slowed the car down and pulled into the driveway of a swanky Pacific Heights Victorian. As he pushed the gearshift into park I noticed the crime-scene tape, the swarm of cops and onlookers, and then it hit me: there's probably a dead person inside that house. I clamped my mouth shut, feeling my teeth begin to chatter. My heart started to speed up again.

He killed the engine, pulling the key out of the ignition. Hayes kicked open the car door and stepped out, then dipped his head back inside and looked at me. My feet were bolted to the floor, my eyes boring through the windshield at the one-car garage door in front of me. My palms were damp, and I held them firm against my thighs.

"You coming, Lawson?"

I tried to lick my lips, but I had no saliva. I prayed to God, Buddha, Oprah—whoever might be listening—then forced my lips to move. "Is it still in there?" My voice came out raspy and low.

Hayes's dark eyebrows shot up, almost lost in the soft brown curls that tousled against his forehead. "It? You mean the perp? No, he's not still inside."

Hayes sat down again in the driver's seat and looked at me, his blue eyes warm and concerned. "The place was clean when the guys got in here. From what I hear, the vic may have been dead awhile." He reached out and touched my arm softly, his fingertips soft and trailing up my forearm.

"You're fine. You've got practically every cop in the area looking out for you." He grinned. "Plus one very adequate detective."

My stomach flip-flopped, but not in the delighted, hot-guy-touching-me sort of way. It was just that I had never seen a dead person who was actually . . . dead.

"The body," I whispered, "will it still be in there?"

Hayes looked confused, his dark eyebrows knitting together. "Of course. This is a crime scene. They won't have moved anything—or anyone—until we go through. Is that what you're afraid of? Seeing the body?"

I bit my lip. "Um, no." I forced a nonchalant lilt into my voice, not wanting to appear the meek, freaked-out little girly girl that I actually was. "I was just checking."

Hayes blinked, a small smile playing on his lips. His voice went soft and I was touched by the kind warmth in it. "It's never easy walking into a crime scene, Lawson, but we really need you here to help with this. You'll be okay, I promise."

I nodded, certain that if I opened my mouth to answer properly, my thundering heart would fall out onto the car floor.

Stepping out of the car, I followed behind Hayes, who stopped to talk to an officer guarding the door.

"It's our second time out here in as many days," the officer was telling Hayes. "The owner called it in. It seems there was an attempted break-in here yesterday."

"Or an attempted murder," Parker said solemnly.

The officer nodded his head slowly and then stepped aside. He looked from Detective Hayes to me, his tired eyes going a bit softer as he looked at me. "It's pretty gruesome in there."

"Aren't you people supposed to be impartial at stuff like this?" I leaned up on my tiptoes to whisper into Hayes's ear.

"Come on, Lawson," Hayes said, ushering me inside.

My mood wasn't helped when we were each handed a pair of latex gloves and papery booties to cover our shoes. I struggled into the gloves and slipped the booties on. Hayes already had his on when he looked over his shoulder, studying me. "You sure you're ready?"

My deodorant went into hyper drive as a bead of sweat rolled down my back. "Yep," I whispered, following him through the front door.

When we walked into the foyer, I sucked in a breath—not at anything crime-related, but at the sheer beauty of the place. Although the room was littered with cops unfurling yellow-and-black crime-scene tape, the opulence of the house still shone. My entire apartment could fit in the enormous, open entryway, and from the looks of it, I could park my CRV in the guest bath with room to spare.

"Whoa," I whispered under my breath.

Despite the paper booties covering them, my heels clattered on the marble floor and echoed up to the high, vaulted ceilings.

"This place is unbelievable," I told Hayes.

"And secured like Fort Knox," he replied, glancing at a sophisticated-looking jumble of wires and flashing lights hung in a metal box on the wall. He shook his head. "Whoever it is that's doing this is not the least bit fazed by modern security. This is certainly not the work of your run-of-the-mill opportunist perpetrator." He closed a metal door over the alarm system and slid a painting back over it. "Not a single wire has been tripped or cut."

"Is that bad?" I asked.

Hayes took me by the elbow, steering me out of earshot of the other officers as they milled about.

"You tell me. Do"—his voice dropped—"your *people* have the ability to get around technology?"

I chewed on my lower lip. "Well, not exactly. I mean I'm pretty sure there are spells to get around that kind of thing. Witches and warlocks would know, I suppose. And a vampire could certainly trance or glamour a human into turning off an alarm system. A fairy or pixie might be able to do that, too, with a glamour, but they usually wouldn't have the patience. And I've heard that on occasion, certain demons can wreak havoc on an electronic field."

Hayes's expression was suspicious, and I hurried on. "But the bottom line is that it's not exactly standard operating procedure. Alarms—and disarming alarms—that's really more of a human thing, don't you think? I mean, demons are pretty much old school."

"Old school, huh?" He seemed to consider this and then said, "Come on," one paper-bootied foot poised on the bottom stair. "We're going upstairs."

I followed Parker up the winding staircase, our booties making a soft *shoosh-shoosh* sound as we sunk into the lush ecru carpet. I glanced down, noticing fresh vacuum lines and stared behind me, seeing the lone trail of our footprints.

"Who vacuumed?"

"The maid. She told the officer who's with her that she vacuums before she leaves each night."

"Is there another way up?" I asked. "A back set of stairs or something?"

Hayes wagged his head. "Not that we've found. Why do you ask?"

"No footprints on the carpet. I mean, other than ours."

"Good catch." Parker grinned, chucking me on the shoulder.

I nodded, a bit proud, feeling very junior sleuth.

Maybe I could get used to this detecting.

"The maid said she found the vic when she let herself in this afternoon. The discovering officer didn't mention another set of footprints." Parker glanced down, pointing at his feet. "I've been walking in the prints already left here." He picked up one foot. "See? No tread. Those marks are from the booties."

"And there were no footprints."

Parker nodded. "So, the victim was either killed last night while the maid was in the house," Parker paused, frowning. "Or it could fly. Are we looking for something with wings now?"

I looked around Hayes at the undisturbed carpet. "Not necessarily. Vampires have no quantifiable weight. They wouldn't leave any tracks." I thought of Nina, the silent way she flitted around our house. "Lots of other mythical creatures wouldn't leave footprints, either," I said quickly.

We crossed the hall and I glanced through an open door where the maid, in a crisp, pale blue uniform, was sitting on a rose damask loveseat. She was sobbing loudly, working a rumpled handkerchief between her thick, stubby fingers while an officer stood by, taking notes.

At the end of the hallway, we paused in front of a set of double doors, and Hayes looked over his shoulder at me. "Ready?" he asked.

I nodded and he pushed open the doors.

The master suite was phenomenal, even in its dimmed-light state. The huge bay windows were obscured by pale gray floor-to-ceiling curtains that only let in a few meager shards of sunlight. An imposing carved-wood bed took up one whole wall, and tucked daintily into the bed a woman rested, peaceful, eyes closed, pale lips drawn, her golden hair spread out in fairy-tale swirls on her white silk pillowcase.

"She's so young," I said, frowning, looking around the pristine room. Delicate antique perfume bottles were lined up on a glass tray, and a vase full of tulips—not a single petal lost—arched over the night-stand. Not a thing was out of place. The calm of the room was palpable.

"Why do they think this was a murder?" I asked, stepping closer to the sleeping woman. "She looks so peaceful. Maybe it was natural causes? Heart attack, cardiac arrest, choking . . ." I ticked off all the causes of death I could think of from watching *Grey's Anatomy*. "And she's got eyeballs, right? This doesn't look like our guy." I clapped my hands, a prickly wave of relief washing over me. "I guess that's it, right? Should we head back to the station? Grab a cup of coffee from the diner? I'm buying."

Hayes ignored me and moved closer to the bed, putting one gloved hand on the bedclothes carefully folded over the woman. In one swift motion, he folded them back.

I gasped, my heart lurching, my knees buckling. The hardwood floor felt cool through my skirt as I sat down hard and my feet kicked away, trying to shove my body farther from the offensive scene.

"Oh. God," I gasped, then clamped my mouth shut. "Oh God, oh God, oh God."

Hayes looked back at me, panicked. He crouched

down next to me, his knees touching mine, his hands on my shoulders. "Lawson, are you okay?"

I wagged my head and fought to get up, one hand still clamped over my mouth. Hayes stepped out of the way, and I found the bathroom door, shoved it open, and vomited.

Chapter Six

I was splashing cold water on my face when Hayes appeared in the doorway, a combination of concern and amusement washing over his face. "I barfed at my first crime scene, too," he said companionably.

"Good for you," I said, swishing water in my mouth and then spitting it into the sink. "But I don't think I'm cut out for this." I turned off the tap and wiped my hands on a towel—*a dead woman's towel*—and felt the urge to vomit again. It passed and I pressed my hands against my heart in an effort to keep it from thundering through my chest. "This was a bad idea. I'm an administrative assistant. I don't do murders. I file papers. I take fingerprints."

Hayes leaned against the door frame and crossed his arms. "Demons have fingerprints?"

"Everyone has fingerprints. Except hobgoblins because of the slime but—" I glanced up at Hayes's amused face and frowned, fists on hips. "A woman is dead here, Parker. I'm having a severe panic attack. Can you be serious for like, one minute?"

Hayes came toward me and bundled me into an

awkward, one-armed hug. His lips were right at my hairline and he whispered, "It's okay. I'm here, Lawson. Everything is going to be okay. We'll get this guy."

A rush of warmth washed over me and I wasn't sure whether it was more nausea or Parker's proximity, but I voted for the latter, then felt immediately guilty for having sexy thoughts in a dead woman's bathroom. I wriggled out of Parker's arm, smoothing my hair back.

"Thanks," I muttered. "I think I'm okay now. Sorry."

"Are you ready to help me with this?" Hayes asked, one hand on the small of my back as he led me back into the bedroom. "Because if it's too much for you . . ."

I steeled myself. "No. I'm okay. Let's just get this over with."

I walked into the room, my eyes immediately going to the bed, to the dead woman. The sheet was still thrown back, and I balled my hands into fists, digging my fingernails into my palms as I willed myself to walk forward, to take in the scene. The woman's peaceful head still rested calmly on the silky pillow, but now I could see that her neck was barely attached. There were horrible-looking bite marks at her collarbone and across her chest; the skin was puckered, torn, and purpled. There were double puncture wounds on each upturned wrist, and more blood than I had ever seen in any of Nina's blood-bank lunch deliveries.

"Who could have done this?" I whispered, unable to tear my eyes away.

Hayes looked sideways at me, his jaw set, that muscle twitching again. "I was hoping you could tell me."

I found myself stepping closer, examining the corpse. I pushed aside a crumple of torn, blood-soaked nightie and gasped.

There was a yawning, bloody hole just under the woman's left breastbone—and her heart had been completely removed.

I wretched and clamped my hand over my mouth again, but the vomit didn't come this time. My knees weakened, and before I knew it, Hayes was holding me up, his calm chest pressed against my heaving one, my head buried in the crook between his neck and shoulder. I felt his hands pressing against the small of my back, massaging in small circles softly, as I was sobbing, gasping, hiccupping. He led me into the hallway, shutting the door gently behind us. It didn't help. The image of the woman's bloodied nightgown and her naked, hollow chest burned in my pinched, closed eyes.

"Oh," I mumbled, sinking down onto the top stair. "Oh, my God." I leaned forward, my head between my knees. I tried to breathe deeply.

Hayes hunched down beside me and brushed a few stray locks of hair behind my ear, his fingertips lingering gently on my skin. The movement was so tender that I wanted to cry.

"I'm sorry," I sniffled, looking up at him. "I guess I'm not a very good detective."

"No one is supposed to be good at this, Lawson. No one should ever be good at this." He stood up. "You stay here. Catch your breath. I'm going to go in and finalize things, and then we'll head back to the station."

I smiled weakly, and Hayes disappeared back into the bedroom.

Once the door clicked shut, I steadied myself enough to stand up and shakily followed Hayes through the bedroom door. Hayes had his back toward me, was hunched over, taking pictures of the body and writing in his little black leather notebook. He glanced over one shoulder at me, his blue eyes clear and focused.

"I think it's vampires," he said.

"No," I said, my eyes following an arc around the body. "Do you see that?" I pointed, and Hayes's eyes followed my finger. He frowned and shrugged.

"What am I looking at?"

I crouched down to the hardwood floor, my fingers brushing a smooth white powder. "There's a pentagram drawn around the bed."

Hayes wagged his head, eyebrows furrowed. "I don't see anything."

"Veil," I said, showing him my chalked fingers. "Someone was trying to cover their tracks—magically speaking."

Hayes swallowed thickly. "So, pentagrams? That's demonic, right? So, vampires."

I looked at the destruction of the body, the dark red splatters of blood on the bottom sheet, the pool of red seeping into the mattress. "I don't think so," I said.

Hayes pointed to the woman's pale arms lying palm up, the delicate skin on each wrist punctured by two tiny, perfect holes spaced equidistantly apart, the skin puckered as though it had been violently sucked.

"Aren't those teeth marks? Fangs?"

I shook my head. "Vampires don't leave this kind of destruction. They generally aren't interested in being caught, in leaving any traces. And the blood—" I swallowed hard against a fresh wave of nausea. "That's a lot of blood to leave behind. Human blood is a life force to a vampire. They aren't going to leave that much—they can't. It's a survival instinct. And the heart . . ." I couldn't finish, and Hayes wagged his head.

"Maybe the vamp was angry, sloppy. Maybe he wasn't doing this to feed. Or maybe he didn't care if he was found out. He certainly didn't care the last time."

"We don't know that it was a vampire last time. Besides, there is no reason that a vampire would gouge out someone's eyes. And if he didn't care whether or not he was found out, why would he bother to put her back in her bed? To veil the pentagram? Why would he bother to make it look like nothing happened?" I found myself whispering the last part: "And why would a vampire take out her heart?"

Hayes blew out a long sigh. "I don't know. But I know it's a vampire. I know you've got a soft spot for whatever reason for the pointy-toothed bloodsuckers, but let's face it: when you hear hoofbeats, you don't go looking for zebras."

I put my hands on my hips. "What is that supposed to mean?"

"It means that if there are teeth marks, I'm going to go looking for vampires."

"Vampires. Crap!" I slapped my palm on my forehead and glanced at my watch.

"What?"

"I was supposed to pick up Nina's nephew from the Caltrain station. He comes in in eight minutes."

Hayes shrugged. "We're done here and we're not too far."

"Yeah, but I need to get my car. It's going to take at least forty-five minutes to get back across town now—it's rush hour. And then to get back to the train station. I can't let him just sit there on the platform waiting all alone—he's just a kid."

Hayes pulled his keys from his pocket and dangled them in front of me. "So we'll turn on the siren."

"We're going to pick him up in the squad car?"

Hayes was already heading for the stairs and the front door. "Do you have a better idea?"

Once I had buckled myself into the passenger seat and Hayes had pulled into traffic he looked at me, frowning. "I thought you said Nina was a vampire?"

I nodded, fishing a half-wrapped piece of Trident out of my purse. Better my breath smelled like purse lint and peppermint than barf. "She is."

"So how does . . ."

"How does she have a nephew? Same way anyone else has a nephew. And yes, he's a vampire, too."

"Great. I'm going to go pick up a vampire. And now you're going to have two vampires hanging around?"

I nodded. "It'll be kind of nice, actually. Nina and I have been friends for ages, and I've never met any of her family. I think it might be fun having another member of the LaShay family hanging around—fanged as they may be."

Hayes wagged his head. "I really don't think I'm ever going to get any of this Underworld stuff."

I filled him in on Nina's history with Louis, and by the time I had finished talking, Hayes's cheeks were flushed and we were at the King Street Station, the old trains groaning down the tracks.

"Whoa!" I said, pointing when we were lucky enough

to find a nearby parking space. I grinned at Hayes. "You've got good parking karma. That never happens at rush hour."

He ignored me and stepped out of the car, scanning the hordes of Caltrain riders as they strolled out of the station, beelining for their cabs and buses. "Okay, what are we looking for?"

"*Who*," I said, coming around the car and grabbing Hayes's elbow. "Louis is a who, not a what. And Nina says we should be able to recognize him right off."

"Will he be carrying his graveyard dirt with him, or is he having it sent?"

I socked Parker in the arm and kept on walking, nodding to the janitor who was concentrating on pushing a broom across the tile floor in the train station foyer.

"You know him?" Hayes asked.

"I filed his papers just last week. His wife is going to be coming over from Canada early next month. I'm really excited for them."

Hayes swallowed and lowered his voice. "So he's . . . what?"

"Vampire," I said. "Works the night shift."

"I thought vampires were all hoity-toity. You know, big-time jobs or just independently wealthy or whatever."

"Some are. But all of them are obsessed with cleanliness." I smiled and beelined for the number seven train platform.

"Okay," I told Hayes once we were waiting on the edge of the tracks, "he should be coming off any minute now."

Hayes and I stood on the platform, examining the faces of all the people stepping off. I was looking for someone who bore a vague resemblance to Nina—pixie-nosed, a thick head of blue-black hair, fine-boned—when Parker sucked in a sharp breath beside me.

"That has got to be him," he said, his blue eyes steady.

I followed his gaze and held my own breath, eyeing Louis as he stepped off the train. He was tall—exceptionally so—but shared Nina's slim build and fine, elegant facial features. His marble skin was porcelain-perfect and made the inky black of his eyes, the rose-wine stain of his lips, stand out. The teenaged girls and young women exiting the train around him clamored to stay next to Louis, despite the fact that he was dressed like Bela Lugosi.

I was just thankful that he had decided against the cape.

"Is he wearing a tux?" Hayes asked, leaning into me.

"No. I think that's an ascot. Tuxes have bow ties, right?"

Hayes furrowed his brow.

"Well, maybe that's what all the boys wear where he comes from."

"I'll bet," Hayes snorted.

Indeed, Louis was dressed in carefully pressed black dress pants with a well-tailored black dinner jacket. A red jacquard vest peeked out from underneath the coat, and a silky, patterned ascot was looped tightly around his pale, elegant neck. His dark hair was slicked back, showing off the same widow's peak that Nina routinely brushed her hair over.

There was a thin line of black outlining his dark eyes. "He's wearing makeup," Hayes said. "Do you think where he comes from, all the boys wear eye makeup, too?"

I socked Hayes in the arm again and pasted a welcoming smile on my face. "Louis!" I called, waving my hands over my head.

Louis's dark eyes scanned the heads of the group around him before settling on me. His expression remained blank, unfazed, but he headed in our direction.

"Hi!" I said, smiling brightly when he reached us. "It's so nice to meet you!" I extended a hand that Louis looked at disdainfully. "I'm Sophie, and this is my friend, Parker Hayes. He's a detective."

Parker and Louis exchanged the universally male partial head bob while I chattered spastically. "I'm your aunt's best friend. But I'm sure she's told you that. Do you like to be called Louis or Lou or—"

Louis's dark eyes raked over both Parker and me, the expression on his face that age-old vampire/teenager mixture of boredom and contempt. "Actually," he said, slowly, "its Vlad."

I raised an eyebrow. "What was that?"

"Vlad," Louis said carefully, his fangs pressing against his ruddy lips. "I prefer to be called Vlad. Louis no longer exists."

Parker looked at his feet, but I could see his apple cheeks pushing up into a quiet smile.

"Vlad?" I repeated. "Well, okay, Vlad it is. Are you excited to be here, Vlad? Have you ever been to San Francisco before? We're really glad you're here."

Vlad blew out a bored sigh. "I was here during the big quake."

"Nineteen-o-six or the eighty-nine quake?"

"Both."

"Okay," Parker said, clapping his hands. "How about we head to the car?"

"Are you sure you're going to be okay alone with Count Dracula?" Hayes asked me once we returned to the police station parking lot.

"Be quiet, Parker. I'm sure he's a nice kid."

"Did you get that from his overwhelming silence or from his spitting glares?"

I rolled my eyes. "Look, this day has been long—really long. I just want to get home and get Louis—Vlad—settled. I'll see you at the police station tomorrow?"

Hayes and I stood awkwardly staring at each other until Vlad blew out an annoyed sigh as he stood on the passenger side of my car. "Can we go now, Sophie?"

Chapter Seven

"So, is there anything in particular you'd like to do while you're here, Vlad?"

Vlad ran his fingers over the dashboard, and I saw that his nails were painted black.

"I like your nail polish," I tried.

Vlad glared at me, his eyes dark and flat.

"Aunt Nina got me a job at UDA," he said finally.

"Really? That's great! Doing what?"

"Mail room."

I waited for him to elaborate. He didn't. "Oh. Well, you'll love it there. Everyone at the UDA is great. Like one big family, really. Did your Aunt Nina tell you that I work there, too?"

I felt Vlad's eyes on me, taking me in. "They *let* you work there?"

"Yeah. I work for Mr. Sampson—he's the head of the UDA. I'm his assistant."

Vlad looked at me skeptically and shook his head. "No offense, but I can't believe they'd let someone like you work at the Underworld Detection Agency.

It just goes to show that the demon world is losing its foothold. No offense," he repeated.

I frowned, staring at the road through the windshield. "No offense taken . . . kind of."

Seventy-seven-year-old Mr. Howard, self-proclaimed ladies' man and the building's resident gossip hound, was nuzzling the ear of a giggling, gray-haired woman when we walked into the building vestibule. He pulled the woman—carefully stuffed into yards of cheetah-print spandex—closer to him and gave her a playful kiss on her wrinkled neck.

"Sophie Lawson!" Mr. Howard beamed when he saw Vlad and me. He quickly straightened up, a wave of pink creeping across his high cheeks. He looked Vlad up and down and smiled. "Well, hello, young man. Are you a friend of Sophie's?"

Vlad remained expressionless, and I was secretly pleased that his deadpan demeanor wasn't just reserved for me.

"Mr. Howard, this is Nina's nephew, Vlad. He's going to be visiting Nina and me for a while." I leaned closer to Mr. Howard, stage whispering, "He's very shy."

Mr. Howard nodded and snaked an arm around his woman, then looked down at her, his gray eyes shining with lust as he eyed her heaving bosom. "Lovey, this is Sophie and her friend. Sophie lives in the apartment across the hall from me."

The old woman eyed me suspiciously and offered a limp hand, her wrist-load of bangles jangling as she did so. She looked around me then, her eyes widening when they settled on Vlad. She straightened up and pushed out her large chest as her greasy-red lips crept up into a flirtatious grin. I stepped into her line of vision to break the spell.

Vampires—male and female—have a magnetic draw on average humans. It guarantees the propagation of their kind, though is less beneficial to *our* kind. I heard Vlad quietly grumble behind me.

"Don't you worry, Lovey," Mr. Howard muttered, his hand firmly working the woman's rump, "Sophie and I are just good friends."

"Good to see you again, Mr. Howard," I said, my smile wan. "Nice to have met you, too. Vlad and I should be heading upstairs, though. Time to get settled." I grabbed Vlad by the elbow and pushed him in front of me, then nodded to the couple who immediately went back into nuzzle mode.

"Look," I said under my breath, "You're going to run into a lot of humans here. You've got to keep that"—I wriggled my fingers in front of him—"under control."

"Of course," Vlad said smoothly.

"I'm serious. No glamouring while you're here. At least not while you're here, here."

Vlad eyed me, but his expression didn't change.

"Glad we're clear," I said mostly to myself.

Vlad and I headed up to my apartment. I pushed my key into the lock and dumped my shoulder bag on the hallway floor. *If I can just get into the tub—into the tub and maybe into the liquor cabinet—this day will improve immensely,* I told myself. I ushered Vlad in, then kicked the door closed with my foot, snapping the dead bolt behind us.

"Nina should be home soon. Go ahead and make

yourself comfortable. If you don't mind, I'm going to take a bath."

"Do you have high-speed Internet?" Vlad asked.

"Yeah, of course."

He whipped a MacBook Pro out of his book bag, flipped it open, and settled himself at our kitchen table.

I guess teenagers—dead or alive—are pretty much the same everywhere.

I stripped off my clothes when I walked into the bathroom, leaving them in a trailing heap on the floor. Once I was in nothing but my bra and panties I toed my skirt, blouse, and jacket, noticing an oblong stain of red-black blood on the cuff of my blouse. My stomach lurched and my eyes watered.

"So much for that outfit."

I grabbed the broom and dustpan from the linen closet and swept my clothes into a heap, then dumped the mess—dustpan and all—into the rubbish bin.

I ran the bathwater as hot as I could get it and upturned a bottle of honey-coconut bubble bath under the faucet. I sniffed and then tossed in a handful of pink crystal bath salts and then sunk myself up to my eyebrows in the hot, soapy water, hoping that the mélange of fluffy bath scents and scalding water would wash away any trace of vomit, blood, and memory.

Once I felt adequately boiled—my skin warm, pink, and wrinkled—I snuggled into my baby-blue chenille bathrobe and padded to the kitchen. Vlad hadn't moved from his spot at the table, and now the glow from the laptop reflected off his pale skin eerily.

"What are you playing?" I asked him.

He didn't look up. "Bloodlust."

My stomach lurched. "How nice."

I poured a glass of Sauvignon Blanc and promptly downed it.

"Can I get you something to drink?" I asked Vlad. "Nina stocked the fridge for you. She's got A, B, O pos, and O neg. There's Blood Light too, but . . ."

Do vampires have a drinking age?

"No, thanks." Vlad wagged his head, his eyes never leaving his screen. "I'm fine."

"Suit yourself."

I dumped a half loaf of Wonder Bread on the counter for myself and slathered a few pieces of the fluffy white bread with peanut butter and grape jelly, promising myself that I would go right back to avoiding carbs and eating like a grown-up tomorrow. Then I poured myself a second glass of wine and headed for the couch. "I'm just going to watch a little TV if you don't mind."

Vlad didn't answer.

I was picking the crusts off my sandwich and watching a *Gossip Girl* rerun when I heard the lock tumble and Nina appeared in the doorway, nudging the door closed with her hip.

"Hey," she said, coming in, dumping her purse and keys on the countertop.

I jumped a little, dropping the remains of my sandwich in my lap. "Ugh. You scared me." I licked peanut butter off my hand.

She wiggled her fingers and stuck out her tongue. "Woooo! I vant to suck your blood!" Her Transylvanian accent left something to be desired. She giggled.

"Not amusing," I said, tossing a pillow at her.

"Louis!" Nina squealed, when she saw him sitting at the table.

Louis didn't look up, and I leaned over to Nina. "His name is Vlad now."

Nina frowned. "Vlad? Really?"

Vlad looked over his laptop and stood up, gliding silently toward Nina. "Aunt Nina," he said, grinning, exposing those small fangs.

Nina stood on tiptoes to hug him, and I got a little warm fuzzy from the vampire family reunion. "This is so nice!"

Nina stepped out of Vlad's embrace. "So you're going to be Vlad now? Seriously?"

Vlad nodded solemnly, clasping his hands in front of him.

"Why? Couldn't come up with something more original, like Lord Voldemort?"

Vlad glared at Nina.

"What's wrong with Vlad?" I asked, popping the last bite of sandwich in my mouth.

"Every male vamp under a hundred and fifty calls himself Vlad. It's the Muhammad of the vampire world. You know, Vlad the Impaler? Vlad Von Dracula?"

I shrugged, and she swung her head to Vlad again. "And what's with the outfit?"

"This is the uniform of the Vampire Empowerment and Restoration Movement."

Nina rolled her eyes and flopped on the couch. "Oh, man. You haven't gotten involved with the Movementarians, have you? Ugh, Louis."

"Vlad," he corrected.

"What's a Movementarian?"

Vlad glared at Nina. "We are not Movementarians.

We are soldiers of the Vampire Empowerment and Restoration Movement."

"And that is . . . ?" I tried again.

Nina checked out her cuticles. "It's a bunch of loony vamps that want to drag vampirism back to the dark ages. Hence"—she gestured toward Vlad—"the castle Drac wear. They always talk about going back to the 'old ways'—and are especially against humans."

"Not true," Vlad said with a hungry grin. "We love humans." His dark eyes settled on me, and I shuddered.

Nina glared at Vlad, then climbed up on the couch, standing on a cushion so she was nose to nose with him. She began wagging her finger a quarter-inch from his nose.

"Look, *Louis*, if you even think about drinking the tiniest blood bubble from Sophie, I will stake you and behead you myself."

"You really frighten me," Vlad said, deadpan.

"And I'll turn that human girl who was always trolling around you back home, and you'll be stuck with her whiney, Hannah Montana countenance for all of eternity."

Vlad snarled and went back to his laptop. "I wouldn't have eaten her," he muttered to the screen.

Nina hopped off the couch and smiled down at me. "Teenagers." She shrugged. "So, Sophie, how was your day?" She folded her legs underneath her and kicked off a pair of complicated-looking heels, then sunk onto the sofa next to me. I shivered and pulled my robe tighter against the waft of cool air that came from her marble skin.

"Thanks for not letting him eat me," I whispered, leaning into her.

"I wasn't going to eat you!" Vlad called without looking up from his laptop. "At least not a lot."

"So," Nina repeated, her midnight-dark eyes glittering, "how was your day with Officer Love? Excellent? Wonderful? A freak show of wild, breather sex?"

"I'm sitting right here!" Vlad moaned.

"You're one hundred and twelve, get over it. Humans have sex," Nina called back.

"Gross."

I downed my wine and Nina frowned.

"That bad, huh?" she asked.

"Not with Officer Lo—I mean Detective Hayes. He's fine—straddles that fine line between obnoxious and wonderfully hot—but fine. It's this case." I shuddered. "There was another murder today."

I saw the top of Vlad's head poke over his laptop screen as he listened in. Nina looked away, reaching for an out-of-date *InStyle* magazine on the coffee table. "I still don't see why this is such a big deal. Everyone kills everyone in this city. Everyone's either dead, undead, or dying."

I raked my fingers through my hair. "Nina, this is serious. The crime scene, it was awful. It was a woman our—or, my—age. There was blood everywhere." I tried to swallow, but my throat was dry. "And someone removed the woman's heart."

Nina's eyes flashed. "Removed it?"

"Removed it?" Vlad repeated. "Completely?"

I nodded. "Gone. Hayes is convinced it's a vampire."

"Stupid," Vlad groaned, going back to his computer game.

Nina raised an eyebrow and snapped a magazine page, ignoring Vlad. "Is that so?" She sat forward. "Does this detective even know anything about vampires? Anything at all? *Humf.*" She snapped another page. "He probably thinks we're anti-garlic, too."

"You hate garlic."

Nina pinned me with a glare. "It gives me bad breath."

I pinned her back. "You don't have breath."

Vlad chuckled from his spot at the table.

Nina rolled her eyes. "*Anyway.* We don't do hearts. Or waste blood. Ever. Starving vamps in Africa, you know?" She pointed, her eyes narrowed. "Hobgoblins. That's what you're dealing with. They're sloppy. And into all those weird organ meats."

I could feel my eyes bulge.

"And they're more likely to go rogue. Hobgoblins and zombies. They have no respect for the rules."

"Ghouls either," Vlad supplied.

"What do you think of me in this dress?" Nina folded a page back and held the magazine up to her narrow cheekbone. "Good?"

I sunk back into the couch, my stomach gurgling. "I can't think of fashion right now. People are dying. And other people are thinking it's coming from the Underworld. You know—"

Nina wrinkled her pixie nose. "I know. Delicate balance between worlds, blah, blah, blah." She tossed the magazine and kicked her legs up onto the coffee table, balancing her chin in her palm. "You don't think it's coming from the Underworld?"

"I don't know. There was veiling and a pentagram, so it's got to be someone who knows their magics."

Nina eyed me, the corners of her mouth turning

up. "Pentagrams? How very every eighties horror movie. And any demon could learn to veil; it's magic one-oh-one."

"Can you?" I asked.

Nina looked away. "Any person could learn to do it, too."

"Well, the veiling was one thing, but the rest . . . I've worked in the Underworld for a long time, Nina. I've worked with vampires, werewolves, even hobgoblins, and I've never even seen a hint of this kind of"—I shuddered again—"destruction."

Nina raised a sculpted eyebrow.

"Not even from zombies," I added. "Or ghouls."

"Well," Nina said, sitting forward, "remember when that Chaos demon ate your goldfish? That was pretty destructive."

"A Chaos demon ate your goldfish?" Vlad said. "Cool."

"It was not cool," I snapped. "He swallowed Tipsy whole And the little plastic pirate ship she was hiding in. But the stupid demon didn't rip her heart out."

Nina shrugged, letting one elegantly slim arm hang over the arm of the couch.

"I don't know what to tell you, Soph," Nina started. "It certainly could be human. I've definitely seen a lot of crazy lunatic breathers in my day. Or days."

"And people think *we're* the monsters," Vlad said.

Nina grinned then, her little fangs blue-white against her bright red lipstick. "So, what are you up to tonight?"

I glanced at the clock, then nodded toward my bedroom. "I can't think of anything other than sleep." I tapped my chest. "Breather, remember? We thrive on sleep. What about you?"

Nina gave me a smug smile and headed toward our guest room, which doubled as her enormous, stuffed-to-the-gills closet. "I am introducing my baby nephew Louis—"

"Aunt Nina, it's Vlad!" Vlad moaned.

Nina rolled her eyes. "Whatever. We're going to a new all-night club. It just opened right off the Haight. It's called Dirt."

I wrinkled my nose. "A club called Dirt?"

She raised a pleased eyebrow. "It's strictly pro-vamp. And way more breather-acceptable than its predecessor, Blood."

"Do you have something to wear, *Vlad*?" Nina asked, stressing his name.

Vlad stood, smoothing his vest. "I'm wearing this."

Nina poked her head out of her closet. "Awesome. I'm going to the hottest new club in town with a Halloween costume. Just"—she scrutinized Vlad's suit—"don't walk too close to me."

"Hey," I called, following Nina into her room as she nearly disappeared behind a lacy heap of vintage Betsey Johnson dresses. "How'd it go with Mr. Sampson tonight? Did you have any trouble with the chains? Sometimes the ankle lock sticks."

"Ankle lock?" Vlad asked.

"Sampson's a werewolf," I called over my shoulder.

Vlad shrugged and went back to playing his game.

Nina stopped her rushed plow through her pillaged couture, and her head popped up, a silky cashmere tank top bunched around her thin shoulders.

I crossed my arms, panicked. "You did remember to chain Mr. Sampson, didn't you?"

She gently gnawed on her bottom lip. "It's not even a full moon, Soph. He'll be fine, right?"

"Nina!"

She struggled into her tank top and stepped into a pair of deep-purple suede mules. "So I forgot this one time! I'll do it tomorrow. No big."

"You can't just do it tomorrow!" I threw back the curtains and stared out the window, my eyes searching the inky night sky for the moon. "You have to chain him every night."

Nina came out of her room, straightening her going-out clothes. "I thought that was just precautionary."

I let out a long sigh, rubbing my temples. "It is—kind of. Werewolf evolution is so rapid. But"—I glanced outside again—"we have to do it. Every night."

Nina bit her lip, looking apologetic. I rolled my eyes. "Fine. Don't worry, Nina. I'll take care of it."

"Thanks," she said, wrapping her tiny cold hands around my forearms. "I promise I won't forget again. Besides"—she shrugged, her shoulders delicate and starkly pale against the black straps of her tank—"Sampson will be so happy to see you."

A zip of heat rushed up the back of my neck, and I indulged in the me-and-Mr. Sampson fantasy for a split second before deciding to give up romance novels for good. The surge of estrogen obviously had my hormones in overdrive.

"Come on, Vlad, we're going to Dirt!"

Nina gave me a quick kiss on the cheek and tucked a beaded gold Armani clutch under one arm. She did a quick spin, her glossy black hair fanning around her head, her makeup perfect on her poreless face. "Good?" she asked.

"Good." I nodded, hugging her cold form close to me. "You guys have a nice time. And be safe, okay?"

Nina pulled away and bared her fangs, her delicate features going sharp and bloodthirsty in a split second. Vlad grinned, his own sharp fangs exposed.

"I think we'll be okay," she said, smiling sweetly. "See you in the morning." Nina and Vlad noiselessly disappeared out the front door and I tumbled the lock behind them.

I would have liked to be polished and put together to head down to UDA (especially since it would very likely only be me, Mr. Sampson, and the dim glow from the safety lights). But it was late and wanton comfort won over wanton sexy, so I compromised: a pair of slim black yoga pants and a *clean* University of San Francisco sweatshirt. Impressive, right? I raked a brush through my mass of red curls and then coaxed them into a bouncy ponytail, then hastily swiped on a bit of mascara and let cherry ChapStick stand in for gloss.

I headed to the elevator and realized that I'd never been more thankful to have underground parking than I was on this night, which seemed darker and colder than most city nights.

Within minutes I was in the SFPD parking lot. There was a half-rusted Chevette in my usual parking space, and it seemed as if the majority of the city was spending its Wednesday night at the police station. The lot was nearly full, and squad cars kept coming and going, uniformed officers guiding cuffed suspects through the glassed-in side door. I circled the station once and had to park nearly a block away, wedging my little car between a behemoth SUV and a station wagon packed to the ceiling with newspapers and soda cans.

I shimmied out of the car and wedged my house keys through my fingers like claws, then walked with purpose (and terror) toward the police station. When I got there, I found myself doing a quick scan for Detective Hayes's white SUV and then scolding myself for hoping he was there. First of all: he might be attractively hot with those piercing blue eyes and that sexy, playful half smile, but he was obnoxious, with those beady blue eyes and that smug, cocky half smile. Second of all: I looked like a cross between a redheaded troll doll and college dropout Barbie—not exactly hot-obnoxious-man-impressing material. I slipped into the elevators and headed down to UDA.

When the doors opened on the UDA foyer, the place was deserted. Pale yellow emergency lights hummed from the back corners, but everything else remained completely blanketed in the stiff darkness. I picked my way through the waiting room chairs and vacant desks and hurried down the hallway, my sneakers squeaking on the linoleum. Empty in the shadows, the UDA offices looked far more frightening than they did in broad daylight, dotted with warlocks, vampires, and general demon folk. I shuddered.

I flicked on the light in my little front office and paused when I felt the grit under my tennis shoe. I looked down and my pulse quickened. There was a scattering of broken glass on the floor. I kicked aside the little shards and hugged my elbows, a cold wave of fear washing over me.

"Hello?" My voice came out hollow and tinny in the empty room. "Pete? It's me, Sophie." I picked my way through the pieces of glass and sucked in a breath when I saw five ragged tears in the fainting couch fabric. I fit my fingers over them. "Claw marks," I whispered, my blood running cold.

There was a huge gash on the side of my desk, and my chair had been tossed across the room, shattering a cheery painting of the Golden Gate Bridge. I stepped over the cracked pot of my spider plant and swallowed hard, seeing the splinters along the door frame. Mr. Sampson's office door was hanging by one hinge; the gold letters that used to spell out PETE SAMPSON, PRESIDENT on the door were scratched and shattered. I pushed the door aside and stepped into his office. The room was dark except for the ominous green glow from the bank light on his desk; its little gold ball bobbed on the end of its pull chain.

"Pete?" I asked again.

There was no answer, and the entire room was still as I edged my way behind Sampson's big desk, pushing his chair aside and examining the wall chains.

"Oh no." I sucked in a breath, my fingers running over one open shackle, the metal distorted, folded over itself. I followed the ankle chain to the eyebolt lying on the ground in a shower of powdery cement crumbs, the place in the wall where the eyebolt was held was now puckered and cracked.

"Oh, Mr. Sampson," I whispered. "What happened here?"

I dropped the shackle and headed for the elevator, digging in my shoulder bag for the business card Detective Hayes had given me and flipping open my cell phone. I punched in his number and transferred my weight from foot to foot, counting each ring.

"Parker?" I asked the second I heard the phone connect. "Detective?"

Detective Hayes's voice was sleep-heavy and gruff. "Parker is fine, Lawson."

"Wow," I said, pushing the button on the elevator. "You knew it was me. You are a good detective."

"Good enough to have caller ID. Did your new houseguest take a bite out of you or is there another reason for this?" I heard him pause; then I heard the groan of a mattress, "One A.M. phone call?"

"Maybe." I bit my lip, glancing once more over my shoulder at Mr. Sampson's office. "I think my boss is missing."

"Your boss? You mean Mr. Sampson? Missing? How do you know that? Where are you?"

"At the office. I'm about to get in the elevator. I came down here because Nina told me that she didn't chain up Pete—Mr. Sampson—tonight. I was worried so I came to do it myself."

"It's not a full moon, right?" Hayes let out an inelegant, bored yawn. "Maybe he just went home."

"His den."

"What?"

"His den. He has a den, not a home . . . exactly. And no, I don't think so. The office—something happened here. Everything is broken, shattered and . . . and one of the chains was broken. It had been torn from the wall."

"So what does that mean? I thought you said that Nina didn't chain him up. Why would the chains have been broken if Mr. Sampson never got chained up?"

"Mr. Sampson knows that he needs to be chained up. Always—full moon, or not." I slumped, waiting for the damn elevator. "So, sometimes if we're busy,

Mr. Sampson will start chaining himself. If he does it early enough, it's not a problem. But if he starts to change . . . if he starts to change before he's completely secured—"

"He can do things like tear chains straight out of cement."

"Yeah." The elevator *dinged* and the doors slid open, to my immense relief. I rushed inside, mashing my fingers against the CLOSE DOOR button.

"Do you think he's dangerous?" All the sleep was gone from Parker's voice now.

"No," I said, annoyed, "I think he's *in* danger."

The elevator doors slid shut, the phone still pressed against my ear. "There is a murderer on the loose and frankly, a task force of police officers who are out looking for a giant dog to shoot. I think some-one may have gone after Sampson. Parker?" I frowned into the mouthpiece. "Parker, are you listening to me?" My cell phone went silent, the frowny little *call dropped!* icon on the screen.

"Stupid cell phone," I muttered, riding the eleva-tor to the ground floor of the police department.

I half ran, half walked through the bustling police department offices, my heart thundering in my throat. When I pushed through the back door into the department parking lot, one of the overhead lights was buzzing and blinking annoyingly. I stepped into the outside darkness and hurried through the lot that had emptied considerably, and when I ap-proached my car down the block, the behemoth SUV and paper-stacked station wagon were gone, too. I was about to push my key into the lock when I heard the rustle of feet on gravel, and the unmistakable metallic smell of blood wafting on the air. I resisted the bad-horror-movie urge to yell out *Hello? Is anybody there?* into the darkness, and instead focused on getting my car door open and me behind the wheel before I wet my pants.

I yanked open my car door and was halfway through it when I felt the moist breath against my neck, then the viselike grip on my shoulder, yanking me out of the car. I yelped as fire roared from my shoulder to my chest and I was pulled, my forehead crashing against the hard metal door frame, the skin above my left eye splitting and immediately starting to ooze blood. I couldn't make out the face in the darkness, but I knew that it was coming toward me, teeth bared, fingers gripping. Blood stung my eye and so I clenched my eyes shut, ready for the toothpicklike snapping of my bones. I opened my mouth to scream, but my voice was gone, strangled, lost in my own throat.

And that was the last thing I remembered.

Chapter Eight

When I opened my eyes, the first thing I saw was Opie's face hovering above me, his watery eyes studying my forehead. His big nostrils flared, and I heard him say, "She's coming around, sir."

I tried to sit up, but my head and shoulders protested, the searing pain roaring through my body. My head throbbed, felt raw and cold above my eye, and my stomach seemed to curl over on itself. I blinked twice, trying to avoid the angry fluorescent glare above my head.

"Where am I?" I finally muttered, my lips sticky and stiff.

"She's talking!" Opie said, his small hazel eyes not leaving mine. "What should I do?"

Police Chief Oliver looked down on me next, the dark brown of his eyes highlighting the huge purple bags underneath them. He was an enormous walrus of a man with a heaving chest puffed out and decorated with police paraphernalia, and a fine trail of drying marinara sauce on his navy blue tie. He crouched so that he was eye level with me.

"Are you okay, Miss Lawson?" he asked slowly, enunciating every word.

"I don't know," I said, trying to take in the scene. "What happened?"

The chief stepped back and clapped Opie on the back. He said, "She's going to be okay, Franks. Let's just give her some room," and both men stepped away from me.

I rolled my head, my skull filling with a new needling, angry pain. I tried to blink it away and then focused on the wall in front of me until I realized that I was stretched out on a sticky pleather sofa in an office that smelled of feet and corn chips and was stacked with bargain basement office furniture. "Where am I?" I repeated.

"It's okay, Sophie. You're fine. You're in my office," the police chief answered, and I felt his warm hand closing over my wrist, felt his finger find my pulse point and pause. "Don't try to move," he said when I attempted to sit up again. "You had quite a scare out there tonight."

I struggled to a sitting position despite Chief Oliver's warning, and yelped at the dull ache that blossomed from my shoulder and inched across my chest. I gently touched the cool spot above my eyebrow and winced, pulling my fingers away and examining the sticky traces of drying blood on them. "Am I dead?" I asked mournfully.

Opie grinned stupidly, and Chief Oliver set my wrist down, patting my hand gingerly.

"No, honey, you're just fine. It seems you ran into"—I watched his eyes shift uncomfortably—"a bad element. What were you doing all alone in the middle of the night anyway?"

I thought of UDA, of Mr. Sampson and the broken chains. "Looking for my kitty," I answered finally.

"Well, you should do that in the daylight hours and in a better part of town. You've got a pretty nasty bump on your head and you're a little bruised up, but I think you're going to be just fine. Officer Franks can drive you home."

"No," I said, planting my feet firmly on the floor. "I ran into a bad element? What does that mean? What happened to me? What, exactly, happened?"

I might have been paranoid, but I would almost swear that Officer Opie and Chief Oliver shared a look. I considered that it could have been the "nutty cat lady is getting hysterical" look, but I thought there was more to it. "Please," I said. "I need to know."

"Gangbangers, likely," the chief said, nodding officially.

"Gangbangers?" I asked skeptically.

Though I didn't remember much of the night and admittedly, my experience with gangs could be summed up by the toe-tapping musical brawl from *West Side Story*, I would have been willing to bet money that today's gangs hadn't evolved to bared teeth, claws, and superhuman strength. I winced again when I took a deep breath that sent pinpricks of pain throughout my chest and back. "You're sure it was a gang? Did you see them? Did you see anyone?"

The chief raised one challenging eyebrow, and Opie nodded his head wildly, his strawberry-blond hair bobbing against his forehead. "Gangbangers, definitely. We didn't see 'em, but that's what they were. Definitely," he said.

The chief stepped away from me and eyed Officer

Opie. "Franks, why don't you help Miss Lawson to her feet?"

"I think I'm good." My legs were a little shaky, but I opted to steady myself against a cold metal file cabinet rather than risk my chances with Opie's awkwardly outstretched stick arms.

"Thank you, gentlemen," I said, "but I'm feeling much better now. I just need to get home and rest."

"I'll drive you," Opie said, dangling a chain full of keys in front of me. "We can take my squad car."

I looked from Opie to the chief and realized that I'd be lucky to walk out of this station under my own volition (rather than be thrown over the shoulder and carried out by Opie), let alone be allowed to drive my own car home, so I agreed to let Opie drive me.

"But I need to stop by my car first," I said quickly, "just to grab a few things."

The chief nodded, and Opie led me out of the office and into the cold night air. We walked in awkward silence across the parking lot, and I sucked in a tortured breath when I saw my car in its space on the street.

My car, my little green baby, my first big-girl purchase, was a complete mess of crumpled steel and scratched-up paint. The driver's side door was smashed in like a tin can, and the cut on my forehead throbbed when I examined the forehead-sized crack in the passenger-side window. The driver's seat was shredded, and cotton stuffing bloomed from tears in the passenger seat, too.

"Those gangbangers," Opie said, clucking his tongue, "they can really do some damage."

I nodded solemnly and stuck my head into the car, feeling around on the carpet for my keys. I remembered the sound they made as they fell onto the floor, right before I felt the wind get knocked out of me. I shuddered, then closed my fingers around the keys.

"Okay," I said to Opie. "I'm ready." I cocked my head, swallowing over the lump that rose in my throat when I took a last look at my shredded interior. I blinked.

"Wait." I slid back into the cab of the car and leaned down to where a long, jagged gash had been made in the center console. There was a spray of cotton from the shredded seat, a sprinkling of broken glass, and a tuft of dark fur.

I picked up the fur and stuffed it in my pocket.

After an uneventful—and quiet—drive home in the squad car, Opie pulled up to my apartment building. I plastered a smile on my face and turned toward him, wincing softly as the new bruises on my shoulder and rib cage protested.

"Thanks for the ride, Officer Franks. I can make it from here."

He looked skeptically at the clean, well-lit sidewalk in front of my Nob Hill building and wagged his head, his eyes wide and ominous.

"I don't think so, Sophie. There's a bad element out there."

I squinted out the window at the deserted street, fairly certain a lone tumbleweed would roll by at any minute.

"Gangbangers?" I asked, unable to keep the annoyance out of my voice.

Opie didn't answer, and before he could go for the door handle, I rested my hand on top of his.

"Officer Franks, what really happened tonight?"

Opie stared out the windshield, and I watched as he gnawed on his bottom lip, deep in thought.

I took a chance. "I really don't think it was gang-bangers." I touched the broken skin above my eye, fresh pain blooming at the slightest touch. "I don't think they do this kind of damage. This almost seemed . . . personal. Don't you think?"

"We got to you just in time," was all Opie said.

"Well, when you got to me, what did you see?"

A full thirty seconds of silence passed, and then Opie looked me full in the face and said, "We should get you upstairs."

He insisted on walking me to my front door and standing far too close to me while I pushed the key in the lock. Then Opie slipped in front of me and into the apartment, doing a *Law & Order*-style, guns-drawn exploration of the house while I eyed him disdainfully from my spot in the hall. When Opie was certain no gangbangers were using the plastic ficus for cover, he left.

I immediately fished in my bag for my cell phone and sighed when I saw that Parker had tried to call me six times. I dialed him, and he picked up on the first ring.

"Lawson!" he shouted into the phone. "What the hell? I've been trying to call you for hours! Is everything okay?"

"It's Sophie," I sighed, "and yes, I think so."

"Is everything okay at UDA? Where's Sampson?"

"Yeah, yeah, the UDA is fine. But I don't know where Mr. Sampson is." I slumped into the couch, and found myself bawling.

"I can't understand what you're saying," I heard Parker say between my hiccupping wails. "Slow down."

"Something attacked me!" I sniffed. "They said it was gangbangers! But I don't think it was gangbangers!" *Sniff, sniff, wail.* "My car is broken! Like a tin can!"

"Stay right there. I'm on my way."

Barely fifteen minutes had passed when there was an insistent rapping on my door. My heart thundered as I stood on tiptoes and peeked through the peephole, seeing Parker's head, distorted and huge in my view.

I opened the door timidly, just an inch, and my eyes settled on Parker's. His were deep navy blue and intense.

"You didn't ask who it was."

I rolled my eyes, the relieved joy of seeing him standing in my hallway seeping away. "I have a peephole. And what is this, some kind of after-school special? *I'm* the victim here."

Parker pushed the door open and walked past me. "And *I'm* trying to make sure that it never happens again."

I closed the door and tumbled the lock, glancing once more out the peephole for Parker's benefit. Then I sat on the couch, and Parker settled down next to me.

"Tell me exactly what happened," he said.

But I couldn't.

My eyes were locked on Detective Parker Hayes sitting on my couch at 3 A.M.: dark hair disheveled and unabashedly sexy, his square jaw littered with razor stubble, T-shirt on backward, his undershorts sticking out of the top of his sweatpants.

"Is that Daffy Duck?" I asked, eyeing the black cartoon ducks on his waistband.

He zipped up his sweat jacket and crossed his legs. "Geez, Lawson, can you keep your mind off my shorts for five minutes and let me concentrate? Now tell me what happened tonight."

I opened my mouth to say something haughty and disgruntled, but Parker clapped a hand over my lips, effectively silencing me. "Just tell me what happened tonight, Sophie."

I told Parker again about finding the broken chain and then about the attack on the street. "It was horrible," I said, feeling my body start to shake. "The parts I remember. And then I woke up in Chief Oliver's office." I hugged my arms across my chest, holding onto my elbows. "They said it was gangbangers, but it wasn't." I wagged my head.

"You're sure?"

I raised an eyebrow at Hayes. "You know what we're dealing with."

"Actually," Hayes said, rubbing his palms on his thighs, "I don't. Gangbangers I'm fairly used to. This kind of thing"—he gently thumbed the cut over my eye—"I'm really not. Are you sure you're okay?"

"I'm a little sticky from the blood and sore, but other than that, I'm pretty much fine."

"You shouldn't have been out alone in the middle of the night. It could have been much worse. I don't know what I would have done if . . ."

I raised an eyebrow. "If what?"

Hayes shook his head. "Nothing. Was there anything else you remember? Anything else you can tell me about?"

I blew out a sigh and crossed the living room, digging

my hand into my coat pocket. I sat down next to Hayes again. "When I went back I found this." I held the little tuft of hair out to him.

"What is it?" he took it, examining it from every angle.

"Fur. It was stuck in one of the tears on my console."

"Fur?" Hayes's eyebrows shot up, and he sniffed at the tuft. "Dog fur?"

I looked down at my feet. "I'm thinking werewolf."

"Sampson." Hayes put the tuft of hair down on the coffee table and bounded to his feet, crossing the room in two long strides. He touched me gently, staring deeply into my eyes. "Did he bite you? Are you hurt badly?"

He gently rubbed his thumb over the cut on my forehead again, and I winced—although whether it was from the residual pain of the wound or the screaming desperation of my sex-starved body I wasn't sure. Either way, it was uncomfortable and I stepped away.

"I can't imagine Sampson would do something like this. And if he did, why now? Why not any other time, when we were alone together at the office? He wouldn't attack. Not me, of all people." I swallowed hard against the lump rising in my throat. "He likes me."

The muscle in Hayes's jaw twitched. "If he hurt you in any way . . ."

I pulled at the sleeve of my shirt, and Hayes's eyes went wide at the yellowing bruise on my forearm. "He didn't scratch me or bite me."

"But your eye—"

"That was from the car. I hit my head. If it *was*

Sampson"—I shook my head slowly, trying to avoid the newest flood of tears—"well, it doesn't seem like the person I ran into was the same person who tore that guy limb from limb. I mean, look at me."

Hayes swallowed hard. "I am."

"What?"

"Look, Lawson, maybe the chief and Officer Franks just got to you before Sampson had a chance to really hurt you. You said you don't remember much. And, how much do you really know about werewolves? What they're capable of?"

I opened my mouth and then closed it again, frowning. "My boss is a werewolf."

"Your boss is a man who becomes a werewolf when you leave at night. How much do you know about him when he's dogged out?"

I felt my eyes narrow, and Hayes raised his shoulders as if to say "So?" I blew out a defeated sigh and flopped down onto the couch.

"Not too much, I guess."

"How does he act when you chain him up?" Hayes's cobalt eyes were on mine and they were smoldering. "Is he violent?"

"No," I said, shrugging. "He never has been."

"And his hair—fur, I guess—does it look like this?" Hayes held up the clump of hair again.

"I don't know. He's fine when I lock him up and I—I leave before he changes."

"So you've never actually seen him as a wolf?" Hayes sat down close to me on the couch, his thigh brushing mine.

I clamped my hands together in my lap. "Well, no, not exactly."

"Not exactly?"

"I've seen a little of the change." I stood up, started pacing. "Once, after I chained him up I stood outside of his door. Just to see, you know, I was curious. I heard it happen." My stomach folded as I began to remember the horrible grunts and shrieks that came from Mr. Sampson's office as his body underwent the transformation from man to wolf. "It sounded so awful, so painful. But I forced myself to peek, just for a second."

Hayes was sitting erect now, his jaw tight, his lips pressed into a stern line. "And?"

"And it was dark, but I could see his eyes. They almost glowed. Not horror-movie red glow, but eerie, yellow." I shuddered, remembering. "And his mouth. His teeth . . ." I looked outside, watching the sliver of moon beckoning in the darkness.

I could hear Hayes swallow behind me, his voice going soft. "And how much do you know about Sampson, the man?"

I shook my head slowly. "Hardly anything, really. He's generally very private."

Hayes stood close to me without touching me. Part of me wanted to turn around, throw my arms around him, and crumple into him, all horror-movie-esque. But he was playing the cop and I conceded, following him, going to sit down next to him on the couch as he flipped open his notebook, scribbled a few notes, and looked at me intently.

"You need some better protection," he said finally.

I looked around my apartment, considering the pineapple on the kitchen counter as a weapon in a pinch, perhaps using my Le Creuset grill pan to inflict "blunt head trauma."

"What kind of protection?" I asked.

"Well, let's start with your car. Did you have a security system?"

"Does three inches of dirt, bug guts, and bird shit count?" I tried to grin.

Hayes raised one annoyed eyebrow, and I blew out a sigh. "Does it really matter?" I said. "My car doesn't even have a driver's side door that closes. So no, no security whatsoever."

Hayes looked genuinely pained. "Sorry," he said. "How about this place?" His eyes traveled to my front door, to the ancient brass dead bolt and the chain lock that hung, unfastened. "Do you have an alarm or anything in here?"

"I had a goldfish."

"Ah yes, the attack animal of the toilet. Very dangerous."

I put my fists on my hips. "Well, I'm not exactly a meek and meager girl. I've got two vampires living here—"

Hayes looked around him. "Who are where?"

I glanced at the table, spied Vlad's empty laptop bag. "I have no idea. Anyway, I can fight"—I mean, theoretically—"and this neighborhood is really safe."

"It is unless someone is looking for you."

I gulped. "You think someone is looking for me?"

Hayes put down his notebook and ran a hand through his disheveled, dark curls. "I think it's a distinct possibility."

I slumped down on the couch, dropping my head back and staring at the ceiling. "So what am I supposed to do? Hire an armed guard?" I did a quick mental calculation. If I dipped into my savings, I could pay approximately . . . nothing . . . for round-the-clock protection. "I'm going to be dead before the sun comes up," I groaned.

"How do you feel about guns?"

My eyes went wide, and my shoulders stiffened. "I hate them."

"Have you ever shot one?"

My mind raced to an image of me with amazing Angelina Jolie thighs circled with gun-stuffed holsters, a la *Tomb Raider.* "I guess I could learn to be okay with them." I saw myself doing one of those killer barrel roll things . . . and then shooting myself in the foot. "Or I could cause wanton destruction to my own limbs with one."

Hayes stifled a chuckle and then looked at me seriously. "Well, for all intents and purposes you're on the police force now—at least as far as this case is concerned. And I'd feel much more comfortable if you had a gun, just like any other officer."

I chewed my lower lip, considering. "Would I have to shoot it?"

"Hopefully not, but that is the idea with guns. Generally, they're most effective when used to shoot at someone."

I was horrified. "You want me to shoot *at* someone?" Shooting people was a far cry from just looking kick-ass hot in leather pants and a thigh holster. "Is there an alternative?" *Like a lethal baguette?*

Hayes's hand twitched; he looked like he wanted to grab my hand but didn't. "I want to know you're protected," he said, "even when I'm not here."

His eyes were so soft and comforting that I wanted to do what he said. "Okay," I heard myself say. "I'll at least consider it."

That cocky half grin cut across his face, and when I

stood up he gave me the once-over and muttered, "Besides, there's nothing hotter than a chick with a gun."

I crossed my arms and narrowed my eyes. "And just when I was beginning to like you, too."

"Do me a favor," Hayes said when I walked him to the door. "No more late-night trips to UDA—or anywhere for that matter—without me."

I raised an annoyed eyebrow. "I don't need a babysitter."

Hayes's lips were set in a hard, thin line.

"Okay," I sighed. "Fine. No late-night trips to UDA."

Chapter Nine

The sunlight that streamed through my curtains was warm on my back and I felt myself smile in my half sleep. I rolled over, and the events of the night—as well as the needling, searing points of pain—came flooding back. I kicked back the covers, popped a few Advil, and whipped off my shirt, checking out the waxy yellow and purple bruises on my arm, shoulder, and ribs. I poked at them, winced, and changed into a new tee.

When I padded into the living room, Nina was sitting cross-legged on the dining room table folding laundry, and Vlad—clad in a brand-new three-piece suit and another printed ascot—was sitting behind his laptop.

"Wow," Nina said when she saw me, "someone looks like the dead." She grinned. "Huh. I made a funny."

"You're brilliant. Morning, Vlad."

Vlad gave me a half nod, his eyes not leaving his laptop screen.

"Good game of Bloodlust?" I asked his bent head.

Vlad didn't answer, so I ignored him, helping myself to a cup of coffee.

"I'm going to assume you had a wild late night with Mr. Sampson." Nina spun around on the table to face me, raised her dark eyebrows, and grinned salaciously. "And from the looks of it, he likes it rough. Me-ow!"

Vlad looked up, his lips set hard. "Is sex all you two ever talk about?" he asked.

"If we're lucky," Nina said. "You should be getting ready for work, Louis."

"Vlad!" he moaned.

"Whatever."

I pulled my bangs over the cut on my forehead and caught the sage-green cashmere sweater Nina tossed at me.

"This will be bril with your eyes. You can tell me all about the intricacies of crossbreed love on our way in. Can werewolves even *do it* missionary style?"

"Ugh!" Vlad moaned, shuddering. "I don't know what's worse—my aunt talking about sex or crossbreed love."

Nina pointed to the open door of her room. "Vlad, go change your clothes and get over yourself. We're going to be leaving in a few minutes. It will reflect poorly on me if you're late. And if you're dressed like Thurston Howell."

Vlad stomped out of the room, muttering, "I hate living here," under his breath.

Nina crossed her arms in front of her chest and smiled at me. "We're good parents."

I put the sweater Nina had tossed to me down on the couch. "Nina, when I went to UDA last night Mr. Sampson wasn't there."

Nina blinked and hopped off the table. "We're going to be late."

I grabbed Nina's cold arm and pulled her to the couch. "You don't get it. He escaped."

"He didn't escape. He's a grown man, Sophie. He doesn't have a curfew. And UDA's a job, not a prison"—Nina held up a single finger—"although it can feel that way sometimes." She craned her head over her shoulder. "Are you ready, Vladimir? Come on." She went to the kitchen and rummaged through the refrigerator, pulling out a bottled Starbucks for me and a couple of blood bags for herself and Vlad. "Ooh," she said before she punctured her bag, "Ooh, AB negative!"

Living with a vampire took a lot of getting used to.

Nina's fingers hovered above the key rack. "Want me to drive? I can strand you after work so you can ride in the detective's squad car of love." She wiggled her butt and shimmied with her chest. "He can turn on his love siren and—"

I held up a silencing hand. "It ate my car."

Nina's cheeks went hollow as she sucked the last of the blood from her pouch. "Whoa. Sounds like we're out of UDA and straight into *Transformers*."

I gave her a look.

"I know," she said, tossing her pouch in the trash, "more than meets the eye. Vlad, come on!"

Vlad stomped out of the room, looking more sullen than the usual brooding vampire. He had kept on his suit pants but changed into a fitted black T-shirt and lost the ascot.

"Better," Nina said, examining him. "Almost." She rolled up on her tiptoes and mussed his perfectly coifed and gelled back hair until it stood up around his crown in slick black spikes.

"Gosh," Vlad said, ducking Nina's hand, "Aunt Nina, stop!"

We were halfway down the hall when Nina leaned into me. "So, are you going to tell me what happened or not?"

I looked over my shoulder at Vlad, sullen, earbuds pressed in, black iPod peeking out of his pocket. "I don't know—can he hear us?"

"Yes," Vlad said.

I leaned closer to Nina, whispering. "I don't know if it's appropriate to talk about it in front of him. I wouldn't want to scare him."

Nina scrunched up her forehead. "Soph, he's sixteen."

"One hundred and twelve," Vlad corrected.

"For a long time, he brought ugly death and carnal destruction to the entire eastern seaboard."

My eyes widened. Nina held up her hands, placatingly. "But that was a super long time ago. He's over that now, aren't you, Vlad?"

Vlad simply shrugged and I quickened my pace.

I filled Nina and Vlad in on last night's activities as we pulled into the police department parking lot. Nina's brows were furrowed, and she was gnawing on her lower lip.

"But you're okay though, right?" Her eyes were as wide as saucers, and there was a tiny bit of flush in her normally pale cheeks. "You didn't actually get bitten or anything, did you?"

"Werewolves are always looking to increase their

numbers," Vlad said from the backseat, his eyes focused on his iPod.

I felt myself sink back into the passenger seat as Nina's cold eyes slipped from my face to my collarbone.

"Or scratched?" She shook her head. "It doesn't take much."

"No, I didn't get bitten or scratched, and I'm fine. You mean it doesn't take much to be turned into a werewolf?" I frowned.

Nina pressed her lips together. "A bite, a scratch."

Vlad leaned forward, his cold fingers brushing the back of my neck as he craned his into the front seat. "In the olden days it was drinking rainwater out of a wolf's paw print."

I wrinkled my nose. "Gross." I leaned forward, out of Vlad's reach. "And, Vlad, I'm trying to be a good hostess, but you've seriously upped the creep factor in here by like, a thousand."

He grinned, pleased with himself.

I turned to Nina. "I'm not concerned about me turning into a werewolf. I'm really worried about Mr. Sampson. Did you guys hear anything at Dirt last night, anything about anyone going rogue or new blood in the city or anything?"

"No," Nina said, her fingers trailing over the steering wheel. "As a matter of fact, Dirt was pretty quiet last night." She looked at me sideways. "Do you really think Mr. Sampson could be in trouble?"

"I hope not," I said, staring through the windshield.

The UDA was humming by the time we walked in. Lines were already starting to form, and the waiting room chairs were all filled. There was a wizard snapping the pages of a two-month-old *Sports Illustrated*, a centaur named Nick discreetly nibbling on a *Martha Stewart Weddings*, and a demon with a horrible overbite and a horn through his nose shuffling and reshuffling his papers. I bit my lip, getting the distinct feeling that Sampson really didn't just take a midnight sojourn and head back to work this morning, fresh and shiny.

"Uh-oh," I muttered to Nina, "this doesn't look good."

Nina just shrugged and pointed to the calendar pinned to one wall. "It's the first of the month," she said matter-of-factly. "It's always crazy on the first." Nina grabbed Vlad by the arm. "Come on. I'll take you to the mailroom. You're going to be working with a banshee named Ari. He's super nice. Just don't look him directly in the eye or show him his reflection. It sends him to a parallel dimension, and he gets so pissed when that happens. It also really messes up payroll. Let's go."

Nina skipped down the hall, dragging a very slow-moving Vlad sullenly behind her.

Lydia, a pixie from HR, looked up while handing out papers to a group of Kholog demons. She narrowed her eyes when she saw me, and instantly I heard her voice reverberating in my head.

"Thank God you are finally here," she said. "This place is about to explode, and half the staff is MIA!"

I squeezed my eyes shut; no matter how long I've worked here, I never seemed to get comfortable with her telekinetics.

"What do you mean half the staff?" I said to Lydia after we'd gotten behind the counter.

She stamped the Khologs' papers and slammed her window shut, her blond bangs falling into her eyes.

"Mr. Sampson is out today, and you guys are"—her violet eyes darted to the clock on her desk—"forty-five minutes late. Esme in receiving never showed." Lydia drew her long, slender fingers to her temples and rubbed in little circles. "I swear, this place is a zoo."

"Did Mr. Sampson *say* he was going to be out today?"

Lydia's face went pinched, annoyed. I stepped back, remembering—you should never anger a pixie. "I'm just asking," I said calmly, "for your sake."

Lydia pinched her pink lips together and raised a questioning brow. "Wouldn't you know? You're his little pecksie."

I turned on my heel and headed for Mr. Sampson's office.

I was standing with my hands on hips, surveying the damage in Pete's office when I felt a tap on my shoulder. I whirled, my stomach in my throat. "Oh," I said, clutching my chest, "it's just you."

"And I'm thrilled to see you, too," Parker said, his grin wry.

"I'm sorry. I was just hoping . . ." My eyes wandered back to the broken chains and I sighed, hugging my arms to my chest. "I guess I was kind of hoping last night didn't happen. Or that Mr. Sampson would have come back by now." My eyes raked over the damage, and I swallowed the lump in my throat. "It looks pretty bad in here."

"Sampson must have gotten pretty violent."

I gritted my teeth. "Or the people who came after him did."

Parker opened his mouth and then closed it again;

he patted me awkwardly on the shoulder. "We've got work to do."

"Shouldn't we look for clues here?" I said, stepping over crumpled furniture. "Or maybe we should go back to Sampson's den, check to see if everything is okay over there? I already tried his home phone and his cell phone, and there was no answer on either."

"Lawson," Parker started. "We'll get to all of that. But right now . . ."

"Fine," I said, cutting him off in midsentence, "but give me a sec." I closed the door gently, making a mental note to come back and gather clues. I gestured for Parker to follow me, and I headed to processing, where I found Lorraine, sitting at her desk, her black cat Costineau curled up in her lap. Lorraine grinned when she saw us and knitted her fingers together, elbows poised.

"Hello, Sophie," she said sweetly, "how may I help you?"

Lorraine was a Gestalt witch—of the green order. She was as sweet as pie with honey-colored hair that hung down her back and eyes that flashed from midnight blue to a green that was as clear and as deep as a jeweled pond. She didn't swear, eat cheese or drink, but she was known worldwide for causing two tsunamis and an earthquake that decimated her ex-boyfriend, his new girlfriend, and an ancient civilization. But as long as you stayed on her good side, she was a complete gem.

"Hi, Lorraine!" I said brightly. "You look great! And Costineau!" I reached out to stroke the sleeping kitty. He opened one milky yellow eye and hissed at me, his little cat back arching, black fur spiking.

"Hey, I was just wondering . . ." I felt myself twirling

my hair around my finger and I stopped, shoving my hands into my pockets. "Mr. Sampson has been out the last couple of days. Do you think, possibly, you could do a sweep for him? Just a quick one, just to check?"

Lorraine could send a sweep around the world in record time and tell you exactly where anyone was, right down to the position he was in while lying in bed. Very handy for finding werewolf bosses and checking in on the occasional cheating spouse.

"Sorry." She wagged her head, one long-nailed index finger tapping the sign above her head: ABSOLUTELY NO WITCHCRAFT FOR NON-BUSINESS PURPOSES ON THE PREMISES.

I looked over my shoulder at Parker, who looked dumbfounded, and I blew out a small sigh.

"But it's an emergency," I said to Lorraine, trying my best to make my green eyes look innocent and imploring. I dropped my voice. "We're worried that Mr. Sampson could be in danger."

Lorraine's shining eyes shifted left and right, and she leaned closer toward us so that Costineau squealed and jumped off her lap, settling at her feet under the desk.

"Well, if it's an emergency . . ." She sucked in a breath, letting us hang. "Okay, fine. But just a quick one," she said finally, holding up a single finger.

I nodded quickly, and Lorraine eyed me, then settled back in her chair, breathing deeply and closing her eyes.

I stepped back, letting her work, and I glanced at Parker, satisfied. His blue eyes were wide, terrified, and I looked back at Lorraine, who had paled considerably. Tiny beads of sweat stood out at her hairline and above her lip. Her thin shoulders shook underneath her black shawl.

"Is that normal?" Hayes mouthed. I shrugged.

"No," Lorraine said finally, letting out a gasp. "I can't find him." She blinked repeatedly. "I can't find anything at all on Mr. Sampson." She cocked her head. "It's weird."

"Are you sure?" Parker said, stepping in front of me.

Lorraine raised one dark eyebrow and crossed her arms in front of her chest. "I'm sorry. And you are?"

"Sorry," I said, pulling Parker by the arm. "This is Detective Parker Hayes. He's concerned about Mr. Sampson, too."

Lorraine nodded, her eyes fixed on Parker.

"Thank you, Lorraine, for trying. Sorry we bothered you." I began to pull Parker along with me.

"Sophie, wait." Lorraine was on her feet behind her desk. She pulled a dark pink envelope out of her top drawer and pressed it across the desk to me. "This is for you."

I eyed the envelope. *Clues? A love note from Sampson?* I headed back, holding Lorraine's eye as I took the note. "Thank you," I said, slipping it into my pocket.

I followed Parker out the door. We paused in the hallway.

"So?" Parker asked.

"So, right now I'm really concerned," I said. "Lorraine can find anyone. Anyone who wants to be found—or anyone who's not being hidden."

"Hidden? Someone can hide someone . . . magically?" Parker fell into step with me.

"Yeah. Magic shields hide a lot." I nodded hello to

a gargoyle stepping out of the ladies' room trailing a half yard of toilet paper from her hoof.

"Like that?"

"Yep, like that. They're everywhere. We—norms— just don't think they are, so we don't see them, even if the veils are thin."

"Oh," said Parker, "I'm pretty sure if I saw that walking down South of Market, I'd remember it."

"This is San Francisco. A fire-breathing dragon shimmying down the street beating a tambourine wouldn't even raise an eyebrow."

Parker frowned. "Yeah, you're probably right. But, no. This isn't right."

"Parker . . ."

Parker looked me up and down. "What about you?"

"What about me?" I asked, frowning.

Parker lowered his voice. "Can't you do your hoodoo-voodoo thing, too?"

"Hoodoo voodoo?"

"You know, seeing. Isn't that your thing?"

I crossed my arms. "My *thing* is filing papers and taking fingerprints. And seeing through veils. The whole seeing-people-in-my-mind thing is . . . not there yet . . . with me. Right now Lorraine is the only one who can mind sweep."

"No." Parker stopped and stood, military style, legs spread, arms crossed, lips pursed. "This thing with Lorraine—I don't like it."

"Neither do I. And I'm really getting worried. She should have at least been able to pick up something on Pete. Even she said it was weird."

"No." Parker wagged his head, going into detective mode. "I think she did find something on Sampson— or maybe she found him. I don't think she was telling us everything." He gestured toward my pocket. "Check the note. What does it say?"

"I don't know why she would lie," I said, fishing out the envelope.

"I don't know either, but I'm pretty sure she was. So?"

I peeled open the envelope. "Uh-oh."

Parker's eyes went wide. "What?"

I flipped the note toward him and grinned. "She's having a Tupperware party on Thursday. Shall I pick you up a juicer?"

Parker rolled his eyes and turned on his heel. "Meet me upstairs at one," he said, before heading toward the elevators.

Parker disappeared down the hall toward the elevator, and I turned, heading to my desk—the one that sat outside of Mr. Sampson's office and was now sporting a jagged gash and a spray of broken glass along its side. I kicked aside the tiny shards of glass and rifled through my drawers, stacking up the folders that contained the more personal aspects of Mr. Sampson's life: his car registration, his calendar, the list of client contacts I used to mail out his Christmas/Solstice/Sorry Your Spouse Got Sucked into a Swirling Vortex cards. I was scanning for anything that might give Parker and me some useful information on where Pete Sampson may have gone—or where he may have been taken.

"Ahem," I heard a male voice.

I looked over the top of my desk, saw no one, and frowned. I went back to stripping my files when I heard it again.

"Ahem?"

I slammed the files down and stood up, palms pressed against my desk. I was craning my neck to look out the open door when I saw two dark, bushy eyebrows and a spray of black hair at the edge of my desk.

"Oh, Vlorg," I said, my hand to my heart. "I'm sorry, I didn't see you there."

Vlorg smiled apologetically, his yellowed, snaggled teeth pressed against his pale gray lips. "It happens."

He came around the side of the desk, and my hand went over my nose instinctively. "I'm sorry," I said again, then shoved it in my pocket, feeling ashamed.

Had I mentioned that trolls smelled? Besides bearing the burden of being only three feet tall, having constantly moist skin that grows a downy layer of lichen, and being orthodontically cursed, they smelled. Badly. Like a more pungent combination of blue cheese, belly button, and wet dog.

"Oh good, you're already cleaning out your desk. The boys will be along any minute and we'll move it out for you."

"Move it out?"

Vlorg rolled up on his toes and grinned. "Elpher Brothers Moving, at your service."

"Right." I nodded, remembering my run-in with Vlorg's brother, Steve.

Vlorg rubbed his stubby fingers over the bashed side of my desk and let out a low whistle. "This baby really took a beating." He grinned at me, and I noticed that his two snaggled front teeth were his *only* teeth.

"Who told you to move it?" I asked.

Vlorg shrugged. "Don't know. The work order was

in my box when I came in this morning, and the new desk is supposed to be here on Monday." He looked around. "Are you going to be at the public desk until then or something?"

"Uh no, I'm working on a—another project. Um, what about the new desk? Who ordered it?"

"Don't know that either."

I put my hands on my hips. "Well, someone must have initialed the PO. Mr. Sampson is the only one with that kind of buying power."

"Then it must have been Sampson then," Vlorg said, obviously bored. "In here, guys!" he shouted out the open door, and I slumped into my seat when Olak and Steve filed in.

Olak was a shyer, slightly more stooped version of Vlorg, and Steve, as I mentioned before, was the redheaded stepchild of the troll kingdom—or the velveteen-tracksuit, gold-chain-wearing stepchild. Today he looked like a very tiny adult film producer—only not as charming—with his tracksuit unzipped halfway down his troll sternum, loops of pale green lichen snaking over the zipper.

Steve grinned when he saw me, his gray lips curving up salaciously, his angled tongue sliding over his teeth. He put his tiny troll hands on his hips and sucked in a satisfied breath.

"Steve likes what he sees."

I wrinkled my nose, this time not caring who I offended. "Steve." He stunk in more ways than one.

"Oh, yes, Steve. Has Sophie missed Steve? Steve has missed Sophie." He laced his fingers together and balanced his chin in his hands, donning a look that I think was supposed to look innocent. It came out looking lewd.

"Steve apologizes for not being around more. The business"—he gestured to Olak and Vlorg behind him—"has really been ramping up." Steve rubbed his fingers together. "But Steve has been making lots of money. Would Sophie like a shopping trip? Perhaps a visit to the Sizzler?"

"No, thank you. And really, your absence has been just fine."

"Still—Steve apologizes from the bottom of his heart. Steve will be around from here on out for Sophie. At your beck and call."

I crossed my arms. "Kind of like a stalker?"

Steve crossed his arms. "Steve prefers the term 'mythical protector.'" He waggled his bushy black eyebrows. "Or perhaps beloved boyfriend?"

"Stalker. And why do you always refer to yourself in the third person? Is it just a troll thing?"

Steve raised one eyebrow. "It's a Steve thing. Steve is a lot of man."

I rolled my eyes and pulled out another file folder.

"When is Sophie going to give Steve a chance? Steve can be Sophie's knight in shining armor. Steve would never leave Sophie."

I crossed my arms in front of my chest. "Sophie is— I mean I'm flattered"—I forced a smile—"really, Steve, but no thank you."

"Is it because Steve is a troll? Because, you know, not everything about Steve is troll-sized." The gray corners of Steve's thin lips snaked up in a lascivious, obnoxious grin.

"I'll keep that in mind," I said, grimacing and gathering up my files.

Steve rushed toward me. "Does that mean Steve has a chance? Because Steve can do things to Sophie—"

I dropped my files and pressed my hands over my ears. "Not hearing this!"

Steve frowned. "Steve just wants to make Sophie happy." That salacious grin again. "Very, very happy."

I knelt down. "You know what would make Sophie happy? Steve, leaving."

Steve started to back away, the lewd smile still playing on his lips. "Sophie is going to miss Steve. Sophie is going to miss Steve a lot." Steve disappeared into the hallway.

"That's a risk I'll have to take," I sighed quietly.

Steve poked his head through the open doorway. "But Steve is always just a heartbeat away. You just watch. Steve will wear Sophie down."

I could hear Steve whistling as he strolled down the hall.

Chapter Ten

At 1 P.M. I had an armload of files and was muttering to myself as I walked down the hall at the police station.

"Something is definitely not right here," I started as I pushed my way into Parker's office. "Oh, I'm sorry, Park—Detective—I didn't mean to interrupt."

Chief Oliver, seated on the edge of Parker's desk, craned his neck to look at me and offered a polite smile. "Miss Lawson. Feeling better today, I hope?"

I felt a flush wash over my cheeks, and I hugged the stack of file folders to my chest.

"Yes, I'm feeling much better. Thank you." I peered around the chief at Parker and took a small step backward toward the hall. "Detective Hayes, I'll just wait until you two are finished."

"No, no." The chief used one hand to wave me in, the pinkish folds of his big cheeks pushing up in a welcoming smile. "You're as much a part of this case as anyone else. And"—he glanced back at Parker, whose eyes had wandered back to his computer screen—

"maybe you can make a little more sense out of this than we can."

The chief angled Parker's computer monitor toward me, and I sat in the visitor's chair, squinting at the dark screen.

"What am I looking at?" I asked, trying to focus.

The men exchanged a glance and a hazy gray image appeared on the computer screen. I could make out the outside of a building, faded bricks, and a flickering light. There was a spray of glass on the screen, and then what looked like a big dog tore through one of the windows and disappeared out of the frame. I sucked in a shaky breath.

"What?" I whispered. "Is that—?"

Parker's eyes were soft. "We think it was Sampson."

"This is the surveillance tape taken from one of the cameras just outside of the station." The chief eyed me warily. "It was taken last night, just before you were attacked."

"No." I wagged my head emphatically. "You said it was gangbangers. That's what you told me."

Chief Oliver steepled his fingers and brought them to his pink, thick lips. "Officer Franks doesn't yet know the"—the chief's eyes shifted from Parker to me—"intricacies of the case. But, Miss Lawson, you do. You had to know it wasn't gangbangers."

I sat back against the hard vinyl visitor's chair, all the breath leaving my body. "I know. Of course I knew. I just don't believe that it could be Mr. Sampson. I don't see why Mr. Sampson would attack me. Me, of all people."

Chief Oliver shrugged and put his hand on mine. "Miss Lawson, in this business you learn quickly that you never really know someone." He stood up, nodded to Parker, patted my shoulder, and walked out.

"'You never really know someone'?" I hissed, disgusted.

"Look, Lawson, I know that for whatever reason you have a soft spot for this mutt, but he was going to tear you apart." Hayes gestured to the screen. "It's right there in black and white. Well, kind of."

I smacked the desk with my palm. "You don't know that! And with that, that"—my hand flailed toward the monitor—"tape, you can't prove anything. Sampson could have been running away from me for all we know. Hell, we don't even know that was Sampson. Besides, did the chief or Franks even see any of the attack? It could have been gangbangers!" I could hear my voice rising toward hysteria, and I gulped in several deep breaths while Parker watched, calmly.

"Even so, you need to be prepared." Parker slowly pulled open his top desk drawer and laid a heavy black gun on his desktop.

"Are you kidding me?" I recoiled, standing up sharply, scattering the files on the floor. "You're going to shoot me now?"

Parker rolled his eyes. "I wasn't planning on it, but give me a moment."

I narrowed my eyes at Parker, who waited for me to calm; then I slumped back in my chair. "You're really that worried?" My voice came out as little more than a whisper.

"I'll teach you how to use it."

I gulped, my breath starting to quicken again. "You want me to use it? To shoot people?"

"Hopefully, no," Parker said, leaning back in his chair. "But I do want you to be safe."

"How does having that make me safe? We don't even know what we're dealing with yet. If it really is a rogue vampire or a werewolf, this"—I stared down at the gun—"isn't going to help."

"Fine." Parker stood up, loading the gun into a metal-sided briefcase. "We'll pick up a garlic pizza and some Milk-Bones on the way to the range." He slung an arm around my shoulder and grinned. "That way we've got all our bases covered."

I rolled my eyes and followed him out the door.

"Okay, first things first," Parker said when we got to the shooting range. "Gun safety is our top priority."

I smiled and batted my eyes. "It would be much safer anywhere but here."

He blew out a sigh and removed the gun from the briefcase, laying it on the counter. "Do you know how to hold a gun?"

I crossed my arms in front of my chest. "No."

Parker swung his head to look at me, his blue eyes shining and earnest. "Are you scared? It's okay if you are."

I nodded slowly, softening.

"Don't worry," Parker said. "I'll guide you through it."

Parker's eyes dropped to an almost-sinister cobalt. I might have been imagining it, but I think he licked his lips hungrily. I fought off images of a sharp wind that tore open his shirt, showing off his rippling abs as he embraced me, the smoky heat of the gun between us.

"I don't need any help!" I blurted.

Parker blinked at me. "What?"

Everyone in the entire place—which included a paper-thin cashier with a name tag that said NEWT and a guy in dirty jeans and a trucker hat—blinked at me.

"I'm sorry," I said, dropping my voice and licking my incredibly dry lips. "I guess I just got a little nervous." I rubbed my palms on my jeans and made a mental note to have Nina cancel our subscription to Cinemax.

After Newt had fixed us up with some ultra-fashionable protective eye and headgear, Parker guided me into the shooting gallery. I half expected to see a Western façade, perhaps a line of faux ducks or glass bottles like they had at the boardwalk, but the gallery was long, gray, and concrete, and hanging at the end of a silver line against the back wall of the stall was the black charcoaled outline of a man with a target drawn on his trunk.

I gulped.

"You'll want to aim for the chest. That's where there's the most surface area." Parker glanced at me. "No head shots."

My stomach went sour. "I don't think you'll have to worry about that," I murmured.

Parker loaded the gun, explaining as he went, and I tuned out, breathing out of my mouth to avoid the singed scent of spent powder and casings.

"Come here," Parker said, opening his arms.

I didn't know that it was customary to hug before target practice, but I stepped toward him anyway. He twirled me around, his chest pressed against my back, and I could feel his moist breath as his lips brushed past my ear. He took both of my hands in his and gently pressed the butt of the gun between my palms, lacing my fingers around the trigger space, his fingers warm as they closed over mine.

I hadn't realized how soft his hands were.

"This is how you hold a gun." The stubble on his chin tickled my ear, and I pressed back into him and then stiffened, embarrassed. "Okay," I said weakly. "I think I've got it."

I glanced down at the gun pressed in my hands and eyed the target, then had a very real, very *Charlie's Angels* kind of moment.

Sophie Lawson: Kick-Ass Angel.

I imagined kicking down doors with the stiletto heel of my black patent leather boots; dodging a hail of gunfire with one of those killer tuck-and-roll moves; then landing perfectly, my sexy red hair bouncing around my shoulders as I took down the bad guys, one by one.

Parker's hand squeezing mine brought me back to the smoky shooting range.

"You're going to—"

"I know, I know," I said, impatient, "pull the trigger."

"No, you're going to squeeze it. Gently. And it will recoil, so be careful." Parker stepped away, and I was alone, in full gunslinger stance, aimed and ready to take out my make-believe attacker.

"Yeah," I whispered to myself, "I can do this."

Sexy, stiletto'd, gun-toting me had already taken out an entire community of bad guys in my mind, so I began to squeeze the trigger.

Yanked it, actually.

I heard someone screaming and saw a little bolt of fire ignite, then fade out. My hands were hot. My arms hurt. Something hot and smooth rolled over my wrist and tinkled to the ground.

And there were little chunks of cement raining from the ceiling.

The screaming stopped when I closed my mouth.

"What the hell was that?" I was waggling the gun and jumping from foot to foot when Parker leaned in and grabbed the gun, slipping the safety on.

"That was just the casing rolling over your hand."

"That was so scary!" I yelled. But Parker had stopped listening.

He was laughing.

"Hey," I said, stamping my foot.

"I'm sorry," he said, shutting up abruptly—but I could see his body shaking against his laughter, little tears clinging to his bottom lashes. "You did great. Really."

I put my hands on my hips. "I shot the ceiling."

Parker pursed his lips, and I imagined him gritting his teeth. "Yes, you did. But it was only your first time. You'll get better."

I narrowed my eyes. "Did you shoot the ceiling your first time?"

"Of course not. Let's try it again."

Parker put one hand on my shoulder and turned me around so his chest was pressed against my back again. He wrapped his arms around me and placed the gun in my hands once more. I breathed deeply, memorizing his warm scent of soap and singed gunpowder.

"Okay," he said, his voice low and warm and delicious on my neck. "How do you feel?"

Horny! I wanted to scream. Nina would have said horny, but she had no blood and thus could not turn beet red from follicles to toenails like I could. Also, she had the luxury of eating the source of her angst. Vampires were *so lucky*!

"I'm okay," I squeaked. "I mean, the gun feels okay."

Parker took one hand off the gun and pressed his palm against my rib cage, the tip of his thumb gently brushing the underside of my breast.

I was afraid I was going to fire the gun right then and there.

"Relax. You're okay," he said.

"I just . . ."

"I know. I have that effect on a lot of women." He grinned down at me, that same, lopsided half grin that all at once was lust and hate inducing.

"I'm just nervous about shooting," I spat, annoyed. "Is it going to make fire again? What if the casing hits me in the eye this time? Has anyone ever died from the back end of a gun? What if I shoot *you*?"

Hayes ignored me, but his arms seemed to close a little tighter over me. His hands clamped over mine again, and his thumb stroked mine as he guided my finger to the trigger. "Okay?" he whispered.

I nodded weakly, unsure if the sensation roiling through my body was fear or an intense desire to spend more time pressed up against his firm, warm-blooded body.

"Take your stance," he said, and I felt his leg between mine, pushing against my thigh until my feet were shoulder width apart.

"Ready."

I took a miniscule step back, and Parker made up the distance so his hips were pushed flush against mine once more.

"Aim."

The word was soft, moist, tender against my earlobe.

"Fire!"

I squeezed the trigger, and my eyes shut simultaneously. The gun recoiled hard, but Parker had me, one arm extended and holding the gun, the other clamped around my waist.

"Are you okay?" He looked down at me, his eyes a breathtaking blue. All I could do was nod spastically.

"That was better," he said softly.

I stood up straight, squinting down the aisle toward the target. "Where did I hit him? Can we see it?"

"Actually . . ." Parker stepped around me and pointed at the dirt. "You shot the ground."

"Crap!"

Parker looked away, grinning. "Don't worry. You'll get it; it's just going to take some time. Let's keep working."

Parker spent the rest of the night coaxing my ceiling-and-floor aim to meet in the middle—or, at the very least, to hit the target—and I spent the whole night being folded into his arms and recoiling into his tight chest.

I may never like guns, but I was learning to love Parker's instruction.

"Okay," Parker said, taking the gun and unloading the magazine. "That's enough for tonight. You're doing a lot better."

My arms felt like jelly and shots kept exploding in my head. "Are you less worried about my safety now?"

Parker jabbed at a button, and the paper target came sailing toward us. He held it up to me, and I could see four tiny gunshot holes near the bottom right corner of the paper.

"Not exactly," he said.

I squinted. "I got it on the paper though. That's got to count for something, right?"

Parker chuckled, his smile chocolate-chip-cookie warm and relaxed. "Yeah. Whatever you say, Lawson."

Chapter Eleven

It was dark by the time we left the shooting range, and my stomach rumbled angrily as Parker pushed the key into the ignition. I blushed, feeling the heat rise to my ears.

"Sorry," I said, as a flint of panic washed over Parker's face. "I guess I'm just a little bit hungry."

"Man." Parker's eyes dropped to my stomach. "I thought you were growing a baby dinosaur in there."

"Geez, Parker. You're a real gem. I can't believe a woman hasn't snapped you up yet." I crossed my arms and sunk into my car seat. "Let's just go."

Parker shrugged, turning the key, a hint of smile playing on his lips. "You know what they say: The Lone Ranger rides—"

"Alone?" I finished.

"Come on," Parker said, backing out of the lot, "you're buying me a pizza."

"Is that so?"

Parker ignored me, his grin knee-melting and annoyingly smug. "Yup. Training fee. You should have read the fine print."

I dug into my purse and handed Parker a twenty-dollar bill. "How about you buy your own pizza and we call it a night. I'm exhausted." And frankly, not so sure I could spend another hour alone with Parker Hayes without jumping those alternately frustrating and super-hot bones.

"Don't worry," Parker said as he maneuvered the car through traffic. "We'll eat it at your house. You have cable, right?"

My stomach dropped into my groin, and I clamped my knees together.

This was *not* going to be good.

Twenty minutes later I was balancing a pizza box on my thighs and directing Parker to my apartment. My blood was pulsing, and as astoundingly hot or not Parker Hayes may have been, I had just determined to move him firmly to the Never in a Thousand Years pile. Especially since he really did make me buy the pizza (and a six-pack of beer, to boot). I was slumped in my seat, ticking off Hayes's annoying attributes—sexist, demonist, thinks every woman wants him—when I heard him mutter, "Holy shit."

My head snapped up, and I squinted at the glare from the police lights flashing red and blue into our car.

"Is that your building?"

I nodded, my mouth hanging open, my stomach immediately souring. "Uh-huh. I wonder what happened?"

There was a line of squad cars snaking into the street, and the police were filing in and out of my building, radios squawking.

"Nina," I whispered, gulping. "I have to get in there. Something could have happened to Nina or

Vlad." I began to stand, my hand on the door handle, the pizza box burning a warm trail as it slid down my legs.

"Wait." Parker's voice was stern, his hand soft on my knee. "Let me find out what happened first." Parker turned to me, his grip tightening on my thigh, his eyes firm and dark. "You wait right here."

"No, no, I can't wait." I kicked the car door open and followed Parker, zigzagging into the line of squad cars, weaving around the officers.

Parker found an officer, and I found them both, angling myself closer to Parker. "What happened? I live here," I demanded.

"Break-in." Parker said, looking down at me.

I looked at the other officer, who nodded. "Break-in," he agreed.

I gripped my heart and blew out a long sigh. "That's not too bad." I looked at both the officers, at their hard eyes, both their mouths set in stern, thin lines. "Is there something else?" I asked in a whisper.

Parker took my arm just above the elbow and eyed me. "Do you know a Thomas Howard?"

"He broke in? He wouldn't break in. He lives here," I said.

"The break-in was 6B."

"That's me." I thumped my chest. "I'm 6B. Mr. Howard is 9B. He wouldn't rob me. He's a nice old man. Kind of a dirty old man, but really nice." I blinked. "Right?"

Parker lowered his voice. "Lawson, Mr. Howard is dead."

I felt like someone had kicked me in the stomach, and immediately, my eyes began to water. "No, no, no." I wagged my head, sniffling, barely noticing Parker's arm as it slid behind my back, steadying me.

"We just talked to him—Vlad and I—yesterday, in the hall. He was fine. He's fine. How could he be dead?" In an instant, I thought of Vlad, last night, thought of Nina warning him about indulging in human victims, the way he looked so disdainfully on humankind. There was a sharp pain in my stomach. "What happened to him?" I whispered, terrified.

"Mr. Howard called in a disturbance—the break-in—at your place. When the police arrived, there was no one in your apartment and they found Mr. Howard on the back stairs. His neck was broken. It looks like he fell."

"We think he may have been trailing the intruder, perhaps lost his footing and fell."

"He fell?" My voice was small, and for the first time I noticed the cold night air as it washed over me. "And he died?" I caught Parker's eye and he nodded. I swallowed. "You're sure?" I whispered.

"Yeah, they're sure. There were no other"— Parker cleared his throat, lowered his voice— "circumstances."

A small prickle of relief rushed through me, until I thought again of Mr. Howard, of his toothy smile and him snuggling up to all his women. Parker moved his arm to my shoulder, and I instinctively snuggled into him. "Oh, that poor man. That's awful."

Parker led me away when the ambulance pulled up, and he settled me back on the front seat of his car. "Wait here. The other officers just need to finish up a few things. We should be able to go up to your place shortly."

I nodded, still sniffling, and when Parker came

back and gathered me and the pizza together, I didn't protest, handing him my keys and letting him lead me to my cracked-open front door.

He rubbed his hand over the splintered door frame and looked at me sympathetically. "We'll fix this door and get you a new lock tonight."

I nodded and shrugged out of my jacket, pulling open the coat closet. "I just can't shake the heebie-jeebie feeling," I muttered. I reached into the closet for a hanger when a pair of yellow-green eyes blinked at me from the depths of the darkness and I screamed, my own voice sounding tinny and sharp.

"What the—?" In an instant Parker was crouched beside me, gun drawn.

"Don't shoot Steve, don't shoot Steve!" Steve jumped off a stack of board games, dropping a golf club and raising his small troll hands, palms up.

I put my hand on Parker's and slowly pressed the gun down to his side. "It's okay, Parker. Don't shoot. Yet."

Parker furrowed his brow and leaned into me, lowering his voice. "Who's the dwarf?"

I slapped my forehead with the palm of my hand. "Oh, Parker. Now you've done it."

Parker's eyes widened as he stared from me to Steve. "Uh, little person, sorry. Do you know him?"

I could see the lichen on Steve's thick arms tremble as his eyes darkened, his lips going thin and taut over his yellow, snaggled teeth. His fingers curled into tight little fists.

"Steve is a troll. Steve is not a dwarf," he spat angrily, his eyes glaring fire.

"I'm really sorry—Steve, is it?"

Steve nodded slowly, his little troll body coiled in

anger. I pulled Parker by the elbow and hissed into his ear. "Trolls are especially sensitive to being called dwarves. There has always been a vicious rivalry between the two. Trolls do intellectual work, dwarves do menial labor."

Parker raised an eyebrow. "Intellectual work?" he whispered, looking from Steve to myself.

"They live under bridges and allow passage to travelers who can answer trivia questions. Haven't you ever left the Bay Area?"

Parker's brow furrowed and he shrugged. "I am so not getting this."

"The only thing worse than calling a troll a dwarf is calling him an elf."

Steve's nostrils flared and the stench of blue cheese and old gym socks intensified. "Steve is not an elf! Steve does not even like Christmas! Steve is *all* troll."

"I know, Steve—I was just illustrating a point. What the hell are you doing in my closet anyway? You scared the crap out of me!" I clutched my chest, my heart still beating furiously against my palm.

Parker looked incredulously from me to Steve. "You know this . . . guy . . . well?"

Steve dropped the golf club and inched himself between Parker and me. "Steve was protecting Sophie." He looked over his shoulder, eyeing Parker disdainfully. "Steve and Sophie are an item."

I stood back, edging away from Steve. "No, we are not an item. Steve stalks me at the UDA."

"Steve works at the UDA," Steve corrected.

"Steve, how long have you been hiding in my coat closet?"

"Not hiding. Protecting."

Parker wrinkled his nose and stepped back. "It kind of smells like you were rotting in there."

Steve glared up at him. "Steve's scent is distinct."

"I'll say."

"How long, Steve?" I wanted to know.

Steve shrugged. "Since Sophie left. Steve lost sight of her. Steve should never lose sight of Sophie."

Parker leaned in to me. "What is he again?" he whispered.

"Troll," I murmured.

Steve reached up and laced his fingers through mine. "Lover."

I shook them off. "Not." I paused. "How did you even get in here?"

Steve grinned, rolling up on his toes. "Steve has ways."

I glared at him, and he sighed. "Steve fits through the bathroom window."

"So this"—Parker pointed to the shards of wood hanging from the door frame—"wasn't you? You didn't break into Sophie's apartment?"

Steve wagged his head.

"Then you must have seen who did. Or heard it. Did you? Did you see anything? Did you see who chased Mr. Howard?" I knelt down to be eye to eye with Steve.

Steve's gray cheeks flush a deeper gray. "Steve took a little nap." He grinned. "He was dreaming about Sophie."

I pointed to the open door. "Get out, Steve! And stop following me. And don't *ever* break into my apartment again!"

Steve eyed me and flared his nostrils at Parker. "Steve will go this time, but Steve will be always around. Steve will make this up to Sophie." He pointed a stubby finger at Parker's kneecaps. "And you, breather, you'd better watch your step. Steve has his eye on you."

Parker raised his eyebrows as Steve waddled out the front door. I sighed, made sure Steve was actually gone, and closed the door after him.

"Interesting friend you've got there," Parker said, a half smile playing on his lips. "Parker thinks he might have some competition."

My stomach fluttered despite the stench of gunpowder and sleeping troll hanging in the air. "Right. Now, what about that pizza?"

Parker went for the pizza box he dropped on the counter as I turned around, scanning my apartment. I crossed my arms in front of my chest.

"Everything looks the same in here. I mean"— I picked up Steve's golf club and tossed it back into the closet—"it doesn't look like anything was stolen."

"We think Mr. Howard scared the intruder before he actually had a chance to get in."

I shuddered, glancing around at my IKEA furniture, my collection of overdue library books, the hand-me-down pillows from Grandma's old couch. "What would anyone want to break in here for?"

Parker shrugged, heading into the kitchen and helping himself to napkins and plates.

I swallowed, feeling my muscles tense. I stared at the carpet. "Do you think it was an intruder, or do you think it was Mr. Sampson?"

Parker slid a piece of pizza onto a plate and handed it to me. "You should eat something."

I rested the plate on the table.

"You think it was Sampson, don't you?"

Parker turned his back to me, rattling around in my drawers. "Do you have a bottle opener?"

"Answer me."

Parker's rattling stopped and he turned, his blue eyes sharp. "I think it was Sampson. And I'm not entirely convinced that Mr. Howard fell on his own. I think Pete Sampson really wants to find you." Parker slid the plate back toward me. "You really should eat something."

"I'm too creeped out to eat."

Parker snaked my plate and swallowed my pizza in one gulp.

"Obviously you're not."

He went for a second piece. "I need to keep my strength up. Someone's got to look after you."

I glanced up at Parker as he studied the grain on the table.

"I don't need taking care of," I told him.

Parker swallowed, then took a long pull of his beer. "Yes, you do. That's why I'm staying here tonight."

That familiar anger started to roil again. "Says who?"

"Says me." He leaned back in his chair, kicking his feet onto the table and reaching for the remote control.

"Don't make yourself comfortable." I lifted up Parker's ankles and dropped his feet to the floor. "Besides, I think I'd rather take my chances with the killer, thank you very much."

I stood up, holding the front door open, but Parker didn't move. Instead he just flashed that Cheshire grin and took another swig of his beer.

"You're spunky," he said finally. "I like that."

"I'm not joking, Parker." I crossed my arms in front of my chest. "I appreciate your help, but I can take care of myself." I eyed the open door. "Thank you for the shooting lessons. I'll see you at the station to-morrow?"

Parker stood up reluctantly and slid his jacket off.

"Parker!"

"Relax," he said, striding up to me. "I'm going. But I'm not leaving you unprotected." Parker took my palm and laid his gun, still warm from his chest, into it. "You know how to shoot and you know how to dial the phone to reach me. I really hope you'll do the latter."

I lifted my chin. "Thank you."

"It's loaded, so be careful. Put it somewhere safe."

And then he kissed me.

Parker Hayes closed my hand, pushed my arm to my side, and swept a delicate kiss over my lips.

I wasn't sure whether to shoot him or tear off his clothes.

I wanted to be indignant and angry and feminist, but he smelled so good, like cut grass, campfire, and soap, and his lips were so dizzyingly soft. By the time I had finished arguing with myself, he was gone.

I shut the door, shuddered at the gun in my hand, and tossed it into the freezer for safekeeping.

I spent a full two minutes watching Eric Estrada sell swampland before I speed-dialed Nina. "Hey," I yelled when she picked up, "where are you? Is Vlad with you?"

"Huh?" I could hear the thump of bass, the tink of glasses, and a rumble of laughter in the background. "Sophie? Is that you? I can barely hear you."

I pushed out my bottom lip and sniffed. "Can you come home? I'm scared."

I heard the phone fumble, and then the tink and

rumble were quiet. "Sorry about that—it's so loud in here," Nina said. "Now what were you saying?"

I could feel my lip begin to quiver, the familiar warmth rising in my throat. "Mr. Howard is dead."

"Oh. Well, Sophie, Mr. Howard was like, a hundred and three. He was kind of on his way out."

"No, Nina, he was murdered! Well, not exactly murdered, murdered. He fell down the stairs."

I could practically hear Nina's eyebrow rise. "So he was murdered by stairs?"

"Nina!" I paused, considering. "Where are you? Have you or Vlad been home yet tonight?"

"No," Nina said, stretching out the word. "I haven't. I went straight from UDA out with that were-vamp that came in for his relocation papers last week."

"You didn't even come home to change?"

"I should have. His stupid claws messed up the beadwork on my brand-new Maggie Sottero. I've been leaving a trumpet-bead trail wherever I go. And Vlad met up with some equally moody friends around nine, so I don't think he's been around the house either. " Nina paused. "Why do you ask?"

"No reason," I said quickly. "I just wanted to make sure you both were okay."

"Do you still want me to come home?"

I blew out a long sigh. "No. I guess I'll be okay."

"Don't worry, Soph. I won't be long, I promise."

When I opened my eyes I could see nothing but blackness. I pushed down my cocoon of covers and glared at the glowing red numbers on my digital clock: 3:17. I snuggled back down against my pillow when I heard it: a gentle scraping against the wall, then the sound of—fingernails?—something tapping against my bedroom window.

"Nina? Vlad?" I called. "Nina, is that you?"

No answer.

I pushed off my blankets and padded into the living room but stopped short, standing in the doorway. The living room was silent, bathed in darkness. The scraping sound started again as did the incessant thump of my heart. I hurried to the kitchen, snatching my frozen gun out from between a box of ice-cream bars and vegan corn dogs.

"Nina?" I hissed again. "So help me, I'm going to shoot a hole in your undead head if you don't come out here and stop scaring the crap out of me!"

The scraping stopped, and I let out the breath I didn't know I was holding.

And then I heard my bedroom window being pushed open.

"Oh God. Oh God, oh God, oh God," I whispered, sinking to my knees on the linoleum. I crawled around, gun thawing in my hand, vowing to install telephones in every room of the house from here on out.

I winced, hearing my blinds clatter, the trinkets on my windowsill falling as someone climbed through. "Ohhh . . ." My teeth started to chatter and I pushed myself up, clamping both my hands on the butt of the gun, just the way Parker had shown me.

I heard someone bumping around in my room, and I took a tiny step, inching myself closer to the phone.

Step. Inch. Step.

The gun bobbed in my hands, and I tried to grip

it more tightly, the cold from the frozen steel and my own warm sweat making my palms itch. I was within reaching distance for the phone when I was startled by the sudden silence and then a deep, low breathing. I glanced up, seeing the shrouded figure hunched in the doorway. I stepped back, steeled myself, and leveled the gun. I felt the power roil through me as my fingers inched toward the trigger. I clamped my eyes shut and wrenched my mouth open, letting out a wailing howl as I pulled back and launched. I opened my eyes just enough to see the dark figure over the barrel of the gun as he tore back toward the window, hurling himself over my table and scraping the windowsill before he disappeared into the darkness.

My legs felt rubbery and hot; I sank onto the carpet and crab-crawled into my bedroom. I chanced a glance out the window, but there was nothing below. Whoever had broken in was long gone. So I clamped the window shut, throwing the lock and closing the curtains and blinds for good measure. I crawled to my nightstand, leveled my breath, and dialed the phone.

Chapter Twelve

I opened my front door timidly, just an inch, and my eyes settled on Parker's. His were deep and intense, but that cocky half smile was still playing on his lips.

"See? I knew you couldn't resist me."

I threw open the door, and Hayes sauntered in.

"Look, if I weren't feeling so"—I glanced nervously toward my open bedroom door—"violated, and if I weren't so concerned about the safety of all the other tenants in the building, you wouldn't be here." I tried to stand tall, look fierce, hide the fact that my heart was thumping in my throat and that I'd paced a bald spot in my carpet, jumping at every little sound over the last half hour.

Parker was unfazed and dropped onto the couch, grinning at my pink rubber-ducky pajamas. "Nice jammies," he said.

"Thanks," I said, pulling my bathrobe tighter across my chest.

Parker looked around the apartment. "This place is really nice. I didn't really get a chance to look around earlier. . . ."

I pursed my lips as he stood up again, looking at my books, scrutinizing the photos in frames on my mantle, on the wall. "I guess demon paper pushing pays pretty well."

"Well," I started, "it does. But I've also got a roommate."

Hayes straightened and looked at me, startled. "A roommate? You never mentioned . . ." His eyes wandered to my bedroom door standing open. "I didn't notice another bedroom."

"There really isn't one."

"Oh," he said, his blue eyes wide and apologetic. "I didn't realize you were—that you were living with someone."

"Oh. Oh! No, not like that." I fought the smug smile on my lips. *He thinks I'm sleeping with someone! Well of course.* I straightened up, brushing a lock of red hair from my shoulder. *Why wouldn't he think that? I'm cute, I'm . . . standing here having a conversation in my head while Parker Hayes stands there staring at me.* "She's a vampire," I blurted. "Nina, remember? She's a vampire so she doesn't sleep. So"—I shrugged—"no bedroom."

Hayes looked around. "Then what does she need a place for?"

I strode across the room and pushed open the guest room door, revealing the room that had been completely converted to a walk-in closet, housing the rows and heaps of Nina's couture, collected during the generations of her afterlife.

Hayes let out a low whistle. "Holy crap. That woman can shop!"

I shrugged. "Wait until you've been alive one hundred and forty-odd years. See what you accumulate."

I kicked Hayes's bag off the couch and sat down, Indian style. Hayes followed me and sunk down into the pale yellow cushions, looking tense. "Isn't it kind of weird living with a vampire? I mean, aren't you afraid she's going to bite you?"

"Nah." I kicked my legs out in front of me, crossed my ankles on the coffee table. "They're not all monsters."

Parker nodded slowly, and in the few minutes since he'd been in my apartment my heart had slowed to its regular, calm *thump-thump*. I followed his eyes as they swept over my cheap IKEA furniture, the array of celebrity magazines on the coffee table, the books on my shelves. He blinked at a well-worn porcelain doll high up on the bookshelf.

"She's Nina's," I said, rolling up onto my tiptoes and gingerly pulling down the doll. Her pale, perfect skin mirrored Nina's flawless complexion, right down to the color and cool, slick feel. Her eyes were painted a cornflower blue and wide open in a constant wonder. Her hair was slick and black like Nina's, but she had the corkscrew curls of a little Victorian girl, and they were gathered at the nape of her neck with a limp satin bow. She was dressed in a thread-bare white gown, its hem woven through with a satin ribbon. The pale yellow hue of the once-white garment betrayed its age.

I looked down at the doll. "It was hers from—from before."

"From before she became a vampire."

I nodded. "It's the only thing she keeps from then—from her human life. You know, when I first met Nina—we started at the UDA the same week— she was this tough-as-nails vamp chick. You know, black leather bustier, blood-red nails, the works. I was terrified of her."

"Because you thought she was going to eat you?"

"No." I sat down on the couch, the doll resting on my knees. "I never worried about that."

Parker raised his eyebrows, and I hurried on.

"She was terrifying because she didn't seem to care about anything. Most vampires live in nests or families. Nina didn't. She was always alone. And then one day Sampson gave me an assignment. There was a vampire they suspected was about to go rogue. Going rogue in this case means street hunting. The UDA clientele is strictly forbidden to street hunt—to take their prey from the general population."

Parker gulped. "Well, that's refreshing. I guess."

"This suspected rogue was on the street all night, frequenting a particular spot where a group of runaway kids hung out. Word was the vampire kept trying to get one of the kids alone."

"Separate them from the herd?"

"Right. So I was supposed to investigate and let Sampson know if the vampire needed to be . . . handled."

"Handled?"

"Vanquished. Killed. The UDA takes their rules seriously. Anyway, I went out to the Haight where these kids were, and sure enough, the rogue vampire showed up."

"And it was Nina?"

I nodded. "Yeah. And she *was* trying to separate one from the flock. It was a girl—maybe thirteen, fourteen years old. The poor thing was filthy. Her clothes were torn, her hair was matted. She was a throwaway kid; no one would have noticed if she walked the street one day and wasn't there the next. She looked like every other kid out there."

"So, easy prey."

"That's what I thought. I followed Nina out to the girl twelve nights in a row. I couldn't get close enough to hear what they were talking about the few times they did talk, and I wasn't sure if she were just working slowly. Sometimes a vampire will befriend a human— offer eternal life or whatever—and in return . . ."

"The human brings them fresh meat," Parker finished.

"Right. One night Nina got the girl into a car with her. I followed them, and Nina drove the girl home."

"Just home?"

I nodded. "That's it. She was a runaway. Nina brought her home."

Parker frowned. "That doesn't sound very vampirey."

I smiled. "I know. I was waiting in my car the night she did it. I followed them, and then, thinking I was being real stealthy, parked under a tree on the opposite side of the street, when suddenly Nina was sitting in my passenger seat. Vampires are rather hard to sneak up on. Ssense of smell, lightning speed, you know."

Parker smiled.

"Nina told me if I told anyone at UDA what she did, she'd kill me. And believe me, when that much leather bustier and fang is in your passenger seat threatening death, you believe it. I asked her why though—why that girl, why bring her home. Nina just shrugged and said, 'Little girls need their moms.'" I swallowed the lump that had formed in my throat. "We both knew how it felt to lose our moms. Nina couldn't go back to hers once she'd changed and I—well, you know about my mom. I guess we bonded over that."

Parker patted my hand softly. "That's really nice. And I don't mean to be callous, but sweet-as-pie or not, how do you decide to *room* with a vampire?"

I shrugged, tucking the doll back to her space on the shelf. "Are you kidding? Have you seen what a two-bedroom goes for in San Francisco? I'd room with Satan himself for a view like that."

Parker raised his eyebrows but chuckled, following my gaze to the glistening lights of the Bay Bridge outside my front window.

"I guess."

"And vampire or not, Nina is my best friend."

Parker grinned that cocky half smile again. "Well, okay then."

I sat down next to him, basking in the warm fuzzy of the moment.

"So . . ." Parker brushed a lock of hair across my forehead, his touch and his voice gentle and sweet. "Are you going to tell me what happened here?"

Thump-thump.

I swallowed, telling myself that the beads of sweat that just pricked the back of my neck were scary-monster related and not close-to-Parker related.

"Someone was in the apartment," I started.

Parker nodded and his hand dropped from my forehead, his fingertips casually trailing along the exposed skin on my thigh.

Thump.

"I don't know what it was." I was shaking my head so fiercely that I could see my red hair, in rats-nest snarls, bobbing around my cheeks. I blinked, feeling the tears start to form. "He pushed open the window—my

bedroom window—but I was already out here. I heard
him climb in, and he was huge—and—and—" The
tears had spilled over and were mixing with snot, both
dropping in big blobs on my legs.

Sophie Lawson: Badass Angel. Not.

"You said you got out your gun. Did you fire it? Are
you okay?"

I pointed a shaky finger toward my bedroom door
and sniffed vigorously, trying to hold back the hysterical hiccupping that always came when I cried.

Parker stood up, going toward the open door. He
slid his palms along the pristine eggshell-white
walls, studying them carefully. "No holes." He
turned to me, throwing a grin over his shoulder.
"Did you hit him?"

"Maybe," I said slowly.

"How many rounds did you fire?"

I tasted the salty tears on my lips. "None."

"None?"

I wagged my head and hiccupped, then buried my
head miserably in the soft folds of my bathrobe. "I . . .
threw . . ."

Parker came back and knelt down in front of me,
both his hands warm on my knees. "You threw up?
Again? That's okay. Lots of people barf when they're
frightened. It happens all the time." He sat back on
his haunches. "Sometimes they pee. Did you pee?"

"No!" I yelled, annoyed. "I didn't throw up *or* pee.
I threw the gun!"

Hayes stood up, his eyes intense and narrowed. He
bit his lip and cocked his head. "Come again?"

"I was scared. I was going to shoot. But then . . . I
threw my gun at the guy."

"You threw it?" Parker seemed to savor the words. "Where?"

I gestured toward the bedroom. "There."

I dropped my head in my hands again and waited for Parker's lecture on gun safety, but it didn't come. I looked up, and Parker was doubled over, his hands on his bent knees. He was wheezing, and the redness from his face was seeping all the way to his scalp.

"You threw your gun at him?" He was blinking furiously now, using his palms to wipe his eyes. "You threw it at him?" he repeated.

I felt the anger roil in my chest, and my hands went into fists so tightly that I could feel my fingernails digging half moons into my palms. "I panicked!"

"Obviously!" Parker snorted. "I'm sorry, I'm sorry," he said, holding up his hands and sniffling. "This really isn't funny. This is serious. There was someone in your apartment and your gun could have gone off. This"—he stifled a girlish giggle—"is no laughing matter."

I stamped my foot. "If I had it to do over again I'd shoot you!" I said, feeling indignant and embarrassed.

"Well," Parker started, growing more serious, "being willing to actually *shoot* the gun is a step up from throwing it."

I narrowed my eyes. "I hate you."

Hayes disappeared into my bedroom and returned with the gun. He frowned. "It's freezing." I kept my mouth shut while he unloaded the magazine, handing me the bullets. "Next time you're in a throwing mood, try tossing just the bullets. They're cheaper."

I slipped the bullets into my robe pocket, and he

handed me the gun. I snatched it from him and threw it into the freezer, slamming the door.

Parker was incredulous. "Seriously?"

"Oh." I dug into my pocket and emptied the handful of bullets into a box of Skinny Cow Mint Dippers.

Parker pointed at the freezer. "You know, you shouldn't—" He sucked in a sigh and shrugged, gathering his jacket. "Never mind. You going to be okay?"

I swallowed thickly, looking over my shoulder at my bedroom. "I'm pretty freaked out," I admitted.

Parker leaned against the doorjamb. "Can I take you somewhere? Friend? Boyfriend?" He grinned. "Steve's place?"

I shook my head. "No."

Parker's left cheek pushed up into one of his trademark half smiles. "Oh, I get it. Fine." He stepped back into my apartment, pushing the door shut behind him. "I'll stay." He slinked out of his jacket and tossed it onto a chair. "You know, you could have just asked."

"What?"

"You didn't have to concoct the story. But the gun throwing"—he wagged a finger—"good effect." He disappeared into my bedroom. "Coming?"

I rammed my fists against my hips and stomped after him. "Where do you think you're going?"

Parker's eyebrows shot up in innocent arcs. He jerked a thumb over his finger toward the bed—*my* bed—and yawned. "We've got a big day tomorrow . . . er"—he glanced at his watch—"today." He looked back at my bed. "Looks comfy," he said with a big, goofy-guy grin.

"It is. For *me*."

Then Parker Hayes dropped his pants.

I sucked in a shocked breath and clamped my

hands over my eyes, making sure to spread my fingers just wide enough to peek at Parker's tight quad muscles flexing underneath his *SpongeBob SquarePants* boxer shorts.

He peeled off his socks and snuggled into my bed, a big, satisfied grin on his face. "Mm, comfy."

I gaped at him. "Aren't you forgetting something?"

Parker pursed his lips and then sat up. "Right." He whipped his T-shirt over his head and dropped it onto my floor. "It's going to be hot tonight."

I stepped onto the bed and planted my heel firmly against Parker's butt cheek—his very, very firm butt cheek—and started to push.

"Get. Out. Of. My. Bed!"

Parker opened one eye. "Shh, Lawson, I'm trying to sleep. And can you get the light, please?"

I flopped down beside him. "Parker, you are not sleeping here."

Parker rolled over, looking deliciously comfortable framed by my fluffy down comforter, his head cradled on my baby-blue pillow. "Didn't you want me to be here for your protection?" he asked.

I blew out a resigned sigh, eyeing the silky skin on Parker's naked shoulder, ripe for nuzzling. *But who's going to protect you from me?*

I pulled an extra pillow and a blanket from the foot of the bed, then gestured toward the open bedroom door. "I think it'd be better if you protected me from out there."

Parker kicked off my blankets and stood up, brushing past me, grabbing the blanket and pillow as he went.

"Fine," he said, yawning. "Call me when the creepy

crawlies show up. Better yet"—he reached down, picking up a sneaker—"throw that at them."

Parker slammed the door behind him, leaving me standing alone in my darkened bedroom. *It's better this way,* I told myself as I climbed into bed. There was a murderer on the loose, my boss was missing, and someone just broke into my house. The last thing I needed was a hot, half-naked detective lying in my bed.

Right?

Chapter Thirteen

I woke up with a start, and Nina was sitting cross-legged on my windowsill, her bone-white back pressed up against the window glass.

"Who's the tasty morsel on the couch?" she said when I opened my eyes.

I yawned. "That's the detective from SFPD."

Nina opened her mouth, the tip of her pink tongue touching one of her razor-sharp incisors. "I thought he smelled familiar!" Her red lips curved up into a sly grin and I shot her a look. Nina held up both hands and wagged her head. "Reformed, remember? Whew." She checked out her cuticles. "I knew you loved him."

"I don't love Parker Hayes," I said, kicking aside the covers and standing up. "And what are you doing in here anyway?"

Nina shrugged. "Dirt was dead. The general manager took off about a week ago—and their blood-stock is going low. They only had O pos on tap. And, there's a man-lump sleeping on our couch. Where else was I supposed to go?"

I rubbed my eyes and stared at the dawn as it broke outside my bedroom window.

"Is Vlad here?"

Nina shook her head. "Nah. He met a two-hundred-year-old fifteen-year-old girl. Last I checked they were staring morbidly at each other and talking about how everyone sucks."

"Sounds fascinating. Ugh. I need coffee," I mumbled.

I carefully opened my bedroom door and tiptoed into the living room, where Parker was sprawled on the couch, his breathing a low whoosh in the dim, silent room.

"He's cute," Nina said, grinning over my shoulder.

I looked back at Parker, at the blanket wrapped around him.

"Coffee," I said again. But I was having a hard time stopping my eyes from wandering back to Parker, to his chiseled chest, toward the blanket twisted over his . . .

Wasn't he wearing anything?

"Really cute." Nina was licking her lips in a delicious snack kind of way, and suddenly my dry mouth started to water.

I could make a meal out of Parker Hayes myself.

I eyed Parker's blanket, partially rumpled over his nearly hairless chest, as it rhythmically rose and fell. The sheet dropped open at his naval, exposing a delicate trail of black hair, and then was rumpled and folded again, covering him up.

Nina narrowed her eyes. "Stupid blanket."

"Ahem."

Nina and I both jumped, and Parker blinked sleepily at us, his face breaking into an amused smile.

"Oh. Parker," I said, looking at Nina. "This is my roommate, Nina."

She wriggled her fingers in greeting. "I remember you!" she sang.

"We were just—and you were just—" I stumbled.

Parker arched up on one elbow, his shoulder and pectoral muscles flexing. If Nina had any breath, I'm sure she would have sucked it in like I did.

"Do you want some breakfast? What do you like to eat?" I turned on my heel and raced for the kitchen, pawing through the cupboards. Finding nothing, I yanked open the refrigerator and stared in there. "Nina can help me cook. Right, Nina?"

"Mmm." Nina's lips were pursed, her eyes locked on Parker.

I went back to rummaging through the fridge.

In my imagination our refrigerator was stocked with farm-fresh organic eggs, whole-wheat bread, thick-cut bacon, and fruit salad. In actuality, there were several bottles of blood, a soggy-looking box of baking soda, and two pudding cups.

"Uh-oh," I mumbled.

I looked over my shoulder at Nina, who had inched away, but was still staring intently at Parker. I joined her, and from the safety of a potted plant we both watched Parker stand up and stretch, the blanket falling away and revealing those *SpongeBob* boxer shorts.

"Rats," Nina hissed under her breath.

"Whatever you have to eat is fine," Parker said, stepping into his jeans. "But I really need some coffee." He yawned heartily. "Do you two always get up at the crack of dawn?"

Nina's head swung toward me, and she grinned,

snagging a bottle of blood from the fridge. "Don't forget to put the coffee on," she told me, one eyebrow raised slyly. She disappeared into her closet/room while I put the coffee on and grabbed a couple of mugs. I was about to bring them to the table when I turned and ran full-force into Parker.

Smacked, into Parker Hayes's naked chest.

"Oh, my," I heard myself mutter as my nipples sprung to delighted attention.

"Indeed." Parker was eyeing my pajama top and I hugged my elbows tightly, my cheeks pulsing hot with blood. "I'm going to go get my sweatshirt," I said.

I tossed on a sweatshirt and fixed my hair, swabbed on a bit of deodorant, and gave myself a once-over in the mirror. I could probably do without the sheet creases on my pink cheek, but other than that, I didn't think I looked half bad.

When I walked into the kitchen, Parker was leaning against my counter, shirtless. His jeans hung low on his slim hips, his legs were crossed at the ankles, his feet bare. He studied me from beneath lowered lashes and sipped his mug of coffee, looking very *GQ,* very man-I'd-like-to-roll-in-the-hay-with. I swallowed hard and did a mental finger shake, reminding myself that Parker Hayes was my partner and my workmate and therefore completely off-limits.

Mostly.

"Morning, sunshine," Parker said with a grin.

"Good morning *again,*" I said.

"So, where's the fabulous spread you promised me?"

I opened the fridge and knocked over Nina's Blood

Light while snaking the two remaining pudding cups. I offered one to Parker.

"I'm afraid this is as fabulous as it gets this morning." I raised my coffee mug and smiled. "But at least there's coffee."

Parker took the pudding cup and the spoon I offered. "Chocolate pudding. The breakfast of champions."

We stood in the kitchen eating in silence for a moment until Parker said, "So Nina. She's the vampire?"

I nodded, licking my spoon. "Uh-huh. And Vlad, of course."

"Isn't living with a vampire—or vampires—a little weird, though?"

"Oh no," I said, leading Parker into the other room. "Nina is the best roommate I've ever had. I never have to worry about waking her up, she never hogs the mirror, and best of all"—I raised my pudding cup—"she never eats my food."

"I don't know," Parker said, slumping down at the kitchen table. "I couldn't sleep if I knew the vampire was there. I'd be sure it was just a matter of time until she ate me."

"All you breathers are exactly the same!" Nina shouted, stomping into the living room, pale nostrils flared.

"She's also super quiet," I said, licking the chocolate pudding from my spoon.

"Look, buddy," Nina said as she gathered her dark hair into a long, slick ponytail. "We've been around awhile. You breathers aren't the only ones who've evolved."

Parker's eyes narrowed, and for once, I thought I

saw genuine terror in them. I considered intervening, but I wasn't done with my pudding cup.

"Whoa, I didn't mean to insult you. I'm just trying to figure this whole thing out," he said, palms up, placating.

"Well, you no longer have to go all bow-and-arrow around dinnertime"—Nina shrugged—"and neither do we."

Parker looked from Nina to me and back again and dropped his voice. "Vampire restaurants?"

"Something like that," I said.

"See? This is what I can't stand. We're not all crazed maniacs, you know. When you walk into a grocery store, do you start ripping everything off the shelves, tearing into a box of Frosted Flakes with your teeth? No! Sure, when you're hungry you might make a few bad decisions"—Nina rubbed her stomach and winced—"but you can control yourself. So can we."

Parker shuddered. "But don't you . . . like . . . the thrill of the hunt?"

Nina's eyes went wild, primitive, and her lips parted, the pink tip of her tongue touching her sharp incisors. "Do I ever!" She kicked out her right leg and pointed at it. "Dolce and Gabbana slouch boots, forty percent off!"

The color returned to Parker's cheeks, and he groaned, tossing his pudding cup in the trash. "I don't know why I was worried. You chicks are all the same—dead or alive."

Nina cocked her head, her nostrils fluttering as Parker passed her.

"What?" he asked, eyes wide.

"You smell . . . different."

Parker's cheeks flushed, and I tossed Nina my "it's impolite to sniff our guests" look. "So, Nina, how was Dirt last night?"

"Wait. One more thing," Parker started, taking a large step back from Nina. "What about the no-sunlight part? Is that true?"

Nina crossed her arms in front of her chest and nodded. "Yeah. You know the whole UV-sunburn thing?"

Parker nodded.

"Well, it's like that, times, like, a billion. And then we burst into flames."

I grimaced, but Parker seemed unfazed. "And what about the no-aging part? People have to wonder about that. How do you get around that one?"

"Most vampires are nomadic for that reason. But it's not as big a problem as you might think. Men never question it; it's the women who always ask."

"And what do you tell them?"

"Pilates."

Parker's eyebrows shot up. "Pilates? Really?"

"If I even hinted at the truth there wouldn't be a drop of blood left in the entire hemisphere and I'd be stuck with an undead army of cougars in Juicy Couture. That's another thing—when you live forever, you become very skeptical of who you want to take along for the ride." Nina blew out a sigh. "Forever is a very, very long time."

I stared into my pudding cup and grinned while Parker squirmed.

"Forever, huh?" he asked.

Nina shrugged. I refilled Parker's and my coffee mugs, and then the three of us settled at the dining room table.

"Okay then," I said to Nina, "back to Dirt. Anything we should know about? Has there been anything interesting going on?"

Nina shrugged, pulling the morning paper off the counter. "That's just it—nothing. Apparently there was some big fight there earlier—Thor demons, I heard—so the place was basically emptied out by the time we got there."

"Thor demons? Fighting? That's weird. They're generally pretty peaceful."

Parker's eyes flashed, and I sipped my coffee, continuing, "You know, as far as demons go."

The lock tumbled on the front door, and then Vlad was standing in the middle of the living room, his black-Drac uniform obscured by an ankle-length leather duster.

I pasted on a smile as Parker's eyes widened. "Vlad, you remember Parker."

Vlad's nostrils flared as if he was smelling something unsavory. "Uh-huh."

"Nice coat," Parker said.

Vlad's eyes flashed. "This is the official uniform—"

"We know, we know, Vlad. It's the official wacky uniform of the Vampire Empowerment and Restoration Movement," Nina said.

Parker's brow furrowed. "VERM?"

"Yeah, that's why we don't shorten it."

Parker leaned back and sipped his coffee. "And what is it that this movement wants to do, exactly?"

"We seek to restore vampires to their former glory and power, when humankind was rightfully subservient to our superior race."

"Well, la-di-dah," Parker said under his breath.

"It's just a lame excuse for a bunch of vamps to run around in capes and top hats," Nina said.

Vlad glared, his blue-white fangs bared. "We are restoring a centuries-old balance of power. Our race has been practically obliterated, forced to flee, to live underground."

"I thought sunlight killed vampires?" I piped up.

"That's beside the point," Vlad said sharply. "The Movement welcomes all vampires"—he eyed Nina—"no matter how far from the flock they have fallen."

Nina snorted and flipped a page on her newspaper. "Lame!"

"If you're not with us, you're against us, Auntie."

"Fine!" Nina threw up her hands. "Put me down for a bumper sticker."

Parker chuckled, and Vlad rolled his eyes, crossed the living room in a burst of cool air, walked into Nina's closet bedroom, and slammed the door behind him.

"Charming kid," Parker said, raising his coffee cup.

"You should see him when he's in a bad mood," Nina said, scanning the paper.

"Are these VERMS—"

"We don't shorten it!" Vlad moaned from behind his closed door.

Parker lowered his voice to a near whisper. "Are they violent? Could they possibly be responsible . . . ?"

Nina wagged her head. "No. Like I said, it's really nothing but a bunch of spoiled rich vamp kids with nothing better to do."

"I heard that!" Vlad whined.

"Good," Nina returned. "Then maybe you all will forget this stupid movement and decide to do something worthwhile with your afterlife!" She shook her head at Parker and me. "This new generation of vampire—they think they're so entitled." She went back to reading her paper, then fingered the edge of her mug and casually looked up at us. "So, have you two had any luck with your case?"

I wagged my head. "No, not really."

Parker swallowed and glared at me. "We're doing okay. Hey, what's Dirt? You mentioned it a minute ago, before Mr. Dark and Broody blew in."

"Club," I said. "Underworld friendly. Mostly vampires, demons . . ."

"The occasional zombie." Nina wrinkled her nose. "They have *got* to get better security at the door."

Parker looked at me. "Maybe our perp . . ."

Nina's head snapped up. "What was that?"

Parker cleared his throat, pushed his empty coffee mug away. "I think our perp might be"—his eyes studied Nina, her slick black hair, her ruby-red lips pursed and heart-shaped—"of the nonhuman persuasion. Have you heard anything around the club? Any chatter about . . . conquests, attacks?"

"Conquests?" Nina snorted. "We're demons, not Vikings."

Parker raised an annoyed eyebrow. "Fine. Have you heard anything?"

Nina sat back in her chair. "I guess there has been some chatter. I don't really pay attention though; the band was actually pretty decent last night."

The bedroom door opened, and Vlad poked his head out. "Chatter? I heard a few things."

"Now he's Mr. Helpful," Nina muttered.

I looked at Vlad. "Heard about what?"

"Lucy—this little glampire I was hanging with last night—mentioned something about a couple of norms harassing her, asking her if she'd do them a favor."

"What's so weird about that?" Nina asked. "Breathers are always asking us for stupid stuff—love potions, to feed on someone."

Parker looked green.

"But I never do," Nina continued.

"They were asking her about the demons at Dirt, and then they wanted to know about the Sword of Bethesda. If she knew where to find it. They were obviously idiots."

"Why is that?" Parker asked.

Vlad snorted. "Because they couldn't even tell a real vampire from a glampire. Lucy didn't know anything."

Nina slapped her hand on the table. "Wait, let me get this straight. Vlad Count Chocula, Mr. Vampire Empowerment, was hanging out with a breather? If you're so pro-vamp, why the heck would you be wasting your time with a breather?" She held up a placating palm to Parker and me. "No offense. Isn't that against, like, your bylaws?"

Vlad steepled his fingers, his porcelain face remaining unchanged. "The weak-willed breathers are used to doing our bidding. They will be properly compensated when their services are no longer needed."

"*You* have bidding?" Nina asked, incredulous. "What the hell kind of bidding do you have, Louis, seriously?"

I blanched. "Compensated? Like, changed?"

Nina's face was fierce. "Oh no. No one is getting *compensated* that way. No one is getting bitten."

Vlad raised a single eyebrow. "Perhaps you think she would prefer a puppy?"

"What is it with you two and baby animals?" I shouted. "No kittens, no puppies, and no turning humans into vampires, capisce?"

Nina went back to reading her paper, but I could see the smile playing on her lips. "She's tough, Vlad. I'd do what she says."

"What's the Sword of Bethesda?" Parker asked.

Nina shrugged. "Don't know, never heard of it."

"Don't you know anything? The Sword of Bethesda is a charmed sword," Vlad said.

"Great," Nina said, bored. "And why would I want a charmed sword?"

I gulped. "Maybe to gauge someone's eyeballs out?"

"Or slit their throat?" Parker asked.

Nina looked pained.

"I didn't mean *you* would use it to gouge someone's eyeballs out." I looked from Nina to Parker. "I'm just thinking maybe that's what it would be used for."

Parker shook his head. "When did these guys talk to your friend?"

Vlad shrugged. "Dunno. A couple of days ago, I guess. You can ask Lucy yourself. We're going out tonight."

"Thanks, Vlad."

Vlad slammed the bedroom door. I glanced at Nina, then at Parker, and my eyebrows shot up. "Hey, what if we go to Dirt? I mean Parker and me. You know, like, undercover?"

Nina and Parker looked at me, both their expressions set on "Are you crazy?"

"Just listen. We could slide in, just for a night, and listen to what everyone is saying. Maybe we could get some clues or ask around. I certainly wouldn't mistake a fanpire for the real thing. Maybe I could find out more about this sword, who's looking for it—or who's got it."

Parker looked at Nina. "Why don't we just send Nina in?"

Nina crossed her arms. "Why don't we not?"

I laid my palms flat on the table and knitted my brows. "Come on, Parker. This might be the only way to break this case—or at least to help rule out whether or not the killer is human. And Nina—" I worked the puppy-dog eyes on her. "This could be our only chance to find Sampson. Someone has to know where he is, has to have heard something. A werewolf doesn't just disappear into thin air."

"That's true," Vlad called from behind his closed door. "That one's impossible. Dell goblins can, but they're pretty much the only ones."

Parker blew out a resigned sigh while Nina looked contemplative.

"Okay," Nina said finally, licking her lips. "Tonight's a good night for visiting anyway. Vlad's going to be there with Lucy, and who knows, you two might like it. Heartstrings are playing and they are fantastic. The keyboardist used to feed on Mozart."

Parker went pale.

"Okay, great." I forced an excited smile. "What time do we leave?"

"Wow," Nina said as we drove to the UDA office that morning, "you're glowing."

"What are you talking about?"

"Woke up with Coptastic, have a hot date tonight . . .

I can practically *hear* the blood coursing through your veins. You're all atwitter."

I frowned. "I'd appreciate you not listening to my innards; it really freaks me out. And it's not a date. It's undercover work."

"And this morning?" Nina wanted to know.

"More work. And speaking of this morning, why were you smelling Parker? It's hard enough to tout the benefits of a vampire friendship without you sniffing around him like he's dinner."

"It's just that he smells weird," she said, frowning. "Not like dinner weird, either. I can't put my finger on it. It's different."

"It's Buffalo. That's where he's from."

Nina looked at me sideways.

"I smell it, too." Vlad said, turning down the death metal on his iPod. "What is he, anyway?"

"He's a detective!"

Neither Nina nor Vlad looked convinced.

"Look, you two, I don't know what's stranger—you guys thinking that he smells weird or you guys smelling him at all."

"He doesn't smell like a detective," Vlad murmured, turning up his iPod. "He doesn't even smell human."

"What does he smell like?" I asked.

Nina shrugged. "Just weird."

"He's human," I said. "You guys are nuts. I've even felt his heartbeat."

Nina's eyebrows waggled. "Sexy."

"Gross," Vlad contended from the backseat.

We rode in silence until Nina pulled her car into the police station parking lot, maneuvering over to the UDA-reserved spaces.

"Hey." I grinned, relief washing over me. "That's Pete's car. At least one thing is back to normal."

"Our boss is back at work," Nina moaned, pulling her key out of the ignition. "Yippee."

I headed straight for Mr. Sampson's office when we walked into UDA but stopped short when I got to his closed office door. I knocked timidly, then poked my head in. "Mr. Sampson?"

I pushed the door open when there was no answer and stared at the empty room.

"Sampson's not in," Lorraine said from behind me.

I whirled, clutching my heart. "Oh. Lorraine, sorry, you scared me."

Costineau whined as he circled around her ankles, throwing me dagger glares with his yellow cat eyes.

"I saw that he—at least his car—is here. Do you know where he is?"

Lorraine held the file folders she was clutching close to her chest and pinned me with her stare. Finally, she simply said, "No."

I strode toward her. "Really, Lorraine? Because this could be really important. I'm worried about Sampson. Did you see anything, anything at all, when you did that scan?"

Lorraine's eyes shone. "Yes."

My eyebrows rose in the universal "Well?" fashion.

"I think you need to ask your detective friend." Lorraine smiled thinly and stepped away, Costineau following after her.

"What does that mean? Ask him what?" I yelled, tailing her.

But Lorraine didn't turn around. Costineau jumped onto Lorraine's shoulder and hissed at me as they disappeared down the hall.

By one o'clock I had made eighteen passes in front of Lorraine's empty desk and listened to Parker's voice mail greeting twenty-two times. Nina was sitting on the end of my desk, swinging her long legs and sucking on a plasma pop, when I finally got Parker on the line.

"Parker, thank God! I've been calling you all day."

"Sorry," Parker said, sounding distracted, "I've been tied up. What's going on?"

"Sampson's car is here. In the UDA parking lot. But Sampson never showed up to work."

There was a short pause, and then Parker said, "Okay, show me. Meet me in the lot."

I tightened the belt on my sweater against the damp air while Parker reclined on a white SUV, looking all at once Abercrombie attractive and *CSI*-cocky. I showed him to Sampson's car, and he circled it, scrutinizing it from every angle while I jumped from foot to foot, trying to keep warm.

"Well?" I asked.

"Well, it looks like the dog drives a nice BMW, while I—a perfect angel—get a 4Runner with a transmission problem."

"Fabulous. Can you do your male comparisons on your own time? What does the car tell us about where Sampson is?"

"It tells us that Sampson is not here." I gaped at Parker, and he grinned at me.

"Real smart," I said.

"Ask a stupid question," Parker said as he shook his head and sunk down to his knees. Before I could blink he had jimmied the driver's side door lock.

"Parker!" I hissed as he slid into Mr. Sampson's

front seat. "What are you doing? Get out of there. You're breaking and entering."

He grinned up at me and kicked open Mr. Sampson's glove box. "You call it breaking and entering, I call it being thorough. Besides, I'm a cop. This is totally legal." He handed me a stack of registration papers. "Here, make yourself useful."

I slid onto the passenger seat and looked out the front windshield nervously, holding the papers in my lap. "So, I talked to Lorraine today."

Parker didn't look up while he rifled. "Oh yeah? What did she have to say?"

"She said to ask you about the scan."

"What scan?"

I put the papers down and blew out a sigh. "When she scanned the other day, looking for Sampson, remember?"

Parker paused. "Yeah. Didn't she say she couldn't find anything?"

"She said that yesterday. Today, she told me to ask you."

"I have no idea what she meant by that. Look at this." Parker extracted a glossy postcard and handed it to me. "Looks like Pete Sampson was a VIP guest at the grand opening of Dirt."

I tucked the postcard back into the glove box. "So?" I asked.

Parker raised his eyebrows, and I rolled my eyes.

"So I guess it's a good thing we're headed to Dirt tonight."

After work Nina and I had dinner together—well, I had two mini cheeseburgers and a half order of fries while Nina pouted her lips and rapped her fingers on the table, grimacing at every bite I took.

"How can you eat that stuff?" she asked me, her cute little ski-jump nose wrinkled.

"Like this," I said, shoveling in a few more fries. "Look, when I decide to go all liquid, you'll be the first to know."

"Can you at least hurry up? Parker is going to be back here at eleven and I want to get to Dirt before they run out of AB neg."

I raised my eyebrows.

"It's the Cristal of blood."

"Delicious," I said, my burger churning in my stomach. "I'll go get dressed."

I stared into my closet, frowning at my collection of smart button-down blouses and Martha Stewart–esque knit twin sets. Not very vamp. After digging for a bit I struggled into the black sheath that I had worn for my Uncle Fernstad's funeral six years ago.

Hm, must have shrunk in the wash.

I sucked in heavily, slid the slim dress down over my hips, kicked into a pair of Mary Janes and shrugged in the mirror. Not great, but it would do.

"Okay," I said to Nina, doing a quick spin when I walked into the living room. "Vamp enough?"

Nina tinkled the ice in her cup and licked a drop of blood from her lip. "Not even close." She wrinkled her nose. "Not even troll worthy."

I frowned, looking down at myself. "What? It's black, tight, short . . ."

"Off-the-rack, dull, linen. You look like you're going to a funeral." Her eyes dropped to my ankles. "In sensible shoes."

I flopped onto the couch. "This is the best I can do.

Besides, I'm working, remember? I'm not exactly there for fun, and besides"—I glanced at the remains of Nina's bloody cocktail—"do I really want to stand out?"

Nina set down her cup and stood up. "Yes, you do. That"—she eyed my ensemble dismissively—"is going to get you eaten. Come with me." Nina's cold hand wrapped around mine, and once again, I was shocked by her strength as she pulled me off the couch and behind her to her room.

"Never fear," she said, kicking open the door. "Haute couture is here."

Nina's enormous closet was more organized than most clothing stores with all her pieces grouped by designer, color, and decade. She had an entire wall dedicated to shoes, and I lovingly fingered the butter-soft leather on a pair of high-heeled boots from the Victorian era while Nina zipped past me, draping garments over her arm, holding them up to me and tossing them aside.

"Off," she said, pointing to my funeral dress. I wriggled out of it while she handed me a delicate slip dress, deep purple and cut on the bias.

"A little skimpy, don't you think?" I asked, as the fabric swished a few inches below my butt.

Nina bit her lip and headed over to the portion of the room draped in the heavy, jacquard fabrics of the French royals (circa 1700) and found a complicated-looking corset.

"Put this on."

I started to slide the straps of the dress off my shoulder and Nina rolled her eyes, grabbed the corset and smoothly wrapped it around my waist, her pale fingers moving quickly and methodically as she laced it up. I sucked in deeply, wondering if my eyes were bulging or if my ribs would implode.

"Excellent," Nina said, her fangs exposed. She handed me a pair of black hose and a pair of killer boots. I gazed at the four-inch heels skeptically.

"I'm going to get a nosebleed wearing these."

"Better not," Nina said with a smile that was meant to be reassuring.

I gulped and yanked on the hose and boots. Once I was dressed, Nina looked me up and down, nodding, thrilled with her handiwork. "Perfect," she said.

I took her word for it. Having no reflection, Nina had no need for a full-length mirror.

There was a knock at the door, and Parker was in the foyer before I had the chance to scrutinize myself in the bathroom mirror and tie a trench coat over my hooker-vamp makeover. My eyes widened as he leaned against the door frame, his jeans dark-washed and sitting low on his narrow hips, his black T-shirt stretched taut against that mouth-watering chest. His dark hair was still wet, pushed back over his forehead, a few curls snaking over the tops of his ears. I felt Parker's cobalt eyes slide over me, then watched his pink lips press together and as he let out a low whistle. "You look hot, Lawson!"

I felt the burn in my cheeks and looked at my toes in Nina's fancy black boots.

"It's Nina's," I murmured to my shoes.

"You can thank me later," Nina said as she brushed past us in a cool wave. "Come on. We'll go over the ground rules in the car."

"Ground rules?" Parker asked, his eyebrows raised.

I shrugged and stepped through the door, feeling a little shudder when Parker put his hand on the small of my back, took my keys, and locked the door behind us. His smile was sweet as he looked down at me and my legs turned against me, going all Jell-O-y and warm, setting my heart off in a series of nervous pitters.

"We should go undercover more often." Parker's eyes were fixed firmly on my breasts, and when I caught a glimpse of myself in the vestibule mirror, I saw why.

"Nina!" I hissed. The corset had pushed my normal, barely-B's into voluptuous, chin-skimming C's that seemed to jiggle appreciatively with every move I made. Although I had every intention of being indignant and Gloria Steinem–pissed, I must say my cinched-in waist looked extra slim with my new, top-heavy body, the effect being a pretty hot hourglass in a butt-length skirt. Either way, I crossed my arms in front of me and scowled.

"Pervert," I muttered to Parker.

"Tease," he muttered back, that devilish half grin on his face, his hand on my ass. I swatted it away and slid in next to Nina in the front seat of her black Lexus.

"Nice car," Parker said.

"Keeping a little in the bank for one hundred and sixteen years—plus my twenty-nine real life years—can earn you a bit of interest," Nina said, smoothly pulling into the midnight traffic.

"I'll bet." Parker nodded.

"Okay," Nina said, her dark purple fingernails drumming on the steering wheel. "First things first: you're going to stick out like sore thumbs."

I frowned down at my vamp makeover. "Then what was all this for?"

Nina pulled the car onto a dark, slick street,

headlights cutting yellow rifts through the fog. "I might be traveling with breathers, but I do have an image to maintain."

"What do you mean we're going to stick out?" Parker was leaning over the front seat, his eyes wide, a bead of perspiration forming on his upper lip. "Is that safe? Don't we not want to stick out? Like, really not want to?"

"Well." Nina's eyes found Parker's in the rearview mirror. "You're obviously not vampires."

"Because we're not dressed right?" I asked.

"Because you're breathing. That's a hard one to miss amongst my crowd. That and your overwhelming stench of first-life."

Parker wrinkled his nose. "Okay . . ."

"And your lack of horns, fangs, uncontrolled slobber, slime trails, or lichen sets you apart from the general demon population."

"So what does that mean for us?" Parker asked.

Nina shrugged. "It means you don't make a scene. Don't ruffle any feathers, don't get on anyone's radar and don't go anywhere alone. Generally no one will bother you—certainly not the vampire set."

"See?" I told Parker. "I told you. Vampires are very rule oriented."

"Well, when the options are follow the rules or spend eternity running for your life—being hunted by pithy little blondes or mocked by the high school goth set—the decision becomes quite simple, really." Nina looked up into the rearview mirror, but there was no return reflection.

"So we should be okay?" Parker asked.

"Should be. But you will be recognized."

I shuddered. "Is it really that bad?"

"Not usually, but sometimes the service at the bar can be so slow and"—Nina rolled her eyes—"some demons have no self-control. Either way, most vamps will just dismiss you guys as fanpires."

"Fanpires?"

"Breathers who pretend to be vampires. Anytime a new vampire movie comes out, they're out in droves. Thanks a lot, *Twilight*."

Chapter Fourteen

Dirt was located in an old church just off the Haight on a dark side street. The high ceilings and large, Gothic windows of the old structure made for one heck of a bar. Which would have been incredibly swanky if it weren't for the bloodless clientele and the occasional three-horned Asimian demons delivering drinks.

We strolled up to the front door and my breath caught in my throat when Vlad—dressed entirely in black, as usual—stepped out of the shadows, a pale-faced young woman curled around him. The girl blinked at me, her crimson contacts barely obscuring her blue eyes. Her hair had been dyed Crayola black, the blunt-cut ends streaked with deep red. Her white pancake makeup made her pretty face look flawless; the heavy coal eyeliner made her large eyes swim under her pointed bangs and long false eyelashes. She looked me, Parker, and Nina over slowly, her matte, deep purple lips pursed, then rested her head against Vlad's chest, exposing a thick, red, satin ribbon tied around her neck.

"This is Lucy," Vlad said by way of explanation.

"Oh, please," Nina groaned. "And I'm Van Helsing."

"Hi there, Ms. Helsing."

We all turned to look in the direction of the sultry voice and I looked at my shoes, hiding my smile when Nina's eyes went big.

"It is Ms., I hope." Standing directly in front of Nina, staring her down with his beady hazel eyes was a "breather," dressed to kill in a stretchy red velvet T-shirt pulled over a pair of black skinny jeans leaden with chains. He may have been Nina's height originally, but his feet were stuffed into boots with a four-inch stacked heel.

"Oh my gosh," I whispered.

"Is he hitting on her?" Parker muttered into my ear.

Nina's breather friend propped his elbow against the wall and fiddled with his shoulder-length black hair, grinning the whole time, his eyes boring into Nina's. He scanned our group quickly and then went back to staring Nina down.

"The name is Reggie, and you know, you and I seem to have a lot in common."

Nina crossed her arms, jutted out one hip. "Is that right, Reggie? You think so? Now why would you think that?"

"Well, it looks like you and I are both the odd men out in our respective groups."

Nina peered over Reggie's shoulder. "I don't see any group with you."

He just shrugged, an arrogant smile playing on his thin lips. "So, what's say we make this foursome a six-some?"

I tried to fight the bubble of laughter that started in my stomach. I leaned against Parker and could feel his body shaking with silent laughter. I gripped his hand, willed us both to remain silent.

"You mean, because we have so much in common?" Nina asked Reggie.

"We're both obviously good-looking people. Both have this whole"—his eyes slid over Nina from tip to toe appraisingly—"dark-side vibe going on." He licked his lips. "I think you and I could have a lot of fun together."

I saw Nina's lips purse, a single challenging eyebrow raised. "Well, all that may be very true, but there is one very significant difference between us."

"Oh yeah?" Reggie asked. "And what would that be?"

"That I could eat you for dinner." Nina smiled broadly, her white fangs standing out against her deep red lips.

Reggie paled and stumbled backward, his hazel eyes wide and terrified. "What the hell?" He angled a shaky index finger at Nina. "You're a vampire?"

Nina just continued her bloodthirsty grin until Reggie spun on his stacked heel and began pushing through the crowd of patrons waiting to get into Dirt. "That chick's a vampire," he mumbled into the blank, ignoring faces of the crowd. "She's a real fucking vampire!"

We heard "Idiot!" and "Drunk" rumble up from the crowd before Reggie disappeared down the street.

Nina turned to face us, still grinning. "Now, where were we?"

"Lucy," I said, stepping forward, "Vlad told us that some people—uh, breathers—talked to you the other day."

Lucy turned her big eyes toward Vlad. "She says yes, that's right. It was two days ago."

Nina slapped her palm to her forehead. "Oh God. First Reggie the loser and now this?"

"Can vampires read minds?" Parker whispered.

"No, we can't," Nina confirmed angrily. She widened her stance, put her hands on her hips, and stared Lucy and Vlad down. "We can't read minds, we don't turn into bats *or* mist, we don't sparkle, fly, or dress like Count Chocula. And we never miss a meal." Nina bared her fangs at that last part, and Lucy stood upright, a tiny squeal escaping her purple lips. "So spit it out, wannabe."

Vlad put his hand on Lucy's shoulder, and she started to babble. "I was here, two days ago, and these two breathers approached me. Guys. Um, one fat and one thin, but otherwise, I don't remember too much. Except that they came out of a limo—a black limo—and someone was inside there waiting for them. Whoever it was wasn't too pleased that I didn't know anything about the sword thing."

"What happened after you talked to them?"

Lucy shrugged, still watching Nina who was still baring her fangs. "Nothing. They got back in the limo and drove away."

I looked back at Parker. "Well, that doesn't really tell us anything."

"Thank you for your help, Lucy," Parker said over my shoulder. And then, to me, "I don't think we're going to get any more information here. Maybe we should just go."

"No. If Lucy got that far outside the bar, there is a good chance we'll get more information inside. Something we can really use. Right?" I raised my eyebrows.

"Well, we're here," Nina started.

"Might as well," I said.

Vlad and Lucy pulled open the doors, and Nina followed them in.

"I'm still not entirely sure about this," Parker said, his lips pressing into my hair as we followed behind.

I looked over my shoulder, and I was nearly nose to nose with Parker, his blue eyes fierce.

"Nina wouldn't let anything happen to us," I told him. "And neither would Vlad . . . maybe."

"That's right," Nina said, her voice cutting through the din of the bar. "But follow the plan. Stay close, go nowhere alone. And don't be so liberal with the fact that I brought you here." She smiled sweetly in the dim light, her white fangs nearly glowing.

I followed behind Nina, pressing through the throngs of clubgoers while Parker stayed behind me, a breath away. His hand brushed against mine and my heart did a little flip-flop as I felt his fingers interlace with mine and hold on tightly.

"I don't want to lose you," I heard him whisper in my ear.

"I knew it was just a matter of time before Sophie came for a roll with her troll."

I wrinkled my nose while my stomach lurched.

"Hi, Steve," I said as Steve smiled lasciviously, his gray tongue darting over his lips, his yellow troll eyes intent on the too-short hem of my skirt.

"And usually Steve only gets the pleasure of running into Sophie behind a desk." He wiggled his caterpillar brows. "Or running around a desk." Steve leaned back, the sharkskin weave of his tiny suit catching the metallic light of the overhead disco ball, his gold chains nestling in the pale green lichen on his chest.

I frowned. "Nina and I were just—" I blinked in the dim light, but Nina was gone. I went to tighten my grip around Parker's hand, but he was gone, too. I scanned the bobbing heads, looking for Vlad, for Lucy. "Um, my friends are . . ."

"Right here," Steve said, stepping closer, his troll stench engulfing me. "Care to dance, my breathing baby?"

"Actually—" I looked around wildly, deciding that if Nina and Parker weren't dead already, I was going to kill them. "I should really go find my friends."

Steve lurched toward me, and I stepped back, suddenly feeling the heat prick at the back of my neck, for the first time noticing how Nina's borrowed corset was making it difficult for me to breathe. I thumped into a zombie, who stared at me, his cold, dead eyes milky, his stiff, purpled arm rising slowly until his cold, wrinkled fingers touched my forearm and started to dig into my flesh. I whimpered, pulling away, feeling the blood rush to my cheeks and the tears to my eyes as faces swirled around me—vampires with blood-red eyes and slick white fangs bared; zombies with their purpled, decaying flesh; all manner of demons thriving, salivating. I felt a pair of arms encircle my waist tightly, pulling me hard, and I kicked wildly, thrashing through the crowd.

"It's okay, it's okay." Parker's voice was soft and warm in my ear, his lips pressing against my lobe. I felt his arms soften around me, his palms pressing against my abdomen.

"Sorry, buddy." Parker grinned down at Steve who

looked up, dumbfounded. "Looks like my girl has had a little too much to drink."

"Your girl?" Steve's one eyebrow rose quizzically.

"Your girl?" I turned, craning my head to stare incredulously at Parker.

Parker didn't miss a beat; his long eyelashes batted once and he eyed me. "Sorry, my *lady.*"

"Steve didn't know you were seeing anyone," Steve told me, skeptically. "Steve is not so sure about all this."

Parker's grip tightened around my waist, and the pulsing embarrassment I felt a minute ago had turned to rage. "Oh, you know Sophie." He nuzzled my neck, and I had to work to keep angry as the shiver went down my spine and directly into the pit of my stomach. "Shy, shy, shy."

Steve crossed his arms in front of his chest and jutted out one short leg. I saw that he was wearing tiny alligator-skin cowboy boots that skimmed his knees. "Steve thinks you might be pulling his leg. Steve doesn't think you two are an item."

I opened my mouth, and Parker clamped his hand over it, then stroked my face lovingly. "An item? Maybe. If you can call soul mates an item."

"Soul mates?" I worked my way out of Parker's grip, but he was quick, rearranging his hands so they were firmly cupping my butt and my breasts were crushed against his chest.

"She can't keep her hands off me," he said to Steve.

"I—" My mouth was open, and then Parker's mouth was on mine. His lips were gentle at first, but as I tried to speak he pressed harder against me, his lips hot and insistent, his tongue darting into my mouth, effectively silencing me.

The man was a genius.

I felt his fingers travel up my back and then entangle themselves in my hair, and before I could command them otherwise, my arms were wrapped around Parker, my hands splayed on his back, feeling, caressing every chiseled inch of him.

I heard him groan, and I wanted to do the same as his fingers trailed down to my neck, his forefingers and thumbs working little circles, creating sparks all the way down my spine.

"Ahem. AHEM!"

I broke away from Parker's incredible lips and looked at Nina, whose coal-black eyes were narrow, black brows raised, a pink drink poised in one hand. "If this is how the whole SFPD works, it's no wonder you haven't caught this guy."

"Nina!" I broke out of Parker's grip. "It's not like that. We were—it was just for Steve's benefit. He's been following me. Stalking me. He was in our house! And Parker was—" I leaned in, the top of my head brushing against Parker's chin, and I lowered my voice. "Steve wants to dance with me and Parker is pretending to be my boyfriend so we don't get split up. We're undercover, remember?"

Nina took a long swig from her drink, her eyes sweeping the dance floor. "You know Steve left with his brothers about ten minutes ago, right?"

I looked at Parker grinning down at me, his one hand still on my rump. "Thoroughness is the hallmark of a good undercover operation," he told me, squeezing playfully.

I yanked Parker's hand from my butt and stepped aside. "Pervert!" I hissed.

Parker used one finger to wipe his lips—those luscious, bee-stung lips. "Professional," he corrected.

I went to break away from Parker, but his hand was around my waist again, his lips at my ear. "Admit it—you loved it." His voice was all at once playful and deep and sultry. It stirred something deep inside me, and I wished my skirt were a little longer.

"I was working," I said, my mouth wanting him. "That's all."

Nina rolled her eyes. "Look, can you do your he-loves-me, loves-me-not thing somewhere else? I thought you wanted to get to the bottom of this case."

"We do." I stepped away from Parker and crossed my arms in front of my chest. "We definitely do. Did you hear something?"

"There's been a few interesting conversations going on over there." Nina nodded in the direction of the bar, and we followed her, zigzagging across the dance floor.

"Sit here," Nina said before pressing me onto a red velvet bar stool. She shook the ice in her empty glass over my head, and the bartender turned around, his yellow eyes fixed on her glass. "Another?" he asked her.

I looked up at the bartender. "Ooh." I felt myself cringe and then go red.

The bartender narrowed his eyes at me, the green scales on his face slick, his thin-slit nostrils flaring. "Is there a problem?"

I wagged my head. "No, no. Not at all."

The bartender shrugged, handing over Nina's re-filled drink. He narrowed his eyes at me. "Hey, we can't all be Rob Pattinson."

Nina took her drink and sipped slowly.

"Is that blood?" Parker wanted to know.

"It's a Cosmo," Nina said, annoyed.

"You can do that?"

"God, I should write a handbook. Anyway, just pay attention. Those guys over there—" Nina's midnight-dark eyes darted toward two gentlemen, heads bent, sitting at the end of the bar. "They're talking about a murder."

"How do you know that?" Parker asked. "I can barely hear myself think in here."

Nina tugged at her ear.

"Vampire perk," I told Parker. I bit my lip. "I can't hear anything." I looked at Nina, listening intently, at Parker, seeing the slight bulge of his gun underneath his coat. I frowned, feeling powerless—and then I thought about Mr. Sampson. He believed in me. He assigned me to this case.

I was Sophie Lawson, *CSI.*

"I need to get closer," I said. "Come get me if it looks like I'm about to be drained or beheaded." I was up before Parker—and my own good sense—had a chance to stop me. I edged my way through the bar crowd fringe and squeezed myself between the two men.

"Excuse me," I said, batting my eyelashes and doing my best dumb-and-hot routine. "Is anyone sitting here?"

One of the men smiled down at me, and I could see one of his sharp white fangs glimmer. "No one but you, sweetheart."

I sucked in a nervous breath but pushed ahead. "Thanks." I jumped up onto the bar stool and settled myself, taking an extra couple of minutes to re-arrange my legs so I wasn't flashing the entire dance floor in Nina's miniskirt. Once situated, I widened my eyes and tried to smile softly. I looked at the man to my left. "Don't I know you from somewhere?" I started.

"Oh," the man said, shaking his dark head, "I don't think so. But that doesn't mean we shouldn't get to know each other now. I'm Hank," he said, offering me his cold, undead hand, "and this is Malcolm."

I shook hands with both men and glanced back at Nina and Parker, who were sitting at the other end of the bar, agog. I'd like to think they were riveted and awed by my total control over the situation, but even from this distance I could see that muscle twitching in Parker's jaw, and Nina gnawing on her lower lip. I smiled sweetly at them.

"So, does anything interesting ever happen around here? You know, anything fun?"

Hank and Malcolm exchanged a look over my head. "Sometimes you've got to make your own fun."

"Like, pummeling the occasional norm?" I said casually.

"Funny thing for a norm to say, don't you think, Malcolm?"

I felt the heat prick at the base of my neck. "Norm?"

Malcolm had leaned into me, and I felt the tip of his nose, his cold marble lips brush against my neck, sending terrified shivers down my spine.

"You smell nice," he growled at me. "Real nice. I bet we could have a lot of fun together."

And that's where my plan went awry.

I hopped off my bar stool and stepped back, my stomach playing the accordion, my heart pumping so much blood into my cheeks that I probably went from "tasty" to "irresistible" on the vampire delicious-food meter in less than a second. "It's getting awfully late, fellows. I think I should be going."

Hank narrowed his eyes at me, and I could see Parker standing up on the other side of the bar, Nina in tow, both looking a combination of frightened and exasperated. They were trying to make their way toward me, slowly edging between a throng of hob-goblins who were doing body shots.

"You can't leave now. It's still early, and we were just about to get to the fun part. Weren't we, Malcolm?" Hank's bloodless hand closed around my wrist, and he squeezed, the motion making my veins bulge blue in my arm. He licked his lips, and Malcolm chuckled.

"Thanks, but I really think it's about time I go. It's been really fun. . . ." I tried to struggle away, tried to fight Hank's grip, but Malcolm took my other arm and my hands went cold as both men stopped the blood flow. "Guys, I've really got to—" But my protest was lost in the chorus of shouts and growls that started on the dance floor.

"Damn zombies! You're nothing but hangers-on! Freeloaders!"

"Who are you calling a freeloader?"

"You, freeloader!"

Malcolm and Hank let go of me to watch the commotion just as the dance floor exploded into pushing, pulling, punching chaos. Blood bags were punctured, and drinks were splattering everywhere. I saw a Heat demon blow a mouthful of fire, incinerating the DJ stand. A vampire crumbled and turned to dust when an irate, six-inch pixie drove a wooden chair rail through his heart. Malcolm and Hank stood up, and I used the opportunity to drop down to hands and knees and crawl toward the back hall. Once I was sure the vamps weren't missing their snack, I began yanking on doors in the hallway, looking for a way out. After three locked doors in a row, finally, a knob turned.

"Thank God!" I breathed.

I yanked open the door and was immediately pummeled. I heard the unmistakable crack of bone on bone and felt the searing pain of a head butt. Whoever had thrown himself at me had done so with all their strength, and I was pinned to the floor under his weight—his solid, dead weight.

I struggled underneath the body, and the skull that bonked mine lolled over my chest and gazed up at me with milky, sightless eyes. I howled and started kicking, skittering—anything to get the dead guy off of me.

"My God, my God!" I was panting when Parker and Nina ran down the hall and found me on the floor, my eyes wide.

"What in the hell is going on here?" Parker shouted.

"Get him off of me! Get him off of me!"

Parker rolled the body over, and I scrambled to my feet, rubbing my arms to get the dead off of me. "Don't touch it!" I screamed at Parker.

Parker was kneeling next to the body, his fingers pressed against the guy's neck. "Yup." He nodded. "Definitely dead."

"Of course he's dead!" I said, exasperated. "Live people don't fall out of closets and pummel . . . other live people!"

Nina sniffed at the air. "And he's fresh, too."

Parker grimaced. "Well . . . that's handy."

Nina knelt down next to Parker. "Do you know how he died?" she asked.

Parker slid the sleeves up the man's arms, and I wanted to barf. He checked the man's neck for bites, and my knees started to quiver. "You guys, I need to get out of here."

"No bite marks," Parker told Nina, both of them ignoring me.

Nina gave the man's veins a once-over. "He's bleeding though."

I looked at my own heaving chest. "Oh, God, so am I."

Nina and Parker stood up and rushed to my side, examining the heart-shaped smear of blood on my chest. Nina dragged her index finger through it and then sucked heartily. "Not yours though," she said finally.

My heart skipped a delighted beat, and then my mouth went dry. "Should I be concerned that you know what my blood tastes like?"

Parker fell back on his knees, pushing the dead man's leather jacket aside. "Here. He's been shot. Looks like through the back with a small-caliber rifle."

"So what does that mean?" I asked. "A dead man, shot, stuffed in the closet of a demon bar?"

"It means that this isn't the work of a demon," Nina said, hugging her elbows.

Parker sat back on his haunches. "It means this is probably not our guy."

"Because we're dealing with a demon," I said slowly. "Right?"

Parker's eyes flashed, locked on mine.

"Maybe," Nina said.

"So far we know that our killer drinks blood," Parker said.

"Takes blood," Nina corrected. "We don't know what he did with it."

"Okay," Parker continued, "a killer who takes blood, tears one of his victims to shreds, removes the heart of a third. A shooting victim for number four just doesn't add up."

"And the eyeballs," I said solemnly. "Don't forget the eyeballs."

"So, blood, eyeballs, heart, gunshot wound? No. Definitely doesn't make sense."

I sat back. "It certainly seems like we're dealing with more than one killer. And our dead guy . . ." I glanced down at him, sprawled on the floor, mouth gaping open and I blinked.

I knew those vacant eyes. The pale skin, the meager attempt at a mustache.

"That's Officer Franks!" I said, pointing. "From the front desk at the PD! Don't you recognize him, Parker?"

Parker crouched down, studying. "Yeah. Yeah, you're right."

Nina stooped over, feeling for Officer Franks's wallet and badge. "Yeah," she said, once she retrieved them, showing them off. "Officer Kevin Franks. Kind of cute."

Parker felt around the body, and I winced. "But he's not carrying," he said finally.

"So we're pretty sure it's not our killer. The MO is totally different, right? Maybe it was just a case of the wrong place at the wrong time."

Nina wagged her head. "No, the clientele at Dirt is too smart for that. No one kills in a public place like this, and even if they did, with a gun?" She looked disgusted. "Wouldn't happen."

"All the other murders have been demon–human, right? Or at least seeming that way." Nina and Parker both nodded. "So I guess the real question is, what's a norm doing hanging out at Dirt?"

"No," Parker said, handing me Opie's wallet. "The real question is, what's a police officer doing hanging out at Dirt?"

Chapter Fifteen

"I need a shower. Stat," I moaned the second I sunk my key into the lock. By this time the blood had dried on my chest and flaked off in a brown shower every time I moved. Also, though I was doing my best not to think about the dead guy who was rolling on me less than an hour ago; my skin still crawled and I couldn't shake the feeling that I had dead-guy cooties seeping into my pores.

"Need help?" Parker asked.

"Charming," I said, slamming the bathroom door in his face.

I melted into the hot water, starting to lather up, but every time I closed my eyes Opie's milky, vacant eyes floated into my mind. When I tried to blink the image away, it was replaced by the heartless dead woman from the day before. I shuddered, my skin prickling with goose bumps in spite of the hot water.

And then I remembered that I had kissed Parker Hayes.

The goose bumps prickled again, but this time the feeling could only be described as effervescent—or maybe delicious—and my mouth started to water. I blew out a long, exasperated sigh and decided that Parker's kiss—his tasty, pressing, passionate kiss—was the lesser of the two evils to think about, and I savored the memory of his lips crushing against mine, of the way his chest felt pressed up against mine, of the way his hands found the perfect spot at the base of my neck, the spot that made the erotic touch of his fingers send shivers from my neck to my head, right down to my toes and back again.

We've got to crack this case, I told myself. *I can't take any more bodies, I can't take any more attacks, and if I have to spend any more time with Parker Hayes—well, it might be his body being attacked.*

When I padded into the living room Parker was sprawled on the couch eating a slice of leftover pizza and Nina was perched on the floor in front of her open laptop.

"Did you get all the dead guy off of you?" Parker asked with a grin.

I raised an eyebrow and took a slice of pizza from the box. "Mmm," I said, taking a big bite. "This is the best pizza ever. I can't remember the last time I ate."

"Nina and I are trying to figure this thing out," Parker said, crumpling his napkin.

I sat on the arm of the couch. "Since when did you get interested in police work?" I asked Nina.

She glared over her shoulder at me. "Number one, I'm not that interested. Number two, Coptastic over there is bonding with our couch and I'd like to have it back someday soon. The sooner this guy is caught, the sooner I can stretch out and watch *The View*."

Parker glowered at her. "Don't you have a coffin you should go sleep in?"

Nina narrowed her eyes. "Don't you have a donut to eat?"

I jumped in between Nina and Parker, breaking their daggerlike stares. "Guys! Come on. You can deeply offend each other later. We've got a case to solve. Let's get to work."

Both Nina and Parker let out long, resigned sighs. Nina went back to scanning her laptop, and Parker snaked another slice of pizza.

"Okay." I flopped onto the couch, tucking my legs underneath me and snagging a pepperoni from Parker's slice of pizza. "We're looking for a murderer who's kidnapped Sampson."

Parker's eyes flashed. "Lawson . . ."

I narrowed my eyes at him, my words tight. "We're looking for a murderer who's kidnapped Sampson. What do we know?"

"We know that none of the murders have been exactly the same. Different MOs, different crime scenes, vics don't seem to have anything in common."

"So, random killings?" I asked.

Parker wagged his head. "I don't think so. There's got to be some pattern, something about the victims that we're missing. I mean, most killers—your garden-variety sociopaths—are opportunists."

"And there's not much opportunity to murder a man on the twenty-third floor of his highly populated office building. And the woman from Pacific Heights— I believe the term you used was Fort Knox?" I said.

"Right. The victims must have had something the killer wanted very badly."

I grimaced. "Like their eyeballs."

"Let's take the first victim—the lawyer."

"What's his name?" Nina piped up, her fingers flying over the keyboard.

Parker extracted his leather notebook from his jacket pocket "Um, Alfred Sherman, esquire," he said.

I frowned. "Alfred Sherman? Doesn't that name sound familiar?"

Parker bit the end of his pen. "Well . . . Alfred Pennyworth was Batman's butler."

"No, that's not it. . . ."

Parker went back to scanning his notebook. "Alfred Sherman, attorney. Worked down in the Financial District, right across from the—"

I blinked. "Transamerica building. He worked right across from the Transamerica building, right?"

Parker referred to his book and nodded. "Uh-huh, that's right. How did you know that?"

I went to the bookshelf and slid out my grandmother's photo album and began to thumb through it. I stopped, snapping out a yellowing photograph of Grandmother and myself standing out front of the Transamerica building when I was nine years old. I was grinning with a crooked ponytail. The sun was glaring off the plate-glass windows of the building, and there was a man standing with us, wearing a seventies-style seersucker suit. I jabbed my index finger at the man. "Is that the attorney who was murdered?"

Parker reached into a manila envelope, rifling through crime-scene photos. He slid one out, and my stomach lurched as I caught sight of the man, in Parker's photograph, his skin purpled and pasty, laid out on a coroner's gurney. He was older and more weathered, but he was certainly the same man.

Parker's eyes went wide. "Alfred Sherman," he said slowly. "How did you know him?"

"He was my grandmother's attorney. He took care of her will, her assets. He was the only"—I sucked in a breath—"he was the only norm who knew about what she could do."

Parker took the photograph from me and whistled, holding the two together.

"Well, I'll be," he said.

"I haven't seen him since my grandmother passed away—and that was almost ten years ago. Now I guess I never will."

Parker stroked his chin. "He knew about your grandmother's powers?"

I nodded.

"Did he know anything about you?"

"About my complete lack of power? I don't know." I shrugged. "I can't see how it would ever come up."

"Interesting," Nina said from her spot on the floor. "Alfred Sherman was kind of the premier attorney for the Underworld."

"What?" I said, standing.

"Specifically, he was a go-between for UDA and the San Francisco DA's office."

Parker's eyebrows shot up. "I can't believe the boys missed this."

"They wouldn't have known," I said, chewing on my lower lip. "But I should have."

"If he was a go-between, he would have known Sampson, right?" Parker asked.

Nina and I nodded.

Parker shrugged. "So Sampson knew the first victim."

"A lot of people would have known Mr. Sherman.

Anyone high up at UDA. Any of his clients. Any of them could have had a grudge against him."

Parker rested his hand on my forearm, and I sat down. "Calm down, Lawson, I'm just trying to lay out the facts. We're not accusing anyone."

"Tell me again about each of the murders," Nina called over her shoulder.

I must have paled because Parker put his hand on my thigh and massaged it gently. "Why don't you go lie down? You've had a hell of a night. You could really use some rest."

I wanted to protest, to help with the case, but the idea of hearing Parker detail the grisly murders again made my stomach quiver dangerously.

"Maybe lying down is a good idea," I said, standing up. "For just a minute or two."

I shut the door softly behind me and then opened it a crack, so I would be able to hear if Parker and Nina come up with something exciting. Or, frankly, to hear if Nina and Parker's work conversation jumped the boundary to friendly, sexy banter. The kind that *I* was getting used to with Parker.

I slipped out of my robe and crawled into my bed, relishing the way the cool sheets felt against my naked skin. I was fairly sure I wouldn't be able to sleep, what with the vortex of swirling dead-guy thoughts and the adrenaline of the evening, but before I knew it, the clock on the bedside table read 3:43 and I was cuddling up to Parker's naked chest. I knew I wasn't dreaming because my left foot was asleep and I was sprawled out, naked, except for a pair of faded yellow panties with cupcakes on them that I had the brilliant sense to slip on after my shower.

"Parker," I hissed in the darkness. "Parker, what are you doing in my bed?"

He stirred and his arms tightened around me, his lips gently nuzzling my hair. "Back to sleep, Lawson," I heard him mutter.

"I can't sleep with you in here," I said, wriggling out of his grasp. "Isn't there some sort of police rule about not sleeping with your partners?"

"Only if you're HR. Now can you turn it down? I've got to be up in two hours." He nestled his dark head against my pillow, his breathing immediately going even and soft. "Besides," he added, his voice low, "you're awfully comfortable."

His palm stroked my naked back and I saw stars.

"Go back to sleep," he murmured. "Relax. Just don't try and get fresh with me."

I glared over my shoulder, seeing the apple arc of his cheek as it pushed up in a smug grin.

"Parker," I tried. But as his palm worked its gentle circles down my spine every single synapse in my brain was firing; every nerve ending was on red alert. I was completely convinced that spontaneous combustion was a very real probability lying there in my bed with Parker Hayes.

I extracted myself from Parker's warm arms, slipped into a nightshirt, and blew out a long sigh.

"Parker," I started, "this has to end here and now. Look, I really do like you. First of all, you're an excellent detective and I am thrilled to be working with you. But that's just it. I really don't ever mix business with pleasure. It's not that I don't want to—to have a personal relationship with you; it's just that I think it would be a better idea if we kept our relationship on a professional level, at least for the duration of the case. Maybe after that we can try something, you know, start with a regular date and all. Do you understand, Parker?"

Parker answered me with a long, low snore, his eyelashes fluttering softly.

"Christ," I said, flopping back down on the bed.

The sun was streaming through my curtains, and I blinked, yawning, stretching my arms across my empty bed. I sat up with a start.

Had I imagined Parker here last night?

"Hey," Nina padded into my room and sat daintily on the edge of my bed, handing me a steaming mug of coffee. "So, you're welcome," she said, grinning.

I took the mug and eyed Nina. "I'm welcome for what? The coffee? Thanks." I took a big swig.

Nina shook her dark hair toward the empty side of the bed. "No, silly, for your roll in the hay with Coptastic. Though I must say—you two were very quiet. Didn't hear a word." She narrowed her eyes. "Or a squeal."

"Ugh, Nina!"

Nina's pale face fell. "Oh, was it not good? I really thought he'd be good."

"He was fine," I said, then, holding up my palm, "not that anything happened." I took another sip of coffee.

"Boo," Nina said, frowning.

"I can't believe you forced him in here!"

"Give me some credit," Nina said, tucking her thin legs underneath her. "I don't force. I'm not scary. Okay, well, yeah, I'm a little scary. But let me tell you—Officer Hot Stuff did not need to be asked twice to come in here with you. Besides"—she stretched—"I needed a little alone time. You norms can be exhausting. So it was all for naught?"

I rifled through my drawers, collecting my clothes for the day. "I'm not answering that. Sex is just not my priority right now. Finding this killer is."

"Sex is always a priority. Especially when you've got a tasty delicacy like Parker Hayes to snack on."

I eyed Nina. She rolled her eyes. "All I'm saying is that if I can't have sex with Parker someone should." Nina stood up. "You coming into work today?"

I showered and dressed quickly, then met Nina in the living room. I looked around. "Where's Vlad?"

Nina shrugged. "With Lucy, I think."

"Is that . . . safe?"

Nina looked up at me. "I was just asking," I said quickly. "You're the one who said he was kind of troubled."

"Troubled, like he dresses like a Halloween store bargain bag. Not troubled like he's going to feed on a teenaged glampire. He's smarter than that. Pickier."

"Great." I grimaced.

"I'll be sure to check on him when we get into work." I glanced at Nina and she sighed. "And I'll check on Lucy, too."

We drove to work in silence until Nina pulled up at a red light and looked at me, exasperated. "Really, you're not going to tell me anything?"

I grinned. "That's why you were so quiet this whole ride?"

Nina frowned. "I was giving you space. Space over. Really, nothing happened?"

"Really."

"But you love him," she moaned. "You're attracted to him, right?"

"Okay, yeah, I'm attracted to him. But who wouldn't be? He's a warm body—a warm, delicious body with chiseled muscles and a head of hair just screaming for your fingers to run through it. . . ."

Nina snapped her fingers in front of my face.

"Oh." I grinned sheepishly. "Sorry. What I meant was, yes, Parker Hayes is attractive in a hot-model kind of way. But I know nothing about him."

"You know he's a cop, so that's good."

I frowned. "I'm starting to have a real hard time figuring out who the good guys and who the bad guys are lately. Being a cop doesn't prove anything."

"You know"—Nina pressed her foot on the gas and gnawed on her lower lip—"I wouldn't expect you to know this—I mean, I've been around a lot longer than you have—but there is a way you can find out a few things about ol' Parker Hayes."

My eyes lit up. Another spy mission? Ages-old romantic insight? Sometimes it paid to have a roommate who'd been around the proverbial block seven or eight hundred times.

"Really? How?" I asked.

"Try talking to him. I find the classic question-answer approach works wonders in this kind of situation."

"Wow. One hundred and forty-five years and that's all you've got for me?"

Nina rolled her eyes. "Fine then. You just leave it to me. I'll pin down Parker Hayes."

I raised my eyebrows.

"Metaphorically! God, you breathers take everything so literally."

Chapter Sixteen

"Are you freakin' kidding me?" Nina had her small hands on her hips, her black eyes wide.

"My God."

I was staring at the chaotic remains of the UDA offices. The glass partitions that separated staff from clients were cracked and in some places, caked with yellow goo mingled with drying blood. The velvet ropes that demons so patiently waited behind were shredded, and someone had tossed a potted ficus so hard it was sticking like a spear out of one wall.

"What happened here?" I asked, my feet crackling against the spray of plaster on the floor.

"Oh, Sophie, Nina, it's you two." Lorraine crawled out from underneath one of the half-crushed desks, and Costineau curled around my legs. I reached down and scratched him, then helped Lorraine to her feet.

"Hello, ladies," Lorraine said sweetly, picking bits of drywall off of her blouse. "Did you get your invitations to my Tupperware party? There's a whole new line of product. It's called Calypso Cool."

"Yeah, thanks," I said, my brow furrowed. "Lorraine, what happened here?"

Lorraine pulled a Post-it note from her hair and bit her lip. "Well, things got a little out of hand last night."

"I'll say," Nina snorted. "Look at this place! Who did this? Zombies, right? I knew we should have barred them from the Underworld. Let them stay up top where they belong. They have no manners."

"It wasn't zombies. Well, it was . . . zombies, witches, a centaur family, a couple of trolls. Basically, our whole clientele went a little"—Lorraine's eyes raked the destruction—"batty."

"Why, though? Why now?" I wanted to know.

"Well." Lorraine wringed her hands. "It seems that someone let on that Mr. Sampson is no longer in control of UDA."

"That's not true!" I protested. "He's still in charge. He's just . . ."

"Indisposed," Nina finished for me.

"Who would say that?" I asked.

Lorraine smiled thinly. "Vlad."

"Vlad?" I groaned.

"What, exactly, did Vlad say?" Nina asked.

"Well, it seems he was holding a Vampire Empowerment meeting in the lunchroom. Something about taking back the Underworld, laying our stake to what rightfully belongs to demonkind up top . . ."

"Oh, hell."

"It was rather interesting, actually."

My eyes bulged.

"From an historical angle," Lorraine quipped. "I don't believe in all his separation-of-demon-species propaganda or anything like that, but it did seem to rouse the masses—some of them."

"I'll say," I said, scanning the room.

"But anyway"—Lorraine leaned in, lowering her voice—"then word got out that Sampson has gone missing and that he did so right about the time that the murders in San Francisco went supernatural. After being a bit incensed by Vlad and the Movement, well, I guess our clients and staff started to think that if the head of the UDA doesn't have to keep order, why should they? I mean, the rule is you go rogue and the Underground sets you straight. But if the leader of the Underground has gone rogue . . ."

Nina's coal-black eyes were wide. "Whoa."

"And the demons started to get anxious."

Nina and I nodded.

"And then we were so short-staffed . . ."

I swallowed guiltily.

"It was like a powder keg, and Mr. Sampson going rogue, well . . ." Lorraine smiled weakly. "I guess that was just the spark that they needed."

"What happened to Vlad? Where is he now?" Nina asked.

Lorraine shrugged, gesturing to the half-crushed desk from which she had climbed out. "You'll understand when I say that keeping an eye on your rabble-rouser nephew wasn't high on my priority list while demonkind was tearing apart our offices, screaming about Sampson going rogue."

I felt like someone had punched me in the stomach. Was I the only one who had any faith in Mr. Sampson at all?

"So everyone in the Underworld thinks Sampson is responsible for the murders, too?" I could hear the hysteria rising in my voice, yet again.

Nina took both my hands and led me to the

remains of a waiting room chair. She sat beside me, her brow knitted.

"Sophie, I know how much you care for Mr. Sampson."

I looked at my knees. "He's been the best boss I've ever known. The only boss."

"Look, I know better than anyone that people—even people we love—aren't always what we think they are. Sometimes the demon in us takes over. Sometimes it's just too hard—or too exhausting—to control anymore. Maybe Mr. Sampson had had enough."

I shook Nina's hands from mine and stood up. "No. No, I don't buy that. Just suddenly, after all this time? And why the eyeballs? The blood, huh? Why the heart? Has Mr. Sampson not only become a crazed killer but some kind of disgusting part collector, too?"

Lorraine cleared her throat; up until that moment, I had forgotten she was there. "Add demon skin, crossbred blood, and the Sword of Bethesda and he's not collecting, he's creating."

Both Nina and I swung our heads to gawk at Lorraine as she casually stroked Costineau.

"Creating?" Nina asked, disgusted.

My stomach rolled. "Like Frankenstein? Body parts? He's making a monster?"

Lorraine wagged her head. "No. Well, not exactly. He's not making a demon—he's creating a pathway."

"That's what the Sword of Brunhilda is for? Creating a pathway?"

"Sword of Bethesda," Lorraine corrected. "It's a special, jeweled sword. Forged specifically for the purpose of opening portals, charmed by Irish Meers, etcetera, etcetera, etcetera."

Nina crossed her arms in front of her chest. "So this stuff—the eyeballs and sword and stuff—it does what, exactly?"

Lorraine shrugged, nuzzled the cat. "The pathway, once open, will give the opener ultimate power—over demons, humans, whoever. Very enticing, but very dangerous. Most demons are too smart—or too frightened—to dabble in that kind of stuff, but to some the draw is just too great. That kind of power is . . . alluring."

"Black arts," Nina said with a shudder.

"No. Whatever is a shade darker than black—that's what he's working to open with the sacrifices. This kind of magic makes the black arts look downright PG. This kind of stuff will suck out your soul or what's left of it. If you have any humanity—and some demons still do—it drains that out, too," Lorraine informed us.

"But," I said, licking my dry lips, "we haven't found any demons hurt. Or"—I winced—"skinned."

Lorraine smiled. "Actually, if Mr. Sampson is working the spell, he could use a bit of his own pelt. He is, after all, a demon, too."

My mouth dropped open, a whoosh of air escaping. Nina rushed to my side, closing the gap between Lorraine and me. "But Mr. Sampson is not going to do that." Nina's eyes were hard and she swung her head toward Lorraine. "Is he, Lorraine?"

Lorraine shrugged. "I was just making an observation."

I hugged my elbows. "No, I just can't imagine Mr.

Sampson doing something like this. And for more power?"

"Ultimate power," Lorraine corrected. "Over anything."

Nina raised her eyebrows. "He already lords over the entire Underworld."

Lorraine didn't meet my eyes. "Maybe he was ready to move on."

"He has always been fair. And the whole Underworld looks up to him—he was *voted in* as president of the UDA. He didn't even ask for it. He isn't power hungry! Not enough to"—I looked sadly at the ruins of UDA—"not enough to cause this kind of destruction. He had to know what leaving UDA would do to our clients."

"Maybe he just didn't care," Lorraine said quietly.

I bit my lip, pausing, before knocking on Parker's office door. With Sampson going missing, the murders, and the imminent heart attack that was Parker Hayes, I wasn't sure how much more I could take. I popped another Tums, chewed, and rapped on the door.

"Come in."

Parker was hunched over his desk, his big hands cradling his head.

"Oh, Lawson, it's you," he said without looking up.

"Did you hear about UDA?" I asked, taking a seat across from him.

Parker nodded, and I saw that his eyes were bloodshot. His tie was crooked and his face was pale. "The chief let me know earlier. I don't know how we're going to put all this together. I don't know if we're looking for a vampire, a werewolf, a troll, the bogey-man . . ." He wagged his head, blowing out a sigh.

"Well," I said, trying to pump some cheerfulness into my voice, "the bogeyman isn't real. So, we can strike that one from the list."

"Up until a week ago vampires, werewolves, and trolls weren't real either. What about the Loch Ness monster, Sasquatch, the abominable snowman? I mean, who are we looking for here?"

"Well, I don't want to shoot down all your child-hood fantasies. . . ."

"Seriously, Lawson, how do you deal with this and keep your head screwed on straight?"

I shrugged, and a tiny smile escaped Parker's pressed lips. "Oh, that's right—you're a little left of center."

I wanted to be annoyed, but it was good to see him smile.

"So," I said, lacing my fingers together. "Have you heard anything more about Officer Franks?"

Parker wagged his head. "It's only getting weirder and weirder. Franks was scheduled to work last night. He was, at some point, armed. He was still wearing his holster, but the gun is missing."

"Oh. Why would a killer who rips out hearts and eyeballs suddenly need a gun? Seems kind of . . . an-ticlimactic, don't you think?"

Parker shrugged.

"Do you think he really was a victim of our killer? Maybe Franks wasn't on the killer's hit list, but he got too close? It doesn't seem right. No gore, no"— I wrinkled my nose—"missing body parts, lack of fluids. Maybe he was just in the wrong place at the wrong time?"

"Nina says that kind of stuff doesn't happen with . . ." Parker paused, choosing his words carefully. "Those people. And besides, there just aren't coincidences like that. In my experience I've learned that there are only three main reasons why people kill: love, power, or money."

I crossed my arms. "What about the truly depraved who kill just for the fun of it?"

"Four main reasons then."

"Well, supernatural or not—closet cop not included, maybe—it seems to me like we're dealing with a hard-core number four. I have a hard time figuring out where eyeballs, blood, and a human heart fall into the love-power-money spectrum."

"Good point."

I bit my lip. "But I might know where they fall in the supernatural spectrum. Nina and I saw Lorraine today—the witch, from HR?"

"Right." Parker sat back in his chair. "The one who knows more than she lets on."

"Well, she's letting on more. She said that the stuff—that the stuff taken from the victims? It can be put together to create something."

"Like some kind of macabre macaroni necklace? Gross."

I sighed. "No. Like something that can give the creator—or gatherer or whatever he would be—absolute power."

Parker's eyebrows rose. "Well, that sounds ominous."

"It's been your experience that people tend to kill for three main reasons. Power . . ."

"Power and power." Parker ticked it off on his

fingers as he spoke. "Miss Lawson, I think you've just given us a motive."

Parker Hayes bounded over his desk and gathered me up in his arms, my breasts crushing against his solid chest. His breath was moist and warm on my neck as he muttered, "Baby, I knew you could do it." Then his lips were on mine. . . .

"Lawson? Lawson?" Parker was on his feet, waving his arms airline traffic controller style. "Are you okay?"

My face went hot and red. I cleared my throat and clamped my knees together. "Sorry just . . . trying to work on the case."

Parker's face broke into that sexy half smile and he leaned against his desk. "Sophie Lawson—dedicated player. We make a good team."

"If you only knew," I muttered under my breath.

"Okay, great. We've got motive. But where do we go from here?"

I raised my eyebrows. "I think I know. Lorraine mentioned that in order to perform the ritual, the demon needs not only the"—I shuddered—"stolen body parts, but to use a certain sword. It has to be charmed, the steel has to have been forged by one of the Meer demons in a remote part of Ireland, and it has to be inlaid with a purple quartz stone."

"That sounds awfully specific."

"Specific and rare. Not the kind of thing you pick up at the local Target."

Parker rubbed his hands together. "Okay, then where would someone pick up something like that? It seems to me we find the sword, we find our killer."

I nodded and flipped open my laptop. "There are a lot of demons in San Francisco but not a whole lot of demon retail. There's a place in San Jose where Nina used to go, though. . . ."

"A place where Nina used to go, huh?"

I nodded.

"You think Vlad might know about this place, too? Maybe know a little something about the sword?"

I looked up from my laptop. "I really don't know anything anymore, Parker. Vlad wasn't even here when the first two murders happened. Besides, he's just a kid."

"A hundred-year-old kid?"

"I don't know," I moaned, going back to my laptop. "Okay, got the address." I jotted down the address to the Crystal Ball and held up the paper to Parker. "Feel like a road trip?"

Parker shook his keys between his thumb and forefinger. "Let's go."

I buckled myself into Parker's white SUV when he pulled out of the police station lot, and turned away from the freeway. I jabbed my index finger toward my passenger-side window. "Parker, you're going the wrong way. The freeway on-ramp is right over there."

Parker's eyes remained fixed on the road, but I could see his cheeks push up in a grin.

"Haven't you even been on a road trip before, Lawson? The first rule of travel is road food. Can't drive on an empty stomach." He patted his trim stomach, then maneuvered the car into the McDonald's parking lot, swinging through the drive-through entrance.

"San Jose is only forty-five minutes away!"

"Right," Parker said, his eyes scanning the lit-up menu board. "I should get two cheeseburgers. You want something?"

I blew out a sigh. "Strawberry shake, please. And a small fry."

Parker patted my thigh jovially. "That's the spirit."

Parker called our order out of the driver's side window and handed me our spoils. Once the car filled up with the overpowering scent of grease and salt, we turned onto the highway, heading south.

"I know I keep asking this," Parker said, mouth full of French fries, "but how is it that the whole Underworld —and UDA—can exist, and the regular world not know about it?"

"They know about it," I said, sucking strawberry through my straw. "They just don't think about it. Works in the demon's favor. And besides, the demon world was around long before the human one ever was, so they—the demons—kind of have the upper hand."

Parker furrowed his brow. "Where'd you get that?"

"I guess everyone has their own Big Bang Theory. Demons, too. According to the Underworld, demonkind existed long before humankind. The demons grew so arrogant—their words, not mine— that humans were created to replace them."

"That's rough."

"Yeah. You can see why a lot of demons are a little upset and make humans offer them sacrifices or pay for favors or protection. After the humans were created, the demons were used to carry man's prayers to the gods and the gods' wills to mortals."

Parker fished another fry from the bag. "I don't know if I believe that."

"Well, then Christianity spread, and all the spirits were demonized and shoved downward—into the Un-

derworld, caves, eventually into sewers and cellars—
and angels were created."

Parker's head swung toward me, and he swallowed
hard. "Angels, huh?"

"Eyes on the road," I said, turning his jaw forward.
"Angels were supposedly created to replace the
demons. They inherited the demon function of carrying messages and prayer. The demons were obviously upset that they, real beings, were replaced by a
mythological, made-up creature."

Parker smiled. "So angels aren't real?"

"Not that I've ever seen."

"But centaurs, wizards, trolls—they're real?"

I finished the last of my milkshake. "As real as you
and me."

We drove along in companionable silence for a few
minutes until Parker said, "What about you, Lawson?
Do you believe in angels?"

"Of course not. I believe in God—but the whole
winged angel thing?" I shook my head. "Silly."

"Silly?"

"I'm sorry, did I offend you? I didn't think—"

"No," Parker said, "not at all. I was just asking. This
is our exit, right?"

I nodded as Parker steered the car off the highway.
"Right there, that's the street. Turn there."

We pulled into the Crystal Ball parking lot and
jumped out of the car, pausing in front of the scarf-
covered front door.

"Ready for this?" I asked Parker.

"If you are," he said, his hand on the knob.

We walked in, a tinkling of bells signaling our entrance into the incense-filled shop.

Long counters and shelves were lined with all

manner of trinkets—magical and non—plus minia-
ture statues of stern-faced gargoyles and trolls inter-
spersed with baskets full of crystals and rocks.

"Would you get a load of this?" Parker said, picking
up a troll statue. "Remind you of anyone?" He grinned,
and I took the troll doll—which did, in fact, bear a
striking resemblance to Steve—and put it back on
the shelf.

"Stop playing around, Parker. We're here for a
reason."

"Yeah, but is anyone else?"

Parker was right—the store was deserted. No cus-
tomers except for the two of us; no shopkeeper or
employees standing behind the counter. "Hello?" I
called out. "Is there anyone here?"

A young woman—younger than me, at least—
pushed out from behind a curtain. "Sorry," she said,
chewing, and putting down a Chinese takeout box
with chopsticks sticking out the top. "I didn't hear
you come in." She wiped her hands on her skirt.
"What can I do for you?"

I blinked when the woman smiled a dazzling, welcoming smile that made her hazel eyes crinkle attractively. She nodded to me and then focused on Parker,
her grin growing broader. "Wow, we haven't had one
of you in here before."

The woman pushed her long, corn silk hair over
one shoulder, and I glanced at her beaded name tag:
KISHI. She remained focused on Parker, and he was
quiet, his eyes intense, entranced.

"Parker," I whispered, shaking his arm.

"Oh, sorry." He blinked, then grinned. "My partner"
—he chucked me on the shoulder, locker-room
style—"and I are looking for something in particular."

"Oh yeah," Kishi said, her eyes never leaving Parker. "What would that be?"

"A sword," I interjected, stepping in front of Parker. "A jeweled sword that can be charmed. It's called the—"

"Sword of Bethesda," Kishi supplied, "and I don't have one. Not anymore, at least."

"Not anymore? Did someone buy it?"

"Yeah, just a few days ago, actually."

My heartbeat sped up. "Who bought it? Can you tell us?"

Kishi cocked her head. "No, I really can't. The patrons of the Crystal Ball expect a certain degree of anonymity."

"But this is serious. It's detective work. Parker, show her your badge."

Parker tore his eyes from Kishi and dug out his wallet, flashing his badge.

Kishi half smiled. "And you're a cop, too." She leaned forward and rested her elbows on the counter, her chin in her hands. She pressed her breasts together seductively, and I noticed Parker's eyes skim over them. "How does that work?"

"What is she talking about?" Parker whispered to me. I held up a silencing hand.

"Please, Kishi, lives could be at stake here. We could come back with a search warrant, but by then it might be too late, and you could have a portal to hell opened and a lot of innocent blood on your hands—human *and* demon." I steeled my eyes. "You wouldn't want that, would you, Kishi?"

Kishi blew out a long sigh and looked past me at Parker. She slid a crystal bowl full of pomegranate seeds toward him. "Fruit?"

I slapped Parker's hand away and held on to it, staring Kishi down. "Who bought the sword?"

She rolled her eyes. "Fine. Give me a second." She backed away, disappearing behind the curtains.

"Wow, she's really something, isn't she?" Parker said with a grin.

I slapped his chest. "And so are you. She's a demon, Parker, a very, very bad one, and she's entrancing you."

"Kishi? Nah," Parker said, reaching for the pomegranate seeds.

"Don't!" I grabbed his hand, slapping a spray of pomegranate onto the floor. "If you eat food from a Kishi, you can't get away. She looks beautiful, but she's two-faced. Literally." I leaned closer and lowered my voice to a barely audible whisper. "She will eat you."

"Okay," Kishi said, slipping back through the curtain with a receipt in her hand. "Whoever bought the sword paid cash. I sold it myself."

I laid my palms on the counter. "Do you remember anything about the buyer?"

Kishi shrugged her shoulders. "Not much. It was a woman. Youngish, I guess. Black hair."

I frowned. "That's it?"

"That's it." Kishi looked around me at Parker and held up the crystal bowl again. "Are you sure you wouldn't like something to eat, angel?"

Parker paled and I mashed my foot on top of his. "No, thank you," he said finally. "We should probably be going. Thank you very much for your help, though, Kishi. We really appreciate it."

Kishi's beautiful features went cold as she frowned. "Fine. Have a nice day," she said sharply. Then she turned on her heel, and I grabbed Parker by the wrist, dragging him out of the Crystal Ball. I slammed the door behind us, and he turned for one last glance at the beautiful Kishi, and paled.

"Did you see that?" Parker breathed, pointing at the store. "Kishi, she—she's—"

"Two-faced," I finished.

Kishi was behind the counter, reaching for her Chinese takeout box. Her back was toward us, her rump perfect and perky under the loose folds of her skirt, her waist trim. Her long hair was parted neatly over her shoulders and a face—dark-eyed with salivating, pointed teeth—peered out from the back of her head.

"I told you. Kishis have beautiful faces on the front to lure their prey. On the backside, usually underneath their long, Pantene-commercial hair is their other face. The one they use to eat their prey."

Parker's breath was quick, and I crossed my arms in front of my chest, satisfied. "Guess you were lucky I was here, huh, 'angel'? She must have really liked you. By the way—if you eat anything they offer you, you can't escape them." I leaned up on my tiptoes, my nose just inches from his. "Ever. So, you're welcome."

Parker pushed his hands into his jean pockets as we walked to the car. "Can Kishis . . . see things . . . about people?"

I grinned. "Like your angelic façade?" Parker's eyes widened and I laughed. "Obviously not."

After we had pulled back onto the highway, Parker looked at me. "So, how do you know all this about demons and the Underworld, anyway? I'm a detective, but I couldn't tell you much about it or, you know . . . detective history."

I smiled, remembering. While most kids my age were falling asleep to Disney movies on the VHS, Gram was in bed with me, telling me stories about the Underworld and the creatures that lived there. She told me about the pink-and-blue-bodied Oni, from Japan, who drinks too much, eats too much, and is known for occasionally drinking Japanese rivers dry, and the oversensitive, shape-shifting Bori, who likes to playact as a human just for fun. She told me which demons couldn't be referred to by name (lest you trap them as your slave), and that you should always whistle when approaching certain members of the demon world. Fairies, pixies, ghouls, and crouchers were generally peaceful if left alone but quickly resorted to violence when snuck up upon. Gram had volumes of knowledge about the Underworld and treated each being in it with reverence and respect— always reminding me that the Underworld, with its thousands of demon species, survived because demonkind followed a code of respect that had been lost on humankind.

Parker tapped his fingers on the steering wheel and looked at me sideways. "So, the person who bought the knife was a woman."

"Right," I said, yawning.

"With long black hair."

"Uh-huh."

"Kind of like your roommate."

I looked at Parker incredulously. "You can't be serious. There is no way Nina, of all people, would be involved in something like this. Look at her! She's five-one for God sakes!"

"She's a vampire. Weren't you the one who told me they have superhuman strength?"

"She's also my best friend," I said, staring out the front windshield, "and I know her a lot better than you do. This has nothing to do with her."

Chapter Seventeen

The light was fading in the conference room where Parker and I had the contents of the evidence boxes spread out between us. Well, the contents of the evidence boxes, two empty bags of peanut M&M's, the remains of an Ali Babba falafel platter, and two frozen mocha lattes melting in Styrofoam cups. I rubbed my eyes and blinked out the big glass window into the police station vestibule.

"Looks pretty dead out there," I muttered.

"Pretty dead in here," Parker said, pushing the latest heap of crime-scene photos out of his way. "There's no rhyme or reason to this. Maybe we should just call it a night."

I glanced at my watch. "Ooh, I almost forgot. I have a Tupperware party over at Lorraine's in half an hour."

Parker's nostrils flared. "What do witches need Tupperware for?"

I stood up, gathering my sweater. "I don't know. To keep their eye of newt fresh?"

Parker grinned. "At least you have a sense of humor about your weird life."

I paused. "What's that supposed to mean?"

"It means that you have a weird life. And that you have a sense of humor about it. Face it, Lawson, as far as normalcy goes, you're zero for zero."

I put my hands on my hips, my eyes raking over the grisly selection of crime-scene photographs that Parker was shoving into his briefcase. "And I suppose you're as normal as they come?"

Parker nodded. "Heading out to grab a beer, then picking up my date, probably getting a bite to eat and then a little—"

I raised a hand, stop-sign style. "Don't," I started. "I don't want to hear about your big-breasted concubines."

Parker's face split into that half grin, which tonight I found grating. "How'd you know she's big-breasted?"

"You're right. I might be abnormal, but you're down right stereotypical. Give Bambi my best." I snatched the manila file folder that Parker held out to me and stuffed it into my shoulder bag. "See you tomorrow."

I was fuming when I pushed through the double doors of the police station and into the cold night air. I gulped heavily and then blinked, surprised by the moist trails on my cheeks.

Was I crying?

I sniffed angrily, then wiped my nose on my sweater sleeve, rubbing the tears away with my fists. I would not cry over Parker Hayes. I would not cry over that demon-hating asshole. I was just tired.

And completely normal.

I speed-dialed Lorraine on my cell phone and let her know that I wouldn't be able to make it to her party tonight. "But put me down for a juicer and a salad spinner," I said before hanging up. Normal people juiced fruit and spun salads, right?

Stupid Parker Hayes.

I drove home with my radio blaring, trying to quell the hot anger that roiled in my stomach, but with every turn I saw Parker, saw that stupid half grin and heard his comments about my abnormal life roll through my head.

Normalcy had always been a problem for me—not that I didn't try. Like every other eight-year-old girl I wanted a princess party. I remembered how Grandmother swathed the house with white twinkle lights and countless yards of pale pink tulle. She set out glittery crowns and little paper cups filled with pink M&M's, but where most little girls would have been okay with a paper cutout of a fire-breathing dragon in front of their Crayola castle, Grandmother figured, why bother with fake when she knew a perfectly good dragon who lived in the Sunset and owed her a favor? The party was going well until Nelia Henderson (yes, *that* Mrs. Henderson—fresh from the UDA) lumbered in, forked tongue flicking, tendrils of smoke curling up from her nostrils.

At first my party guests were thrilled—even the uber-popular Allison Baker (my wildcard invitation and whose friendship, I prayed, would vault me into normal social standing) squealed with delight. It was controlled chaos until Mrs. Henderson downed a bottle of grape soda and then burped fruit-scented fire right down the center of my pretty pink princess table. Allison Baker never spoke to me again—not even after her singed eyebrows grew back.

School wasn't any better. I despised Mother and Father's Day, when my teachers would look at me with those stupidly sad expressions and suggest that I make cards for my grandmother instead. My grandmother, who would show up for parents night dressed in a ridiculous array of rainbow-colored scarves and tinkling gold jewelry and stand alongside all the other little girls' mothers, who were dressed in pastel twin sets and elegant pearl studs, their slim, unwrinkled throats wrapped with dainty pearl rope necklaces. Grandmother would always talk too loud or laugh too loud, and I was labeled the girl with the weird grandma—and the girl with no parents. It was Cathy Stevens in the seventh grade who dubbed me "Special Sophie"—said with a snicker and a wave of her Barbie-blond hair.

By high school I had tested into an exclusive private school where the girls on the brochure had waist-length, stick-straight hair and wore cardigan sweaters and pleated skirts. I thought it was my Special Sophie escape. Chelsea, the twelfth-grader who led the Mercy High tour, talked about how all the girls in the school were like sisters, and I had visions of sleepovers and field trips and normal best friends with pink skin and heartbeats. I kept up my "normal" façade through spring semester by having the carpool drop me off in a slice of suburbia nine blocks away from Grandmother's house with the blinking neon eye in the window. My normal façade was effectively shattered when a group of popular girls thought it would be a hoot to have their palms read—and walked right into my living room. My school pictures hung on the wall between pictures of Grandmother hugging a warlock and shaking hands with a centaur, so my plan to act as a curious patron was dashed. I finished out my high school life as Loser Lawson, and the moronic monikers and life abnormalities just went on from there. Now I was nearly thirty-three years old, living with a vampire, being hunted by something else, and being hounded by an obnoxious but blindingly hot cop.

"Yeah," I snorted, "I can do normal."

By the time I got home I was spitting mad. I kicked open my front door and tossed my shoulder bag onto the floor, the manila file folder tumbling out, splaying crime-scene photos all over the hallway floor.

"Ugh!" I said, tossing my jacket over the heap and heading for the kitchen.

"That's it," I said, banging open cupboard doors and yanking out pots and pans. "Normal. I want normal. No werewolves, no demons, no murders, and certainly no Parker Hayes."

I pulled open the freezer door and narrowed my eyes, scrutinizing the frosty contents: veggie dogs. Skinny cows. A frozen gun. Two paper-wrapped packages from the Ferry Market Butchers.

"I want pot roast," I said, reaching into the freezer. "Normal, human dinner." I took out one of the paper-wrapped packages and dumped the frozen hunk of meat on the counter. "And peas." I snatched a bag out and sailed it over my shoulder, hearing it land with a satisfying thud in the sink. "And potatoes." I stood in the center of the kitchen, hands on hips, frowning at my bare countertops. "Okay, so no potatoes."

I tossed the frozen pot roast into the microwave and set it to defrost, then sat down with a sleeve of Ritz crackers and some cream cheese. A nice, normal snack, for a nice, normal girl.

Parker Hayes didn't know what he was missing.

I was halfway through my second sleeve of crackers and nearing the end of a bottle of St. Supery Sauvignon Blanc that I was saving for a special occasion when my cell phone chirped. I glared at the readout and tossed it on to the counter, then poked the pot roast as it spun in the microwave. It was effectively leathery on the outside but frozen solid on the inside, so I dumped a bottle of A1 over it and set the microwave to thirty minutes, then pre-heated the oven. My mouth watered thinking about the juicy, tender pot roast that Grandma would make on Sundays, and I frowned, thinking of poor Alfred Sherman and his disastrous fate.

"Normal," I reminded myself while the pot roast spun.

I heard the deafening pop of the gunshot a millisecond before I felt the searing pain at the side of my head. My stomach lurched angrily, and I shakily touched the open wound, my fingertips immediately mingling with oozing blood.

"Oh my God," I whispered. "Oh my God—I'm going to die!"

I crumpled to the floor, the pain at my temple hot and thundering, my warm blood rushing in rivulets to my ears. I felt the lump grow in my throat, felt the tears wash over my cheeks as I reached for the cell phone, then rested my throbbing head against the cool linoleum floor. "Nina," I whispered to the empty kitchen. "Help me."

* * *

When I woke up I was staring at my kitchen ceiling with Parker's concerned face looming over me.

"Lawson? Lawson?" I could hear his voice, but it sounded foggy, a million miles away.

I tried to move, but everything hurt. My stomach was churning, my head felt as if it weighed a thousand pounds, and everywhere around me was the stench of burning, of wounded flesh.

"How bad is it?" I murmured.

I saw Parker look around, his blue eyes big and wondering. "It's pretty bad," he said solemnly. "It's a mess in here."

I felt the lump forming in my throat, and before I could stop it, my eyes went moist again and I could feel the hot tears as they trailed down my cheeks for the second time this evening. "Am I going to die?" I whispered.

Parker bit his lip and then—smiled?

"From pot roast? I doubt it."

I blinked. "Pot roast?" I sat up on my elbows and looked around my kitchen. The exploded, smoky remains of my pot roast was everywhere. I touched the wound on my head and came away with a handful of shredded meat and sticky A1 sauce.

"Ugh!" I dropped my head back with a thunk on the linoleum floor. "God, I can't even do normal right!"

Parker leaned over and waved the empty wine bottle in front of me. "As a matter of fact, I think you do normal quite well."

"I didn't drink all that."

"Then you exploded a defenseless pot roast just for the hell of it?"

"What are you doing over here anyway?" I asked, picking a piece of gristle out of my hair. "Aren't you supposed to be out with Boobarilla?"

Parker eyed my forehead and avoided my gaze. "Took her home early. And I'd appreciate it if you stopped talking about my baby niece's breasts."

"You were out with your niece?"

Parker shrugged, his cheeks a pale pink. "We have a date once a month. Her parents are divorced, and my brother's kind of an ass."

"So Uncle Parker to the rescue? Why didn't you tell me that?"

"You were awfully busy storming out. Besides, I wouldn't want to stand in the way of a woman and her Tupperware. How was that, by the way?"

I raised one eyebrow suspiciously. "Why are you here again?"

"I was passing by on my way home and saw your light on." He shrugged. "Wanted to make sure everything was okay."

"Well, aren't you the Boy Scout?"

Parker grinned and offered me a hand. I tried to stand but slid on some exploded meat. Parker's arms were around me in a flash, holding me steady.

"And aren't you the lucky one?"

"Yeah," I said, tossing my arms around Parker's neck, liking the woozy feeling in my head. "Aren't I?"

Parker grinned down at me and I noticed how perfect and white his teeth were. I brushed his lips with my fingertips, and he caught my hand, gently kissing my palm. The touch of his lips sent a little quiver down low in my belly.

"I like you, Parker Hayes," I said, working hard to lock my eyes to his. Parker brushed his hand over my hair, shaking a few strands of charred pot roast off his sleeve.

"You're all right, too, Lawson."

I was leaning heavily against Parker, loving the feel of his warm, muscular pectoral muscle against my cheek and maybe drooling just the smallest bit when Nina walked in.

"Nina!" I wailed, throwing my arms around her and stiffening against her chilled skin. "I have been looking everywhere for you. Do you know Parker Hayes?"

Nina wriggled out of my embrace and narrowed her eyes at Parker. I had never seen that smoldering look, and I slumped down, sitting hard on a kitchen chair. "Are you mad?"

"What did you do to her?" Nina ignored me, her words sharp and directed at Parker.

"Me?" Parker wagged the bottle in front of Nina's nose. "Don't ask me, ask Robert Mondavi."

Even in my less than optimal state I could feel the heat as Nina's eyes raked over me.

"It was St. Supery," I whispered.

"She's had a little too much to drink," Parker explained in a low voice.

Nina's dark eyes slid to the ceiling.

"And an issue with the microwave."

"I made pot roast!" I said brightly. I looked at Nina's white fangs and frowned. "It's too bad you don't eat."

"No, it isn't," Parker and Nina said in unison.

"This is nice," I said, pulling my legs up onto the chair and curling my arms around them. "It's like we're all having a dinner party. A nice, normal dinner party."

The last splat of pot roast peeled off the ceiling and hit Nina right between the eyes.

"Come on, Lawson," Parker said, tugging on my arm. "Let's get you into bed."

"Let's!" I said, standing up quickly.

Nina grabbed my arm. "That's fine. I think you've done enough, Detective Hayes. I can get my roommate to bed."

I linked an arm around each of them, feeling lighter than air as they dragged me into the living room. "My friends," I said, happily.

Nina stepped away from me and stooped, her dark eyes focused on the scatter of crime-scene photos I had left on the floor.

"Are these from the murders?" she asked, her head cocked.

"Yeah," Parker said. And then, to me, "They were supposed to be confidential."

"Whoops!" I sang. "They must have fallen out of my safe."

"We know the first one is Alfred Sherman—"

"Sophie's attorney friend," Nina supplied.

"Right. The second was a vagrant. Forensics just came back with an ID. Dauber. Dauber Sawyer."

Nina leaned down, her bare feet making no indentation on the soft-pile carpet. "Dauber Sawyer is no vagrant." Her eyes were wide, matter-of-fact. "He's the general manager of Dirt. He went missing over a week ago."

"He went dead about a week ago," Parker said, straightening up.

Nina's eyebrows went up. "How dead?"

My stomach gurgled. "How dead is there? Isn't there just dead and"—I looked at Nina—"undead?"

"Really dead," Parker finished. "Was Sawyer a demon? How well did you know him?"

Nina shrugged. "He wasn't a demon. He was a seer."

I felt the saliva go hot and metallic in my mouth. "A seer?" I whispered.

Parker looked hard at me. "A seer whose eyeballs had been gouged out."

"I think I'm going to be sick," I said, weaving my way toward the bathroom.

Chapter Eighteen

I locked the bathroom door behind me and then sunk down onto the cool tile, cradling my head in my hands.

Sophie Lawson, General Failure.

I clamped my eyes shut, feeling light-headed and odd, and that was when I saw Mr. Sampson.

With my eyes closed I had a perfect image in my mind of Mr. Sampson, though not from any memory I'd ever had. He was chained, but not against the chocolate-brown walls of his UDA office, and he looked disheveled and forlorn. He was in his human form, but his clothes were ragged and torn, and his usually pink-scrubbed skin looked sallow and was streaked with dirt and blood.

"Sophie?" he whispered, his lips dry and cracked, his voice low and hoarse. "Sophie, can you hear me?" His brown eyes were searching in the dim light.

I could see my own head nodding and then hear my own voice. It reverberated, dreamlike, through my skull.

"Mr. Sampson! Are you okay?"

"Oh God, Sophie, you've got to get me out of here. We've got to stop him."

"Where are you?" I heard myself say. "Stop who?"

"I've got to get out of here before the next moon cycle. If I turn into a wolf down here, I won't be able to turn back. Not ever. That's what he wants."

"Who? That's what who wants? Mr. Sampson! Tell me where you are!"

I could see the terror in Mr. Sampson's wild eyes. "I've got to go," he said, his voice going low again. "Please, Sophie. Hurry!"

I blinked, and I was standing upright in the bathroom, my bare feet lost in the pink shag bath mat. Nina was knocking on the door.

"Soph? Soph, you okay in there?"

I nodded and tried to speak, but my throat was parched and dry. I steadied myself against the sink, taking a long swig directly from the faucet. "I'm okay," I finally croaked, pulling open the bathroom door.

Nina and Parker peered in at me.

"Sophie, you look awful." Nina wrapped her hand around my wrist, brushed her cool palm against my forehead. "And you're burning up."

"It's the pot roast," I said, avoiding both Parker and Nina's studying gazes. "I just need to clean up. I'm fine, really."

Parker narrowed his eyes. "But your eyes . . ."

I couldn't tell if the look on his face was interest or disgust, but he seemed to be keeping his distance. I blinked, pressing my fingertips against my cheeks. "What's wrong with my eyes?"

Nina pushed me into the bathroom and I blinked into the mirror. My usual clear-green eyes were a deep amber color, the irises outlined in a glaring crimson. I blinked a few more times and they faded back to green.

"Weird lighting," I said, pushing past Parker and Nina. "Um, I'm going to go to bed now. Nina, can you show Parker out, please? I'll just see you at the station tomorrow, Parker. Right now I just really need to get some sleep."

I closed my bedroom door on Nina and Parker, both their faces drawn and concerned.

I couldn't worry about them right then.

I had to find out what this meant.

I fell onto my bed and squeezed my eyes shut, calling out Mr. Sampson's name in my mind. Nothing happened. I pulled my knees up to my chest and clenched my hands into fists. "Mr. Sampson, Mr. Sampson, Mr. Sampson," I murmured into the darkness. "Mr. Sampson, can you hear me? It's Sophie. Mr. Sampson, please, answer me!"

"Um, Sophie?"

I opened one eye and peered at Nina, standing with her arms crossed in my doorway.

"Go away," I told her. "I'm trying to talk to Mr. Sampson."

Nina came into the room, using her naked toe to raise the dust ruffle on the bottom of my bed. "Is Mr. Sampson under here?"

"No," I said, blowing out a long sigh. "I don't know where he is. Is Parker still here?"

Nina wagged her head, her eyes still focused intently on me. "I sent him home like you asked. Sophie, what's going on with you?"

Nina sat on the edge of my bed and I swung my legs over, sitting shoulder to shoulder with her. "In the bathroom, a few minutes ago. I could hear Mr. Sampson talking to me . . . in my mind."

"Are you sure it was Sampson and not the bottle of white wine you snarfed down?"

I propped myself up on my elbow, excited, in spite of myself. "Nina, I think I'm getting my powers."

Nina bit her lip. "ESP?"

"It would make sense, right? If my grandmother was a seer? And my mother?"

Nina yawned. "And you're the most powerful wizard at Hogwarts. Sophie, I think you need to get some sleep. And take a couple of aspirin."

I flopped back onto the bed. "I thought of all people you would understand."

Nina flopped down beside me. "I'm not people."

"I don't know what it is—ESP or whatever. All I know is that I heard Mr. Sampson's voice. I saw where he was and he said he needed help. We were *communicating*."

Nina sat bolt upright and sprung off the bed. "You saw where he was? Well let's go save us some werewolf!"

"Well, I saw the room he was in. Not like an address or anything."

Nina sat down again. "Well . . . is it anything you can describe? Is there anything significant about it?"

"I keep trying to look for something, to see if there is something that I've forgotten about what I saw, but I don't think there is. If I remember something worthwhile, then maybe I can have Parker *CSI* my vision."

Nina looked down, tracing the pattern on my bedspread. "Sophie, I think we should leave the detective out of this."

"Leave Parker out of the case? But it's his case!"

Nina swallowed. "I don't trust him."

I crossed my arms. "Because he's a breather? Because he smells funny? Come on, Nina, you don't trust anyone who has blood but doesn't drink it."

Nina frowned. "I trust you."

"Only because I haven't staked you in the heart yet."

Nina snorted. "Like you could. But really, Sophie, I'm serious." She stood up, silently crossed the room. "I thought there was something weird about him from day one."

"On day one you thought he was a tasty snack cake."

"Really though, what do you know about him?"

"I know he's a cop, so he's one of the good guys." I smiled weakly. "Cops are always the good guys, right?"

"Only if vampires are always the bad guys."

She had me there.

"Like I said, I've been around awhile and there's something about this Parker Hayes that's off." She wrinkled her nose. "Something that doesn't sit right. I just can't quite put my finger on it yet."

"Look, while my luck with men hasn't exactly been"—I licked my lips—"stellar . . ."

"Like the Mentos commercial guy."

I glared at Nina, who ignored me, pulling her long black hair into a ponytail. "Sorry. Go on."

"I don't think I'd overlook the signs of homicidal mania in a potential boyfriend."

"Now he's a potential boyfriend?"

"Potential platonic work friend," I corrected.

Nina shrugged her small shoulders, looking away.

"Oh, and I'm supposed to take dating advice from the woman who dated Lenin *and* Stalin?"

Nina's eyes were wistful. "Oh yeah, my Russian phase." She shuddered. "Such drama queens, though. But my feeling about Parker isn't exactly based on . . . feeling."

My heart beat a little faster. "What's that supposed to mean?"

"I looked Parker up, Soph. He's not a detective with the San Francisco Police Department. He was an officer with the Buffalo Police Department in New York."

"I know. I told you that. He transferred over here. I even saw the fancy cardboard boxes in his office."

Nina licked her lips. "Sophie, Detective Parker Hayes was killed in the line of duty three and a half years ago."

I couldn't help but go all Haley Joel Osment on her. "You mean, I see dead people?"

"No." Nina brushed a glossy lock of hair from her forehead, uncovering a sharp widow's peak. "*Your* Parker Hayes—or this one—isn't dead. He's very much alive."

I flashed back to the day Parker and I first met, to our meal at the diner. I thought about how he took my hand, slid my palm into his shirt so I could feel the warm beat of his heart—very much alive.

"Yeah." My voice came out as little more than a whisper.

"And he's telling us that he's a detective. He's lying to you, Sophie. He's been lying all along. Detective Parker Hayes isn't who he says he is."

"No." I wagged my head. "That's wrong. I saw him at the police department. I saw his name on the door. I even saw the police chief in there talking to him. Don't you think they would know if Parker isn't . . . Parker? Or if he isn't even a detective?"

Nina shrugged. "I don't know. But I do know that we need to find out who he is and why he's here."

I nodded, fear pulsing through my body, a cold sweat breaking out on my upper lip. I sucked in a shaky breath. "Parker is looking for Sampson."

Nina looked at me, her dark eyes cold. "We need to find him before Parker does."

She didn't say it—didn't need to—because we were both thinking the same thing: *Could Parker Hayes really be the collector?*

Nina put her hand on mine, and her cold touch ran all the way up my arm. I looked at her, at her pale, milky skin, at the tiny white triangles pressing at the corners of her lips. Nina and I both stared out the bedroom window, watching the city lights press through the thick San Francisco fog.

"Okay, then. Where do we start?"

Chapter Nineteen

Nina fished around in her Birken bag and pulled out a file folder, pressing it close to her chest. "Are you sure you want to see this?"

I nodded, and a warm heat roiled through my body. "I'm sure. I want to see it."

I took the folder with shaking hands, opening it slowly. Looking up at me was a four-by-six-inch head shot of a smiling man with spiky blond hair and a tight smile. His narrow shoulders barely seemed to fill out his navy blue police uniform, and printed in clear, careful scrawl across the bottom of the photograph were the words *Officer Parker Hayes, Buffalo, NY.*

"That's Parker Hayes," I whispered.

Nina nodded, her eyes warm.

"But it's not Parker Hayes."

There was no doubt about it. This man was not the man I knew. I gingerly put aside the photo and scanned the dossier about Officer Hayes—eye color: blue; hair color: blond. I noted his birth date, hometown, and then, with unsteady breath—the date he died.

"I don't get it. Why is Parker pretending to be a dead guy?"

Nina took the file from me and thumbed through it. "It says that this Parker died while investigating . . ." Her voice trailed off, and when I looked up, she was gnawing on her lower lip.

"Died investigating what?" I asked.

Nina closed the folder. "Parker Hayes died while investigating a string of strange murders in Buffalo. Two victims. One completely drained of blood."

I gulped, my saliva tasting metallic. "The other missing his eyeballs?"

"Remember the other night at Dirt, when we were trying to figure out what all these victims had in common?"

"Yeah," I said, "and we really couldn't come up with anything."

"*We* couldn't, but I found something interesting when I was looking for Parker's info. Alfred Sherman filed a police report two days before he died—reporting a stolen wallet."

"Okay, so?"

"There was a break-in at Dirt a few days before Dauber went missing. He called the police, and they came out, but they couldn't find anything. Just came around to take a report."

I frowned. "And the woman in Pacific Heights— the officer there said the police had been there just the day before investigating an attempted break-in. So all the victims had petty theft issues just before their murders? What does that mean? Security was compromised, information could be missing. . . ."

Nina's eyes were hard and I gulped. "Or that in every instance, the police had been called."

"Kind of convenient that Parker didn't bring that up in your investigation, isn't it?"

My stomach dropped to my knees. "Yeah," I whispered. "I guess it is."

"He was probably setting them up. Checking to make sure all these people had what it is he needed to open the portal."

I stared hard at the carpet. "Oh. But we went to the Crystal Ball. We were looking for the Sword of Bethesda and they said a woman bought it."

"You don't think Parker could know a woman?"

I bit my lip. "He did say he goes out with his niece about once a month."

"Maybe Parker's niece is the type who occasionally does his shopping. Did whomever you talked to know who bought the knife? I mean, other than it was a woman? Did they tell you anything else?"

I looked at Nina, at her blue-black hair hanging over one shoulder. "No," I said simply. "Nothing else."

Nina began gathering up the files and slid them to me. "I'm going to lurk around, see what more I can find out. Vlad should be back in a little while. Until then, are you going to be okay here alone?"

I nodded, barely feeling the file under my fingertips. "Do you think Parker—this Parker—is really after Mr. Sampson now"—I sucked in a breath—"for his skin?"

Nina crossed her thin arms in front of her chest. "I don't know, but it certainly would explain why he's here—and why he wanted to hook up with you."

A lump formed in my throat. "I led him right to Mr. Sampson."

Nina wagged her head definitively. "We don't know that, Sophie."

My eyes went wide. "Parker might already have Mr. Sampson. Then all he'd need—all he'd need is—me." *A crossbreed.* My voice was barely a whisper.

"No. Stop talking like that. No one is going to open any kind of portal or hell hole or whatever." Nina's eyes were fierce, and she knelt down in front of me, her palms cold as she gripped my thighs. "Do you hear me? We're going to be fine—*you're* going to be fine. We're going to stop this guy, whoever he is, and go on our merry ways, maybe do a little shopping, hit the white sale at Macy's. You got that?"

The light glimmered off of one of Nina's fangs and I nodded. "Yeah," I said.

But I wasn't entirely convinced.

I was poking at a nuked blob of meat loaf when I heard the front door open. I stood up quickly, my stomach knotted.

"Vlad? Nina? Is that you? Did you find him? Did you find some—" I sucked in a breath so sharp I felt the ache in my rib cage. "Oh. Parker. Hi."

"You know," Parker said, tapping on the door frame with his index finger. "We had a deal. You're supposed to keep this door locked at all times. It seems like you want me to be mad at you."

I forced a smile. "Oh yeah—I mean no, I don't want you to be mad. I'm sorry. I guess I just forgot."

Parker's face broke into that half smile, and he strode toward me, slinging an arm around me. "Lighten up, Lawson—I'm not really mad at you. Sheesh, you look like you've seen a ghost. Although I guess that would be kind of old hat to you, huh?"

I stumbled backward, out of his grip. "No. No. No

ghost. Do you want"—I snatched the plate off the dining room table and whirled around with it—"Meat loaf?"

Parker and I both watched the grayish blob slide off the plate and ooze onto his shoe.

"No thanks, I'm"—Parker shook off the meat—"fine." He leaned down toward his oily shoe, and I brought the plate up over my head, cracking it hard over the back of his skull.

He howled, his hand finding a fine cut and an ooze of blood inching through his hair. "What the hell is wrong with you?"

Parker lunged for me, and I jumped back, tumbling over a dining room chair and landing hard on my rump. "Stay away from me!" I said, wagging a shard of broken plate at him.

"Lawson." Parker took a step toward me.

"Stay away!" I shouted again.

"Okay." Parker raised both hands, palms facing me. "I won't come near you, but you have to tell me what is wrong with you. Lawson—Sophie, it's me, it's Parker. We're friends, remember? Partners?"

"You're not my partner! You're not my friend! You're not even Parker Hayes!" I yelled, scrambling to my feet, cutting blindly at the air with my broken plate. "Parker Hayes is dead!"

Parker's eyes went wide, and I saw his jaw twitch. His hands dropped to his sides, tightening into fists. He took another step forward, and I dove behind the other chair, holding it like a cage in front of my body. When Parker finally spoke, his voice was low.

"Sophie, you've got to let me explain."

"You've explained enough!" I shouted, wincing at the cliché.

Parker put both fists on his hips. "I haven't explained anything."

My heart was pounding in my throat. "Explain it to the police!" I spat.

My eyes traveled to the phone on the end table a few feet away; Parker followed my gaze. "Sophie, no," he said in a gravelly, deep voice. "You don't want to do that."

I looked from the phone to Parker, his cobalt eyes gone wild and fierce. His lips were set in a tight, thin line. I remembered kissing them, and suddenly I wanted to cry.

"Yes, I do," I whispered hoarsely. "Get out of here or I'll call the police."

"Now, Sophie, listen to me. I'll explain everything, I will. But right now I think I have a lead on Sampson."

My eye twitched and I glanced up through my bangs at Parker. "Where is he?"

Parker shook his head and held out a hand. "We have reason to believe he headed back to his house before moving on. I need you to take me to Sampson's house, Sophie." He beckoned for me, curling his fingers. "Come on?"

"Is he there? Tell me. Just tell me where he is."

Parker's stance was firm, the muscle in his jaw twitching again.

I wagged my head, my voice lost in a body-wracking sob. I tried to blink back tears, but they came rushing over my cheeks in hot trails. "Just go."

Parker's feet were still rooted, and he held his palm out to me again. "I just need you to promise me you won't call the police. If you call the police, it will ruin the whole case."

"You mean it will ruin your little collection."

A smile broke the ferocity in Parker's eyes. "Is that what this is about?" He crossed his arms in front of his broad chest and rolled back on his heels. "Come on, Sophie, you don't really think I'm responsible for all these murders, do you?"

"I don't know anything about you. I don't know what you might be responsible for. All I know is that you're not who you say you are, and, and, everyone says you smell weird and Lorraine thinks you know something about Sampson. . . ."

Parker nodded slowly, savoring my answer. "Okay, truth time. I'm not Parker Hayes."

"I knew that."

"But I am a detective. Well, sort of."

I nodded, silently sweeping the apartment for a way to escape. Parker noticed me eyeing the phone again and stepped to the side, his body covering my access to it. I swallowed hard, watching as his hands balled into fists at his side. "I told you, Sophie, you really don't want to do that." His words were stiff, cold. "I don't want to scare you, but you really do need to trust me. You trust me, right?"

I nodded slowly, dumbly. "Sure, Parker," I whispered, "I trust you. So, you're sort of a detective?"

Suddenly Parker was a hairsbreadth away from me, his fingers closing over my wrist, his blue eyes focused and exploding with color. "This is going to sound strange and you should know that I've never told another human being this before. I don't even think I'm allowed to."

I raised one barely interested eyebrow. *What? Now he's a zombie? Werevamp? Shapeshifter? Wizard?*

"Sophie, I'm an angel."

There was an agonizingly long pause as Parker held

my gaze. His lips were pulling into a calm smile, and I watched his Adam's apple bob as he swallowed slowly. "Did you hear what I said?"

I heard myself start to giggle, and then it was a full-blown guffaw. "An angel? You think because I live with a vampire and work for a werewolf, I'm going to buy that?"

Parker's eyes were set, the smile on his lips serene and unyielding. "Well, yes."

"Okay, brilliant. Nice halo, by the way."

"No halo," Parker said, freeing my wrist and moving to the phone.

"And no wings," I observed. "What are you doing?"

Parker unplugged the phone from the jack. "I need to be sure you're not going to call the police." He turned to face me. "And you're right—no halo, no wings. I'm a fallen angel."

I snorted. "I'll say."

"You don't believe me?"

"Oh no, I totally believe you. Why wouldn't you be an angel? My roommate's a vampire. A gargoyle cuts my hair. Hell, my great aunt was the tooth fairy."

"Now you're just being silly."

"You're right. *I'm* being silly." I was also being held captive by a demented human-parts collector who thought he was an angel.

"You believe me then?"

I shrugged, and a slight smile crossed his lips.

"Good. Let's go get Sampson and I'll explain the whole thing." Again, Parker stretched out his hand to me, and this time, I pushed myself up on shaky legs and slid my hand into his.

"See?" Parker squeezed my hand. "You don't have to be afraid of me."

"No," I said, my heart thumping in my throat. "I don't know what I was thinking." I tried to shrug nonchalantly, but it came out as more a spastic trembling.

I crouched down and picked up the meat loaf, and then found the fork sinking into the carpet. I slid it into my hand and followed Parker toward the door.

"You know how to get to Sampson's place?' he asked me.

"Uh-huh," I said, gripping the fork in my palm. Angel or no, I was on the offensive.

Parker snaked my keys from the key hook and closed the door behind us. When he leaned down to lock the door I struck, plunging the tines of the fork as hard as I could through his pants, feeling the tough strain of the fabric and the smooth plunge as the tines dipped into the flesh of his thigh. He howled, throwing my keys and pushing me backward, both of his hands diving for the fork shoved in the tender inner flesh of his thigh. I crab-walked to snatch my keys and pushed myself up to my feet. I sprinted down the stairs, Parker's screams and footfalls thumping behind me until I pushed through the front doors, gulping in lungs full of cold, night air.

My hands were trembling as I worked to push my key into the ignition of my rental car; I tore my eyes from the rearview mirror long enough to careen out of my parking space and onto the street. I remembered Parker's and my first car ride together, and I was crying as I pushed the gas pedal to the floor now, ignoring the honks and screams of angry drivers as the tears and snot rolled down my chin.

The light turned red at the end of my street and I considered running it, but careened to a stop when the Fulton 5 bus groaned through the intersection, just inches from tearing off my rental car's bumper. I was looking over my shoulder at the glass vestibule doors of my apartment building, hoping Parker wasn't coming out, when I heard the pounding thump of fists on metal. My heart lurched, and when I looked out the front windshield, Lucy was there, her hands pressed into fists pounding, working the hood of my car.

"Sophie! Sophie, please let me in, you've got to help me!"

Lucy's eyes were wide and terrified; her smoky black eye makeup was halfway down her cheeks, her tears leaving pink tracks in her white pancake makeup. "He's going to get me!"

She screamed, and when she looked over her shoulder, I could see that her blouse was torn around the collar, and her neck and chest were covered with fresh blood.

I pushed open my car door and grabbed her by the wrist. "Get in!"

Lucy dove through the open driver's side door and scrambled across my lap, panting, crying, trembling. "Close the door, close the door, close the door," she was mumbling. I slammed the door, locked it, and hit the gas, hearing the squeal of my tires as we raced through the intersection.

"Lucy, what happened to you?"

Lucy had curled herself against the passenger side door, her bird legs pressed up against her chest, her arms cradling them. She was whimpering and shaking uncontrollably.

"It's Vlad," she said finally. "He's gone crazy. He tried to bite me. Sophie, he thinks he's a real vampire."

I looked sideways at the terrified girl who looked

like a tiny child curled up on the seat. "Lucy," I started softly, "Vlad is a real vampire."

She took the news better than I expected, staring blankly out the windshield. "Where are we going?" she asked finally.

"My boss's house. I have to find him. I'd drop you off, but there's no time. I think he's in danger."

"More vampires?" Lucy whispered.

I swallowed, my eyes on the road. "Worse."

By that time I gathered my composure enough to maintain a nonlethal speed, but when I glanced down and noticed the line of fresh blood smeared on my steering wheel, I wanted to cry again. Instead I took a deep breath, resigning myself to be strong for Lucy.

"Is it bad?" I asked her.

She looked at me, blinked. "What?"

"Your neck. Is it bad, do you need to go to the hospital?"

Lucy shook her head, her long black hair dancing around her shoulder. "Uh-uh. He didn't really bite me, bite me, just sort of nicked me." She produced a Kleenex and dabbed gingerly at the blood.

"Even so, I need to call my roommate and warn her about Vlad—and Parker—and maybe we should call you an ambulance."

I looked around for my purse and remembered it hanging on its little hook by the kitchen counter, my cell phone comfortably charging in its cradle. "Damn it! My cell phone is at home."

Lucy smiled weakly at me. "That's okay, Sophie. I'll be fine. I was just really scared is all."

I nodded, thinking of Parker, of Mr. Sampson. *I've got to warn him,* I thought. *If only I could contact him . . .*

When we pulled up to the next red light I clamped my eyes shut and tried.

"Mr. Sampson! Mr. Sampson!" I said in my head, hoping that my power would kick in. "Mr. Sampson, I'm so sorry. It's Parker, Parker Hayes is the killer and I—I—I stabbed him with a fork!"

"What are you doing?" Lucy wanted to know.

I looked at her, rested my hand on her knee reassuringly. "Lucy, there is a lot about this town that you don't know. Vampires are real, demons are real, and me—well, I'm a seer. I can contact people with my mind. That's what I was doing just now. Although"— I bit my lip—"it didn't really work."

Lucy smiled warmly at me and snuggled back into her seat.

The lights of the Golden Gate Bridge swirled in front of my eyes, and I pushed the gas pedal down once more, hearing the angry groan of the car as it reached higher speeds. I sucked in my breath and focused hard on the road in front of me.

"I'm coming for you, Mr. Sampson. I'm coming for you, I promise," I whispered.

Chapter Twenty

I had managed to get my breathing under control as Lucy and I crossed the bridge, heading toward Mr. Sampson's ritzy, hilltop house in Marin. I'd spent many a UDA Christmas party running dishes under the kitchen faucet, imagining a brood of half-werewolf kids with shocking green eyes running under foot as I stared over the twinkling lights of the city. It wasn't exactly that I was obsessed with my boss; it's just that I'd never lived anywhere with a view.

I pulled my car to a jerking stop in Mr. Sampson's super-sloped driveway. I saw Lucy's eyes widen as she took in the house. "Is this where your boss lives?" she asked.

"Yeah. I'm just going to go inside and get him. Do you want to wait here? I'll lock the doors for you."

Lucy wagged her head. "No, I can help you inside. Besides, I'm way too creeped out to stay here. Vlad said he would get me." She shuddered, and I stroked her arm.

"It's going to be okay, Lucy. I'm really sorry you had to get involved with that. Come on."

Lucy followed me out of the car and looked on while I fished around for the outdoor key that I knew Mr. Sampson left for his housekeeper, Fortuna. After turning over a slew of damp, mossy stones and sinking three inches into the front lawn, I found the spare key on the porch, under the *Wipe Your Paws!* welcome mat.

"Provincial werewolf," I muttered, plugging it into the lock.

I inched the door open, poking my head in first. "Mr. Sampson?" I whispered. And then, louder, "Mr. Sampson, it's me, Sophie. I'm here to rescue you!" I bit my lip. "From your house."

When nothing but silence answered me, I stepped in, ushering Lucy behind me, and kicked the door shut behind us both. I walked a snaking trail of grass and mud across Fortuna's sparkling handiwork on the marble entry floor before kicking off my shoes, even though walking barefoot in someone else's home didn't seem very detective-like.

I gestured toward the hallway. "Lucy, why don't you go on down the hall. The bathroom is the first door on the left." I pulled a half roll of paper towels from the kitchen counter and handed them to her. "You can clean up your neck, and then we'll see if we need to take you to the hospital."

"Thanks, Sophie," Lucy said, taking the paper towels from me. "You're really sweet."

Once I heard the water running in the bathroom, I crept back into the kitchen, hoping that Mr. Sampson had pinned an *I am at . . .* note to the refrigerator. No such luck. I opened the fridge, impressed by his stash of highbrow groceries. It wasn't that I expected Alpo and Milk-Bones; it was more that I didn't expect thin-sliced prosciutto, a selection of fine cheeses, and a filet mignon nearing its expiration date. Mr. Sampson certainly did not plan on vacating the house for any period of time. I poked at the steak, grimacing as a blob of purple-red blood rushed around the raw meat.

"Okay," I said, slamming the fridge door shut, "Mr. Sampson is definitely not in the fridge." I went into the home office and started opening drawers and file folders, finding a detailed and organized collection of check stubs, timely payments, and platinum plus cards just waiting to be activated, but no giant map with a flag on it, directing an amateur sleuth where to find Mr. Sampson should he ever go missing.

"Crap!" I muttered, fists on hips.

I padded down the hall and popped my head into the last room on the right: Mr. Sampson's bedroom. Before I realized it I was in the room, my toes disappearing into the lush, mocha-colored carpet. I tiptoed to the bedside, palming the soft fabric of the bedspread: Calvin Klein Home Collection. Egyptian combed cotton. One thousand thread count—if I had to guess. I was very accurate because by that time I was lying on my back, making snow angels in Mr. Sampson's silky sheets. Sinking my head in his luscious, down-filled pillows. All the tension was seeping out of me and I felt the heaviness in my limbs, the dull ache of my bruised skin and healing muscles. It was while I was reveling, rolling around in my Goldilocks moment that I looked up, seeing Lucy standing in the doorway.

I rolled over onto my stomach and grinned sheepishly. "I was just looking for clues."

Lucy crossed her arms in front of her chest, her expression unreadable. "So, where's the wolf?"

I sat up. "What?"

"Your boss. The wolf. Where is he?"

"Uh . . . how did you know about Mr. Sampson?"

Lucy crossed the room, and we were eye to eye, hers set and hard. "Get up," she said.

I swallowed, my eyes dropping to her neck. Clean. Scrubbed pink. No puncture. No cuts.

"I thought you said Vlad—"

"Shut up!" Lucy shouted.

"Lucy—" I went to reach out to her, but suddenly my teeth were rattling in my head, my whole body receiving a ridiculous surge of electricity. I felt my blood boil, every hair on my body standing up on edge.

When my teeth stopped chattering, I looked up at Lucy, incredulous. "You Tased me?"

She smiled, giggled girlishly, and pressed one hand against her mouth. "That was neat."

"I don't understand."

Lucy's hand dropped to her side. She was still smiling at me, and for the first time, I noticed her two pointed incisors. They were longer and thinner than the fangs every other vampire I knew sported, and a weird, pale yellow.

"Caps," she said, her tongue darting out of her mouth and licking the pointed edge of her left fang. "For now."

"Vlad wouldn't change you, would he?"

Lucy's smile dropped. "No. But I don't need him to now. And once I'm changed—" Lucy used her thumb to kick on the Taser again, a crackle of blue light zipping across the metal tines. I automatically shrunk back. "Vlad is going to be the first vampire I tell."

"Who's going to change you?" I wanted to know.

"There isn't a vamp in this town who's going to cross that line." *There isn't a vamp in this town who'd want to spend eternity with this whiny little twit either,* I thought.

"Wouldn't you like to know?" Lucy asked me.

"Yeah," I said, "I would. That's why I asked."

Lucy stamped her black-booted foot. "Shut up!"

"Or what?" I challenged.

Lucy flipped the button on the Taser and my stomach dropped. "Or I'll Tase you again."

Well, she had me there.

"What do you want, Lucy? What do you want from me?"

Lucy grinned, the Taser gun held steady in her outstretched hand. "I don't want anything from you," she said. "It's what I'm going to get *for* you."

"Huh?" I asked.

"There's a bit of a price on your head, Lawson."

I gulped. *Lucy was working with Parker?* "Are you an angel, too?" I said slowly.

Lucy furrowed her brow when I heard the lock tumble on the front door. "Sophie?" I heard a familiar man's voice sing. "Miss Lawson?" Then the unmistakable sound of footsteps clattering across the foyer's marble entryway.

As Lucy cocked her head to listen, I saw my chance. I sprung on her, going chest to chest, my arms tightening around her waist, pinning them to her sides. I heard the Taser clatter to the floor; heard the "ooaf!" of air that came out of Lucy's purple-lipsticked mouth when my body collided against hers. We clattered to the floor, me on top of her, her thrashing wildly, angrily, her black boots pushing against Mr. Sampson's expensive comforter.

"Let me go!" Lucy groaned.

"Hello?" I called. "Who's there? Help! Please, I need help!"

Lucy struggled against me and then lurched up, her lips locking against my neck, her fake fangs pressed hard against my skin. I stared down incredulously. "Are you trying to bite me?"

Lucy bit harder, and I struggled against her, the irony of living with a vampire and being bit by a human just an inch away. I let one arm go and used the heel of my hand to push against Lucy's forehead, working to peel her and her fake teeth off of me. "Stop biting me!" I yelled at her.

"It's okay, Sophie," I heard. "It's the police."

I gave Lucy a hard smack on the side of the head, and she unhitched herself from me. I scrambled from on top of her toward the bedroom door. "I'm here! I'm in here!" The words were barely out of my mouth before Lucy was on top of me again, sitting on my back and grabbing fistfuls of my hair.

"Yeooooowww!"

"That's enough, that's enough!" I heard the words and felt Lucy being pulled off of me; I flopped flat onto my stomach, gasping.

"Are you okay, Sophie?"

I lifted my head barely an inch and stared down at the spit-shined shoes of Police Chief Oliver.

"Chief Oliver!" My cheeks hurt from the size of my grin.

The chief crouched down next to me. "It's okay, Sophie. Everything is going to be okay. Are you hurt?"

I wagged my head and struggled to get up on hands and knees. "No, I'm not hurt. But Sampson—" I started.

"It's all right. Mr. Sampson is just fine. I'm going to

take you to him so that you can see for yourself. He's doing just fine."

"And Lucy?" I asked slowly. I looked over my shoulder to where Lucy was standing in the corner, just off the chief's shoulder. Her arms were crossed, her lips pressed into a colorless, fierce line, and she was glowering at me, eyes fixed. I pried my eyes from her and looked up at the chief, relaxing as he slid his meat hook of a hand underneath my arm and helped me up. It took me a few seconds to steady myself on my jellied, quivering legs.

And then I was looking down the greasy-black barrel of a gun.

"Shouldn't you be pointing that at her?" I whispered, my eyes going to Lucy, whose lips were now curved up in a satisfied snarl.

"Oh. Wait. It's okay," I said, looking back at the chief, my voice suddenly even. "You know about Parker. Don't worry; I'm not with him. Parker's not here." I angled my head around the barrel of the gun, shielded my mouth with my hand. "I think Lucy might be working with him. We have to find him. We have to find him and get to Sampson. You know where he is. You know where Mr. Sampson is, right?"

Chief Oliver grinned broadly at me and cocked the hammer.

The breath left my body.

"Chief Oliver?"

"Don't worry, Sophie. I know exactly where Sampson is. I can take you right to him. Would you like that?"

My eyes widened, held by the black gun barrel. "Lucy?" I whispered, my dry lips trembling, my eyes starting to water. I chanced a look over at her, and her eyes were fixated on the gun, her expression a freaky mix of terror and pleasure. At this point, I would really rather take my chances with the impish fake-vamp than with the chief and his exceptionally real gun.

"Don't you worry about Lucy," the chief told me. "Lucy is doing exactly what she was supposed to do."

I gulped. "And that would be?" My voice was little more than a hoarse whisper.

"That would be to bring you here, bring you to the chief. Didn't I do well?" Lucy asked.

I just nodded dumbly, falling against Chief Oliver as his fingers dug into my shoulder.

"And you, Sophie, did everything you were supposed to do, too. You led Sampson right to me."

I felt my eyebrows rise, and I shook my head. "No."

The chief grinned. "Yes. That night by your car? I was just out looking for some half-breed blood. Didn't even count on getting the dog, but lo and behold—you hurt the owner and the dog comes running."

I felt my lower lip start to quiver, felt the ache in my head. "Mr. Sampson rescued me . . . from you?" I whispered.

"Oh, yes. Beautiful moment, really. Would have been nicer, too, if I hadn't had to Tase the son of a bitch. He did put up quite a fight." He clucked his tongue, shaking his head. "Tough to see a dog whimper like that."

I heard Lucy simper in the corner, her hands pressed up against her mouth, her small shoulders trembling under the weight of her laughter.

"She's with you?" I murmured, fitting the whole scene together.

"Anyway," the chief continued, ignoring me, "I guess I should thank you. Really, I couldn't have done it without your help. Sampson was going to be a tough one."

My stomach lurched, and I swallowed a miserable wail.

"Oh, but enough revelry. Come on now." Chief Oliver pushed me in front of him. "Lucy?" he said, and I stiffened, feeling the gun angled between my shoulder blades. He tapped it harshly against me. "Step lively, demon girl, I don't have all night."

"Oh, Chief Oliver, I'm not a demon." I wagged my head, feeling a hysterical giggle escaping my lips. "Is that what you thought? No, I'm human. All human. I'm just an administrative assistant at the Underground. I file papers. I can prove it." I took a chance, craning my neck to look over my shoulder and smiling hopefully into the chief's stiff grimace. "Do you have any papers you'd like me to file? Alphabetically, chronologically? I'm really very good."

He nudged me with the gun again, and I stumbled into the hallway.

"Just keep moving. I know exactly what you are, Miss Lawson. I know who you are, and I knew who your grandmother was."

I paused and then winced as the chief drove the gun hard into my spine. "Keep walking," he growled, the stubble from his chin grazing my ear. "You don't want to make this difficult for yourself, do you?"

I wagged my head and gulped, feeling the lump growing in my throat. "Is Parker a part of this, too?"

Chief Oliver snorted. "Parker Hayes. A detective from Podunk, New York."

"Buffalo," I whispered through dry lips.

"What was that?"

I cleared my throat. "Parker Hayes is from Buffalo."

"Whatever. He's nothing to worry about." The chief snorted. "He thinks he's been chasing a mythical killer? That idiot's been chasing his tail all this time." The chief shook me hard, and I squealed. "Parker Hayes is nothing to worry about," he repeated.

A fresh round of tears burned at my eyes. *He's nothing to worry about because he's got a fork shoved in his thigh.* I sniffled, and as we walked into the foyer, Chief Oliver wound his free hand in my hair and yanked. I bent down backward, wincing as my spine protested.

I heard another unmistakable, gleeful giggle escape Lucy's lips, and from the corner of my eye, I could see her helicoptering around the chief and me, angling for the best vantage point.

"Now, you're not going to do anything stupid like run away or scream, are you?"

"No," I said, feeling strands of my hair snapping in Chief Oliver's palm.

"You know, I'd like to believe you." He shoved me so hard against the wall that I lost my breath and immediately tasted the hot blood that rushed from a fresh cut on my lip. "But I've learned that you never can trust a demon." Chief Oliver leaned in, his breath moist and hot on my ear. "Even just a half-breed," he muttered.

I heard the tinkle of his belt and then felt the searing pain in my shoulders as the chief twisted my arms hard and locked cold metal cuffs around my wrists. He spun me around and frowned, his bushy caterpillar eyebrows coming together.

"You're bleeding," he said, and for a brief moment

I thought that the chief might actually feel bad for me. But then he rubbed his hand roughly over my lips and sucked the excess blood from his thumb and grinned. His smile was hungry, ferocious, and my blood had tinted his teeth a freaky, glowing pink. He smacked his lips. "Yeah, that'll do quite nicely."

He pulled a handkerchief from his back pocket and shook it out, tenderly dabbing at my nose and lips. "We don't want to waste it," he said.

"Why are you doing this?" I moaned as Chief Oliver shoved me toward the front door. "Aren't you supposed to be the good guy?"

The chief snorted. "Good guy? Huh. In this city, it takes more than good guys to keep everything in line. Forty-seven square miles of demon-infested city?" Chief Oliver shook his head, his distaste obvious. "And you demons act like you own this town. Looking up to that damn Pete Sampson like he's some kind of god . . ."

"But—"

The chief spun to face me, and I could see the spitting hatred in his eyes.

"You know, I'm getting awfully tired of listening to you."

"I'll be quiet," I said, my voice small.

He smiled that twisted, grotesque smile and used one hand to pin me to the wall, the other to beckon for Lucy.

"Lucy, sweetie, do me a favor and watch over our little friend for a second here, will you?"

Lucy skipped—*skipped*—over to me, her dark hair bobbing around her shoulders, her wide lips spread in a pleased grin. I looked her over as the chief disappeared out the front, considered whether—cuffed or not—I could take her. My query was cut short when she pulled out that Taser again, flicking the on switch so the electricity between the two wires shivered and made my teeth ache with memory.

"Come on, Lucy. You don't have to do this."

"I know," she smiled broadly, and I could see that one of her fake vampire fangs had broken off. "But it's just so much fun."

"Chief Oliver is a murderer," I said, dropping my voice to a stage whisper. "Do you know that? Do you know that he's already killed at least three innocent people? Lucy, you've got to get yourself out of this."

Lucy's grin didn't falter. "Oh, Sophie, it's all for the greater good. And they weren't people, they were demons. And all those demons had something we needed."

"I don't understand why you're doing this."

The smile abruptly dropped from Lucy's lips, but she still held the Taser just an inch from my exposed skin. "Look, you demons have your restoration league."

"VERM? That's for vampires."

"Haven't you read the literature? It has tiers for all of you demons. So you have your thing for empowerment and restoration and so do we. The UDA has controlled things for too long and is losing its foothold. It's time for something bigger."

"And where do you come in with that?"

Lucy smiled, the pointed pink tip of her tongue curling over her remaining yellowed fang. "I get my own powers. What I get makes vampiracy look like child's play. The chief promised me."

"The chief is lying to you."

Lucy's small palm snapped against my cheek, and she leaned in, the Taser a millimeter from my neck.

"Don't you say that about Chief Oliver. All he's concerned about is protecting the people—the human people—of this city. You have no idea what you're talking about so just shut your mouth!"

The chief wandered back in, his red-rimmed eyes taking in Lucy and me. "You two getting along in here? Not that I care . . ."

Lucy stepped away from me, but her fierce eyes were still on mine. She held the Taser so tightly that I could see her knuckles had gone white.

"Chief Oliver, I—"

The chief put his hands on his hips and stared at me. "You know, Sophie, I'm really getting tired of listening to you." He angled his gun at me again, and I cringed, pinching my eyes closed tightly. When a full second passed without gunfire, I chanced to open an eye. I saw the chief, gun still steadied and trained on me in one hand, the other rummaging through a duffel bag left open on the hallway table. Chief Oliver produced a silver roll of duct tape and tossed it to Lucy, who caught it and peeled off a piece, tearing it with her teeth.

"Doesn't matter if you're a demon or not, all you broads talk too much," the chief said.

I was about to protest, to plead my non-talking-broad case, but Lucy smacked a piece of tape over my mouth, smoothing it with her delicate hand.

The chief came up behind her, grinned, and patted her on the shoulder. "Good work, kid."

Lucy beamed like a proud kindergartner.

"Now take her car and get out of here."

The smile abruptly dropped from Lucy's lips. "But I wanted to see the ceremony!" she whined. "You said I could be there when the portal opened and I'd get my powers." Lucy was stamping her foot again, her black hair bobbing. "I got the stuff you wanted!"

I blinked.

I remembered Kishi's voice that day at the Crystal Ball in San Jose. I remember her saying that the woman who bought the Sword of Bethesda was rather nondescript, but had long black hair.

"Lucy," I murmured.

"Huh?" she called over her shoulder, annoyed.

I tried again, then realized with the tape stuck over my mouth I was probably letting out nothing more than an incomprehensible moan. The chief blew out an annoyed sigh, aimed his gun at my nose, and whipped the duct tape from my mouth.

"Ow!" I moaned. "Geez."

Lucy raised a perturbed eyebrow. "That's what you wanted to say?"

"I wanted to say that it was you, Lucy, who bought the Sword of Bethesda."

Lucy smiled, looked lovingly at the chief. "Uh-huh. Good on you for figuring it out way too late." She tossed a hard glance over her shoulder. "I'm staying. No one's going to come looking for her car, and even if they do, so what? The ritual will be completed and no one will be any match for us."

"They won't, will they?" the chief looked amused and patronizing at the same time while Lucy nodded.

"Lucy, I—" I was barely able to get out the second syllable when the chief slapped the tape over my mouth again. He patted both my cheeks and smiled, and in one quick motion, yanked a pillowcase out of his duffel and dropped it over my head.

I blinked in the immediate darkness.

Suddenly we were moving again, the chief's hands

clamped over my arms, tight, cutting off my circulation
as I stumbled in front of him. I heard Lucy scampering
behind us, complaining about how to dispose of my
car, about how she wanted to stay and be a part of "the
ceremony." The chief remained mostly quiet, grunting
occasionally, until I heard him open a car door. Almost
immediately I felt myself being launched inside, sliding
on my belly across a foul-smelling leather bench seat
and cracking my skull on what I can only assume was
the other car door.

"Sorry 'bout that," I heard him mutter before I felt
the door slamming against the soles of my bare feet.
I groaned, them immediately strained to hear the last
few seconds of the chief and Lucy arguing outside.

"But it's what you promised!" I heard Lucy whine.

"Stop it. I don't have time for this."

"But—"

"I'm warning you. . . . Just get in the car and drive
away like we talked about. I'll come and get you when
everything is through."

"Chief!" Lucy's whine was high-pitched and
piteous. I heard a few more muffled words, a quieted
howl, a scuffle. Then a gunshot rang out through the
night. I blinked in the darkness of my pillowcase, felt
the cool heat as all the hairs on the back of my neck
pricked. I felt my heart thumping wildly in my chest
and made a mental note that if I were to ever get out
of this situation alive, I'd keep a cardiologist on
speed dial. And also surgically attach my cell phone
to my hand.

I worked to sit up, then scooted myself across the
bench seat, leaning my pillowcased head against the
cool glass of the window. Not surprisingly, I couldn't

see anything except for a splotch of yellowish street light and a single dark figure standing in the night.

My heart continued to thump, and my mouth fell open as the figure slowly lumbered toward the car. I pressed the soles of my feet against the car door and launched myself across the seat, cowering against the other locked door. I was breathing hard and sucked in a mouthful of cotton pillowcase while the tears spilled from my eyes. Was Lucy dead? Was I next? The chief had murdered before—horrendously murdered— three innocent people, and now Lucy's foot stomping and demands had gone deathly silent.

I pinched my eyes shut and waited for my life to flash before them. I waited for the split-second feeling of calm that was supposed to come when you accepted fate.

Neither came.

So I went with the next best thing: spastic movements. I had learned in a self-defense class (or by watching *Oprah*) that a moving target was hard to hit, so, when escaping an attacker with a gun, you should run zigzag. I wasn't going to let the fact that I was trapped in the coffin-sized backseat of a police car hamper my best defense so I threw myself spastically around the backseat the second I heard the click of the car door open.

"What the hell are you doing back there?"

I kicked. I thrashed. I bobbed. I weaved. I panted a little and wished I'd spent more time at the gym working up my cardio. I heard the groan of the leather seat and I cringed, imagining Chief Oliver as he leveled the gun and shot me dead, too. With a second burst of adrenaline I dove for the floor mats, and then heard the jangle of the key as it slipped into the ignition, the groan of the engine as it turned over.

"You're fucking nuts," I heard the chief mutter. "You're all fucking nuts."

I lay still on the floor of the car, the industrial carpet scratching my bare arms as the chief kicked the car into gear and headed down the drive. I wanted to ask him about Lucy. I wanted to ask him if I'd be next. Instead, I lay with my cheek pressed against the car seat while the tears rolled down my cheeks.

I'm going to get out of here, I told myself, *I have to.*

I stiffened and scooted forward, pressing one ear against the car door. As we rode, I struggled to listen to every sound, to count every jerking movement of the car—turns, stoplights, anything that could be used to identify where he might be taking me. But there was a sickening, sweet scent inside the pillowcase that I hadn't noticed before and it was making me tired, making my eyes so heavy.

I wonder if this is how it happens on CSI, I thought, before falling off into darkness.

Chapter Twenty-One

I woke up to a soft voice calling my name.

"Sophie? Sophie?" I heard.

I stirred, and realization hit me. "Mr. Sampson? Mr. Sampson, is that you? I can hear you in my head." I had to work to move my dry, heavy lips.

There was a soft hand on my shoulder, and then I heard the jingle of metal, the clank as it brushed against concrete. "Sophie," Mr. Sampson said, "I'm not talking to you inside your head. Can you open your eyes for me?"

I tried, wincing at the star of pain that blossomed above my right eye, that stung my swollen, dried, blood-caked lips. Mr. Sampson came into focus looking disheveled and broken, his face marred by fresh pink scratch marks. He smiled softly at me, and I noticed that his usually perfect teeth were replaced by a mouthful of heavily pointed incisors, that a thick shock of brown fur was circling out of the tears in his shirt.

"Oh my gosh." I lifted both my wrists, grimacing at the thick chains encircling them. "Oh my gosh." I gaped at Mr. Sampson. "What the hell is going on here? What is this?" I rattled the chains. "I've got a whole Jacob Marley thing going on. And you!" I gingerly touched the heavy cuff around his neck, and he pulled away, ashamed.

"Sophie, do you have any idea where we are?"

I scanned our concrete enclosure, frowned at the pentagram etched out in chalk dust on the floor. "Hell?" I asked weakly. "Although I think if that were the case, the pentagram would be a little cliché."

Mr. Sampson tried to smile, and I felt the tiniest bit of relief at being alive. "I'm not dead, right?" I confirmed.

Mr. Sampson shifted his weight, the clank from his chains reverberating in the silent, cement room. "No, you're not."

"I was attacked by a fake vampire, and now I'm here." I looked around, incredulous. "This doesn't happen," I continued softly. "This shouldn't happen. This is real life." The words were out of my mouth before I had time to stop and consider that I was crying to a man halfway through a werewolf transformation, chained to a metal wall in what looked like a giant kennel.

"What the hell is going on here?" I shouted.

Mr. Sampson clapped a hand over my mouth. "Shhh," he hissed. "Let him think you're still out. It might buy us some time."

I slumped against the wall, my chains rattling. "Time for what?"

Mr. Sampson crawled over to me. "Does anyone know you're here?"

I frowned. "I don't even know where here is. And even if I did, 'going out, getting chained to wall'"—

I rattled my chains, for emphasis—"wouldn't be high on my list of usual activities."

Mr. Sampson looked at me with those warm, chocolaty eyes, and I sighed. "Sorry. It's just been a really rotten day."

"I'm fairly sure we're still in the city limits. I was hoping maybe Nina could pick up your scent if we're not too far."

My eyes widened. "Oh, wait! I can contact her! I can do it, I know I can."

Mr. Sampson looked puzzled. "Can you reach your cell phone?"

"No," I said, perching on my knees. "I can call her with my mind. I did it with you, remember? I finally got my powers." I squeezed my eyes shut.

"Sophie—"

"No, just wait. It's pretty new to me so I still haven't perfected it." I bit my lip. "I just wish I had something of hers to hold on to. I bet that would help. I mean, I think it would. Although I didn't need it with you."

"Sophie, I—"

I held up my palms. "I know, I'm babbling. Okay, I'm getting an image of her. I'm going to try to get her attention." I pursed my lips, hearing my voice echo through my mind as I imagined Nina, sitting on our couch at home watching *The View*. "I was able to talk to you. You asked me to help. Don't you remember? I found you with my mind." I frowned. "Nina doesn't seem to be listening."

"Sophie, I called you."

I opened one eye. "Excuse me?"

"Sophie." Sampson reached out for me, his fingertips brushing my thigh before the chain pulled him back. "Werewolves can mind meld. From a distance if it's someone they care about. It's . . . it's just one of our powers."

A shiver of delight went up my spine. *Mr. Sampson cares about me!* Which would have been the most romantic thing in the world if we weren't chained together in a giant kennel, balancing on the precipice of death.

If we ever got out of here, I was going to need *so much* therapy.

"I called you," Mr. Sampson was saying. "I came into your mind and called for you. I was hoping you would be able to help me."

I forced a smile, sitting back on the hard concrete floor. "Mission . . . accomplished?"

"Where were you when the chief came after you?"

"I was at your house when he nabbed me. I was with Lucy—the fake vampire—trying to save you from Parker. Or whoever he is."

Mr. Sampson sat back on his haunches. "Sophie, Parker is a good guy."

I tried to bite back the hysteria in my voice. "He's not a good guy." I looked around wildly. "I'm not even sure there are good guys anymore. But Parker Hayes—he's not even who he says he is! His name is not even Parker Hayes. I think he might even be working with the chief."

"No, he's not. And I know that he's not Parker Hayes." Mr. Sampson's calmness sent my near-hysteria into a full-on tizzy.

"You *knew* that?" I used both my hands to push my hair out of my face. "When did you know that? Why didn't anyone bother to tell me?"

"He's a field agent with the FBI. He needed to pose as a police detective to gain the chief's confidence."

I was still agog. "And you *knew* this? The whole time?"

"We couldn't risk telling you. Any suspicion about Agent Grace's identity could have undermined the whole operation—and nearly a year's worth of prep and tracking work would have gone down the drain."

I rattled my chains. "Brilliant plan. Executed flawlessly. Like we will be."

Mr. Sampson smiled apologetically. "Well, apparently we all missed one thing the chief was after."

I tried to cross my arms in front of my chest, but the chains yanked me back. "And that was?"

"Me."

I slumped. "With all due respect, sir, then what the hell am I doing here? I'm just the secretary."

Mr. Sampson smiled thinly. "Administrative assistant."

"Look who's awake!"

My head snapped toward the booming voice in the doorway, at the chief waddling down the stairs toward us. I wanted to be afraid, especially when I saw the long, thin sword he carried in his hand, but I couldn't.

The man was wearing a Snuggie.

You know the blanket with sleeves as seen on TV? I frowned.

"Are you wearing a Snuggie?"

The chief faced me now, his eyes narrow, angry slits in his pink cheeks, the hem of his burgundy Snuggie brushing the concrete floor.

Mr. Sampson leaned into me and whispered, "It's a ceremonial robe."

"Silence!"

I was slightly more frightened, especially when I

saw the glow from the naked lightbulb above my head reflecting off the blade that Chief Oliver held in front of my nose. I recognized the quartz crystal and the jeweled handle immediately.

"That's the Sword of Bethesda."

The chief grinned down at me. "Well, Sophie Lawson. Aren't you the smart one? Glad you're awake and welcome to the party."

Chief Oliver raised his arms and a glimmer of hope sliced through me—maybe this has all been for a wild surprise party? Maybe?

Nothing happened, and I felt a cold bead of sweat run between my breasts. "Can't you do something?" I whispered out of the corner of my mouth to Sampson.

Chief Oliver grinned. "No," he said, answering me, "he can't do anything. He won't be able to do much of anything ever again." The chief's eyes slid to the tiny sliver of window close to the ceiling of our little dungeon. "Two more sunsets and good ol' Sampson here will be nothing more than what he's always been—a common dog. That is"—the chief twisted the sword in his hand, so the light glinted off the narrow blade—"if he makes it through this."

"You're crazy, Oliver," Sampson said through gritted teeth, the chain coiled around his neck pulled taut.

Chief Oliver swung his head from side to side, his dark eyes glittering and set on Sampson's. "A common dog."

Sampson gritted his teeth. "To think I used to envy you, Oliver."

Chief Oliver's eyebrows rose, and I swung my head to Mr. Sampson. "Envy him?"

"Trying to butter me up won't work at this point,

Sampson, but okay, whatever. I'll bite. Why did you envy me?"

Mr. Sampson swallowed hard; I watched his Adam's apple bobbing through the thick tuft of werewolf fur curling out from his collar. "Back when we were in college. I hadn't been changed yet. We'd spend our nights at the Grog, trolling for coeds, heading home at dawn. We'd make it to a couple of classes, and then when the sun set we'd do it all over again."

I thought I saw a hint of a nostalgic smile cross the chief's puckered face. "Those were pretty good days."

"One night you took off with that engineering student from Berkeley—remember her? I left, took the long way around Lone Mountain to give you guys some privacy."

My stomach churned as I heard the chief chuckle. "Doreen. She was a pretty little thing."

"Out there behind Lone Mountain was when I was bitten. The wolf came out of the woods. For some reason, I wasn't frightened. It was like I knew it was supposed to happen to me. I was bitten, my blood intermingled with the werewolf's saliva, and from that night on I knew nothing would ever be the same for me. Nothing would ever be normal for me again."

"Oh, Sampson, that's so sad," I mumbled.

"Yeah," Chief Oliver said disgustedly, "I really feel for you."

"I envied you because you still had your entire normal life ahead of you. You could do anything, go anywhere at any time. You could graduate, get married, have kids. And here I was, trapped. Chained"—Sampson raised his arms, the heavy chains rattling—"to an alter ego that I couldn't control."

"Chained to a power that was all consuming," the

chief spat. "Didn't you know that I could see what was happening to you? I saw the changes, saw the hungry way you looked at people—because you were no longer like them. You wanted them. Wanted their flesh."

"I wanted to be *like* them again. That was it."

The chief gritted his teeth. "And when I asked you to change me, you wouldn't."

Mr. Sampson bit out his words. "You were my best friend. I wasn't going to do that to you. This is not a life I would have chosen for myself; I wouldn't choose this life for anyone."

"What? Immortality? Superhuman strength?" The chief's eyes were hard.

"Loneliness. A body and spirit that betrays you with the changes of the moon."

"No. You wanted the power for yourself, Sampson. That was obvious. You couldn't take anyone challenging you, challenging your power or your precious Underworld."

"That wasn't it. I was trying to protect you. I only wanted to protect you."

"Well, aren't you the saint, Pete?"

I sucked in a breath. "So the paw prints, the scratches that the police found around the first body. Was it—were they—?" I looked at Sampson, at his chained hands.

"You thought it was me."

"No, I—" I spun around, looking at the chief. "You framed him. You wanted me to think it was Mr. Sampson so I wouldn't trust him."

The chief angled himself to look around me. "To your credit, Pete, she really stuck by you. Nice woman you've got there. Too bad you both have to die. We could have played golf or something."

Sampson narrowed his eyes at the chief. Chief Oliver grinned and stepped on the chain that snaked around Sampson's neck; Mr. Sampson jerked back violently, beads of sweat standing out on his forehead and upper lip.

"Mr. Sampson!" I tried to reach for him, but my chains pulled me back. "Why are you doing this?" I yelled at the chief. "Just because he wouldn't make you into a wolf? I bet he'd bite you now. Right, Mr. Sampson?"

Mr. Sampson was breathing hard. He didn't answer.

"Why, why, why," the chief moaned. "Why do anything?" Then that grin crept across his mouth again. "Because I can. Because I have the eyes of a Seer. The heart of a priestess." His eyes slid over Sampson. "The hide of a changeling and"—Chief Oliver pointed the edge of the blade at me, letting it settle against my cheek—"the blood of a half-breed. Pete Sampson will no longer be more powerful than me. No one will be more powerful than I am."

I angled my head back, trying to put as much space as possible between my cheek and the glittering edge of the Sword of Bethesda. "But what about Alfred Sherman?" I wanted to know. "You killed him and took his blood. Why do you need mine?"

Chief Oliver's nostrils flared, his lips pursing into a disgusted line. "Easy mistake." He shrugged. "Who knew that the half-breed wouldn't be the sour old ambulance chaser who dropped his business card all over the Underworld, but the granddaughter of one of his demon clients?"

My muscles tightened. "My grandmother was not a demon."

This seemed to delight the chief, and he chuckled, the blade of the knife shaking in front of my face.

"And Mr. Howard? Did you—was that you, too?" I asked, thinking that if I kept him talking, it might keep him from stabbing—for now.

The chief frowned. "Howard?"

"The old man in my building. He was completely innocent. He didn't know anything about the Underworld. He couldn't have been in your way."

Chief Oliver just shrugged. "It's the blood of the innocent that waters the fields of the new world."

"What does that even mean?" I wailed.

The chief glared at me. "I made a mistake, okay? The old bastard was faster than he looked. But you," the chief said, changing the subject and swinging his gaze—and the sword—toward Mr. Sampson, "you are just poetic justice, Pete. The ruler of the Underworld. My old college roommate. The hide that will make me the most powerful thing on the planet—man, demon, or god—just happens to come from law-abiding, demon-regulating, good ol' Pete Sampson. Really, it is absolute poetry. I couldn't have written it better myself."

The chief snatched the blade away and clapped his hands, looking expectantly from me to Mr. Sampson. "What's say we get started? I don't know about you two, but I'm just giddy."

"Wait!" I said, holding up a hand that made my chain waggle. "What about Officer Franks? Did you know he was found dead? At Dirt?"

Chief Oliver feigned sadness. "Yeah. That poor kid." He tapped his fingers against his cheek. "Surprisingly, not as dumb as he looked. He was almost on to me. Almost. I could have forgiven him that—it wouldn't have mattered after tonight anyway—but really, it was simply a case of wrong place, wrong time."

My satisfaction at being right—wrong place, wrong time—was fleeting as one of my cuffs was chafing my right wrist. I winced, shaking my arm.

"Sorry about those. Rather uncomfortable, aren't they?" Chief Oliver gestured toward my cuffs. "You won't be in them for much longer." Again Chief Oliver's eyes slid toward the little window. "I'd really like to get you drained before sunrise."

"Actually," I said, my voice high, "I'm very comfortable right now." I held up my hands and wiggled them. "These are actually quite nice. There's no need to rush."

The chief seemed amused by me, his Snuggie bouncing as his belly jiggled with laughter. I laughed too, with hysteria and sheer terror, until in one fell swoop the chief was silent, the blade was exposed, and he'd sliced through the front of my sweatshirt.

I stared down incredulously at my exposed belly, at my sweat-soaked white bra. I hunched over and tried to cover myself as best I could when I heard the chief laughing again. When I looked up his eyes had gone to a hazy, smoky gray and he was licking his lips, a distorted, grotesque smile on his moist face.

"Juicy," he finally said. And then, his eyes raking me up and down, the chief said, "I think I'm going to need a bigger drip tray." The chief looked at me as though I were a child denied the circus. "I know you're excited to get started, but this will just take a moment. Talk amongst yourselves," he said as he turned on his heel and headed up the stairs.

Chapter Twenty-Two

Mr. Sampson scooted closer to me, keeping his eyes averted while I tried to pull my sweatshirt back together. "Are you okay?"

"Yes," I sniffed, realizing that I was crying. "Mr. Sampson, what is he going to do to us? Are we going to die? I don't want to die. There's so much I haven't done in my life. I've never even ridden the Matterhorn!"

Mr. Sampson put his hand on my cheek, and I melted into the soft warmth of his palm. He looked deeply into my eyes and sharply bit off each word. "Sophie, you are not going to die. We are going to figure out a way out of here. And if *we* don't, Parker and Nina will come looking for you."

I stuck out my lower lip, and Mr. Sampson disappeared behind a fresh torrent of hot tears. "Parker won't come looking for me."

"Yes, he will, Sophie."

"No he won't. Why would he? I stabbed him."

Mr. Sampson's eyebrows shot up. "You stabbed him?"

I nodded. "I'm sorry. I didn't know he was a good

guy. I was trying to get away and so I stabbed him. With a fork."

Mr. Sampson tried to hide his smile. "Well, I'm sure all you did was slow him down a little bit. I'm certain it will take more than flatware to get Detective Grace off the case."

We both stared up as Chief Oliver came thundering down the stairs. He paused midstep and wrinkled his nose, frowning. "Detective Grace?" he asked.

Mr. Sampson's eyes went hard and flat as he stared Chief Oliver down. The chief blew out a sigh that ruffled his fat cheeks. "Never mind." He spun a set of rubber tubes in his hands, and my stomach dropped.

"Okay," the chief said, stepping down and positioning himself in front of a heavy velvet curtain. "Showtime."

My mouth went dry as Chief Oliver pushed the curtain aside with a delighted flourish. He exposed a long table draped with chains and then turned and grinned at me over his shoulder. My heart thumped, and I pushed myself back until my shoulder blades went flush with the concrete wall behind me. Chief Oliver pushed the sleeves of his Snuggie up and came toward me. I scrunched my eyes shut, dipping my head into the folds of my torn sweatshirt, my breath ragged, my heart thundering. I prayed to disappear, to wake up, for the earth to open up and swallow me—anything—to keep Chief Oliver from getting any closer to me.

I heard chains rattle and the scratch of fingernails dragging across concrete. Then a low, menacing growl. "You stay away from her, Oliver."

I opened my eyes and tried not to gape; Mr. Sampson's shirt was splitting all the way down the arms, exposing bulging, pulsing muscles lined with soft, brown downy fur. His pants had split the same way, and I was staring at hind flanks and thick legs that were pulling taut against his chains. Mr. Sampson's elegant hands had morphed into heavy, clawed paws, with long, black nails gripping at the concrete. His lips were thin and curled back against a row of sharp canine teeth, glistening with saliva. Even hunched on all fours, he was taller than I was standing up.

"Mr. Sampson?" I whispered.

One pointed, brown wolf ear twitched, but Mr. Sampson did not turn to face me. He kept his dark eyes trained on the chief, those sharp teeth exposed, the growl still low and rumbling as it emanated from his thick barrel chest.

Chief Oliver bent down and slapped his knees with his palms, laughing. "Aw! The puppy is very protective of his little girlfriend, isn't he?" He wiped his eyes with his balled fists and chuckled some more. "That's just precious."

Mr. Sampson's eyes narrowed, and his growl rumbled even deeper, louder, his shoulders tensing. I could hear the slow tear of the fabric of his shirt as his thick shoulder blades, covered still with that downy brown fur, became exposed. He nipped at the air, just a few centimeters from Chief Oliver's fat jowls. Mr. Sampson's jaws clamped shut with a frightening snap, bits of saliva spraying on the concrete. Chief Oliver's head jerked back, and then he laughed, a roaring, horrible laugh and delivered a closed-fist thump to the top of Mr. Sampson's head. The sound of the heavy smack of hand to head made my eyes water, and my heart broke when I heard Mr. Sampson's pained squeal.

"I'm done with playing. Come on, you." Chief Oliver dug his fingers into my arm, and I gasped, the pain reverberating through my body. He sunk a skeleton key into the lock, and my cuffs snapped open. I tried to squirm away, but his hands were over me immediately. He lifted me up easily and tossed my whole body over one shoulder as though I were a sack of potatoes. My ribs crunched against his shoulder, and I let out a pained, "Ooaf!" My forehead snapped against the chief's spine, and in one fell swoop he tossed me, flat-backed, onto the table and clicked a new set of cuffs around my ankles. The breath left my body as he whipped off my sweatshirt, and before I could react, he clipped a new set of cuffs around my wrists.

I could hear my heart thundering in my ears, my blood hot and pulsing through my veins. My throat started to close, but I didn't think I even had the will to cry anymore. My eyes were raw and painful. I glanced to the left, seeing the jeweled handle of the Sword of Bethesda on the table next to me.

The chief pulled off another velvet cloth, this one covering a small table lined with thick black candles and a large shallow metal bowl. A wave of nausea washed over me as I spotted two glass jars on the table as well—one containing a semi-fresh set of eyeballs, the second, the bloody remains of a human heart. My gag became a wail as I felt myself being jerked by the ankles off the table, my head thunking with each lurch of my body. The chief was hunkered on the other side of the table, turning a large crank. My body slid with each turn, and soon I was completely upside down, my red hair skimming the tabletop, my arms dangling over my head.

"Oliver, please!" Mr. Sampson said as I hung from my ankles. "Please don't do this to Sophie."

The chief's eyes, now narrow slits, went to me and then to Mr. Sampson, chained and pleading in the corner.

"You don't have to do this, Oliver, please. We can work something out."

"Don't worry, Pete. There'll be time for you. Once our little half-breed here"—Chief Oliver poked my chest with his index finger—"is bled dry, you'll be up." He smiled jovially. "Of course you'll be a dog by then. But not to worry; I've always been an animal lover." He snatched up the sword he'd been fingering all night. "The Sword of Bethesda will make quick work of skinning you"—he frowned—"unfortunately. I was, in fact, hoping it'd be a little rougher for you. Oh well, can't win everything."

"This will never happen, Oliver," Mr. Sampson snarled.

"Because of you darned kids? Get over it, Scooby Doo—it's done." He tapped the jar of eyeballs with the tip of the sword. "Things are already set in motion. Now—" Chief Oliver positioned the metal bowl just under my head and then softly poked my collarbone with the knife. His tongue darted over his lips, and he eyed me. "You ready for this?"

I started to tremble when the chief laid the cool blade against my jugular. I tried to angle away, but my body went leaden as I felt the pressure build against my skin. The chief eyed me and licked the edge of his tooth as he angled the tip of the sword against my vein. I saw the muscle in his arm flex, felt the cool, tingling prick of metal on skin—and then saw him frown. He used the tip of the sword to poke at me again, this time hard enough to send my body swinging.

"What the hell?" he muttered, staring at the blade. He poked the tip with his hand, pulled back when a velvety cap of blood surfaced on his index finger.

I swung from my ankles closer to the chief and his sword, and he reached out with it, this time poking me in the ribs.

I giggled freakishly, the cold blade tickling me.

The chief blinked, his caterpillar eyebrows crawling together. He looked at his sword and then up at me and then eyed Sampson.

"What is this?" he snarled.

Sampson sat back on his haunches. "I have no idea what you're talking about."

I swung back once more, and again the chief poked the sword into my flesh. Again, it bounced off.

The chief stepped forward and in one fell swoop, sliced the blade over the top of Mr. Sampson's head.

"Sampson!" I shrieked, watching a cascade of newly shorn dark hair flutter to the ground.

"Why won't this work on her?" the chief asked, ignoring me.

Sampson shrugged, the tiniest smile playing on his curled lips. The chief held the blade to Sampson now, and I could see the chief's knuckles pale as he pressed the blade hard into Sampson's flesh, thin streams of blood rushing over the blade.

"It won't work because the blade is charmed!" I yelled. "Leave him alone!"

The chief turned to me now. He looked at the blade and then at me. "It is charmed. And you are?"

I smiled weakly. "Unaffected by charmed objects. And most magics."

The chief crossed his Snuggie-clad arms in front of his chest. "Well, I'll be. That's a new one."

"So . . ." I said, my eyes scanning the chief's table de horrors. "You might want to let me go. I'd probably mess up your whole little operation here. You know"—I tried to shrug—"since the magic won't affect me, my blood is probably useless for you."

The chief cocked his head. "Or that much more powerful. Magical immunity," he mused, "I hadn't thought of that. This is really my lucky day!"

He dropped the sword onto the floor and reached into his Snuggie, producing a Leatherman. He grinned as he swung out a three-inch blade. "You're not immune to this, are you? It'll take longer and hurt more, but I'm a very patient man."

All the blood had rushed to my head, and a tear rolled up over my eyebrow and landed with a thud in the metal bowl. This seemed to amuse the chief even more. He grinned, then laid the Leatherman blade flat across his outstretched palm and tugged it through the skin in one slick, elegant slice. He closed his eyes as though savoring the ecstasy of the pain as his blood dripped in thick, velvet-red drops into the metal pan.

"Oliver, no! If you mix your blood with Sophie's this way you will bleed out your humanity—and hers!" Mr. Sampson said, his face contorted in anguish.

The chief glared at Sampson, his narrowed eyes a rich mix of violet and crimson, his lips held in a disgusted, grotesque grin.

"Trust me—Sophie won't need hers. And what has humanity ever done?" Chief Oliver spat. "It puts murderers back on the street; it sends rapists back to the raped. It seeps through the gutters; it slices"—his eyes washed over his open wound—"through the demons of this city as they tear out the throats of our children. Humanity shouldn't exist in this city. Humanity should be stamped out." He clenched his fist, the blood oozing like red ribbons through his fingers and pooling into the bowl.

"Oh God," I moaned, wriggling from my ankle chains. "Oh God!" I wrinkled my nose against the noxious stench of Chief Oliver's blood—metallic, with the unmistakable waft of—mold?

I squirmed again, and the chief glared at me. "Stop that!" he barked.

I waggled anyway—really, what did I have to lose? And craned my neck to peer behind me out the little window. And there, pressed up against the glass, was the most beautiful face I'd ever seen: gray, with thin black lips encircling yellowed, snaggleteeth, caterpillar eyebrows framing beady black eyes. I sucked in a mold-scented breath, and Steve pressed one stubby troll finger up to his pursed lips, silencing me.

I turned my head back around, coming nose to nose with the dull tip of Chief Oliver's Leatherman blade. If I had any saliva left in my mouth, I would have gulped. Instead, I opened my mouth and let out a wailing scream while doing my best to flop around like a caught fish, bashing my arms around in the air in front of me.

"Ahhh! Help me, help me, help me! I'm down here! The chief is crazy! He's going to kill us!" I continued flopping and waggling, hoping to buy myself some time, while the chief stabbed wildly at the air in front of me.

"Stop!" The blade came slicing down a half inch from my ear. *Doing!* Slice, slice. "That!"

"Agh!" I shrieked as the end of the blade caught my shoulder, ripping into the flesh. I yanked myself back while the chief grabbed at the knife, stuck in my flesh.

"Steve!" I howled. "Steeeeve!"

There was a crash and then the tinkling of broken glass. The chief and I both craned our necks, staring down at Steve, lying on his side, showered with shards of glass. In a flash Steve was up on his small troll feet and in full karate stance. The chief grinned down at Steve.

"This is the cavalry?" Chief Oliver put his hands on his hips, yanked the Leatherman from my shoulder, and picked up the Sword of Bethesda again. He held one knife in each hand, battle stance ready, and grinned.

I howled.

"Steve is Sophie's hero! You will not hurt my Sophie!" Steve yelled before launching himself, snaggleteeth bared, into the chief's shins.

"Yeooooowwww!" The chief howled, pounding his fist against Steve's bald head.

"Get him, Steve!" I shouted, flopping around ineffectually, my shoulder wound gaping and cold.

The chief centered his narrowed, hateful eyes on me, and I heard the whoosh of wind and then felt a cold tingle from collarbone to armpit. I arched my head forward and saw little pearls of velvety blood beading from a crooked gash across my chest.

"Oh!" I wailed.

"Sophie!" My name was nearly lost in the gurgling growl of Mr. Sampson's voice as it deepened.

I heard the unmistakable clank of metal clattering

against concrete, the splintering of wood, and all at once the chief was laid out on his back, pinned by a fearsome wolf, the brown hair along its spine prickled and raised, its snapping jaws sinking into Chief Oliver's shoulder, washing the wolf's fur in a deep red. Steve rolled along on the concrete and ended up on his back, then bounded up, scurrying under the table.

"Oliver!"

I was flopping around, my vision going hazy from the blood rushing to my head and the little rivulets of blood dribbling from my chest and shoulder, but I thought I saw—

"Parker?" I mumbled.

He was standing at the top of the stairs, gun drawn, a gaggle of men in black clothing standing behind him. My head flopped back to where Mr. Sampson was, to the broken chains—and to the enormous werewolf pawing at Chief Oliver.

"Oh God," I said. "Mr. Sampson?"

The werewolf cocked his head at me, his jaws set hard, the fur around his lips damp with crimson blood and quivering. The velvety brown eyes looked at me, and I could see the familiar crinkle in the corners. The wolf lowered its head, and then, in one fell motion, he bounded from hind legs against the chief's chest, onto the table underneath my head, and out the broken open window. I choked a cry, the faint scent of Mr. Sampson's cologne wafting by.

Chapter Twenty-Three

Parker cuffed the moaning police chief and handed him off to a herd of SWAT officers in black flak jackets who came down the stairs, helping to load him on a stretcher. Steve stepped out from under the table and barked directions as Parker came over to me, cobalt eyes wide.

"You're cut," he said. "I'll get a medic."

I flopped—my best upside-down attempt at a shrug. "It's not deep," I said. "I'd just like to get down." I looked at my blood-stained bra, scanned the room full of police men. "And maybe get a shirt on."

Parker shrugged out of his flak jacket and whipped off his T-shirt, draping it over me. I was hanging upside down, just a hairsbreadth away from having been drained of my blood by a power-hungry psychopath, and my body betrayed me. It went goosebumpy and a little flutter in my stomach went down (or up?) to my nether regions as Parker's fingertips brushed over the naked skin on my abdomen.

Sophie Lawson: Sex-Starved Side of Beef.

"I'd really like to get down now."

Once Parker and the other SWAT officers had me out of the ankle cuffs and right side up, I sat down hard on the concrete floor, feeling the blood rush back to my limbs. I took a deep breath and rubbed my eyes, then blinked, for the first time noticing Vlad—black clad, as usual—as he stepped out from the group of SWAT guys and eyed me.

"Vlad, you're here."

He looked away sheepishly. "I'm sorry, Sophie. I told Parker as soon as I put it together about Lucy."

"Lucy!" My eyes went wide. "Vlad, I'm sorry. I think—I think she's dead. When I was with the chief, he threw me in his car and she was arguing with him. I heard a gunshot. I think he must have shot her."

Parker leaned into me. "We'll check into it, Sophie. Where did this happen? Up at Sampson's place?"

I nodded. "Yeah, outside."

Parker stepped over to one of the SWAT officers and told them about Lucy, asked them to check Sampson's house for any traces of him. I shivered, wrapping my arms around my knees.

"It was terrible, hearing the sound of the gun. I know Lucy tried to kill me and . . . suck my blood, but, honestly, I hope she's okay."

Vlad frowned. "She tried to suck your blood?"

I rubbed at my neck. "It was more like a violent hickey; she didn't even break the skin. She told me you wouldn't change her."

Vlad looked away from me, studied his shoes. "We do have rules."

"Even the VERM?" I tried to smile, but everything was starting to hurt.

"She thought she wanted to be changed—thought it was a great alternative to her life. She got angry when I wouldn't do it, when I wouldn't feed off of her. She smeared blood all over her neck, begged me to change her that night."

"She told me you bit her. I believed her."

"Yeah, well, I guess I never gave you reason to think otherwise about me. I knew I should have gotten to Parker sooner. Lucy and I kept fighting, and she started talking about the sword, about all the things that were needed to open the portal—including you. She told me if I didn't change her that I would be sorry—dead, finally—or sorry. Until she started talking about you, about draining your blood to open the portal, I figured she was just another breather who was convinced she knew how to access the demon world. When I finally realized that she knew what she was talking about, she was already gone. We were both heading to your apartment, but as it turns out, she found you and I found Parker."

"So you knew Lucy was in on this? Did you know she was in cahoots with the chief?"

Parker stepped up behind Vlad, was silently looking on as Vlad shook his head. "No, not at first—not until I talked to Parker. But I knew she was the one who purchased the Sword of Bethesda."

I was incredulous. "You did? How? When?"

"It took a while, but I was able to put all the clues together. At first she was questioning me, wanting to know where someone would find the sword. She knew an awful lot about it for—"

"A breather?"

"Yeah. I realized it had to be her. I thought about it, and it all clicked. When you've been around as long as I have, you learn to read things about human nature, about primitive desires. I knew Lucy was the one who had the Sword of Bethesda."

Parker raised an eyebrow, pinning Vlad with a stare.

"And also, she stabbed me with it."

Parker looked at the ground, smiling.

Vlad rubbed his abdomen. "Kind of ineffectual, but still rather offensive."

"Oh, Vlad, I'm so sorry." For the first time I realized that under his black, ankle-length leather duster he was wearing black denim jeans and a *Buffy the Vampire Slayer* T-shirt. There was a three-inch gash through the fabric at Buffy's slim midriff. I smiled. "Nice shirt, though."

Vlad tried to hold his blank expression steady, but I could see the hint of a smile playing at the edge of his lips. "The irony pleases me."

Parker bent down next to me, his face drawn with concern. "Okay, enough. We can sort everything out later, and I've got a couple of cars headed over to Sampson's place now. How are you? Are you okay? Are you hurt very badly?"

I swallowed. "I'm okay. Just a little wobbly. I would really just like to get out of here."

I went to push myself up, but Parker smoothly slid his arms underneath me, cradling me against his chest and picking me up in one motion. "You shouldn't walk," he murmured into my hair, "not until we get a medic in to see you."

Parker carried me up the stairs and out into the cold night air as Vlad followed behind us. People stood on tiptoes behind a police barricade, watching, and squad cars were creating a makeshift perimeter. I craned my neck and realized that we were at City Hall.

"We were under City Hall the whole time?"

"It seems Chief Oliver had a whole setup to go along with his plan of opening up a portal. We've been tracking him for over a year."

"That's right!" I leaned back as far as I dared from Parker's smooth, naked chest. "You're not Parker Hayes! You're not a detective. Who are you?"

Parker gently set me down on a stretcher in front of one of the ambulances. "She's been cut," he told the paramedic. "She needs attention. Sophie, Neils here is going to take care of you." Parker stepped aside, and Neils—with an Elvis-worthy pompadour and a pair of latex gloves—came at me with an alcohol-soaked gauze strip.

"This might sting a bit," Neils warned me.

"Wait!" I tried to stamp my foot, to glare at fake Parker, but the bulbous bouffant of the paramedic was in my way. "Who are you?"

My mind raced as Parker stared at me, blank faced, lips drawn.

He was an angel. A liar. Loony toons.

"I'm an FBI agent," he said finally. "My name is Alex Grace."

Or he was an FBI agent.

I raised my eyebrows. "Weren't you a—"

Parker pursed his lips and pressed his finger against them, his eyes sparking that brilliant blue.

"Sophie!" Nina squealed.

I looked up to see her rushing across the parking lot toward me, the moonlight glinting off her pale skin. Her black hair framed her face—eyes wide, brows furrowed, ruby lips held taut. She edged herself in front of Neils and threw her arms around me when she reached me, crushing me against her cold, tiny chest.

"Nina," I gasped as a whoosh of air went out of me.

"Sorry!" she said, softening her grip. "After what Vlad said about Lucy, I was just so worried about you! You must have been terrified—I could smell you a mile away!"

I sat back, my cheeks burning red. "Because I was scared," I explained. "She can smell fear." I was attempting to explain to Parker—er, Agent Grace—and the bewildered Neils when the man standing behind Nina caught my eye.

"Nina?" I asked, still staring at the man behind her.

Nina turned, weaving her arm through his. "Sophie, this is—"

"Officer Franks!" I exclaimed, examining Opie's smooth, undead complexion, his strawberry-blond hair standing out fiercely red against his now-pale forehead. He grinned at me—that same goofy, toothy smile—and I could see delicate fangs pressing against his lower lip. He tipped his head to look lovingly into Nina's eyes, and I could see the two tiny puncture wounds on the side of his neck.

"Nina!" I hissed. "You didn't!"

Vlad glared, put both of his hands on his hips. "I can't turn anyone, but *she* can? God! There is such a double standard around here!"

I smiled, shared a private look with Vlad while Nina looked sheepish, kicking at the ground with brand-new black leather peep-toe ankle boots. "I know I shouldn't have, but he had hardly been dead an hour when we found him," she said, staring up into Opie's black marble eyes, "and then I just couldn't resist." She snuggled close to him. "He's just so darling!" She inclined her head toward me and whispered, "Isn't he just luscious?"

Nina turned, her dark eyes settling on Alex's naked chest. "Speaking of luscious . . ."

A blush of crimson washed over Alex, and he shrugged back into his flak jacket. He looked from me to Neils, his blue eyes reflecting the dark sky. "Is she going to be okay?"

"She would if she'd hold still," Neils answered.

"Wait," I said, edging away from Neils after he smoothed a long white bandage across my wound. "What about Mr. Sampson? Has anyone seen him?"

"Miss," Neils said, "you need to relax." He draped an itchy, folded blanket over my shoulders.

"Wait," I said again, ignoring Neils and staring from Nina to Alex. "Please?"

Alex leaned against the ambulance and raked a hand through his dark, tousled hair. "Sophie . . ."

I stood up. "He's okay, though, right? You were able to find him, just to make sure he's okay?"

Nina looked at the ground, and my heart jumped into my throat, constricting my breath. My eyes started to moisten and itch. "Right?"

"I'm sorry, Sophie. We haven't found any trace of him," Alex said.

I looked at Nina. "You?"

She shook her head sadly. "I haven't been able to trace him. Other than the scent—it got really strong a few minutes before we found you—but then it was gone. *He* was gone."

My hand went to the bandage across my chest. "When the chief cut me."

"Sampson must have had a surge of emotion

when he thought you were being"—Nina winced—
"drained."

I blinked, staring past the assembled officers and squad cars, the San Francisco streetlights blurring under my tears. "It changed him. When the chief cut me, he changed. He broke through his chains to save me."

"Sampson's going to be fine," Alex said. "I'm sure of it."

Nina nodded. "He'll probably even be right back—after the dust settles."

I let my friends' assurances wash over me, let the weight of the night sink in. I felt the moist, cool night air on my skin and breathed deeply, rested my head against the open door of the ambulance.

"Rough night," I whispered.

"Rougher than pot roast night?" Alex said with a grin.

I saw Neils's eyes go large as Steve strolled up to us, lacing his thick gray fingers through mine. He dipped his head against my thigh and looked up at me, batting his slate gray eyes.

"Steve," I said, "thank you." I crouched down to hug him, wincing at the warm ache that surged through me. "Thank you so much for rescuing me."

Steve nuzzled against me, and I held my breath against his troll stench as he patted my back softly. "Steve wouldn't let anything happen to Sophie. Steve is Sophie's hero."

Alex squeezed in between Steve and me. "I like to think I had a little something to do with this rescue mission, Steve."

Steve crossed his arms and stared Alex down. "Mr. Superhero likes to think."

"How did you find me, anyway? And why"—I looked at Alex—"why did you come to find me after the way I treated you?"

"You mean when you stabbed me?" Alex's face broke into the Parker Hayes sexy half grin, and a shiver went up my spine.

"Yeah."

Alex shrugged. "I knew you didn't mean it."

"And when you stabbed Park—Alex"—Nina smiled sheepishly—"you must have cut yourself."

I looked down in bewilderment at the ragged split in my palm. "Oh, right."

"It made it easy to trace you."

"I helped, too!" Alex protested.

"Sophie was never in any real danger," Steve said, rolling up on his heels. "Steve had his eye on Sophie the whole time." He widened his stance, his small hands on his hips, looking satisfied.

"He was hiding in my trunk," Alex said.

"Steve knew he was not Sophie's boyfriend," Steve said, shaking his head toward Alex and then wrinkling his nose. "Something just didn't smell right about that. Steve decided to trail Alex."

"Yeah," Alex repeated, "hiding in my trunk."

"When I got back to our place, Alex and Vlad told me what happened. Alex had a lead on Sampson—where he might have gone—and Vlad knew that Lucy was after you. We were hoping to catch up with all of you at Mr. Sampson's. But when we got to Sampson's place, the smell of your blood and your fear was really strong. And Alex had a feeling about the chief, so"—Nina grinned, her fangs standing out against her red lips—"lucky guess."

"Lucky twelve-months-of-research guess," Alex said, his lips close to my ear.

Neils was completely engrossed in our conversation as Steve's eye narrowed at Alex. I knelt down so I was eye to eye with Steve.

"Look, Steve." I took both his hands in mine and squeezed gently. "You're a really great guy—really great. But I just don't think things are going to work out between us, Steve. Really, it's not you—it's me. I'm just not ready for someone as gallant as you."

I tried to find Steve's eyes and then followed his gaze over my left shoulder, directly to the impressive cleavage of a female paramedic who was bent over, replacing things in her bag.

Steve looked at me quickly. "Steve could never be the man for Sophie," he said, his voice and his eyes trailing. "Steve knows that now. Steve only wishes that Sophie would release him from her heart's vise-like grip."

I smiled and released Steve's hands. "Consider yourself free, Steve."

I watched as Steve unzipped his velour track jacket to mid-navel, fluffed up the lichen on his chest, and beelined for the busty paramedic.

Neils stepped in between us, looking from Nina and Franks, moonfaced, swooning, to Steve sauntering down the street, to me. He looked me up and down and crossed his arms in front of his chest.

"So what are you?" he asked finally. "Some kind of she-wolf or something?" Neils was keeping his distance from me, his eyes raking me up and down carefully.

I wagged my head and sat down on the ambulance

tailgate. "Nope. Nothing. I'm not special like that. I'm just your average girl."

Alex rearranged the blanket on my shoulders and snuggled me close to him, his lips a hairsbreadth from my earlobe.

"Sophie Lawson," he whispered, "there is nothing average about you."

Chapter Twenty-Four

I was mashing potting soil around the new spider plant in my office when Alex knocked on the door frame.

"Agent Grace," I said, grinning up at him.

"It's Alex," he said, striding up to me. His blue eyes slipped over me. "You look good. How are you feeling?"

I leaned against my desk. "Surprisingly well given the circumstances." I felt the broken skin on my lips with the tip of my tongue.

"So, no word from Mr. Sampson yet?"

I wagged my head, glancing toward the still-broken door to his office, his furniture still sitting empty, desk vacant. "Nothing. I heard they still haven't been able to find Lucy, either."

Alex nodded. "That's true. The guys have been out at Sampson's house a couple of times—it's clean. They recovered the shell casing, but weren't able to find Lucy's body."

I shuddered. "Her body. Part of me hopes she just took off—I mean, she's just a kid."

Alex's eyes flashed.

"A terribly misguided, slightly sociopathic kid. Maybe she learned her lesson." I tried to smile. "I kind of think we should go look for her, you know, maybe while we're looking for Sampson? I bet we could—"

"You know I'm not really an FBI agent, Sophie."

"Right," I said quietly.

Alex sat on the edge of my desk, and I tried to keep my eyes on my potting soil—tried desperately not to glance at the way his quadriceps bulged underneath his jeans, or the way his biceps mercilessly stretched at the arms of his olive-green T-shirt.

I cocked my head, studying. My fingers touched the warm skin on his arm, leaving a dusty trail of soil. "I never noticed this tattoo," I said, tracing the elaborately etched wing that poked from underneath his sleeve.

Alex turned, taking both my hands in his, lacing his fingers through mine. He pulled me close so that I could feel the warmth of his chest as it burned through his T-shirt, could taste the sweet crisp-apple scent of his breath.

"Sophie, I am an angel," he whispered.

I tried to think of a sexy retort, but Alex held my gaze steady, his eyes bluer and more firecracker-startling than ever.

"You saved my life, Alex. You might be a hero, but an angel?"

"I'm serious," Alex said. "You know I am."

"Angels don't exist," I replied, extracting my hands from his and going back to my spider plant.

"Neither do vampires," he answered.

I sat down hard, brushing my palms on my jeans. "So first you're Parker Hayes, the San Francisco detective."

"By way of Buffalo," he interjected.

"Then you're Alex Grace, the FBI agent. Now it's—what? Gabriel the angel?"

"Gabriel is an archangel. And kind of a drama queen if you really want to know the truth. One website calls him 'exalted,' and that's all he ever talks about."

I could feel myself gape. "Oh holy Lord, you're completely serious. And what about your niece?" I made flapping motions with my hands. "Is she an angel, too?"

Alex wasn't amused. "She's a pseudo-niece. Friend of the family. Her father asked me to check in on her after he passed away."

"Passed away? You mean died." I was incredulous and Alex cracked that half smile. I stood up and looked over his shoulder.

"What are you looking for?" he asked.

"Wings."

"Earthbound angels don't have wings."

I crossed my arms in front of my chest and sat down again. "Right. That's convenient. No wings, no halo. And I suppose you don't have one of those bow-and-arrow things, either."

Alex raised an amused eyebrow. "That's Cupid. He's actually a cherub—that's different."

"Of course it is," I groaned, my eyes narrowed, studying. "Very convenient."

Alex blew out a long sigh and in one swift motion, pulled off his shirt, leaving me face-to-face with his impeccable (okay, *fine*, "angelic") pectoral muscles. He turned his back toward me and my mouth watered—and my eyes found their way to two, four-inch scars, each running vertically just underneath his shoulder blades.

"They took your wings?" I ran my index finger gently over the waxy, silver scars, the warmth from his skin roiling through my entire body. I swallowed slowly. "They took them off?"

Alex turned to face me again. "I'm earthbound." His bright eyes suddenly clouded. "You call us fallen. When that happens, your wings just . . . just come off."

"Looks like I came right in the nick of time!" Nina swished through the office door and stood, legs spread, hands on hips. "What is going on here, and why wasn't I notified of beefcake nudity?"

Alex slid his shirt back over his head, and I sat back down, kicked my feet up on the desk. "Apparently, Alex is an angel now."

Nina slapped her forehead with the heel of her hand. "Oh! *That's* the smell! I couldn't place it for the life of me. Makes perfect sense."

Alex raised his eyebrows at me. "Smell?"

"Oh, vampires. They have this whole smelling thing. It's no big deal."

Nina yanked a blood bag from my mini fridge. She popped a straw into it and started to drink, her dark eyes fixed on Alex. "So an angel, huh? So do you like, know Lucifer?"

"Vampire, huh?" Alex asked, looking Nina up and down. "So do you, like, know Dracula?" There was a hint of smile playing on Alex's lush lips.

"Touché," Nina said, chewing on her straw, her eyes fixed but playful.

"Can you give us a moment, please, Nina?" I asked.

Nina stomped out into the hallway. "Fine! But you're telling me everything the moment Coptastic—

or Angeltastic—or whatever the hell he is—flies off."
She poked her head back through the doorway, her
fingertips pressed against her mouth, her lips twisted
into a wide grin. "Oh, I said hell—sorry, does that
offend you?"

I rolled my eyes. "Nina . . ."

Alex smiled softly at her, and I got up, closed the
office door.

"Geez!" I heard her bellow in the hallway.

"Okay, Alex, you're an angel. My werewolf boss has
run away. Yeah, okay, I see what's going on here."

Alex's face brightened. "You do?"

"Yup. I'm a nutter."

"Your vampire roommate just walked in here down-
ing a bag of AB negative. Why is *this* so hard to believe?"

"Look around! This is the Underworld. Demons,
zombies, bastions of hell. Don't you think I would
have been notified of angels? We don't even have a
form for that. And we have forms for everything."

"We operate on different planes. If it makes you
feel better, I really didn't know the Underworld existed either. Demons, vampires—a complete world
consisting of monsters? All legend to us on the celes-
tial plane." Alex chuckled. "And man, no one is going
to believe this. Are they going to get a kick out of
hearing about the Underworld when I get back."

I felt my heart skip a beat. "When you get back?"

Alex's eyes were soft. "Well, yeah, Sophie, that is
the eventual idea."

I paused, considering. Then, "Angel, huh? So were
you . . . born that way?"

Alex bit his lip. "No. I was born human. The angel
thing happened after I passed."

I swallowed. "You died?"

Alex nodded.

"So let me get this straight: you lived, died, went to heaven, became an angel—"

"Fell from grace," he said softly.

"And returned to Earth? Man, I feel so unaccomplished."

"So?" Alex asked, looking at me sideways.

"So, I guess it's good to know that the man I'm involved with thinks he's an angel."

Alex grinned. "We're involved?"

"No. No, not anything like—I mean, as coworkers. Or, you know, detectives. Or whatever we are." I offered a thin smile.

Alex frowned. "That's too bad. I was already thinking about what to serve at the wedding. It's going to be hard to feed the vampires, I'd expect. I don't know how blood would go over on the buffet table. . . ."

"Can angels even—wait—at the wedding? *Our* wedding? Alex, I'm not even sure I like you, let alone would be willing to—one day, in the far, very far, very distant future—have a wedding with you."

"Oh," Alex said, his warm arms encircling my waist, his lips cool and moist against my earlobe. "I think you like me, Lawson. I think you like me a lot."

For the first time in a long time my heartbeat sped up and the feeling was delicious and welcome—rather than precipice-of-death horrific. I looked up into Alex's earnest blue eyes. "Angel, huh? I guess I could get used to that. It's not the strangest thing I've ever heard."

"Well," Alex said, "if it makes you feel better, I could just leave you to your relationship with the troll."

I socked Alex in the arm and stepped back, awkwardly

breaking our embrace and regretting it immediately. I rubbed the warm spot on my waist where Alex's arms had been.

"So, if you're going to be hanging around here"— I was careful to keep my eyes focused on the grain of my desktop—"I should probably know what happened."

Alex's eyebrows went up. "What happened?"

"To you. What happened to make you . . . fallen."

His eyes clouded. "Sophie, I really don't think you need to get involved with all this. It's really . . ."

"Weird? Hard to understand?" I licked my lips. "Slightly left of center? You saved me and my werewolf boss from the scheme of a crazed killer, and you had to enlist the assistance of a smelly troll and a brooding teenage vampire to do it."

"I didn't *have* to enlist their help. They just . . . wanted to . . . assist."

"Whatever. All I'm saying is that there really is nothing you could say that's going to shock me. I'm pretty sure of it."

"So you really want to know?"

"Yeah. If we're going to hang out"—I held up my palm, stop-sign style—"just as friends, for now, I'd like to be sure that you weren't, you know, tossed out of heaven for kicking puppies or eating babies or something terrible like that."

Alex hid his grin behind his hand. "You really think I'm the type to kick a puppy?"

"Or eat a baby," I finished, and then narrowed my eyes. "Alex Grace, I'm not entirely sure what kind of guy you are. So, go ahead. Spill it."

Alex blew out a resigned sigh. "Well, it was close to two years ago when it happened. I was . . . kind of a security officer, I guess. A protector. And well, my loyalties were . . . called into question."

"Called into question? And for that they sent you packing? Geez, that seems a little harsh."

Alex crossed his ankles. "It wasn't just me. I was supposed to protect something—something that was very important. And I . . . trusted the wrong person— I guess that would be the best way to put it."

"And that someone betrayed your trust?"

Alex bit his lip, bobbed his head. "Yeah. My trust was betrayed, and because of that, something very precious was lost. It was my fault, and I was deemed untrustworthy—actually, more like an enemy to the hierarchy."

"Wow. What was lost?"

"An amulet."

I snorted. "Jewelry? God—or whoever—seems pretty nitpicky if he did all that over an amulet. Can't he just"—I snapped my fingers—"whoosh! Whip up a new one or something?"

"The amulet is actually a keeper of souls. It's the place where you go when your fate is being decided. In some religions they call it limbo or purgatory."

I scratched my head. "So when you're in limbo you're in costume jewelry? Hm. Imagine that."

"Good and evil are constantly warring, and the souls trapped in the amulet—well, the claimant of those souls can tip the scales in their favor and take over both worlds. Up until recently, the amulet was held on the angelic plane—balanced between the archangels and the fallen. There was a pact made in blood so that if either an archangel or a fallen angel touched the amulet, it would tip the scale and destroy their own world."

"So, sort of like a super-duper security device."

Alex smiled wanly. "Sort of. But I was taught a way around it, a way to claim the amulet. And I thought I was doing the right thing. I really thought I was stepping in for the good of humankind."

"But you were betrayed."

He nodded.

I raised my eyebrows. "So, as punishment you're destined to wander the Earth forever now?"

Alex shrugged, crossed his arms in front of his chest. "It's not that bad. I have cable." He grinned and I eyed him expectantly, but he didn't continue.

"Wow. An eternity of *Sex and the City* reruns. Lucky you."

"I will be offered redemption when I find and return the amulet. Provided I do it in time."

I frowned. "I don't understand. If you're out looking for this amulet thing, why did you get involved with the collector case? The chief was after power—and eyeballs and human hearts—not an amulet, or you know, souls. He never even mentioned it when we were trapped with him."

"The collector—Chief Oliver—was working to open a portal to hell; to gain power over everything—the human plane, the demonic plane, *and* the angelic one."

"He knew about the angelic plane?"

"Like the Underworld, there are all sorts of legends about it, people claiming to have been there, but it can only be an actuality if . . ."

"You're dead?" I wondered.

"We prefer the term chosen," Alex continued. "As for the chief, well, I had been tracking him for nearly a year. He was committing similar murders in other parts of the country—I think he was looking for each piece of his puzzle somewhere where an odd death wouldn't draw so much attention. There was talk that possibly the amulet had ended up in his hands. I thought I was going to be able to find him, find the amulet, and then find my way back home."

The sadness in Alex's voice cut to my bones. "I'm sorry you didn't find the amulet. So . . . what happens now?"

Alex focused on me. "Now I keep looking."

"Okay," I said, standing shoulder to shoulder with Alex. "Where do we start?"

Alex smiled wistfully. "Thanks, Sophie, but you don't need to . . ."

"No, really, it's the least I can do. You saved my life. I can, you know . . . get one of those metal detectors and go amulet searching. Maybe the chief buried it in Golden Gate Park or something." I grinned.

"To be honest, I don't even know exactly what the amulet looks like."

"Weren't you protecting it?" I asked.

"I was, but we weren't able to see it. It's charmed, so even though it's called an amulet, it could really be anything. It's a security thing."

"Like Fort Knox?"

He smiled. "Something like that."

I stood up. "I could still help you. I mean, there's a good chance that maybe the amulet—or whatever it is now—has fallen into demon hands. Maybe the UDA can help you. And if it's charmed, then I'll be able to see through it. You know, if they got all squirrelly and decided to hide it in plain sight of something." I was starting to dip back into my *Sophie Lawson, CSI* revelry. Although, maybe when working with angels I wouldn't need a gun. Maybe just a bow and arrow or a sword or something. Yeah, I could deal with a sword. . . .

Alex put both his hands on my shoulders and squeezed gently, bringing me back to reality. He looked at me, his cobalt eyes bright and clear, his smile soft.

"Thank you, Sophie. I appreciate you wanting to help. Your life is here, though." He rubbed his thumb against my jawline, cradled my chin in his palm, and then his lips were on mine.

If I didn't believe in angels before, I did now.

Chapter Twenty-Five

He had a shock of my hair wrapped around his knuckles, yanking so that my chin rose toward the ceiling and my neck stretched and elongated uncomfortably.

"Please," I murmured, my eyes traveling to his glistening fangs as they pressed hungrily against the corners of his mouth. "You're getting soap in my eye."

Gerard angrily slapped the faucet off and draped a towel over my head; I could hear his sigh from under my pink terry cloth towel.

"All you breathers ever do is complain," he moaned, wringing my hair in the towel. "Where's Nina with my lunch?" He eyed my neck again, and I felt myself inch a little farther back in my chair.

Gerard was a recent UDA hire. He had transferred in from our Los Angeles office as part of the new team called in to keep things flowing in Mr. Sampson's absence. In addition to being the executive assistant to our current UDA head, he was the king of the makeover. Or so Nina had convinced me.

Gerard and I were set up in the UDA bathroom, and today, in addition to running a meeting on how to handle a group of unruly banshees terrorizing the Castro, he was in charge of turning my carrot-colored hair into a lush mane of rich auburn during today's lunch hour.

"How does it look?" I asked, sliding the towel from my head and beginning to turn toward the mirror.

Gerard's eyes widened, and if he had had any blood in his undead cheeks, I'm confident it would have drained. He put both his hands on my shoulders and smiled a bright, dazzling smile, fangs bared.

"You can't look until it's all finished," he said. "Stylist's rules." He pushed me down hard into the office chair Nina had wheeled in. Gerard chewed his lower lip and cocked his head, using a long, slender finger to brush a lock of pink hair from my shoulder.

A lock of hot pink, finger-in-a-light-socket-frizzy hair from my shoulder.

"What the—?" I sprang up, kicking my chair out from beneath me, and glared in the mirror.

"Holy crap!" Nina exclaimed when she kicked open the bathroom door. I turned around and her pale hands were pressed hard against her mouth, her coal-black eyes wide. She looked desperately from Gerard to me. "You look fabulous!" she finally squeaked, her brow pinched.

I swung back to the mirror, my heart thundering in my chest. "I look like a troll doll. My hair is pink. *Hot pink!*" I tried to run my fingers through the cotton-candy mess. "And it's curly."

"Well," Nina said, fluffing the mess affectionately around my shoulders, "you said you wanted a change, and it is certainly . . . different."

Gerard frowned at the empty tubes of hair color dumped in the sink. "I have no idea what went wrong," he said. And then, quickly, "Not that there's anything wrong with it. Really, you do look smashing. It really brings out your eyes. You know, the red part." He smiled politely. "I like it."

I blinked at the pink halo in the mirror. The hot pink mess made my pale cheeks paler, my red eyebrows redder, and the lime Jell-O green of my eyes that much more limey. "I don't know what I expected," I sighed, plopping down into my desk chair. "Nothing ever goes my way."

"Oh no," Gerard said, carefully brushing a lock of his immortally perfect blond hair from his bony shoulder. "Here we go again—pity party. Nothing works out for Sophie. Sophie was almost killed by the power-crazed chief of police. Sophie fell in love with a dude who turned out to be a fallen angel. Sophie's the only employee at UDA who actually breathes. Whine, whine, whine, whine."

So, Gerard was right—kind of. But this wasn't going to be a pity party.

My lower lip stuck out, and I could feel the moist heat of tears beginning to form. "I'm not having a pity party," I huffed.

Nina perched herself delicately on the arm of the chair and went to pat my head, thought better of it, and patted my shoulder instead. "I know you're upset about Alex, Sophie. But it's not like it would have worked out between you two anyway. He's a fallen angel and you're . . . you. You know, regular."

I frowned. "You really need to work on your pep talks."

"Besides," Nina continued. "I think the pink is very chic. I'm sure your date will love it!"

My stomach dropped. My date.

Generally, there are two things I don't do: date, and sing in public. But since I had been a little bit hermitlike since the whole Alex Grace/chief-trying-to-kill-me incident, Nina had cajoled—cajoled, pleaded, begged, forced, kicked—me into accepting a date with the sweet, unassuming UCSF resident who had moved in upstairs from us.

It was either that or perform a half-vamp mash-up of "I Will Survive" and "Brick House" at a demon karaoke bar. I chose the lesser of two evils.

"Ahem."

Gerard, Nina, and I all swung our heads to the open bathroom door as Lorraine poked her head in, her mane of enviable, honey-colored locks swishing smoothly over her shoulder, Costineau circling territorially around her feet.

"Nina, you're needed up front." She grinned shyly at Gerard. "Hi, Gerard." Her eyes widened and her cheeks flushed when she saw me. "Oh. Wow. Sophie."

Nina and Gerard filed quietly past Lorraine, and I rushed toward her, gripping her arms. "Lorraine, can you fix my hair?" I begged. "Please? It's pink. It's pink."

Lorraine stepped in the bathroom, letting the door snap shut behind her. "I don't do hair," she said apologetically. "Besides . . ." She tried to brush a finger through my candy mess, but it stuck. She had to yank to remove it. "It's really . . . perky."

"No." I wagged my head. "Spell it out! Magic it out! Anything!"

Lorraine raised both her eyebrows, and I slumped down in my chair. "Oh. Right," I muttered. "Damn magical immunity. Thanks anyway."

* * *

I pulled a hat down low over my forehead and glared out the window. Leave it to the weather gods to open up the rare portal of San Francisco sunshine the one day I actually *needed* to wear a hat. I was back at my apartment after spending the final three hours of my workday being goggled at by trolls, centaurs, and three Kholog demons and spending another day staring at my phone, pretending I didn't want it to ring. Pretending that I wasn't waiting for a phone call from Alex.

"Nice," Nina said as she walked in the front door, Vlad following sullenly behind her. "I hear the bank robber look is very in this fall."

Vlad tried to keep up his brooding countenance, but even he couldn't keep his eyes from widening when he saw the wisps of pink hair poking out of my hat.

I narrowed my eyes at Nina. "This is all your fault."

"The pink hair or the date?"

"Both."

She yanked open the refrigerator door and pulled out a blood bag, tossing it to Vlad, who punctured it like a Capri Sun. They both drank and stared me down while I glowered in the corner.

"Couldn't you just let me be a hermit?" I moaned. "I never make you do anything you don't want to do."

Nina sucked the last of her blood bag and patted me on the shoulder, heading for the front door when the bell rang. She snatched the hat off my head. "You'll thank me for this," she said, pulling open the door and shoving me through.

Eric's eyes widened as I mashed up against his chest. "I'm sorry," I said quickly. "Nina, my roommate is—" I looked behind me as Nina slammed the door shut. I pasted on a reassuring smile and turned to Eric. "Are you ready to go?"

Eric Bowers was all California surfer: disheveled, sandy-blond hair, ocean blue eyes, and berry-stained lips set in golden, sun-kissed skin. He was lanky, thin, and wiry, and had no problem filling out the pale blue button-down and pressed chinos he was wearing.

"Wow," he said, his blue eyes studying my hair.

"Oh, it's—"

"No, no. I mean, you look great. That's a nice dress. Why don't we go?"

I nodded gratefully, and Eric walked me to his car.

As we drove to the restaurant, I squinted into the darkened streets, my heart skipping a beat. I sucked in a sharp breath and bonked my head against the passenger window.

"Are you okay?" Eric asked.

I rubbed my forehead. "That was stupid." I forced a smile. "I thought I saw . . . an old friend out there."

An old friend. Huh.

I thought I saw Alex. Alex Grace, angel: fallen from grace, destined to walk the earth until he made his peace with heaven, buns of steel, lips that made my mouth water just thinking about them. Alex Grace who had walked out of my office and disappeared into thin air.

"Are you sure you're okay?" Eric asked again. "You look a little glazed."

I hoped the heat radiating through my body wasn't apparent, and I clamped my knees together. "I'm fine, thank you."

I glanced over my shoulder out the window again

and sighed when the man I thought was Alex turned and grinned a toothless, definitely not-Alex smile.

It had been six months since Alex left San Francisco, and I had been mostly fine until about two days ago. Suddenly, I saw Alex everywhere. He was the barista at the Starbucks on Geary. He was eating a ham sandwich at Mel's on Lombard. Folding laundry at Wash'n Royal on Fillmore. Walking a three-legged beagle on Chrissie Field.

I turned to Eric and forced a smile. "So, Eric, tell me a little about yourself. We're neighbors, and other than the fact that you read the *New York Times*, I don't know anything about you."

Eric smiled, and I liked the stern set of his profile. "I *get* the *New York Times*," he said. "I rarely have time to read it. I'm a resident over at UCSF. Um, I'm from Pacifica, on the coast, originally. I like long walks, puppy dogs, and thunder showers turn me on. Now you."

I raised an eyebrow. "Thunder showers, huh?"

He waggled his eyebrows.

"Okay, well, I'm not particularly turned on by weather patterns, but puppies are all right. And I'm originally from"—I pointed toward the red glow of the towers on Twin Peaks out through the front windshield—"over there."

We drove in uncomfortable silence for a moment until Eric tried again. "So, what is it that you do for a living, Sophie?"

Oh, right.

Well, Eric, I considered saying, *I work at a demon detection agency. My boss—recently gone missing—is a werewolf. There's blood in the office fridge, someone brought eye of newt to the office potluck, and I know, firsthand, that it is nearly impossible to get hobgoblin slobber out of linen.*

"Oh," I said instead, "administrative. But you're a doctor—that sounds way more interesting. Tell me about that."

I listened to Eric describe his medical career all the way to the restaurant, and pasted on a smile as he continued while the maitre d' showed us to our table. I tried to keep my eyes focused on Eric's shiny, disheveled hair while a guy, who looked very much like Alex Grace, bussed the table over Eric's left shoulder.

"Could you excuse me for a moment?" I asked Eric, breaking into his breathtaking description of the cyst he had lacerated yesterday.

When Eric nodded, I crumpled my napkin and hurried to the women's restroom, my stomach in knots, my palms sweating as I rubbed them against the Banana Republic sheath dress I had borrowed from Nina.

"You're not here, you're not here, you're not here," I muttered as I sank down on the toilet seat, my index fingers making manic circles against my temples. "You're a figment of my undersexed imagination." I clamped my eyes shut. "Figment of my imagination . . ."

"Are you through?"

I opened one eye, and my heart dropped to my knees as figment-Alex, now in the women's restroom stall with me, raised an eyebrow.

"What?" I stood up, the backs of my calves ramming against the cold toilet, the automatic flusher going crazy. "You're not here," I tried, jabbing a shaking finger at figment-Alex. "You're not here. . . ."

Figment-Alex grinned and took my index finger in his hand, kissing the tip. His lips were warm, moist, and they felt very real.

"Alex?" I asked, my heart starting to thump.

"Hi, Sophie."

"What are you doing here?" I rose up on tiptoes in a halfhearted effort to look over the stall wall. "You shouldn't be here. And you really shouldn't be here, here."

Alex looked unfazed.

"I have a date out there," I hissed.

Alex shrugged, looked nonchalantly over his shoulder. "Shall I tell him you've been detained?"

"No! No! You can't tell a guy that I went to the bathroom and never came back. He'll think I have explosive diarrhea or something."

Alex leaned an elbow against the stall door. "So tell him you have to end your date because you ran into an ex-boyfriend."

I could feel my eyes bulge, feel the color rising in my cheeks. "Ex-boyfriend? Look, buddy, you were not my ex-boyfriend, let alone any kind of ex—"

"Buddy," Alex chuckled, stepping closer to me.

"Boyfriends do not poof! Disappear. And they do not return again in a public restroom. Especially not in the ladies' room." I dropped my voice. "What are you doing here anyway?"

"This was the only place I could get your undivided attention."

I blew out an annoyed sigh. "Not *here,* here." I spread out my arms, my fingers banging the stall walls. "Here. In San Francisco. On Earth."

Alex looked around, the corner of his mouth pushing up in that deliciously annoying half smile of his. I hadn't realized how much I missed it.

I unlocked the stall door, steadied my hands on Alex's chest, and pushed him out. "You shouldn't be here."

"Oh!" A woman pushed through the bathroom door and gaped at Alex and me. "You people are disgusting!" She turned on her heel and sped out of the bathroom, clucking the whole way.

I pointed to the bathroom door as it clapped shut after the disgusted woman. "Isn't it things like that that are going to keep you out of heaven? Or, wherever it is you're headed?"

"Sophie, I need your help."

I glanced at myself in the mirror, frowned at the bright-red blush of my cheeks as the blood surged through. "You know what? I don't care. I don't want to hear it. You disappeared. Gone—without a trace. Or a phone number."

"I'm sorry. I'm sorry for leaving the way that I did. I just didn't think you'd understand. I thought it would be easier if I just . . . wasn't there."

I put both my hands on my hips. "I work in the demon realm. I live in San Francisco. There are very few things that I don't understand. But, ironically, you disappearing was something that I didn't understand."

"I have a chance to go back. To restore my grace."

"To go back to heaven?"

Alex nodded slowly.

"Heaven?" I said again, one eyebrow raised.

"Can we talk about this, please? Maybe somewhere that isn't"—Alex looked around the she-she pink powder room—"here?"

I tried my best to stay solid, not to lose myself in the cobalt blue of his eyes, in the firm set of his jaw. "Meet me back at my apartment in about an hour," I muttered.

Alex grinned. "What about your date?"

"I'll think of something," I told him.

* * *

Eric was gnawing on a breadstick when I went back to the table.

"Everything okay?" he asked, his mouth full of bread.

"I'm sorry, Eric, but I'm just not feeling very well."

Eric swallowed, his eyes sympathetic and locked on mine. "Oh."

"I think I just need to lie down. I must have eaten something that didn't agree with me."

Eric stood up, flattened his palm against my belly. "It's okay," he said when I flinched. "I'm a doctor."

"Oh, right."

"Where does it hurt?"

Eric grinned down at me, and I thought momentarily about how nice it would be to date a doctor. Who breathed. Who came from a place with an actual postal code and who didn't *pouf!* into thin air and who wouldn't (theoretically) sprout wings when all was right with his world again.

"You know what?" I said, sinking down into my chair. "I think it passed. Why don't we have a drink?"

Eric and I had had two rounds of cocktails and were sharing a crab appetizer when I felt my phone buzzing in my purse. I fished it out, glanced nonchalantly at the readout.

"I'm sorry. It's my roommate. Do you mind if I grab this? It'll just be a second."

Eric wagged his head and I connected.

"Nina?"

"Sophie."

I lowered my voice, hunching behind my arm. "What do you want? I'm on a date with Eric."

"I know. Do you know where I am? At home. With an angel. Your angel."

I dropped my voice. "He is not *my* angel."

"Whatever. He's on *my* couch. And he said you were coming home to talk to him."

"I am. Eventually."

Nina blew out a sigh. "Would eventually be before or after *Glee*? He might be an angel, but he's a complete remote-control hog."

I groaned. "I'll be home in a few minutes."

When I got back to my apartment, Nina, Vlad, and Alex were assembled around the kitchen table, staring at each other. I dumped my keys on the counter and walked in, hands on hips. "Okay, Alex, what is so important that you have to pop back into my life and interrupt me on a date?"

Nina swallowed hard, and I sank down into the only empty chair at the table, then slapped my palm against my forehead. "Oh, wait, let me guess—it's Eric, right? He's evil? He's actually Satan or something? Of course. I meet a nice guy who seems to breathe, seems to have regular old blood coursing through his veins, and there is something paranormally wrong with him."

"No," Nina said, "he's a breather."

"And his blood is fine," Vlad confirmed.

I grimaced. "Okay, then what is it?"

Alex's eyes were hard. "It's Sampson."

"Pete?" I asked, my voice sounding small. I looked from Alex to Nina. "What about him? Have they found him? Is he okay?"

Nina hung her head, and I felt my lower lip start to quiver, felt the choking lump in my throat. "That's what you came to tell me?" I whispered. "That Mr. Sampson is dead?"

"Sophie, I'm sorry."

I stood up so quickly my chair flopped onto the floor behind me. "I don't believe it."

"It's true. I'm sorry. I hate to be the one to tell you this. You don't understand how hard it is for me to see you hurt—to make you hurt—again. But I needed to be the one to give you the news."

Vlad righted my chair, and I sunk down again. "Why? Why did it have to be you? In person?"

Alex opened his coat and pulled a long, thick envelope, folded lengthwise from his pocket. "Because Mr. Sampson wanted to be sure that you got these." He pushed the envelope across the table toward me, and I just stared at it, until it swirled in front of me, lost in a rush of tears.

"What is it?" I asked.

"It's an answer to most of your questions," Alex said.

My eyes flashed. "So, you saw him? You saw him before he died? Was he okay? What happened to him?"

Alex looked at his lap and wagged his head. "I didn't see him before he died. This was something I had promised to do long before any of this—even any of this with the chief—ever happened."

I sniffed and nodded my head, then used my fists to wipe the tears from my cheeks.

"What's in the envelope, Soph?" Nina asked.

I swallowed heavily, unhooked the latch, and peeled out a tri-folded stack of papers covered in very carefully handwritten script. "It's from my grand-mother," I said, fingering the paper.

While Alex, Nina, and Vlad looked on, I smoothed the letter against the table, licked my lips, and learned the truth about my life.

Please turn the page for an exciting sneak peek of
UNDER GROUND,
the next novel in the
Underworld Detection Agency Chronicles,
coming in November 2011!

It's nearly impossible to get hobgoblin slobber out of raw silk.

I know this because I had been standing in the bathroom, furiously scrubbing at the stubborn stain for at least forty-five minutes. If I could do magic, I would have zapped the stain out. Heck, if I could do magic I would zap away the whole hobgoblin afternoon and be sinking my toes in the sand somewhere while a tanned god named Carlos rubbed suntan lotion on my back. But no, I was stuck in the Underworld Detection Agency women's restroom—a horrible, echo-y room tiled in Pepto pink with four regular stalls and a single tiny one for pixies—when my coworker Nina popped her head in, wrinkled her cute ski-jump nose, and said, "I smell hobgoblin slobber."

Did I mention vampires have a ridiculously good sense of smell?

Nina came in, letting the door snap shut behind her. She used one angled fang to pierce the blood bag she was holding and settled herself onto the sink next to me.

"You're never going to get that out, you know."

I huffed and wrung the water from my dress, glaring at Nina as I stood there in my baby-pink slip and heels. "Did you come in here just to tell me that?"

Nina extended one long, marble white leg and examined her complicated Jimmy Choo stilettos. "No, I also came in to tell you that Lorraine is on the warpath, Nelson used his trident to tack a pixie to the corkboard, and Vlad is holding a VERM meeting in the lunchroom."

I frowned. "This job bites."

Nina smiled, bared her fangs, and snapped her jaws.

Nina and I work together at the Underworld Detection Agency—the UDA for those in the know. And very few people are in the know. Our branch is located thirty-seven floors below the San Francisco Police Department, but we have physical and satellite offices nationwide. Word is the Savannah office gets the most ghosts but has the best food. The Manhattan office gets the best crossovers (curious humans wandering down), and the good ol' San Francisco office is famous for our unruly hordes of the magnificent undead, mostly dead, and back from the dead. However, we're rapidly becoming *in*famous for a management breakdown that tends to make incidents like the fairy stuck to the corkboard barely worth mentioning. Some demons blame the breakdown of Underworld morals. I blame the fact that my boss and former head of the UDA, Pete Sampson, was killed last year and has yet to be replaced. Thus, we've been privy to a semi-permanent parade of interim management made up of everything from werewolves and vampires to goblins and one (mercifully short) stint with a screaming banshee.

So am I a demon? Nope. I'm a plain, one hundred percent first-life, air-breathing, magic-free human being. I don't have fangs, wings, or hooves. I'm five-foot-two on a good day, topped with a ridiculous mess of curly red hair on a bad day, and my eyes are the exact hue of lime Jell-O. My super powers are that I can consume a whole pizza in twelve minutes flat and sing the fifty states in alphabetical order. And that I'm alive. Which makes me a weird, freakish anomaly in an Underworld office that keeps blood in the fridge and offers life insurance that you can collect should you get the opportunity to come back to life.

"There you both are!"

My head snapped to the open doorway, where Lorraine stood, eyebrows raised and arched, her emerald green eyes narrowed. Lorraine is a Gestalt witch of the green order, which means that her magiks are in tune with nature and are deeply humane. Usually.

Her honey blond hair hangs past her waist and her fluttery, earth-toned wardrobe reflects her solidarity with natural harmony.

Unless you got on her bad side, which, today, I was.

Lorraine glared at my slip. "Can you wrap up your little lingerie fashion show and meet me in my office, please? And you"—Lorraine swung her head toward Nina, who was holding my damp dress under the hand dryer—"can you please break up Vlad's empowerment meeting and get out to the main floor?"

I looked at Nina. "Vlad is still into the Vampire Empowerment Movement?"

Nina gave me her patented "Don't even start" look, punched her fist in the air, and bellowed, *"Viva la revalucion!"* while slipping out the bathroom door.

I pulled my dress over my head under Lorraine's annoyed stare, and then worked quickly to rearrange my mass of unruly hair. When Lorraine sighed—loudly—I wadded my curls into a bun and secured it with a binder clip, following her down the hall.

"Okay," I said as we walked, "what's up?"

Lorraine didn't miss a step. She pushed a manila file folder in my hand with the blue tag—*Wizards*—sticking out.

"Nicholias Rayburn," I read.

"Ring a bell?"

I frowned. "No. Should it?"

"How about 'Three-Headed Dog Ravages Noe Valley Neighborhood'?"

"Mr. Rayburn did that?"

"No," Lorraine said flatly. "You did."

I raised my eyebrows, and Lorraine let out another annoyed sigh. "Nicholias Rayburn was here last week. Old guy, blue robe, pointy hat?"

I cocked my head. "Oh yeah. Now I remember him."

"You should, because you allowed him to renew his magiks license."

My stomach started to sink.

"Yeah. With his three-inch-thick cataracts and mild senility. You were supposed to withdraw his license and strip him of his magiks, but you didn't, and he walked home, thought a fire hydrant was following him, and unleashed the hound of hell on the land of soccer mom. Not exactly great for our reputation."

I felt my usually pale skin flush. "Whoops."

Lorraine stopped walking and faced me, the hard line of her lips softening. "Look, Sophie, I know you've had a hard time. I understand that with all you've been through you're going to make some mistakes, but you've got to be more aware."

The events of the last year of my life flooded over me, and I blinked rapidly, trying to dispel the imminent rush of tears.

It *had* been rough.

While I had gone for nearly thirty years with nothing so much as an overdue library fine to raise any eyebrows, in the last twelve months I had become involved in a gory murder investigation, been kidnapped, attacked, hung by my ankles in an attempt to be bled dry—

"And I know it's got to be hard, what with Alex out of the picture and all."

—and I had fallen in love with a fallen angel who had the annoying habit of dropping into my life with a pizza and a six-pack when things were supernaturally awful, and dropping out when things shifted into relatively normal gear.

I sniffed. "Thanks. It won't happen again. I promise."

"Let's hope not. But why don't you head out a little early today?" she said, squeezing my shoulder. "Get some rest and regroup." Lorraine bit her lip and danced from foot to foot, then leaned in close to me. "Okay. I'm really not supposed to say anything, so this is just between you and me, okay? The main offices have found Sampson's replacement. We're supposed to have the new management in place by the end of the week. But its super hush-hush so don't tell a soul."

I mimed locking my lips shut and then turned on my heel, heading out to find Nina.

* * *

Nina was perched on the end of her desk when I found her, legs crossed seductively, her shoe dangling from one toe. She was winding her long black hair around and around her index finger and interviewing a werevamp, who was sitting in her visitor's chair. Nina was the only person I'd ever met who could make the sentence "Please tell me about your previous employment history" sound sordid. She was nearly purring as the werevamp—who looked dashing in a steel gray suit and had the chiseled profile of James Bond—ticked off a forty-seven-decade-long employment history that included being a project manager for King Henry the VIII and ended with "software programmer."

I tried to catch Nina's eye, but she glared at me— nothing is icier than a vampire glare—and I rolled my eyes, heading down the hall toward the elevator. I was skirting the hole in the linoleum where a High witch blew herself up when I ran chest to chest into Vlad and his Fang Gang—nine vampire staff members of UDA who were currently enraptured in the Vampire Empowerment and Restoration Movement. Loosely put, VERM members were dead set on bringing vamps back to their glory days (think Dracula, graveyard dirt, and ascots). Though UDA code was adamant about vampire/human relationships (the former was not allowed to eat the latter), I generally tried to steer clear of VERMers—Vlad, being Nina's nephew (and a longtime resident of our couch), was the exception.

"Whoa, sorry about that, Sophie. Hey, have you seen Nina?"

I gestured toward Nina's office door that had mysteriously closed. "She's interviewing a werevamp."

Vlad smoothed his perfect hair. "I didn't think we had any open positions."

I shrugged. "I'm pretty sure we don't."

Vlad fell in step beside me. "So, did you hear about that three-headed dog in Noe last week?"

"No," I said quickly, stepping into the elevator.

I knew psychologically that there were only two things that could help the kind of day I was having, so I had a bottle of Chardonnay in one hand and a package of marshmallow pinwheels in the other in record time. The surge of chocolate and alcohol helped but not enough, so I beelined for the bathroom, filling my mouth with cookies and peeling my clothes off as I went.

I drew a bath as hot as I could stand it and upturned a bottle of cucumber-melon bath goo under the tap. Then I positioned my wineglass next to the remaining marshmallow pinwheels and eased myself into the tub. "Ahh," I moaned, closing my eyes, breathing in the heady scent of cucumber and chocolate. "Much better."

I dunked a washcloth, wrung it out, and placed it over my eyes, then sipped contentedly at my wine. I was reaching out for another pinwheel cookie when I heard the rustle of cellophane and felt a cold prickle of fear creep up my neck, despite the hot water.

Someone placed a pinwheel in my outstretched hand, and I sat bolt upright in the tub, the washcloth falling from my eyes, the poor pinwheel reduced to chocolaty, marshmallow ooze dripping through my fingers.

"Didn't mean to scare you," Alex said, perched on the side of my tub, his pincher finger and thumb hovering above my half-empty pinwheel package. "May I?"

Alex Grace was gooey, chocolaty goodness if ever there was. He was an angel—of the fallen sort—with cobalt blue eyes and hair the color of milk chocolate, swirling in wondrous, luxurious curls over his forehead, snaking over ears just perfect for nibbling. His build was fairly slight but wrought with wiry, rock-hard muscles that made his jeans look mouthwatering, and stretched out the chest and arms of his T-shirts mercilessly.

"What the hell—why are you—" I fluttered and floundered, splashing bits of cucumber-melon-scented fluff and bathwater all around.

I worked to get my panicked breathing under control. Alex and I had shared some steamy moments and every glance or touch of his skin electrified me, but he was bad news—fallen angels always are. And his whole disappearing-reappearing thing really got on my last nerve.

And then I realized I was naked.

I sunk lower into the water, pushing the bubbles over my girly bits and glowering at Alex, who looked at me, that obnoxious, adorable half smile playing on his lips. He helped himself to a cookie.

"What are you doing here?"

He chewed thoughtfully. "I needed to talk to you."

"I have a phone. Or an e-mail address. Or, hell, a carrier pigeon. Do you always have to show up in the bathroom?"

"I needed your undivided attention."

I raised an annoyed brow. "Or you needed a naked-lady fix. And did you lose your ability to knock along with your wings?"

He grinned, took a swig from my wineglass. "Is that a ninety-eight?"

"Get out!" I screamed, "I'm not going to talk to you while I'm naked."

Alex's grin widened. "So you are naked . . ."

"I'm in the bathtub," I snarled. "What did you expect?" I was sitting forward now and vaguely aware of the cool air touching my breasts. I hunkered down in the water again. "You're a pervert."

Alex shrugged, finished my wine, and poured himself some more. "Hey, I'm no angel."

I rolled my eyes and snatched my wineglass out of his hand. "Get out."

"I still need to talk to you."

"And I still need you to get out."

"Can I have another cookie?"

"Out!"

Once Alex was safely on the other side of the bathroom door I slipped out of the tub, hastily dried off, and wrapped myself in my baby blue bathrobe. I was tightening the belt and padding into the kitchen when I was treated to a view of Alex's rump poking out of my fridge.

"Can I help you with something?" I asked his butt.

Alex backed out of the fridge, frowning. "There's nothing in here to eat. Are there any more pinwheels?"

I crossed my arms in front of my chest. "No. I threw them away." *Threw them down my throat was more like it.*

I edged Alex aside and peered into the fridge,

coming out with a half loaf of bread and a stack of Kraft cheese slices. "Grilled cheese?"

"Tres gourmet."

"You'd better believe it."

Alex handed me a frying pan and got to work buttering bread.

"So, what are you doing here anyway? I mean here, here, in this realm. In my kitchen."

Alex peeled the filmy cellophane from a piece of cheese and crumpled it in his hand, popping the cheese in his mouth.

"Go ahead," I said. "Make yourself at home."

Alex gave me a sarcastic smile and snagged a couple of beers from the fridge. He handed one over, clinked mine, and took a long pull. I did the same. "Okay, what do you want to talk about?"

"I need your help."

I raised my eyebrows. "Is that so?"

"Remember when I told you about the Vessel?"

"The Vessel of Souls? The one that got you banned from Heaven? Stripped of your wings? That Vessel?"

Alex pursed his lips in annoyance. "Are you through?"

I sniffed. "I guess. What about it?"

"I need to find it."

"I know that. But why now? And why do you suddenly need me?"

Alex let out a long sigh. "The Vessel of Souls houses all human souls that are in limbo. If the fallen angels get their hands on it they can take over everything— the angelic plane, the human plane—even the Underworld. We need to keep the Vessel out of the hands of the fallen."

I looked at Alex. "You're fallen. Why should I help you get it?"

"You know that if I can restore the balance of the planes and get the Vessel back, I can get my wings back. I'm not going to jeopardize that . . . again."

I picked up a spatula. "And you need me why?"

Alex raised his eyebrows expectantly, and I flipped a sandwich, sighing. "Because the Vessel is charmed," I said, answering my own question.

"Even the angelic plane uses magic. They like to hide things in plain sight."

"Really?"

Alex nodded and took a swig from his bottle. "Yeah. Last I heard the Holy Grail was actually a tanning bed in Manhattan Beach."

I narrowed my eyes at Alex's little-boy grin. "Really, Sophie. You're the only one I know who will be able to see through the charm."

Along with my superior pizza-eating and state-reciting powers, I was also magically immune. My grandmother was a seer, my mother was a mind-melder, and nothing could be used on me. Veils, charms, spells, happy endings—anything that could be conjured, wanded, or abracadabraed was lost on me. The magical immunity helped working in the Underworld. The occasional fire-breathing dragon singe or High witch explosion rolled off me like water off a duck's back. Warlocks couldn't use glamour spells to make me fall in love with them and give them extra magiks freedoms or process their paperwork any faster, and I could share a cup of coffee with Medusa and stay perfectly, humanly pink.

"Okay," I told Alex, "where do we start?"